S0-BBH-134

The
Outlaw
Hearts

The Outlaw Hearts

Rebecca Brandewyne

WARNER BOOKS

A Warner Communications Company

Copyright © 1986 by Rebecca Brandewyne
All rights reserved.

Warner Books, Inc.
666 Fifth Avenue
New York, N.Y. 10103

 A Warner Communications Company

Printed in the United States of America

For Mama,
who believed in me.
With love.

The Players

Honor Ashe Colter, *widow of Niles Colter II; sister-in-law to the Colter*
   sisters
Cade Brackett, *husband to Melantha Colter Brackett*
Miss Henrietta (Aunt Hetta) Colter (deceased), *great-aunt of the Colter*
   sisters
An Unknown Yankee Officer

Contents

The Outlaw Hearts

Dreams so bright are broken now,
Like shattered glass, lie at my feet,
Each painful shard a memory,
Cruel and bittersweet.
And all I ever held most dear
Is forever buried deep
'Neath headstones grey and weathered;
Silent watch they keep
O'er those who died too young, too soon,
Their stories yet untold,
While I, who yearned to join them,
Wait for my life to unfold.

The Stars and Bars . . . it waves no more.
The Glorious Cause is lost,
And only we who survived its end
Know just how much it cost,
For it is we who hear the echoes
Of voices hushed and far away,
Of laughter so abruptly stilled—
Yes, all this we keep at bay.
And the nights are long and lonely,
Filled with sadness and repine;
But fancies tinged with madness . . .
Perhaps those alone are mine.

Listen! Do you hear it?
Or is it only in my dreams?
I close my mind to shut it out,
Yet still somehow it seems
There's a wayward wind a'calling,
Singing wild and free,
Rippling 'cross the green grass,
Crying out to me.

Come, it sighs so sweetly.
Leave all your cares behind.
Follow with each breath I take,
And true love you will find.

I doubt and still I wander,
Knowing not where this road goes,
Yet hoping it's the answer
To all my secret woes.
And there at last you're waiting,
Your eyes older than your years.
They kiss my own—oh, tenderly—
And banish all my fears.
We're two against the world, then,
Both outlaw hearts who dare
To ride into the sunset
And seek enchantment there.

BOOK ONE

Echoes

Chapter One

The Ozark Mountains, date unknown

Deep in the heart of the Ozark Mountains, hidden from view by the feathery green boughs of pines, fringed cedars, and acorn-bearing oaks, their trunks enveloped by vines and moss; lapped by the gentle waves of a clear blue spring that ripples quietly in the forest hush, lies a secret, special place.

It is a small place, no more than a tiny breadth of clearing among the stand of close, gnarled trees that surround it like timeless sentries, tall and protective, shielding it from the prying eyes of all unwelcome intruders. Grass, moss, and creeping vines grow soft and spongy upon the ground, fed by the summer rains and the mountain mist and dew, and wildflowers bloom in gay profusion all year long. Even in the coldest of winters, when the snow lies thick upon the fallow earth and the bubbling spring is but a frozen mirror, brave snowdrops blossom to shed their petals in a shower of bright color against the white crystal flakes.

Some say it is a place as old as time, used by the Ancient Ones for worshiping their gods, for here and there are strange rock formations that resemble the animals of the woods, and two sacred stones lie in the center. Others claim it is a fairy ring, wherein the magic of those delicate beings yet lingers, and that the flitting, gossamer-winged butterflies there are, in truth, the spritely creatures. Still others swear it belongs to witches, who have cast a spell upon it, so those who dare to enter the circle are forever trapped within its confines by a silken web from which there is no escaping.

Only the old-timers, those aged, bent hermits and wiry trappers who are one with the hills, know none of this is so. But they are a close-mouthed lot and not wont to speak of the place lightly, lest the two who rest there be disturbed by those who have not the understanding of bonds more powerful than the worldly ones known to most mortals.

For it *is* a place of enchantment, a place where those things that cannot be touched, but must be felt with the heart prevail, and it is this that has given rise to the tales of sorcery that are whispered about it.

Few are those who dare to seek it out, and fewer still are they who find it, for the Ozark Mountains are dark with forests and strewn with caves as well, so one may easily lose one's way in the hills and wander endlessly till claimed by dust and ashes. But, if pressed and having imbibed more than a swig or two from a moonshine jug, the old-timers will, slyly, sometimes reveal their knowledge of the place, and one can then learn of the narrow, twisting path that must be followed to reach it.

It is a solitary place, a fitting spot for the two headstones that rise up like obelisks in the center, old and grey and weathered, so the inscriptions chiseled thereupon have faded like long-ago memories. Only with difficulty, fingers tracing the letters, can one make them out. Some, however, need not kneel upon the ground amid the wildflowers to read the words—or so the old-timers declare. For these few are the chosen, and they need only to look and listen with the heart to see and hear the secrets of the place.

But, the old-timers warn, they must dare to dream and to believe truly in the power of love, and they must arrive at sunset, that hour between the daylight and the darkness when the earth's mysteries are sometimes revealed. To arrive at another time is to see only the two old graves nestled among the woods and to hear only the quiet sounds of the forest: the harmonious chirruping of the birds and insects, the creaking of the branches of the trees, and the rustle of the leaves in response to the breeze.

But at sunset wondrous things may be beheld—or so the old-timers insist. Then, if one were of the chosen and drew near to the place where the grey headstones keep silent watch over those who rest beneath, that is what one would see.

The green carpet of grass, moss, and vines, damp with twilight dew and the beginnings of the evening mist, covers the two graves like a blanket, as though those who lie within are but sleeping and will soon awaken. The setting sun stretches its fingers over the land, touching the trickling waters of the spring and causing them to glow like pink-orange flames, bathing the place in their luminescent reflection, so all is vibrant and alive. Slowly the wind begins to sough, and, like a woman's perfume, the sweet, subtle scent of honeysuckle fills the air, wafting to one's nostrils. The spring gurgles, becomes the sound of a woman's low laughter, and, turning, one can see her sitting there among the wildflowers, her gown spread in soft folds about her.

One senses instantly that she is of the earth and wise in its ways. Her hair is the brown of the woods and loam; her eyes are the grey of mist and dew and rain, filled with knowledge and emotion and shadowed just a little with pain, as though they have sometimes seen things she wished they had not. She is young yet old, as are all those of the earth. There is a beauty about her, but it comes from within, lighting her face so she seems not of this world—and she is not. Touch her, and she would evanesce into the twilight. So those who believe remain still.

Presently a man appears beside her. He is of the sky and all-encompassing. His hair is the gold and silver of the sun and moon; his eyes are the blue of the firmament, ageless and timeworn, as though, like the woman's, they have seen too much and been hurt by it. He is strong yet tender, as are all the elements that may bring life or death to the earth. He is so handsome, so godlike, surely he cannot be real—and he is not. Like the woman, he is a vision seen only by those who believe.

He holds out his hands to the woman, takes her in his arms, and kisses her, deeply, passionately, and the air grows hot and expectant with desire. But it is not this alone one feels. It is something more, something that reaches into the heart and soul with a bittersweet caress that can be felt only by those who have loved as the two spirits love and thus can understand that without this, life is not worth living and death is truly nothingness, the end of all.

The man's mouth moves gently upon the woman's, his tongue outlining her trembling lips lingeringly before parting them to taste of the honey within. Slowly, tantalizingly he explores her mouth, searching out its moist, heated crevices and filling them with his tongue, so that with just a kiss he becomes a part of her and she of him, as they have always been.

Her arms creep up to twine about his back and neck, holding him even nearer as fervently she returns his embrace, his kiss, her lips fusing with his, her tongue seeking his own. Her body quivers like an arrow fitted to and drawn back by a taut bowstring, and, shuddering like a bow when bent before release, the man steadies her and himself as well, lest their passion be too quickly spent.

He wraps his fingers tightly in the brown hair streaming past her slender hips, reveling in the feel of the soft tresses, and his lips slash like a Bowie knife across her cheek, as warm and pink as the sunset. The woman moans a little, deep in her throat, as his mouth brands her eyelids and her temples, finds her ear and nuzzles it, opens to whisper words of love and sex within.

His breath is like the summer air, hot and humid, smelling of whiskey and tobacco, tickling her and causing her to laugh softly once more as she writhes against him, her nipples hard buds against his chest, her face twisting playfully to escape from his lips.

The man laughs too, huskily, before claiming her mouth again, urgently now, demandingly, his tongue shooting deeply between her lips, his hands, still tangled in her hair, gripping her forcefully and compelling her to acquiesce to his desires. Satisfied that she is his, his palms begin to caress her body, sliding down her back to cup her buttocks and pull her to him so she can feel the hardness of his passion pressed close against her thighs.

The woman flings back her head, offering her bare throat up to the man, and he devours it hungrily with his mouth and teeth, nibbling and kissing the column feverishly, his lips traveling ever lower, roaming down the valley between her breasts until he finds the full ripe mounds that beckon to him so enticingly.

Impatiently his hands tear at the bodice of the woman's gown and the silk lacings of her chemise until nothing remains between his mouth and her flesh, flushed and damp with the heat of her desire. His palms take possession of her twin spheres; his thumbs flick the two stiff peaks, circling, teasing, till they strain against him, aching for more. His lips capture one dark honey crest; his tongue taunts it, savors it. The woman arches against him, her fingers curling wantonly in his blond hair as she hugs him to her bosom, whimpering with the emotions he is unleashing inside of her.

A flame of excitement burns where the man's tongue lingers, begins to radiate from the center of her nipple until her whole body feels as though it is on fire. Her flesh tingles as though it has been scorched; her blood boils. An almost painful ache starts to blaze at the very core of her being, growing hotter and hotter until she feels as though it will consume her with its intensity. She cries out, but still the man's mouth moves upon her, sears its way across her breast to claim its counterpart.

Once more his hands rip heedlessly at her gown, rending it still further, until it cascades down like a waterfall to lie in a pool at her feet, her white undergarments floating like waves atop.

The sun descending on the far horizon reaches out to touch her naked skin, to caress and kiss each delicate curve and indentation of her body. Like the earth and the spring, the woman is bathed in a pink-orange glow so her flesh seems almost translucent in the dying light. An incandescent mirage, she shimmers in the man's arms, as fluid as quick-silver as his fingers part her thighs, his lips find the shallow swells of her womanhood, and his tongue probes the warm wet chasm secreted therein.

The woman gasps sharply, then cries out again, her melodious voice sweet in the twilight, mingling with the songs of the birds and the locusts, the croaking of the frogs and toads, all of whom are witness to this mating as old and primitive as time.

Then slowly, purposefully the man stands, kissing the woman's breasts and mouth once more before undressing, so he too is naked beneath the sun. His body is lean and bronzed and glistens with the sweat of his passion, making him seem like a brown-and-gold idol, gleaming and beautiful. The woman runs her hands over his chest, her fingers enraptured by the feel of the soft, crisp, dark blond curls that mat his torso, trailing down his belly to the strong proud shaft between his narrow, muscular flanks.

She kneels before him, her long brown hair a satin shadow hiding her face as her hands claim him shyly, tenderly, and her lips and tongue bring to him the joy he has given her earlier. Now it is the man who moans and murmurs, a willing slave of her and the moment. She smells of honeysuckle, and the heady scent drifts up from her, enveloping him, so he is wrapped in a cocoon of her weaving, and the place is still, holding its breath as one with the man, lost in the magic of the woman's spell.

He inhales raggedly, quickly pressing the woman down upon the blanket of the soft sweet grass, the spongy moss, the creeping vines, her head pillowed upon the wildflowers. Her thighs open in invitation, lur-ing him on with love and wanting. He fits her perfectly, as though they have been made for each other. Powerfully he spirals down into her, feeling the smooth, fluid heat of her desire close around him as she takes him deep inside of her so he may know the mysteries of her being. Over and over they join, meld into each other, become one, as the earth and the sky are one.

The sun glimmers upon the two lovers, the dreamers, blessing their union as they cry out rapturously together, swept away upon the wings of their passion, carried to the heights of ecstasy and beyond. Enchant-ment fills the air as the secret of their bond is revealed as the simplest yet the most complex of all emotions. Their deep love has surpassed all worldly boundaries; it has brought them to this quiet place and kept them here, where once they trod and dreamed and whispered vows all lovers speak. This is why only those who believe can see the two whose place this is.

Slowly the fire of the sun dies to embers as the great, flaming ball slips below the western horizon, leaving the earth cloaked in the beginnings of darkness, black and velvet in its silence as inexorably it starts to descend.

The two who loved and laughed here earlier are gone, and it is as though they never were. As the stars ignite to fill up the heavens, one wonders if the lovers were ever there at all—or if one only imagined them.

Presently, awed, hushed, and filled with emotion, one turns to begin the long, winding trek down through the hills and forests to where lesser men abide. From an ancient, tin-roofed cabin set into the mountainside, a grizzled old-timer, moonshine jug in hand, calls out from his dilapidated front porch, where he has been rocking and waiting.

"Come on over," he invites. "Come on over, 'n' sit a spell. Don't see too many furriners in these here parts."

Gratefully one sinks down upon the knotted, roughhewn planks of the porch and waits respectfully for the old-timer to speak again. The night sounds echo in the stillness as the full silver moon climbs higher in the firmament, causing the darkness to shift its soft black mantle slightly, so its folds drape less securely over the hills it has gathered to its breast as though they are children in need of protection. The night creatures stir, their howls and hoots mingling with the sighing of the wind, the groaning of the trees, and the distant murmur of the mountain streams. At last the waiting grows unbearable.

"Tell me about the two lovers," one addresses the old-timer breathlessly, reverently, for one can see by his eyes, ageless and wise, that he knows the true story of the special place.

The old-timer squints, assessing his questioner sharply for a moment, his rheumy eyes seeming to pierce the heart and soul. No secrets are concealed from him. Then abruptly he nods, as though satisfied.

"I figgered you'd be askin' sooner or later." He chuckles slyly, as though pleased. "They always do." He pauses, then continues, his voice quieter now, less gregarious. "So you want to know 'bout the outlaw hearts," he says. "Well, 'tis many a story's been told 'bout 'em, some true, some not, I reckon. But, then, that's the way of most legends, ain't it? I guess I know as much as most folks, for I've been the caretaker of these here hills for many a year, through good times and bad. . . ." His voice dwindles away, as though he is remembering days long past. Then he shakes his head, recalling himself to the present.

"But, mind, I ain't sayin' I know the whole tale," he insists. "No, siree. I don't reckon nobody does or ever will. But I do say that, no matter the truth, there ain't never been a more fittin' hero 'n' heroine or a more wondrous story."

Once more the old-timer falls silent, looking out over the hills as though again he is far away, in another time, another place. He blinks his eyes once or twice. Was there a glitter of tears there? Perhaps it was only a trick of the moonlight. He takes a swig from his moonshine jug, swallows it, and clears his throat gruffly.

"Yep. They was a pair, them two," he says, "her as fine a woman as ever lived, and him nothin' but a rogue if ever there was one. You wouldn't of thought they'd ever make a go of it. But they did. Seen sumpin' special in each other that nobody else could, I reckon. But, then, that's how love is, ain't it?"

He is still once more, and the listener is quiet too, patiently waiting to hear the tale, for it is obvious he tells it seldom and reluctantly, as though its magical power might be lost if he shared it with too many. Again he stares hard at his questioner, as though to be certain his earlier appraisal was accurate, that he has indeed found a believer in those things that are truly everlasting, forever cherished in the heart.

Then slowly, his voice rising and falling expressively with each loving word, the old-timer begins once more to speak.

Chapter Two

The Countryside, Missouri, 1870

Jennifer Leigh Colter sat quietly upon her hard bench in the public coach of the train that was carrying her westward to her destination, far away from her past and Faxon's Folly, the plantation where five years ago her life had been shattered into a million pieces.

Just glancing at her slight still figure, a stranger would not have guessed her deep sadness, for there was not a hint in her demeanor of the physical tiredness depression often brings. Her shoulders were firmly squared; her back was straight, and her hands were folded just so in her lap as befitted a young woman of gentle breeding. Her soft dusky-brown hair, pinned up in a low chignon at the nape of her neck and partially hidden beneath her small, feathered bonnet, had been recently washed, and not a single strand was out of place. Though made over from an older gown that had been worn with hoops, her smart grey traveling costume was beautifully stitched and only lightly streaked with the dust that coated so many travelers. Her black leather shoes were a trifle scuffed but neatly polished, and, though carefully mended, the kid gloves and lace handkerchief she held between her clasped hands were spotlessly white. She appeared in every respect what she was: a young lady of good family whose generous circumstances had been sharply reduced by the war.

As such, she was not now an uncommon sight in the South, and, as Jenny was not even passably pretty, she rarely merited a second look. But, had a stranger's gaze returned to her motionless form, it would have lingered on her countenance, and this would have betrayed the fact that all was not as it appeared. Jenny's wide, speaking grey eyes, haunted by dark shadows, were filled with a world of knowledge that should not have belonged to one of her years. Hers were old eyes, terribly old eyes that had faced and conquered with quiet courage things no one ought to have witnessed and survived.

She closed them tightly at the thought of those things and with trembling fingers pressed her handkerchief to her lips as she fought down the bilious gorge that roiled in her belly whenever she remembered.

She just couldn't be ill! Not now—not in front of all the people who shared the public car. But Jenny's sudden queasiness refused to dissipate. Sometimes it happened like that, the past sweeping over her without warning, so she could not control her reactions to it, no matter how hard she tried.

Fearing she was about to vomit, she rose blindly, groping at the tops of seats as, swaying a little dizzily with each lurch of the train, she began to make her way down the aisle to the washroom at the back of the coach.

Briefly Jenny wished she had remained seated, for her somewhat awkward, noticeable limp did not go unobserved by the rest of the passengers, and their surreptitious stares of mingled curiosity and pity made her feel like a freak at a carnival sideshow. Still she stumbled on, her nausea spurring her forward.

With a sigh of relief she finally reached the small closet that was the railroad company's answer to the call of nature. Once inside, she shut the door firmly and locked it. Then, feeling faint, she leaned against one wall of the tiny cubicle to steady herself. Presently her rapid breathing slowed and her churning stomach settled.

Though her hands were still shaking, Jenny managed to pour some water from a pitcher into the shallow tin basin on the washstand. Then, taking a clean cloth from the single shelf beneath the mirror, she wiped the sticky perspiration from her face and the back of her neck.

Soon she saw that the color was returning to her cheeks, which were unnaturally pale, as they always were whenever she relived in her mind that day at Faxon's Folly.

It was a miracle she'd survived at all, Jenny thought. Only the care and encouragement of her great-aunt, Henrietta, and of Cade had kept her fighting for her life when her body had been but a broken shell and her mind had been unhinged by horror and sorrow. Yes, she had come through it all in the end, her internal injuries healing and her bones knitting, albeit improperly, and her sanity returning, though sometimes, like now, she wished it had not.

Occasionally Jenny still experienced twinges of pain in her crippled leg, but these had lessened with time. It was the nightmares that continued to haunt her.

No, she would not think of those, she determined, feverishly burying her face in her hands, as though that were enough to stop the rampaging memories.

She did not want to recall the horrible, unreal images that had been indelibly branded into her mind when her widower brother-in-law, Cade, had lifted her in his arms and carried her from Faxon's Folly. She did not want to remember how her head had lolled listlessly against his shoulder; how her glazed, empty eyes had fluttered open to see what he, emotionally torn apart and believing her more dead than alive, had not thought to conceal from her sight.

Please, God. Not now. Not now.

She tried to halt the flow of pictures as they unreeled before her eyes, hazy and ill defined, as though seen through an out-of-focus lens. They moved in jerky slow motion as well, and that seemed to accentuate their ghastliness.

There was a man, a vile, ugly man. He was laughing raucously, and his strong, cruel hands were—were . . . Nearby, grinning caricatures cavorted and howled encouragement. One of them noticed Jenny, pointed at her. A big black beast from hell, blood spewing from its nostrils, as though it were spitting fire, began to thunder toward her, the devil on its back. . . .

"No!" Jenny screamed and screamed again. "Nooooo!"

None heard the wail of anguish. It was drowned out by the roar of the train clattering over the tracks, wheels chanting rhythmically as it rattled on. For that Jenny was most grateful. She glanced at herself in the mirror, scarcely recognizing the disheveled, grief-stricken woman who looked back at her, ill and wild-eyed.

I've got to get hold of myself, she thought. I've just got to get hold of myself!

Her body quivering violently, she took several deep breaths to stem the rising tide of hysteria that threatened to overwhelm her. Gradually the horrid pounding of her heart and the frantic jumping of her nerves subsided. Hastily she pushed the loose tendrils of her disarrayed hair back into place.

What would Mr. Horace Peabody, the head of the Tumbling Creek school board, think if he saw her looking like this? Why, he would put her on the first train back to Georgia!

Jenny couldn't afford to let that happen. Her great-aunt, Henrietta, with whom she'd lived for the past few years in Atlanta, had recently died. After the War Between the States it had taken everything the elderly spinster had managed to salvage just for the two of them to survive, so there had been scarcely enough left in Aunt Hetta's estate to pay for her funeral expenses. The house on Peachtree Street, in which she'd lived all her life and which she had single-handedly prevented the Yankees from burning to the ground, had had to be sold. What few possessions that had remained Jenny had given to kindly Doc Whitting to settle the balance still owing on her account at the hospital, where she'd spent so many painful months recovering.

Then she'd set about finding employment, for which Aunt Hetta, old and failing in health yet concerned about Jenny's future, had had the wisdom and foresight to prepare her.

Once her initial shock over that day at Faxon's Folly had begun to turn from a raw, searing wound to a dull, throbbing ache, Jenny had been forced by her great-aunt to face some hard facts about herself and her life.

She wasn't pretty, so it was unlikely she would attract the interest of one of the blockade-runners who'd grown rich and successful during the war. Those few men who were bachelors were having a difficult enough time trying to make ends meet. They didn't want or need the added burden of a wife—especially one like Jenny. Not only was she plain, but she didn't have any money, and she was lame. She hadn't the beauty that would make a man want to cherish and protect her. She hadn't the funds to help ease his lot in life. She could not plow a field or pick endless rows of cotton. She could not even give a man a child born of their love for each other.

No, she was destined to live her life as a spinster; and, unlike Aunt Hetta, who'd at least had her inheritance and her family to fall back on before the war, Jenny had nothing and no one. She would be all alone in the world when her great-aunt died.

Relentlessly, despite Jenny's tears over the thought of losing her only living relative, Aunt Hetta had insisted she prepare for that day.

At last Jenny had given in, deciding to become a schoolteacher, and, after the day's work at the house on Peachtree Street had been finished, she'd studied diligently long into the nights and had earned her teaching certificate. Now Jenny was very grateful she'd obtained it. With her great-aunt dead she must make her own way in the world.

She had been fortunate too in acquiring a position so quickly. Cade's cousin, who owned a general store in Saint Louis, had mailed him several packages of items he'd required for the law practice he'd recently reopened in Atlanta. In one of the newspapers wrapped and tied securely about the bundles had been an advertisement that had caught Cade's eye, and he had clipped it out and saved it for Jenny. The small town of Tumbling Creek, Missouri, was looking for *a qualified young lady of unimpeachable morals* to take charge of its one-room schoolhouse.

The pay was poor, but to offset this disadvantage there was the inducement of *separate living quarters consisting of a parlor, bedroom, gallery, and kitchen, to be provided by the school board at no charge to the employee.*

A house! Jenny would have her own house, not just a room at some boarding establishment. That meant she would be able to take with her Moses and Delcine, her two Negro servants. Jenny had leaped at the chance, for she'd worried over what was to become of them if she couldn't provide for them.

She'd written immediately to Mr. Horace Peabody, the head of the Tumbling Creek school board, and after weeks of waiting anxiously she'd finally received a reply. The position was hers. She was to come at once in order to get settled in before the start of the fall term.

Cade had kissed her cheek gently and, after instructing Moses and Delcine to take good care of her, had put her on a westbound train. How sad and forlorn he'd looked, standing there watching until she'd been out of sight.

For one wild instant Jenny had longed to yank on the brake rope and run back to him. Cade would marry her; he'd said as much the night before she'd departed. But with wisdom beyond her years Jenny had realized it wouldn't work. Cade had been searching for some part of the past in her, and she'd wanted instead something she'd never had and now, at twenty-one, probably never would have.

"Why, Jenny? Why?" Cade had asked one last time before she'd gone, his dark lean visage filled with hurt and anger. "Why did it happen?"

And Jenny, her own sadness etched pitiably on her plain, heart-shaped face, had answered.

"Oh, God, Cade!" she'd cried. "Don't you think I've asked myself that a million times! Why? Why? I don't know. I don't know!" Then, more quietly, she'd said, "I'm sorry, Cade, so very sorry. I wish—I wish it had been me instead of—instead of Mellie. . . ."

Swallowing hard, turning away so she wouldn't see the sudden hot tears that had scalded his eyes, Cade had nodded and told her good-bye.

Now as Jenny recalled him her throat closed up tight, and with difficulty she fought back the glistening beads that threatened to spill from her lashes.

He was a good man, she thought as she remembered what Aunt Hetta had told her during the agonizing days of her recovery: how Cade and Moses had fashioned temporary splints for her damaged legs before carrying her all the way from Faxon's Folly to Jonesboro. How they'd stolen a mule and wagon to bring her into Atlanta when they'd found the only physician in Jonesboro was a filthy old sawbones too drunk to examine her properly. How, after depositing her safely at the hospital and sending for her great-aunt, they'd made the long journey back to the plantation to bury the pitiful remains of her broken life and to search for clues to tell them who had destroyed it and why. How Cade had beaten an orderly half to death to obtain laudanum to ease her pain when the Yankees had refused to part with any of the precious medicine, hoarding it for their own soldiers instead. How he and Moses, who'd had no money, had robbed an icehouse so Doc Whitting could bring down her raging fever and get her delirium under control.

Yes, Jenny had owed Cade a great deal, but it wouldn't have been right for her to have married him. She couldn't have turned back the hands of time. She couldn't even have told him what had happened that day at Faxon's Folly.

Ceaselessly she'd racked her brain, trying to dredge some recollection of the nightmare from her memories—but to no avail. Except for the terrible, blurred images that tortured her still, her mind was a blank. It was as though what she did remember had wiped out everything else.

A sudden loud, jolting noise brought Jenny with a start to her senses. Good heavens! How long had she been standing in the washroom? Even now someone was beating furiously on the door, ordering her to hurry up, that there were others waiting.

Quickly she poured the water from the basin into the slop jar, tidied up the washstand, and tossed the cloth she'd used into a basket perched on the counter for this purpose. Then, smoothing her hair and gown, she unlocked the door of the little closet and, murmuring her apologies, sidled past the large, irate man outside, her eyes averted. He muttered something ungentlemanly under his breath, then slammed the door of the cubicle shut with a bone-jarring bang.

Blushing as the other passengers stared at her censuringly for monopolizing the washroom and causing a commotion, Jenny limped hurriedly toward her seat. She hoped she needn't answer the call of nature before the next stop; she didn't think she dared to make a move toward the washroom again.

"Are you all right, Miss Jenny?"—her maid, Delcine, leaned forward to ask, her speech more refined than that of most Negroes, for she'd once been Miss Henrietta's companion and had worked at learning to speak properly under the spinster's tutelage.

"Yes," Jenny responded, pasting a brave smile on her face to erase the concern she saw in both her servants' eyes. "My stomach's just a mite upset, that's all. Why don't you check our basket, and see if there's anything left to eat. I think a few crackers might help."

Delcine surveyed her mistress skeptically for a minute but made no comment, though she'd guessed Jenny had lied to discourage her and Moses from further prying. Delcine was an astute woman, and she had lived with Jenny for the last few years. She had observed the sudden paling of Jenny's face, the trembling of her hands before, and she knew when that happened her mistress was recalling that day at Faxon's Folly. Time had lessened the impact of the ravaging memories, but perhaps, Delcine mused, a person never fully recovered from the shock of something that horrifying.

"Here." Delcine offered Jenny some crackers left over from dinner. "These ought to quiet your belly. No wonder you're feeling sick, Miss Jenny. Sitting on this hard bench, with this train just a'chugging away like a plow horse, is just about as much fun as riding a swaybacked mule. I declare! I'll be surprised if I'm not chewing with my gums when this trip is over; I think my last tooth just rattled right out of my head!"

To Delcine's relief her deliberately inane remarks brought a more natural smile to Jenny's face and lightened the shadows that darkened her eyes. Moses grinned widely as well.

"Yo sho' is a fine woman, Delcine"—he edged over to whisper in her ear. "Smaht too. Dis heah's one o' Miz Jenny's bad days; Ah cain allus tell dem. But yo perked her right up wi' dat silly talk. Now she looks as happy as dat li'l ole bird her daddy used ter call her aftah."

"Hmph!" Delcine snorted, her speech slipping, as it always did when she conversed with her own people, into the colorful dialect of the Negroes. "Whut does yo know 'bout it? 'Fo' de war yo wuz jes' a field hand."

"Whut!" Moses exclaimed, vastly insulted and drawing up to his full height like a fat old hen ruffling her feathers. "Why Ah wuz not! Nawum. Ah wuz de bes' groom Massah Coltah eber had. Ah drived mah missies purt neah eber day an' perteck'd dem wi' mah life. Whut is yo talkin' 'bout, gal? Ah *neber* wuz no field niggah!"

Slyly the beautiful mulatto turned away so Moses wouldn't see the smile of amusement that curved upon her lips. For five years now

Delcine had loved the big, handsome black man, yet he'd scarcely paid any attention to her. They'd all worked so hard at Miss Henrietta's house in Atlanta, just trying to keep a roof over their heads, that there hadn't been much time for courting. But now, since things were looking up and Miss Jenny had found a good job so they could all live decently again—if they were careful and pinched their pennies—Delcine meant to make Moses take notice to her.

"Hmph!" She sniffed once more, putting her nose in the air haughtily. "If'n yo wuz smaht 'nuff ter be de missies' groom, how come yo ain' smaht 'nuff ter know dat bird Miz Jenny's daddy called her aftah is jes' a plain ole wren? Nawsah. If'n yo ast me, yo is jes' downright dumb, Moses, an' yo sho' 'nuff belonged in de fields, eben if'n dat wuzn't wheah dey put yo! Miz Jenny's got 'nuff problems wi'out yo sayin' she looks lahke dat po' brown bird."

"Why, gal, fo' a house niggah, yo sho' gots a lot ter learn!" Moses retorted, incensed. "Dat li'l bitty bird might not be too much on de outside, but inside, it's gots de purtiest melody yo eber heered, an' when it opens up its mouf ter sing, it jes' meks yo want ter cry—it's so purty. Dat's why Massah Coltah done called Miz Jenny dat name, 'cause dat's whut she's lahke, an' someday she's gwine ter find herself a man ter 'preciate dat fact! Yo wait an' see." Moses nodded wisely. "Yassum. Yo jes' wait an' see."

High on a bald-knobbed hill overlooking Devil's Holler, Luke Morgan squinted his eyes against the glare of the early afternoon sun. It was a lazy summer day, hot and humid upon the top of the bare mound, where there were no trees to offer shade. Below, where thick forests covered the sweeping hillsides, a cool breeze would be stirring, Luke knew, rustling through the leaves to entice the Ozark natives out onto their porches to idle away the hours. But here, except for the buzzing of flies and mosquitoes, the air was still. Luke slapped at an insect that had landed on his neck. Then he pulled his watch from his pocket and glanced impatiently at the hands of the timepiece. He turned to his eldest brother, Jedediah, called J.R. to distinguish him from his father, who bore the same name.

"We'd better get moving," Luke commented. "We've only got a couple of hours before the train comes through."

"Yeah, and it's gonna take some time to fix the rails," Billy Clay chimed in excitedly. "Those spikes are harder than hell to dig outta the ground!"

"I want to go over the spot beforehand too," Tobias said, "to be certain it's suitable for our purposes. You know you really ought to have consulted me about it first, J.R." His voice was accusing and slightly offended.

"Hmph!" J.R. grunted. "You and Luke were in Centerville, skylarking with the Jameses, and there wasn't time to wait around on you. Now let's get going."

Slowly the four brothers trotted their horses down the sloping knoll to the dark green grove of trees that populated the valley below.

The men were a dangerous-looking bunch, their wary eyes glinting like steel and their jaws set with grim determination. Their hands were rough from years of hard riding. Their trigger fingers were callused from frequent use. Obviously these were men who dared to take risks most would have called foolhardy, men who had laughed in death's face on more than one occasion. Wanted posters offered sizable rewards for each of them—dead or alive—and there were nooses waiting in at least five states for the oldest three, should they ever be captured and convicted of their crimes. They were not a group to cross, despite the fact that they lived by a strict code of ethics that was both strangely at odds with their criminal existence and uniquely their own. For nearly twenty years, until Butch Cassidy would make a name for himself with the Hole-in-the-Wall gang, there were to be no other outlaws like the Morgans.

Once on flatter ground, they meandered along a set of railroad tracks that slithered like a snake over the rolling crests and shallow dips of the land. Years of heavy rains had gradually eroded the terrain, and presently the dell narrowed, walls jutting up steeply on either side to create a rocky ravine. Here the woods were so close it was difficult for the brothers to maneuver their horses beneath the tightly woven canopy formed by the green-leafed, moss-hung branches, so they picked their way carefully through the verdant tangle, lest they be knocked from their saddles.

When Billy Clay indicated they'd found the right place, J.R. raised his hand to signal a halt. Then Tobias dismounted to inspect the area. He walked this way and that, his eyes studying intently the planes and angles of the land, measuring, calculating, until at last J.R. grew annoyed by the delay.

"Well?" he queried laconically. "Will it work or not?"

"I guess it'll do," Tobias responded dryly, irritated at having his deliberations interrupted. "But you really ought to have let me check it out first before planning this holdup, J.R. You know Billy Clay is so clabber-headed he can't tell a suck-egg dog from a grind hog, and any fool can see there're too many trees along this stretch of the gorge for us to be able to loosen the railroad spikes and pull the ties free." He rounded on the youngest member of the family angrily. "How in the hell did you think we were going to gallop our horses through these woods, you idiot? Especially when we'd be dragging several feet of heavy lumber behind us?"

"Gee, Toby"—Billy Clay shrugged—"I never thought of that. J.R. didn't say nothing about not having any trees around, else I'd have gone on up the tracks a piece till I come to a clearing. He just told me to look for a spot where the holler walls was real tall and narrow, and that's exactly what I done. Hell! I dunno what you're getting so riled up about—"

"Oh, for Christ's sake!" Luke growled, glaring at his youngest brother, who invariably annoyed him. "Will you shut up! I swear you jabber more than a preacher on Sunday!" He turned coolly to Tobias. "There's no need to get in an uproar about it. We'll just chop down a few of these pines and block the tracks. That'll work out better than yanking the ties loose anyway, because it'll look as though there were a bad storm recently and the wind blew the trees over. Then the engineer won't get suspicious. I never liked the idea of derailing the train anyhow; the locomotive might have flipped over and killed somebody."

"*That* was the whole point of choosing a narrow spot," Tobias elucidated, "so there wouldn't be any room for the damned engine to run wild and turn somersaults. If Billy Clay had just used his brain for once—"

"That's enough!" J.R. spoke sharply, his tone putting a halt to the argument. "We'll just have to improvise, and Luke's idea is the best I've heard out of the lot of you. Now get your axes and get to work. We don't have a lot of time left."

Quickly the three younger men unrolled their tools from their saddle packs and started to hack powerfully at one of the regal mountain pines that stood straight and tall, like a sentry, near the railroad tracks. J.R., still mounted on his horse, kept a keen eye out for the billowing wisps of black smoke that would herald the approach of the oncoming vehicle.

Although since the end of the war the notorious Morgan gang, as the brothers had come to be known throughout the country, had robbed banks, looted county treasuries, burglarized post offices, and assaulted stagecoaches, this was the first time it had attempted to hold up a train. That was why the Morgans' plot was not proceeding as smoothly as the other jobs they'd planned and instigated with such meticulous detail, refining and improving upon the deeds of others like them. Bold tactics chortled over in saloons on rowdy nights of celebration or reckless escapades written up in newspapers the day after their fruition proved sparks to ignite the imaginations of those who lived and died by the gun. But this time, unfortunately, the Morgans hadn't had any specific incidents to aid them, as there had been few train robberies in the past.

The first such endeavor had been successfully carried out in 1866, in Indiana, by the Reno gang, who'd boarded an Ohio & Mississippi train shortly before it had pulled out of the Seymour depot. The Renos, after overcoming the Adams Express Company messenger, had raided the express car. Then at the signal of an accomplice, who'd been waiting with several horses farther down the line, the gang had heaved two safes out of the train onto the ground and had jumped from the moving vehicle. One safe had contained fifteen thousand dollars in cash. The other, which the Renos had been forced to abandon because they couldn't get it open, had held thirty thousand dollars in cash and gold.

Because robbing trains was a rare occurrence, it had not as yet been declared a federal offense, but was considered a crime against the state in which it was committed. For this reason the Morgans were somewhat nervous about holding up the Ozark Mountain Railroad Company on their own side of the Missouri-Arkansas border. Still they simply couldn't pass up this opportunity. There was a tidy sum of gold being sent to the stock exchange in Kansas City, and they meant to steal the shipment. Besides, if anyone pointed an accusing finger at them, the brothers had enough relatives and friends in Tumbling Creek, their hometown, to provide them with alibis so ironclad even the indefatigable Pinkerton agents wouldn't be able to disprove them.

In addition, the Morgans were always extremely careful about the jobs they pulled. Though they were suspected of and wanted for several offenses, it was unlikely the law would be able to pin any of their crimes on them. People might guess who they were, might even hear their names, but there were a lot of Morgans in the South, and because the brothers always kept their faces well hidden when committing a robbery, no one had actually gotten a good enough look at them during a holdup to positively identify them later. This uncertainty over their appearances was enhanced by the fact that the Morgans didn't allow themselves to be photographed, so their pictures were not part of the Pinkerton Detective Agency's Rogues' Gallery, which would have made them more easily recognizable to the public, since such photographs were often published in the newspapers and on wanted posters.

By the time J.R. had spied the smoke wafting up like a long, plumed feather from the smokestack of the unsuspecting locomotive, the other three men had managed to fell a single large pine and two smaller trees. The bushily branched trunks lay in a sprawling heap across the tracks, as though a strong wind had knocked them down.

"Billy Clay, you take the horses, and hide them on back in the woods a ways," J.R. ordered. "You can wait for us by that big rock near the foot of the hills."

"Aw, J.R., why do I always have to be the one who never gets to see any action?" Billy Clay whined, exasperated. "Why—"

"Because you're always hell-bent for election, and your mouth runs like a gully washer, that's why!" J.R. cut him off abruptly, silencing any further complaints. "You get on Luke's nerves; you get on Toby's nerves, and you get on mine. Now get those damned animals out of sight!"

Grumbling heatedly under his breath about the injustice of it all, Billy Clay mounted up and rode off, leading his brothers' horses behind him. The other three men drew their bandannas over their faces, pulled their pistols, and secreted themselves behind several clumps of bushes that straggled like tumbleweeds alongside the tracks.

"I sure hope Raif remembers what he's supposed to do," Luke remarked, his body tensing with excitement as he saw the train round a bend some distance away and come into view at last.

"I wouldn't count on it," Tobias droned, his voice wry. "Sometimes I think he's got about as much sense as Billy Clay."

"If Raif knows what's good for him, he'll do what I told him," J.R. muttered, "or I'll nail his hide to the barn door when we get home."

After that there was no more conversation. Poised expectantly in crouched positions, waiting impatiently for the vehicle to draw near and to reach the point when it must come to a grinding stop, the Morgans mentally primed themselves for their attack.

Inside the hot, stifling cab at the rear of the churning locomotive, the engineer, Quincy Yates, leaning out the window to watch the tracks up ahead, suddenly observed the fallen trees impeding the train's progress. As he was an old hand at his job, having made the Jonesboro-to-Springfield run numerous times since the Ozark Mountain Railroad Company had built the line, he reacted swiftly to the situation, deftly slamming on the brakes and shouting an alarm to the men who stoked the firebox up front.

"Ebenezer! Nathan! Put a hold on the coal! We got us a slight problem up ahead!"

"What's the trouble, Quince?" Ebenezer questioned as he tossed away his shovel and stepped into the cab, wiping his coal-dust-streaked hands on a grimy rag.

"Nothin' serious, but I reckon it's 'nuff to delay us purt near half an hour or more, gawddamn it! 'N' just when we was makin' sech good time too! Mighta pulled in five or ten minutes early, even, 'n' made the boss man right happy. Hell! They musta had a real toad strangler here three or four days ago. There's some trees down, and they's blocking the tracks. Friggin' nuisance, that's what! Well, I s'pose it cain't be helped. You and Nathan'll hafta git out 'n' clear the way."

"Shore thin', Quince. Come on, Nathan. Let's git our tools."

Cars jolting together noisily, the train lurched to a halt, steam wheezing, wheels shrieking in protest.

Inside the public coaches, Jenny and the others were bounced around like marbles hit by a taw as the rapid and unexpected braking nearly jarred them from their seats.

"Gracious!" the girl cried, clapping one hand upon her bonnet to hold it in place as she attempted to right herself. "Whatever can be the matter?" Her voice was anxious, and her misty-grey eyes were wide with apprehension.

Seeing the warning signs that bespoke an onslaught of the irrational fears that were a legacy of that day at Faxon's Folly, Moses quickly poked his head out the window to investigate the cause of all the commotion. Then he hastened to reassure his mistress.

"Now, Miz Jenny"—he patted her hand comfortingly—"der ain' no need fo' yo ter look so skeert, 'cause der ain' nothin' ter be afraid o'. It's jes' some ole trees whut mus' o' been knocked down by a storm. Dey's blockin' de tracks, an' we cain' go no farther till somebody gits out der an' moves dem."

"Oh," Jenny uttered in a small voice, ashamed of her obvious fright —and over nothing at all, it seemed. She couldn't for the life of her understand why she was so on edge today. Usually she had an iron grip on her emotions, for that was the only way she could function normally. The long journey must have tired her more than she'd realized. "Oh, well, if that's all . . ." Her sentence trailed off idly as she settled back onto the bench.

A few moments later all hell broke loose as the Morgan gang sprang from its hiding place to begin its assault. Firing several loud shots from their Navy Colts and yelling the wild cry of "Yip-Yip-Yaw!" made infamous by Quantrill's Raiders, the brothers charged toward the train.

"Don't touch those!" Luke snapped tersely as he swung into the cab of the locomotive in time to see Quincy Yates, who, belatedly recognizing the true reason for the trees lying on the tracks, was cursing a blue streak and fumbling angrily with the controls, intending to reengage the engine and ram through the barricade. "Get your hands up. Get them up!" Luke directed. "And get over there with your buddies." He motioned toward Ebenezer and Nathan. Unlike the grizzled old Quince, they were quaking in their boots at the rear of the cab. "Hurry it up! I don't want to have to shoot you unless it's absolutely necessary."

"Luke"—Tobias raced up to peer through the cab's open doorway, his spectacles glinting in the light—"uncouple the locomotive, and come on. The frigging express messenger is holed up in the goddamned express car, and he's taking potshots at J.R."

"Where in the hell is Raif?"

"I don't know." Tobias shook his head, giving Luke an I-told-you-so look. "He has yet to be seen, and J.R. is fit to be tied!"

"All right. I'll be right there," Luke said.

Then they heard J.R. bellow, "Raiford! You cold-collared bastard! Get your ass out here!" and Tobias started running furiously toward the express car.

Hurriedly Luke uncoupled the engine from the rest of the vehicle, and because the cars were on a slight incline, they began to roll back slowly, moving several yards. Satisfied that he would hear the roar of the locomotive if the engineer, who appeared to be a feisty fellow, dared to attempt to recouple the cars and smash through the barricade, Luke jumped down from the cab and rushed to join the rest of the gang.

By that time his brother Raiford, bandanna covering his face so none of the passengers would recognize him as one of the young men gambling in the smoking car last evening, was finally putting in a dilatory and thoroughly unrepentant appearance.

"Where in the hell have you been?" J.R. asked, a scowl on his face that boded ill for his brother.

Still unabashed, Raiford chuckled, his behavior more suited to a mild prank than a dangerous holdup.

"Well, J.R., you won't believe it," he drawled, "but last night the sauciest little roadrunner you ever did see invited me to join her in her sleeping car, and—Jesus!—I was so plumb tuckered out afterward that I clean forgot about the job. I never even woke up till I heard the shots."

"You damned fool! I've got a good mind to tell Emmalou! She *is* still your sweetheart, isn't she?" J.R. spat, disgusted. At age thirty-seven, he'd been married over fifteen years and was staunchly faithful to his wife, Kate. "Do you realize I might have been killed by that son of a bitch in the express car? I swear, Raif, I'm going to wring your frigging neck when we get home."

"Forget that," Tobias insisted, "and concentrate on the matter at hand. What're we going to do about the express messenger? Goddamn it, Raif! You were supposed to climb through the window earlier, before the attack, and tie the bastard up!"

"Sorry about that." Raiford shrugged, flushing guiltily, although his chin was thrust out defiantly in the face of his brothers' wrath. "Luke'll just have to take him out, I reckon."

"Thanks. You're all heart, Raif," Luke jeered, itching to box his brother's ears for the carelessness that had nearly cost J.R.'s life. "Hey," he then called from the cover of the bushes behind which they were hiding, "you in the express car. Do you know who's out here? You're not dealing with the Jameses or the Youngers, you fool. You're dealing with the Morgan gang. Now, if you know anything at all about us, you know we don't like to kill people, so just lay down your weapons and come on out with your hands up."

"I'm afraid I can't do that, Mr. Morgan," a thin, reedy voice replied waveringly from the window. "If I let you inside the car, the Adams Express Company will fire me."

"Well, if you don't do as I tell you, *I'm* going to shoot you," Luke threatened, his temper rising as it always did at the thought of having to use his pistols on someone. "And I warn you, sir: I'm a damned sight better shot than that rash hothead Jesse James!"

"Oh, dear." The express messenger, August Meeks, sighed, distraught.

He'd defended the Adams Express Company to the best of his ability; surely his employers would be able to recognize that fact. He wasn't used to firearms. He'd had a nice position as a clerk in a naval yard during the war. Still jobs were hard to come by these days; he just couldn't afford to lose the one he had. Besides, outlaws were often fatally unpredictable. He'd heard Jesse James had murdered men just for looking at him cross-eyed. Despite their reassurances to the contrary, the ruffians outside appeared most menacing, and Mr. Meeks had already enraged them with his resistance. For all he knew, the Morgans might shoot him on sight.

"I—I just can't let you in the car," he restated at last. "I have my duty and my family to consider."

"Then stand away from the doors, sir," Luke instructed. "We're going to blast them open." In a lower voice, he said, "Toby, get to work. I'll keep you covered."

In the end, however, Luke's protection proved unnecessary, for with his wild potshots at J.R., Mr. Meeks had used up all his ammunition, and once the doors had been blown apart, he was found cowering timidly in one corner of the express car.

"Luke, you and Raiford start robbing the passengers," J.R. commanded. "Toby and I can handle things at this end."

Indeed Tobias, having decided the petrified Mr. Meeks was stammering the truth about not being able to unlock the safes, was already pouring a fine trickle of black powder along the hinges of the heavy iron boxes. Raiford, still smarting from the sting of J.R.'s anger, didn't wait any longer, but headed for the public coaches. Luke followed hard on his brother's heels, for Raiford had a quick temper, and Luke didn't want him to get carried away and unintentionally kill somebody.

It gave Luke a feeling of pride to know that during all the holdups it had committed over the past five years, the Morgan gang had never murdered anyone. On those few occasions when the brothers had been forced to use their revolvers, they'd always aimed for arms or legs, and, unlike the Jameses and the Youngers, who really weren't good shots, the Morgans knew how to use their powerful Navy Colts and hit their marks every time, wounding instead of killing. This was one of the reasons they were so popular with the people of Southern Missouri, who viewed them as heroes rather than criminals.

Luke too, like Coleman Younger, was remembered for his many acts of kindness during Quantrill's horrendous raid on Lawrence, and this aided the brothers' cause as well.

Because the attack had been sudden and unexpected, it had taken those aboard the train several minutes to determine just what was going on. Those few persons daring to investigate the cause of the shots had informed the rest of the passengers that a holdup was in progress. As almost everyone was unarmed and those who weren't were reluctant to risk their lives for property that did not belong to them, no one had made any effort to halt the robbery. All had assumed the outlaws, once in possession of the contents of the safes, would depart. But this was not to be the case.

Although just as surprised as the others, the conductor, Dooley Newcomb, did hastily try to defend the passengers entrusted to his care. But he was no match for Luke and Raiford. After a brief tussle they subdued him, then expertly, with a length of rope Luke carried slung over his shoulder, they bound the conductor's hands and feet and stuffed him in one of the tiny washrooms, where they ordered him to remain. Their only resistance thus disposed of, they strode purposefully through the public car, guns drawn.

Most of the passengers were so stunned by the appearance of the two outlaws that it did not even occur to them that en masse they could easily have overpowered the men. Since the intelligent few who did recognize this fact were too scared to act, the holdup continued unchecked.

"All right," Luke announced to the passengers, "you all just stay in your seats and remain calm—and nobody will get hurt. Gentlemen, remove your wallets from your jackets . . . slowly, please, and take off all your jewelry. When my brother comes down the aisle toss your valuables into the sack he's carrying."

Though some swore under their breath, no one made any attempt to stop the two outlaws. A few of the women screamed, and one faint-hearted female promptly swooned and had to be revived with a vial of smelling salts by her equally frightened maid; but these were the only reactions to the unfolding crime.

"Ladies . . . ladies, please." Luke shook his head with amusement. "There's no need for all this. Really, I assure you we mean you no harm. We don't even mean to rob you. My brothers and I are Southern gentlemen after all. We don't steal from the fairer sex."

"This, sir, is an outrage!" one old man, braver than the rest, sputtered indignantly but without result.

"Yeah, ain't it just!" Raiford returned, grinning beneath his bandanna as he held out his bag for the loot.

With a muttered oath the old man threw his money, watch, and rings into the sack, regarding with scorn his fellow passengers too timid to protest this assault upon their persons.

The old man's obvious disgust, though he was himself physically unable to fight back, being heavily reliant upon the cane that helped him to walk, at least prodded someone else into action.

When Raiford was halfway down the aisle the large man who earlier, much to Jenny's embarrassment, had beaten upon the washroom door refused to part with his valuables and, shouting, he suddenly jumped up and tried to wrest Raiford's pistol from his hand. During the scuffle the revolver went off with a deafening roar, shattering one of the windows in the train. Glass flew; women shrieked with terror, and a baby started to wail loudly. Frantically the more astute passengers sought cover as the gun discharged again, sending someone's derby sailing across the coach.

"Get down!" Luke yelled. "Everybody, get down!"

Then he sprinted down the aisle to where Raiford was still struggling desperately with his brawny opponent. Luke waited until the man's back was turned toward him, then he slammed the butt of his Navy Colt down hard upon the beefy resister's head. Slowly the man released his hold on Raiford and, staggering a little, slumped to the floor, tiny drops of blood oozing from the wound caused by Luke's blow.

"My God!" a distraught female cried hysterically, running up the aisle to bend over the man's crumpled form. "Caleb! Caleb! Oh, he's dead! He's dead! You've killed him, you monster!" She stared up at Luke accusingly, tears streaming down her cheeks.

"Raif, see if he's still breathing." Luke motioned to his brother, keeping a wary eye on the rest of the passengers.

"Yeah, he's all right," Raiford reported disgustedly as he rose up from his examination of the man's body. "Stop that bawling, lady. He ain't dead—more's the pity." He glowered at the others in the car. "The next idiot who tries anything like that is going to wish he hadn't. Now get back in your seats, all of you!"

Cursing, Raiford kicked the man's fallen figure once for good measure, causing everyone to cower and resume their places. Then he gathered up the items that had fallen out of his bag during the fight. Gradually order was restored in the car, and the robbery proceeded.

Jenny, huddled pathetically on her hard bench, watched, frozen with terror, as the two outlaws began to near her. The pistols in their hands seemed to loom larger and more ominously with each step. Her face was absolutely ashen. Her eyes were big and blank, as though she did not see Luke and Raiford at all, but viewed another scene dredged from the dark chasms of her mind.

Delcine, sensing the girl's rising panic, squeezed her hand tightly in an understanding attempt at reassurance.

"Don't worry, Miss Jenny," Delcine whispered. "They won't hurt us."

But Jenny didn't even hear the words of comfort. She was still caught up in the past, remembering. She opened her mouth to scream, but no sound came out. Her throat was choked with emotion, as though she were suffocating. She couldn't breathe. *She couldn't breathe!*

"You. Yeah, you." Raiford pointed his revolver at Moses. "Empty out your pockets."

"Ah ain' gots nothin' in dem, sah," Moses declared, his voice low as he sidled nearer to Jenny, intending to protect her with his life, if necessary.

"Yeah, that's what all you darkies say," Raiford sneered. "Now empty out your pockets, and be quick about it!"

Slowly Moses turned his pockets inside out, revealing nothing except Kingston Colter's solid-gold pocket watch that Jenny had given to the devoted Negro for helping to save her life that day at Faxon's Folly.

Something inside the girl snapped at the sight of her beloved father's timepiece. It and her mother's delicate, filigreed embroidery scissors, which she had bestowed upon Delcine, were all she and her three sisters had managed to save of their parents' belongings during the war.

"No!" Jenny gasped in a strangled whimper, snatching the watch from Raiford's grasping hands. "You can't have that!"

"Now see here, miss—" Raiford began, only to be interrupted by Luke, who had been silently studying the girl for some time.

"What's the problem, Raif?" Luke demanded, his gaze still taking in curiously Jenny's trembling form, her white, bloodless fingers wrapped too tightly about the timepiece she held clutched to her bosom as though her life depended on it.

She wasn't pretty, he thought critically, for there was nothing the least bit arresting about her except a pair of big, emotion-filled grey eyes, haunted now with dread. Beneath her bonnet her hair, pinned up in a low chignon at the nape of her neck, was a soft brown that would not have drawn attention in a crowd. A sprinkling of freckles danced across her upturned nose and pale cheeks, and her mouth was too generous for her heart-shaped face. But there was something—something *gallant*, yes, that was it!—about her all the same that touched Luke.

It must be those eyes, he decided. They were too large and luminous for the delicate planes of her face, and fathomless too, so that when he looked at her they engulfed him, and he felt as though he were drowning in the twin grey pools. Her full red mouth, its lower lip quivering ever so slightly, was sweet and strangely inviting, and there was as well an odd, pitiable vulnerability about her that made her appear small and helpless, in need of a man's love and protection. It had been a long time —too long perhaps—since Luke had wanted to defend a woman. But for some indeterminable reason he suddenly felt compelled to come to this girl's aid.

She was so tense he believed that if he were to touch her, she would shatter like glass, for she was, he noted, a muscle tightening in his jaw at the observation, absolutely terrified of him and his brother.

Her fear wasn't normal, Luke realized. He had seen that dazed, empty look on men's faces during the war, and he knew the girl was scarcely even aware of him and Raiford—or of her own actions toward them. She was locked in some private hell inside her own mind, a dark, demon-ridden place Luke had visited himself in the past and knew well. War had done that to a lot of men, but he'd rarely seen that lost, stricken expression on a woman's face before.

"What's your name, miss?" he inquired gently, sensing she would respond to a kind tone.

"Jenny," she murmured. "Jenny Leigh Colter."

She spoke her name very fast, as though afraid she might not be able to get it all out otherwise. Then wordlessly she looked up at the man who towered over her.

He was tall and well built. His shoulders were broad and powerful, his arms and chest massively muscled, as though he had labored long and hard during his thirty-two years of living. His firm flat belly tapered down to narrow hips and rounded buttocks that joined thick, corded thighs and calves.

Beneath his brown cowboy hat his tousled blond hair gleamed like spun gold and was streaked with strands the color of flax where the sun had caressed it. Darker blond brows arched over eyes that were far older than his years, eyes the deep clear blue of a summer sky after it has been washed by the rain. Dense brown lashes rimmed the timeworn orbs, making them stand out brilliantly against the bronze of his lean-cheeked, weather-beaten visage. Above the bandanna that covered the rest of his face, what Jenny could see of his nose was slightly aquiline and finely molded. His jaw, she thought, would be strong and set with determination, his lips well shaped and sensual.

His pale blue cambric shirt with its plain wooden buttons was open at the throat to reveal the crisp, dark blond curls that matted his chest. Over his short, dark brown buckskin vest adorned with brass studs, leather ammunition belts crisscrossed his torso. About his waist another leather belt with a brass buckle bore a sharp-bladed Bowie knife. At his hips was a low-slung gunbelt with two tied-down holsters. Tight brown buckskin breeches encased his legs. Dusty brown leather boots were upon his feet.

He was, Jenny reflected with a peculiar detachment, the kind of man she had once dreamed about and longed to make her own, the kind of man who would never look twice at a woman such as she.

But his eyes held hers anyway and went on staring at her, taking in the small pulse leaping wildly at the hollow of her throat, her ripe full breasts that rose and fell quickly beneath the bodice of her gown as she returned his gaze.

To her mortification Jenny felt a tiny flutter begin at the very core of her being, then start to spread with strange, hot, licking flames through her body. The sensation was overwhelming, devastating, and it stunned and confused her, for she had never felt it before. She longed to tear her eyes away from those of the outlaw, but she could not. His contemplation of her was mesmerizing, as though he were reaching inside of her to unlock the secrets of her heart and soul.

It came to Jenny suddenly that for the first time in her life she was feeling desire, and the thought both startled and frightened her. She was uncomfortable with all men but Cade and Moses, and she was deeply fearful and suspicious of their passions. This man looked as though his were many and all-consuming, and without warning Jenny felt as though she were but a morsel he would devour in one bite. There was something hard and unyielding in him, she sensed. If he wanted a woman, he would take every part of her, until she had nothing left to call her own but belonged to him—and to him alone.

The notion sent an icy shiver down her spine as images of that day at Faxon's Folly rose up once more to clutch at her. She would belong to no man—ever! Whatever she felt for the outlaw before her she must trap and suppress in some dark corner of her mind so it would never again surface within her. If she did not, Jenny shuddered to think what would become of her. With desire came surrender, and that she could never face.

This man was a criminal. Her protests would mean nothing to him, as they had meant nothing that day she fought to forget. He might kidnap her, rape her, use her until he'd tired of her, and then kill her. She dared not let him witness her disgraceful, inexplicable reaction to him. He might interpret it as an invitation to take her with him when he and the other men had finished robbing the train. Shaking with apprehension, Jenny swallowed hard and forced herself to wrench her eyes away from his.

"Doan tech her. Oh, please, doan tech her, sah," Moses pleaded with Luke, afraid he would attempt to wrest the timepiece from Jenny's hands and would set off a violent, uncontrollable attack of hysteria. "Let her keep de watch. It belonged ter her daddy. He wuz kilt by de Yankees durin' de war, an' it's all she's gots lef' o' him. She gived it ter me, 'cause Ah done heped ter save her life aftah de war. But it belonged ter her daddy, who wuz kilt by de Yankees," Moses repeated for emphasis, recalling that Luke had mentioned earlier that he and his brothers were Southern gentlemen.

"Is that right?" Luke glanced again at Jenny.

Silently she nodded, once more feeling desire leap between them like a bolt of lightning. The outlaw felt it too, she thought, for he caught his breath sharply, and his eyes darkened perceptibly as they raked her again, this time with more than just a passing interest.

Luke did not miss her attraction to him, but he did not overlook either the fact that the girl was utterly panicked by it, her earlier, all-encompassing fear now sharply defined and focused solely on him. At first Luke did not understand her peculiar reaction to him. Then the importunate words spoken previously by her manservant registered more fully on his brain.

Don't touch her, the darky had beseeched. But his concern had not been for the girl's virtue, as Luke initially had believed. It had been for her mind. She was irrationally terrified of all men, not just of Luke alone and not just because he was an outlaw. But why? There must be something in her past, he guessed, something that had scarred her so deeply she had never recovered from the shock of it. Luke could only think of one crime against a female that would have caused such emotional damage, and his heart ached for her. Even during the war he had never raped a woman, and he had despised all those soldiers who had.

"You may keep the watch, then," he told Jenny, carefully refraining from touching her consolingly, as he suddenly longed to do, and causing Moses to exhale with relief. "In fact," Luke continued, raising his voice so everybody could hear, "anyone who fought for the Stars and Bars may keep his possessions. Only, don't try to deceive us, because all my brothers and I rode with Colonel Quantrill, and we know the names of just about every Confederate regiment there was."

"What in the hell do you think you're doing, Luke?" Raiford asked, his tone frosty. "This here's a holdup, for Christ's sake, not a charity ball!"

"This is also Missouri," Luke reminded him grimly. "Every Rebel here will remember this little piece of gallantry, and when the authorities interrogate them about the robbery, chances are they won't give those goddamned lawmen or those frigging Pinkerton agents one bit of help!"

Solemnly Raiford considered this idea.

"Yeah," he agreed at last, his eyes starting to sparkle devilishly at the thought. "It'll serve those stiff-necked bastards right!"

Quickly, hearing J.R. hollering for them outside, Luke and Raiford filled their sack, questioning each contributor rapidly to determine whether or not he'd actually fought for the South during the war. Then the brothers swaggered to the door, Luke pausing only once, when he reached Jenny's seat.

What he would have said to her she never knew, for it was then that the conductor, Dooley Newcomb, apparently having been freed by some of the braver passengers, suddenly appeared in the doorway of the coach, a carbine leveled determinedly at the two men.

"Halt!" he commanded, though his voice quavered slightly. "Halt, or I'll shoot!"

"Jesus," Luke muttered. Then he raised his voice warningly. "Don't be a fool, man." His tone was steely; his eyes were hard. "I can kill you before you ever even manage to pull that trigger."

The conductor blinked, and the weapon wavered in his anxious grip. But still he knew his duty, and he intended to carry it out.

"Drop your guns, and step back, your hands over your heads," he directed.

Collectively the passengers held their breath as a tense silence ensued, Luke and Raiford making no moves and the conductor licking his lips nervously. Then suddenly, so quickly that no one was even aware of what was happening, Dooley Newcomb fired. His shot went wild, blasting a gaping hole in the roof and sending shards of debris flying. Almost simultaneously a report from Luke's pistol sounded deafeningly in Jenny's ears. She jumped, then cringed as she watched the conductor drop his carbine and stagger back uncomprehendingly against the doorjamb. Blood spurted sickeningly from the wound in his shoulder, gushing out over his uniform and seeping between his fingers as instinctively he put his hand up to staunch the flow of red.

Not even realizing she did so, Jenny screamed, as did several of the other women. Some of the male passengers sprang to their feet, only to freeze when Raiford wheeled rapidly to defend his brother's back. As it had previously, someone's baby began to wail loudly, adding to the general pandemonium.

To Jenny's disbelief she saw Dooley Newcomb, wincing with pain, grit his teeth and reach purposefully for his weapon, which lay a few feet from his grasp. Beside her, Luke fired again. This time the bullet slammed into the conductor's thigh, causing his body to jerk spasmodically as once more he slumped against the doorjamb, blood spraying from the puncture in his leg.

Hysterical now, the present all mixed up with the past in her mind, Jenny leaped from her seat and started to run down the aisle to the door. Heedlessly she lurched past Dooley Newcomb's fallen form and down the steps leading to the ground from the small platform outside.

Wildly she glanced about, spying J.R. and Tobias, who were racing toward the coach. The sight of them only further alarmed her already-confused brain, and she turned and rushed blindly toward the woods, knowing only that she must escape from the unreal scene unfolding all around her.

Hard on her heels, cursing heatedly under his breath, was Luke. He hadn't dared to shoot Jenny, for gunning down a female was not a thing that would have sat lightly on his conscience or endeared him to the public. But he knew he must stop her all the same. Furiously he called for her to halt, but she only kept on running frantically through the trees, her gait hampered solely by her lameness and her narrow skirt.

Branches slapped at her face, scratching it, and tore at her arms and legs, but she pushed the limbs aside, scarcely even feeling the pain. Her gown caught on a bush, but without even pausing Jenny yanked the material free and stumbled on, gasping for breath, her lungs feeling as though they were going to burst from her exertions. Raucous shouts and laughter dinned in her ears, and everywhere she looked she could see gruesome-faced men and blood so thick and red that it was as though she were drowning in a sea of crimson demons. She screamed and screamed as she ran, rasping horribly for air between her shrieks, and Luke thought she surely must be demented. He had seen soldiers go berserk before, during the war, and some dim inkling of what must have happened to her clicked in his brain. But still he pursued her, knowing he must not let her escape. She must remain with the train, like every-one else, until he and his brothers were well away from Devil's Holler.

Panting, he chased after her, his boots thrumming on the hard earth until at last he flung himself upon her, knocking her to the ground.

As all the air was expelled from her lungs at the impact of the blow, for a moment Jenny lay dazed and helpless beneath Luke, petrified by the shock of his weight upon her. Then some dark corner of her mind released her primitive instinct for survival, the instinct that had driven her to fight for her life once before, and she started to struggle desper-ately in his rough grasp, writhing and twisting until she managed to gain some leverage and turn herself around to face him. Without think-ing she clawed at his eyes, her nails raking his skin savagely and tearing away his protective bandanna so the whole of his tanned visage was revealed to her eyes.

"Goddamn it!" Luke snapped, trying to defend himself against her biting nails without injuring her in the process. "Stop fighting me! Stop fighting me, you frigging hellcat! I'm not going to hurt you!"

But Jenny paid no attention to his words, and finally he was forced to pinion her arms above her head and to slap her face to bring her to her senses. Momentarily stunned, Jenny let her head fall back listlessly as she ceased her assault against him, recognizing at last that she was trapped in an iron grip from which she could not free herself. As soft, wrenching sobs shook her, she became aware of Luke's body covering her own, his face and mouth inches from hers, his chest brushing the tips of her heaving breasts, his manhood pressed against her thighs.

She started to tremble, certain he intended to rape her, but, terrified as she was, Jenny gathered her wits and courage, and her hysteria abated.

Luke, his breathing gradually returning to normal, felt her body quivering beneath his, her heart pounding in harmony with his own, and it came to him how fine-boned and fragile she was, like a bird—a tiny wren—fluttering in his arms. She was of average height but slender and soft, with lush, inviting curves that dipped and swelled in all the right places, at odd variance with her plain face. Again the strange compulsion he'd had earlier to protect her rose within him, and in the heat of the instant a sudden, sharp knife of unexpected desire stabbed through his loins, causing him to grow hard against her.

Bemused, Luke stared into Jenny's tear-filled eyes and saw, pityingly, that she understood exactly what was happening to him and was mentally, despite her overwhelming fear of him, trying to prepare herself for his rape of her.

"It seems you've aroused me in more ways than one." He spoke lightly to wipe the awful, blank acceptance from her eyes. "But, then, when a woman angers a man lust usually isn't too far behind."

"Do as you will with me, then," she whispered fiercely, surprising him. "But do not think to have any pleasure from it, for I shall not gratify your lust by screaming or attempting to fight you. There is nothing you can do to me that will be worse than what I have already suffered at the hands of men such as you!"

So he was right about her past, Luke thought, somewhat awed and amazed by her brave defiance of him, for crystal droplets were trickling slowly down her cheeks. What strength of character and will she must have, he mused, traits he admired deeply.

Tentatively, almost caressingly he cupped her chin with one hand, turning her face a little so he could view the purplish blue bruise beginning to darken one side of it.

"I'm not going to hurt you," he repeated quietly. "In fact, I'm sorry I hit you, but I couldn't think of anything else to calm you down. Are you all right?" he asked, shifting his weight slightly so he would not crush her but making no move to release her, afraid she would either strike him or take to her heels again.

Even more vividly now did she remind him of a defenseless bird, ready to lash out bravely with its beak if forced to fight or to fly away if it thought it could escape.

Jenny nodded wordlessly in response to his query, trying to choke back her soft whimpers of dismay.

"Well, then, I reckon I'd better let you up," Luke told her, "before it becomes impossible for me to do so."

Wonderingly Jenny gazed up at him, this action so startling it stilled her tears. She could not comprehend the fact that this outlaw she had just seen coolly shoot the conductor twice did not mean to harm her. It was not until Luke stood and held out his hand to her that she finally believed him.

Curiously she studied him, searching his handsome countenance for some sign of viciousness or deceit, but she saw none. His steady blue eyes were clear, forthright, tinged only with a slight inquisitiveness and concern. There was nothing there of the horrifying purposefulness that had characterized the faces of the men that day at Faxon's Folly. She realized then that Luke, for all his violent, criminal existence, was not as they had been. His courtly offer of assistance reminded her of her sisters' gentlemen callers before the war, and hesitantly, her eyes lighting a little with hope, Jenny laid her palm in his. As Luke did no more than help her to her feet, then quickly loose her hand, she began to breathe a little easier.

Still the taut, awkward silence that had fallen upon them unnerved her, and, not knowing what else to do, she righted her askew bonnet, pinned her hair back into place, and smoothed the folds of her narrow skirt, noticing as she did so that it had been irreparably stained by the grass.

"Oh," she wailed softly. "My dress . . . it's ruined."

To her surprise Luke threw back his head and laughed.

"Now I know you're all right," he explained as Jenny looked at him questioningly, bewildered. "Anytime a woman starts worrying about her clothes is when I stop worrying about *her!*"

Tremulously Jenny smiled, since he seemed to expect it, and he thought suddenly of how her heart-shaped face would glow, lighting up with a beauty that comes only from within, if ever the shadows that misted her grey eyes were to lift. Why had he ever thought her plain?

"Well, I—I guess I'd better return to the train," she said nervously.

"Yes."

Still they stood there, neither one of them making any move to depart. It was the first time in her life Jenny had ever been alone with a man who wasn't a part of her family, and though she was still scared, she felt too a strange mixture of anticipation and, inexplicably, longing.

"Luke!" someone shouted from afar. "Luke, come on! We've got to get out of here!"

"Yes, I'm coming," he called. Then he turned back to Jenny. "Goodbye, Miss Jennilee," he murmured reluctantly, his eyes lingering on her face, as though he would have liked to stay a while with her.

Then he was gone, leaving nothing behind but the new and extremely disturbing memory of his sky-blue eyes kissing her own grey ones tenderly.

Jenny watched him until he was out of sight, shaking once more with the unfamiliar, tumultuous emotions he'd unleashed within her earlier.

His last glance had held promise, she thought, as though it had been just a prelude to the far more exciting things he would do to her, should he ever see her again, and the idea both shocked and fascinated her. Even more mortifying was the terrible knowledge that something deep inside of Jenny even now half wanted him to do them to her. He had been different somehow from all the other men she'd ever known.

Her cheeks flushed hotly with shame as she suddenly imagined herself locked in Luke's powerful arms, yet to her distress she could not banish the unnerving mental picture. She had seen the depths of hell in his eyes—but she had seen the heights of heaven too, and she had responded to both in a way that was beyond her understanding. It was as though something she had not known she'd possessed had been loosed by Luke from the confines of her darker being and would not again be easily caged. Already Jenny could feel it growing inside of her. Resolutely she tried to crush the wicked, wanton thing, but to her sharp dismay she found she could not. It had changed from a shapeless, faceless emotion to a blond-haired, blue-eyed outlaw who laughed softly, mocking her futile attempts to overcome him, and, easily subduing her inner resistance, emerged victorious. She could not put him out of her mind, nor could her body forget his strong embrace.

Jenny shivered. Is this what passion is? she wondered. If so, she wanted no part of it. She must remain in control of herself at all times; it was the only way she could function normally. Yet still the devil of desire that threatened to take possession of her would not be banished.

Feeling as though her life would never again be the same, Jenny began to walk slowly toward the train.

Luke and his brothers, rejoining Billy Clay, who was still fuming over missing all the excitement, loaded their saddlebags with as much of the stolen gold as they could safely carry. The rest they buried beneath the big rock that had served as their rendezvous point. Then they mounted their horses and galloped off into the hills.

"You sure took your own sweet time back there with that girl." Raiford needled Luke, irritated, as they rode along, for he was jealous of Luke's easy way with women and wondered if his brother had gotten something he had missed.

"She was upset," Luke answered coolly, unruffled. "If you hadn't been so damned intent on stealing her darky's watch earlier, you'd have seen then that her reaction to us wasn't normal, that her fear was all out of proportion to a simple train robbery. When all the shooting started she just couldn't handle it, I reckon, so she ran. For Christ's sake, Raif!" Luke sneered with disgust. "The girl was hysterical when I caught her."

"She must have been," Tobias put in dryly. "She marked your face up something good, Luke." He smiled teasingly. "I've never known a woman to do *that* to you before."

"My face," Luke repeated dumbly, his hand tracing gingerly the scratches on his cheeks. With a sinking feeling in the pit of his stomach he realized his protective bandanna, drawn up earlier over his nose and mouth, now lay knotted about his neck. "Jesus, Toby," he muttered uneasily. "She saw my face. That girl saw my face!"

Upon receipt of this information the rest of the Morgans drew their horses to an abrupt halt and stared at Luke, aghast. They could not go back. Those on the devastated vehicle the gang had left behind would be prepared now for that. The brothers could only ride on, spurred by the knowledge that they had committed a savage armed holdup not twenty-five miles from their hometown, and someone aboard the train could positively identify Luke and place him at the scene of their crime.

Chapter Three

Forgotten by the rest of the world, whose gods, Power and Pelf, were worshiped in temples built by progress that had almost—but not quite —passed the small town by, the place known as Tumbling Creek, in Taney County, Missouri, was a peaceful, backwoods hamlet tucked away like an aerie in the high, dark, densely forested hills that formed the heart of the Ozark Mountains.

There were those who claimed the vast, ageless promontories were the oldest in the world. Surely they were the most ancient in North America. Bleak and forbidding in winter; shrouded in the early morning mist of spring, they soared like great pyramids, ever-watchful and mysterious, over the isolated valleys and tangled ravines far below.

To the south lay the twisting White River and the wilds of the Arkansas border just beyond. To the east were the cave and the bubbling, spring-fed rivulet whence the town had drawn its name.

For over a hundred years Tumbling Creek had stood alone against the world, a place apart, unto itself, and it had neither wanted nor welcomed the intrusion of foreigners, as all those who did not belong were called.

Its people, deeply suspicious of strangers, had taught their children to be likewise, and so the circle that composed the closed, tightly knit community had continued unchanged and unbroken through the years that had passed one much like another.

To this day old men still rested their weary bones in gnarled wooden chairs on dilapidated front porches as, moonshine jugs in hand, they boasted of the much-exaggerated exploits of their youth or trounced each other triumphantly in fierce games of checkers and cards. Old women, quilting squares on laps, still gathered in the shabby parlors of two-room shacks to exchange the latest gossip and drink a cup of tea.

And if its traditional customs and beliefs were thought quaint and old-fashioned by those from the outside, Tumbling Creek did not care, for life, though hard, was good.

It was to this guarded, time-encapsulated town that Jenny came when, three hours behind schedule, the train finally pulled into the Tumbling Creek depot.

Slowly, still dazed by the afternoon's events, she drew on her gloves while Moses and Delcine gathered up their few belongings and the dinner basket. Then the three of them stepped outside onto the platform to wait while the two battered old trunks that contained all their worldly possessions were unloaded from the baggage car.

The sun was just setting on the western horizon, sinking like a ship aflame into the dark blue-green sea of peaks that swelled and dipped in jagged crests against the firmament. Below, the sheltered hollow of the land was bathed with vibrant red-orange waves that seemed to ripple to the farthest reaches of the earth until they disappeared in a dazzling, hazy shimmer of light and fire.

Never had Jenny beheld such an extravagance of colors, so rich and majestic, so bold and overpowering that it was almost as though she could have stretched out one hand and touched them. Spellbound, her eyes drank thirstily of the deep purples and blues and greens that cloaked the hills in robes fit for a king, the glowing reds and oranges and yellows that glittered here and there like precious jewels strewn before a queen.

She breathed deeply of the mountain air, fresh and clean and dizzyingly, fragrantly perfumed by the feathery evergreen pines, the tall, acorn-bearing oaks, and the fringed, pungently scented cedars that grew in thick abundance all over the countryside. In the distance, along the cool, muddy banks of the laughing brook that shared with the town the name of Tumbling Creek, sweet anise, mullein, catnip, and pokeweed nestled together in clusters that wafted gently in the breeze, adding their own tangy aromas to the rest.

It was a paradise, Jenny thought, for here man's despoliation had not yet begun.

The town, built of lumber gleaned from the native forests, was like a natural oasis in the midst of the savage splendor, as much a part of its surroundings as though it had been there since time's beginning.

The wide, dusty main street was lined with plank sidewalks along which false storefronts stood, unpainted, the variated patterns of the wood from which they had been made visible. Streaks of light intermingled with dark, and scars and knotholes provided a warm contrast to the hand-rubbed smoothness of the boards. Here the only sparks of color came from the large signs emblazoned across the shops or the smaller shingles that hung less ostentatiously above doors.

Tumbling Creek, for all its isolation, was not, as Jenny had half feared, lacking in amenities. Gazing about, she spied artistically painted signs proclaiming Sweeney's Dry-Goods Store and Ascot & Sons (Fine Furniture), the Razorback Saloon and the First National Bank of Tumbling Creek, among others.

She heaved a great sigh of relief and for the first time in five years felt the fear and tension drain from her body. Here she would be safe, protected by the magnificent mountains that kept this part of Southern Missouri yet a wilderness. Here she would begin her life anew.

She stood a little taller, squaring her small shoulders determinedly and lifting her chin.

"Miss Colter? Miss Jennifer Colter?"

The girl turned at the sound of her name, as a short, balding, bespectacled man hurried toward her, his hand outstretched in greeting.

"Yes," she said.

"I'm Horace Peabody, the head of the Tumbling Creek school board. I'm right proud to know you, Miss Colter, and glad to see you got here safe and sound." He enthusiastically pumped the gloved hand she offered. "I understand you had a most harrowing afternoon, what with the holdup and all. Good grief! I just don't know what the world's coming to. Powder Springs telegraphed us the news, you know, as soon as the train rolled into their depot. I'll bet old Quince—the engineer— was madder than a wounded bear about it!" Mr. Peabody grimaced and shook his head at the thought. "Before today he held the record at the Ozark Mountain Railroad Company for making the most runs on time, you know. And of course Dooley Newcomb, the conductor, must feel like a fool, letting the gang get the drop on him like that. Still he's lucky to be alive. The Jameses would have killed him, you know.

"I guess it must have been a dreadful experience for you too, Miss Colter. I don't blame you for trying to run away. No, sirree. Not one bit," Mr. Peabody stated firmly, putting Jenny at her ease, for she'd wondered if he'd learned of her wild flight from the train, and she had been worried he would think her unstable and thus unable to handle her teaching position. "No doubt you're not used to such goings-on in Atlanta.

"Well, seeing as how you were going to be late," he continued, "I made arrangements to put you up in the hotel just for tonight. I'm afraid there won't be time this evening to drive you out to the cabin. It's some distance from town. It's the only school for miles around, you know, and it's more accessible to the outlying farmlands that way. At any rate, it gets dark real quick in these here hills, and what with the outlaws and the wild animals on the prowl then, a body just ought not travel at night unless it's absolutely necessary—just to be on the safe side, you know. Besides, I figured you'd be tired after your long journey and hungry too, and Mrs. Zee, over to the hotel, turns down a right soft bed and makes a tasty cherry pie to boot."

"How—how very kind of you, Mr. Peabody," Jenny stammered, once she could get a word in edgewise. "I confess I'm extremely weary, and I'm sure Moses and Delcine are too." She turned to her two servants, who were standing quietly to one side. "Did you get our trunks, Moses?"

"Yassum, Miz Jenny." He looked at Mr. Peabody. "If'n yo'll jes' tell me wheah de cah'ige is, sah, so's Ah cain load dem up. . . ."

"Oh, yes, of course. Right this way, please. Right this way," Mr. Peabody repeated, leading them from the platform. "Watch your step there, Miss Colter. I've seen many a poor fellow take a nasty fall in that particular spot—yes, indeed. It's invariably a stranger and usually good for a laugh or two, since we don't much cotton to foreigners here in Tumbling Creek. But of course you'll soon be one of the townspeople, and we wouldn't want *you* to start out on the wrong foot, so to speak." Mr. Peabody tittered with delight at his small joke.

He would have helped Jenny across the rough area, but Delcine, anticipating this and knowing how her mistress shied away from being touched by a man, had already taken hold of the girl's arm. Mr. Peabody, a trifle startled, glanced disapprovingly at the mulatto, then went on.

"We don't see too many coloreds around these parts, you know," he confided to Jenny. "I was rather surprised when you mentioned them in your letter, but since I gathered they've been with you a long time, well, naturally I understood why you wanted to bring them along. It's just as well, I imagine. They'll be nice company for you out at the house. No doubt it gets kind of lonesome out there sometimes. That's why our last schoolteacher left, you know. She was from Chicago, and she just couldn't adjust to our way of life here in Tumbling Creek. She said we didn't have the . . . er . . . sort of culture to which she was accustomed. I hope you aren't going to feel the same way, Miss Colter, what with being from Atlanta and all. It's hard to find a good schoolteacher who wants to live in our quiet little town, and I'd hate to have to go through the hiring process all over again—especially before the start of the fall term."

His tone was a trifle anxious, and Jenny understood now why he had not made more of her irrational behavior on the train.

"I'm certain I'll be very happy here in Tumbling Creek, Mr. Peabody." She spoke reassuringly, somewhat bemused by all his chatter, for she'd never met a man who talked so incessantly. "It seems like a pleasant place, and since I grew up on a—on a plantation, I'm used to living in the country."

"Well, that's just fine, then." Mr. Peabody beamed, then declared, "Ah. Here we are," as they finally reached the buggy. "Now, if you'll just strap the trunks on back there"—he directed these words at Moses —"we'll be on our way."

Shortly thereafter they drew up in front of the Hotel Van Buren, which, the head of the school board breezily informed Jenny, was run by a widow, Zenobia Van Buren, whom everybody called Mrs. Zee.

Anywhere from fifty to seventy, she was a big, rawboned woman with a face like a wizened walnut and breasts that sagged pendulously. She was dressed in a faded black cotton gown trimmed with starched white lace. A plain cameo brooch was pinned to her collar. Her coarse, wiry brown hair streaked with grey was scraped back into a severe bun, and her brown eyes shone with a keenness that missed very little. She was also, as Jenny was presently to learn, extremely blunt and outspoken.

"So you're the new schoolmarm," Mrs. Zee assessed the girl, once Mr. Peabody had made the introductions. "Well, you ain't much on looks, that's for sure. But I reckon you've got a good head on your shoulders and a kind heart in your bosom, which is more than can be said of most folks. Come on in, and sit a spell. I bet you're just plumb wore out and feeling mighty lank too. Sammy. Sammy!" she called to one of her grandchildren, who helped her around the hotel. "Take Miz Colter's trunks up to room number four, then fetch something hot from the kitchen." She turned back to Jenny. "Well, sit down, sit down. You too." She motioned to Delcine and Moses. "I roasted a wild turkey this morning and baked some yams to go with it. I figure that'll fill you up plenty."

"It sounds delicious," Jenny commented as she took a chair at one of the red-checkered cloth-covered tables in the small dining room that was off to one side of the lobby and to which Mrs. Zee had led them.

A few customers were already there, eating supper. They glanced over at Jenny curiously, then returned to their meals, watching her slyly out of the corners of their eyes. All had guessed her identity, she decided, and were silently appraising her to decide whether or not she was going to fit into their community.

After another few minutes of conversation Mr. Peabody announced he must be on his way. He told Jenny he would be by at eight o'clock the next morning to take her out to her new home, and she thanked him for all his help. When he had left she, Delcine, and Moses fell hungrily upon the steaming-hot plates that were soon set before them.

Mrs. Zee continued to sit and talk affably, wanting to elicit as much information from the newcomer as she could. Jenny did her best to answer but deftly fended off the more awkward questions about her family and her past. It was not that she wished to conceal her background, but simply that it was still a very painful subject to her, one she could seldom discuss without bursting into tears. As she was exhausted she knew the wounds that had been the cause of her grief would be all the more easily reopened, and she had no wish to start crying in front of the hotel proprietress and the strangers in the dining room. That would be a most disastrous start to her new life.

Jenny had recognized that Mr. Peabody, for all his verbosity, and Mrs. Zee, for all her brusque kindness, were still suspicious of her and guarded in their conclusions about her. To them she was a foreigner. She knew it would take a long time for her to gain acceptance in the small, reserved society of Tumbling Creek—if she ever did—and that if she did indeed want to belong, she must go slowly and try not to make any mistakes that would earn her the townspeople's disapproval.

Her reticence was not held against her. In fact, it garnered her a slow, grudging respect, for the various residents of Tumbling Creek were themselves closemouthed and would not have dreamed of pouring their entire life's history into the ears of a stranger. Jenny's restraint told Mrs. Zee and the others in the dining room, who were listening intently, although they appeared to be absorbed with their meals, that she was a trifle wary and could be trusted to hold her tongue; and a mark of favor was checked off on the mental columns being tabulated about her.

Jenny had just finished sopping up with a flaky buttermilk biscuit the last of the gravy on her plate when the door to the hotel opened and two men came striding through the lobby into the dining room.

The girl looked up idly at the new arrivals. Noticing little of interest in the flickering shadows cast by the oil lamps that had been lit some time ago, she was just about to turn away when her heart suddenly lurched to a stop, then began to hammer again queerly in her breast.

Why, it was *him!* The man who'd robbed the train! Jenny would have known that handsome, bronzed face anywhere. She shook slightly with trepidation as she saw the red marks upon his cheeks. She had not realized how badly she'd scratched him. Even more disquieting was the fact that when the man suddenly caught sight of her, his deep sky-blue eyes widened in surprise and recognition. He stared hard at her for an instant. Then slowly, mockingly he started to smile, a deliberately jeering, satisfied grin that would have frightened even those made of sterner stuff than Jenny. As he passed her table he nodded imperceptibly, warningly, it seemed, then touched the brim of his hat politely. She inhaled sharply. Her heart seemed to flip-flop in her breast, and her blood rushed like quicksilver through her veins, bringing a flush of agitation and confusion to her cheeks.

"Is there something wrong, Miz Colter?" Mrs. Zee inquired, bristling slightly at the thought that perhaps Jenny had not found the excellent meal to her liking.

"Yes," the girl whispered, afraid and somewhat unsure as to how she should proceed. "Mrs. Zee, I—I don't want to alarm you, but I—I think you should send someone for the law immediately."

"The law!" The hotel proprietress's voice boomed, causing Jenny to cringe and cast her eyes about anxiously to see if the outlaw had heard. "Why, mercy me, child! Whatever for?"

Jenny bit her lip, nervously watching the two men pulling chairs out from a table a short distance away.

"Do you see those gentlemen over there—the ones who just came in?" At the older woman's nod Jenny went on breathlessly. "Well, I'm just positive that tall fellow is one of the men who robbed the train this afternoon!"

"Oh," Mrs. Zee uttered with relief. Then to Jenny's amazement she began to chuckle with amusement. "Is that all? Miz Colter"—the hotel proprietress sobered abruptly and leaned forward conspiratorily in her chair—"you're new here, so I'm going to give you a piece of sound advice: Here in Tumbling Creek it just ain't smart to speak ill of the dead—or of the Morgan gang, and those two men over there are Luke Morgan and his younger brother, Billy Clay.

"Now maybe they committed that holdup—and maybe they didn't— but if you were to go over to the marshal's office and report the matter, I guarantee you those boys wouldn't even be arrested. No, ma'am. They've got a parcel of kith and kin in these here hills, and even if you swore on a stack of Bibles that Luke Morgan robbed that train, there'd be another ten people to swear he didn't, that he was over to the Razor-back Saloon, playing cards, when it happened. No, all you'd get for your pains would be the shame of being made to look like a fool in front of the entire town."

"Why, that's terrible!" Jenny exclaimed, shocked. "Do you mean— do you mean to tell me everyone in Tumbling Creek . . . *knows* those men are outlaws—and yet does nothing about it?"

"That's right," Mrs. Zee replied calmly, "and if you want to stay healthy, you'll do the same. They ain't too keen on killing people, but when them boys is riled there's no telling what they might do. The last time somebody squealed on 'em they went out to his farm—poor old Festus McNabb's place it was—and they tarred and feathered him and hung him up on a butchering hook, along with a sign warning folks that the next tattletale might not be so lucky. It was purt near seven hours before Festus's boy, Matthew, found him, and it took him nigh on a month to get that durned tar off his skin. Festus was madder than a hornet about it, I tell you, but he's never opened his mouth about the Morgans since."

Feeling suddenly faint, Jenny closed her eyes in horror, unable to believe she had been unfortunate enough to come to such a town—and just when she'd been so happy, thinking how safe she was going to be here! But how could she be, when *he* lived here?

Was there no place where justice prevailed? Atlanta, when she'd left it, had been full of carpetbaggers and scalawags who'd made a sham of law and order. And here, it seemed, criminals roamed the streets freely, and nobody even bothered to arrest them!

Jenny clasped her hands together tightly at the thought, but she knew it was not the sole cause of her fear. If she were honest with herself, she must admit the fact that, besides being a wanted man, Luke Morgan had aroused something in her she had no desire to face, and she could not trust herself in his presence. If she were forced to see him on a continual basis, Jenny was afraid she would be unable to control her bewildering emotions toward him. Even now the sound of her heartbeat was ringing so loudly in her ears that she could scarcely think.

How could she stay here? she asked herself frantically. How could she not? a small voice inside of her responded just as desperately. It had taken every last cent she'd possessed to buy the various train tickets she, Moses, and Delcine had needed to journey from Atlanta to Tumbling Creek. Jenny had nothing left. As it was, she'd been counting on a small advance against her salary to purchase the supplies they would need, once they'd reached their destination. No, there was no way for her to leave town at this juncture, even though she wished to.

Her eyelids fluttered open, and her body quivered with alarm as she saw that Luke Morgan was still watching her from across the dining room, that hateful smile still curved upon his lips. His eyes were now unexpectedly filled with humor, as though he'd guessed what Mrs. Zee had just told her about him and his brothers. Yet there was too on his face an odd understanding of her plight and perhaps, Jenny believed, a touch of pity for her as well.

She stiffened her spine with pride at the notion, insulted. She needed no one to feel sorry for her—especially an arrogant, mocking outlaw who could in no way comprehend the tragedies of her life and the scars that had been left upon her soul.

Luke, regarding her intently, did not miss the gesture of indignation, though he did not correctly guess its cause. Instead he assumed Jenny had by this time recovered from the shock of the holdup and was incensed that he was not to be immediately arrested now that she had pointed him out as one of the train robbers. Luke's eyes danced at the thought. Imagine Marshal Farlow trying to take the Morgan gang into custody! Why, the man would sooner chase after a pack of hungry wolves! The new schoolmarm—if rumor had correctly identified her— had a lot to learn about life in the Ozark Mountains. Still the Pinkerton Detective Agency was another matter altogether. Its employees were not noted for their lack of courage, and if the girl chose to talk to one of them, Luke's fate would almost certainly be sealed. He could almost feel the noose tightening around his neck, and he eyed Jenny steadily, wondering if she would indirectly be the death of him.

All the way home from Devil's Holler he had thought about Jenny and the difficulty she presented to him and, by extension, to his brothers. Luke had realized he must locate her, but as there were a dozen small towns between Jonesboro and Springfield and she might have disembarked at any one of them, he had known that finding her would not be a simple task. Nor had he yet determined what he would do with her, once he'd discovered her whereabouts. Luke could not bring himself to murder a woman, and he had shied away from the only other solution he had seen to his dilemma. But now, surveying the girl who had so unexpectedly come back into his life, thus sparing him the trouble of searching for her, Luke began to reconsider his earlier idea.

She was a curious puzzle, he decided. Outwardly she reminded him of a small, helpless bird. With her dusky-brown hair, the smattering of freckles across her upturned nose, and her shy and insecure appearance, she did indeed look ready to take flight at the slightest unexpected movement. Yet she'd had backbone enough to leave her home and to journey to a new position in a strange town, and, though scared, she'd stood up to Raiford and him over the theft of her father's pocket watch. Luke remembered how, desperately, as though knowing full well the horrors of it, she had mentally primed herself to be raped by him, and he thought again that there was a wealth of quiet courage beneath Jenny's unprepossessing exterior. That idea intrigued him, for it had been his experience that valiant women were few and far between and highly appealing.

More than ever, Jenny interested him, although he still didn't know why. She certainly wasn't his usual type at all, he reflected as he went on studying her. Yet he felt he would like to get to know her. In fact, it was imperative he establish some sort of relationship with her. He could not have her blabbing to the Pinkerton detectives about the train robbery. If the girl came to know and like him, perhaps she would keep her mouth shut about this afternoon. Still, Luke thought, even if she did remain silent about him, she would always have that piece of incriminating knowledge tucked away inside her brain, and the Pinkerton agents could be extremely persuasive. No, even if he made a friend out of her, he would never be able to trust Jenny to hold her tongue. Women were just downright untrustworthy; they didn't know how to keep secrets. They invariably confided in someone, and there was no telling who that someone might be.

Before the war Luke, ironically, had been studying law, intending to go into politics. Thus he was well aware that the only certain way to ensure Jenny's silence—outside of murdering her—was to marry her, for a wife could not legally be forced to testify against her husband, and, as such, Luke would make damned sure she kept still.

He frowned as he went on appraising her, as though she were a slave upon a block, brought out for his inspection. She wasn't the least bit pretty, but, then, a woman's looks no longer held any importance for Luke, so he dismissed this as being irrelevant. If she could cook, clean, and keep her mouth shut, it would be more than his nagging first wife had managed to accomplish, and it would suffice, Luke guessed, although he really had no desire to become shackled to a female again.

He wondered what Jenny would be like in bed. She had been attracted to him this afternoon, Luke knew, just as he, oddly enough, had been drawn to her. Even now his loins quickened as he thought of how she'd quivered beneath him in the woods and the way her full round breasts had pressed against his chest. But still he sensed he terrified her all the same—and not just because he was an outlaw. Something in her past made her fear him as a man as well, and that would not be easily overcome.

Inwardly Luke groaned. He did not want to wed anyone, much less a woman who was obviously deeply scarred emotionally and would no doubt shrink from the very touch of his hand! Still, though he racked his brain ceaselessly, Luke could see no other way to extricate himself from the problem of Jenny having seen his face during the holdup—unless he simply frightened her out of her wits about it! Well, that wasn't such a bad plan either; in fact, it was probably better than the one he'd previously been considering.

Smiling to himself, Luke lit a cigarette and dragged on it deeply.

"Thank you for your hospitality—and your advice, Mrs. Zee." Jenny spoke as she got to her feet. "Now, if you'll excuse me, I can hardly keep my eyes open. I believe I'll retire for the evening."

"You go right ahead, Miz Colter," the hotel proprietress insisted. "Your room's all ready, and I've had Sammy set up a cot outside your door for your manservant. If you need anything else, just let me know."

Murmuring her appreciation, Jenny left the dining room, feeling Luke Morgan's penetrating eyes on her retreating figure every step of the way.

She was so intent on escaping from him that neither she nor Moses nor Delcine, who were scurrying along rapidly in her wake to keep up with her, noticed she dropped one of her gloves in the lobby. Luke did, however, and in his haste to retrieve it he nearly toppled over his chair as he jumped up and strode from the dining room.

The glove was worn and much-mended, he saw, but spotless—and dainty as well. He marveled at its smallness. The new schoolmarm, Luke estimated, wore a size five wedding band—if she wore one at all. For a moment, slightly anxious, much to his surprise, he wondered if she did. Then, determining that she didn't, he relaxed. He didn't remember seeing one on her bare left hand this afternoon on the train, and surely he would have noticed if she'd been wearing one. Besides, wouldn't her husband have accompanied her to Tumbling Creek? No, Jenny was unmarried; Luke was certain of it. He felt a strange sense of satisfaction at the thought, and, inhaling deeply of the honeysuckle fragrance that clung to the glove, he glanced upward to the staircase, which Jenny was slowly ascending.

For the first time Luke observed that she limped—and badly. Why, she was crippled, he realized, and felt a pang of pity for her in his heart.

"Miss Jennilee," he called softly. Then, louder, "Miss Jennilee."

Jenny turned and looked down, her heart thudding jerkily in her breast as she saw that the unnerving outlaw had followed her out into the lobby. Why, how dare that dreadful man pursue her—especially after having attempted to rob her earlier today?

Well, she was no longer the hysterical woman he'd dealt with this afternoon. Now that she had regained control of herself and her emotions, she would show him what was what.

"Yes?" She lifted one eyebrow frostily, giving him a frigid look intended to discourage any further attentions.

To her indignation he only grinned in an alarming manner.

"You dropped your glove," Luke drawled, holding it up so she could see it.

"Delcine," Jenny instructed coldly, "will you go and fetch it for me, please."

Then she turned on her heel and flounced up the steps in a huff, the sound of Luke's laughter ringing derisively in her ears.

Once she had gone and Luke had returned to the dining room, Billy Clay, who had not missed his brother's intense contemplation of the girl, edged over to nudge him none too gently in the ribs.

"Hey"—he sniggered—"are you planning on taking up your study of them law books again? Or is it just that you know something about the new schoolmarm that the rest of us don't? You was ogling her so damned hard that I thought your eyes was gonna pop clean out of your head! Don't tell me you're figuring on getting a peek under them prim skirts of hers! Hell! She don't even begin to hold a candle to Velvet Rose, over to Miss Ruby's."

"Put a lid on it, Billy Clay," Luke ordered, irritated, "before I decide to cut me a hickory switch and beat some sense into your brain. I swear Pa didn't whip you near enough when we were growing up."

Billy Clay just grinned and, much to Luke's annoyance, continued to taunt him, growing increasingly more vocal as the rest of the Morgan gang showed up.

"Guess what, boys!" Billy Clay's smug voice greeted his brothers, who were noisily hauling over additional chairs and sitting down at the table. "Luke's after the new schoolmarm."

"Is that a fact?" Raiford's eyes gleamed with merriment at this piece of news, for it was seldom that Luke could be made the butt of a joke. "Tell us more, Billy Clay, tell us more. What's she like? Is she prettier than my Emmalou?"

Emmalou Ivey, of Powder Springs, was the girl Raiford had been steadily courting for the past few years, though so far he'd managed to avoid being hooked by the sweet, curvaceous bait she determinedly kept dangling before him.

"Raif"—Billy Clay guffawed—"when they was passing out looks this gal must have thought they said books and told 'em she didn't need nothing fancy, that she was just a schoolmarm. That's what's so—so funny about—about the whole thing!" he sputtered between gasps of mirth.

"You mean she ain't even cute?" Raiford probed disbelievingly, somewhat surprised, for Luke could pick and choose from among the loveliest women in the county, and his mistress, Velvet Rose, was enough to make a man's mouth water.

"About as cute as that speckled pup Ma had the last time we was home. You know . . . the one with that—that hangdog expression and —and spots all over its face!" Billy Clay managed to get out before falling into another fit of whoops.

"I must say . . . that's not your usual style, Luke," Tobias put in, smiling, though behind his spectacles his eyes glimmered with speculation rather than amusement, for he was far more astute than either Raiford or Billy Clay.

Tobias had not missed the muscle working tensely in Luke's set jaw or the way his hands were slowly tightening, then relaxing about the glass of whiskey he was holding. That dumb Billy Clay was right about one thing, Tobias realized. Luke was inordinately interested in the new schoolteacher, no matter how plain she might be, and he did not appreciate the teasing remarks being bandied back and forth about her, regardless of how good-naturedly they were intended.

"Looks aren't everything," Luke suddenly uttered flatly in such a bitter tone that all jokes and laughter ceased. "I reckon I ought to know that better than anyone."

Then, without any further explanation of his interest in Jenny, he abruptly stood, tossed a few coins on the table, and left.

"You idiots!" J.R. snarled, breaking the stricken silence that had fallen awkwardly upon the table. He glowered angrily at his brothers. "Now see what you've done! Damned fools, the lot of you! Especially you, Toby, because you've got sense enough to have known better!"

Then the oldest member of the Morgan gang wrathfully snatched up his hat and departed as well, his spurs jangling loudly as he stomped toward the door.

The remaining three brothers gazed at each other uncomfortably in the tense hush that followed, their faces red with embarrassment and filled with guilt and grief.

"Gee, Toby," Billy Clay muttered, "I never thought—"

"That's your whole damned trouble!" Raiford spat, enraged at having received such a public dressing-down and blaming Billy Clay for it. "You don't ever use your frigging head—"

"Shut up, Raif!" Tobias hissed. "You and I were just as much a part of it as he was. Lord! I don't know where our brains were. How on earth could we have been so damned unthinking . . . ?" His voice trailed off painfully in self-condemnation.

Luke had once been married to the most beautiful woman in all of Taney County, and he had loved her to distraction. But vain, shallow Maybelle Boothe Morgan, though carelessly fond of the tall, handsome man she'd wed, had not returned his affection. When he'd gone off to war she, easily bored, had looked around casually for other means of entertainment and had found it in the arms of one Yankee soldier after another.

Luke, fighting for his life on hot, smoke-filled prairies and in crazed, blood-bathed towns, had remained blissfully ignorant of his wife's numerous infidelities with the enemy and had joyfully returned home, eager to make love to the body that, unbeknown to him, had been possessed by so many other men.

Maybelle had not been pleased. She'd borne two children during the war, both of them products of Luke's visits home on furloughs, and she'd wanted no more babies to swell within her, grossly distorting the shapely figure of which she'd been so proud. Moreover, she'd grown tired of Luke and the small—and in her eyes dull—farm on which they'd lived. Her craving for excitement, spurred on by Luke's constant absences while he was away on jobs, had been burgeoned beyond control.

Two years ago she had run off with another man and had died some months later, a whore in a Saint Louis brothel. Luke, tight-lipped at the ache of her betrayal, had nevertheless gone north to bring home her body and had buried her in a plot on the farm she'd come to despise with such a passion.

He'd never mentioned her again.

Luke's son, Kipp, deeply hurt and confused by his mother's disappearance and subsequent death, had turned overnight from a happy, boisterous child into a quiet, solemn boy with dark, haunted eyes. His younger sister had suffered even worse emotional damage. For reasons never discovered, the night her mother had vanished Sarah Jane had quite suddenly ceased to talk at all. To this day, despite all of Luke's pleading for her to speak once more, the little girl remained a mute.

It was no wonder, Tobias reflected, that to his brother a woman's looks were no longer important. Maybelle had been so breathtaking she had brought every man within arm's reach to his knees. Yet behind her outward facade there had been nothing at all. Yes, Luke had learned the hard way that beauty was indeed only skin-deep.

Since his wife's death he'd had many mistresses, but they'd meant nothing to him. Certainly he hadn't minded his brothers' sly remarks about any of them, and when he'd grown tired of them he'd passed them along without another thought or care to Raiford or Billy Clay.

But something told Tobias the new schoolteacher was different. He was willing to bet that beneath her unarresting exterior lay something so shyly endearing that only Luke, with his heartbreaking past, had seen it. Yes, if he wanted the girl, he would have her, regardless of her looks, and if that were the case, Tobias pitied any man in Tumbling Creek who decided to wait in line on Sundays for the new schoolteacher.

When Luke Morgan desired a woman he did not lightly step aside for a rival.

Chapter Four

Jenny lay awake for a very long time that evening, listening to the sounds of the hotel, the talk and laughter that drifted upstairs from the lobby and the dining room until at last all was silent save for the snores of Moses, who was sleeping on a cot in the hall. In the small antechamber that served as a parlor and was part of the suite, which room number four had turned out to be, Delcine rested peacefully on the sofa. She was so worn out from the trip that she was not even disturbed by the flickering light shining beneath the closed door from the candle that burned always in Jenny's chamber at night. Jenny wished sleep had come as easily to her, but it had not. Her inner turmoil over the day's events had refused to be stilled and now kept slumber at bay.

She was scared. She had never before experienced the feelings Luke Morgan had wakened in her, first on the train this afternoon and then again in the dining room this evening. By the time Jenny had been old enough for courting, the war had claimed most of the gentlemen who might have come calling at Faxon's Folly. Afterward, after that terrible day at the plantation, she had been glad she was unwed, and when her great-aunt, Henrietta, had pointed out to her that it was unlikely any man would ever marry her now, since she was not only plain, but now crippled and barren, Jenny had been slightly relieved.

She had longed for a home and a family of her own, and had she been able to bear children, she might have managed to force herself to submit to a husband if there had been one in the offing. But since she was sterile Jenny had shrunk from the idea of being a wife—from performing the nightly duties the role would entail—knowing it would all be for naught.

Her teaching would suffice, she had thought, to fill the void in her life. The love and devotion that she once would have given to her

husband and their children she would now bestow just as wholeheart-
edly upon a classroom. She would need nothing more.

How wrong she had been! For now her secure little world had been
challenged by an outlaw, a man whom before the war Jenny would have
considered beneath her! She bit her lip in the half-light as she pondered
the disturbing effect Luke had had upon her. Why should he, of all the
men she'd met the past few days, be the one to reopen the doors of her
wistful, girlhood dreams, doors she had thought long closed, dreams
she had believed long forgotten?

Now vividly Jenny remembered how, once, she had yearned for a
man as handsome as the outlaw to call her own. She recalled her foolish
fantasies, in which such a man had ridden up to Faxon's Folly, swept
her up into his arms, and carried her off into the sunset, where they'd
lived happily ever after.

Always in her dreams she'd been breathtakingly beautiful. Her brown
hair had gleamed with lustrous, striking highlights. Her grey eyes had
glittered with mystery and passion. Her freckles had magically disappeared. Her mouth had pouted slightly, as though aching to be kissed.
She had been dressed in the latest of fashions, and her beau had been so
awe-stricken by the sight of her that he'd been unable to restrain the
words of love that had tumbled from his lips.

But, in reality, she was only plain Jenny Wren, as Papa had used to
call her, and she had never had a beau—or even a gentleman caller.
Jenny sighed at the thought. She had long become resigned to her spinsterhood, and she'd accepted it with dignity and grace, even though,
had things been different, it was not the path in life she would have
chosen. Now, like a pebble tossed into a pond, Luke Morgan had disrupted the still, silent waters of her existence.

Why? What had attracted her to him?

Had it been the timeworn look in his eyes that had mirrored her own,
so that when she'd stared up at him it had been like seeing a reflection
of herself? Or had it been the way his eyes had seemed to kiss her own
gently, with the promise of so much more? Had it been because he was
so handsome? Or because he'd been the first man ever to glance at her
with desire? Jenny had to admit no other man had ever looked at her as
Luke had done this evening, slowly, appraisingly, as though wondering
what she would be like in bed. She blushed at the notion. She didn't
usually have such an effect upon men, nor they upon her, yet she could
not deny the fact that Luke had appeared extremely interested in her
and—worse still—that she'd been aroused by that interest.

Jenny could not understand any of it. She wasn't pretty, so it couldn't be her face that had attracted the outlaw to her, and he hadn't had a chance to get to know her, so he couldn't have seen beyond her plain exterior to the woman within. What, then, had drawn him to her?

Only one answer occurred to Jenny, and it caused her heart to flutter with apprehension. She had been utterly terrified on the train. Perhaps Luke was one of those vicious, perverted men whose lust fed on a woman's fear. Jenny felt sickened and distressed by the idea, especially as it called to mind the dim, horrible images of that day at Faxon's Folly. Was Luke a man such as those men had been?

If that were the case, more than ever must Jenny try to get a grip on her deeply conflicting emotions about him. She knew what such men were like, and she wanted no part of that kind of brutality. Despite her inexplicable reaction to the outlaw, she must put him out of her head. She knew he was a common criminal. What else he might be she had no wish to discover.

She had come here to teach school. It was unfortunate that Tumbling Creek was also Luke's hometown, but she would just have to make the best of it. In the future, if she saw him, she would ignore him. Jenny could think of no other way to suppress that dark part of her being he had freed from its hiding place within her.

Determinedly she closed her eyes and forced herself to breathe evenly as she tried to empty her mind of its chaotic thoughts. But sleep was a long time coming all the same, and when she dreamed it was of a blond-haired, blue-eyed devil who laughed and kissed her passionately until she was aching with desire.

Speculatively Luke gazed up at the open window of the Hotel Van Buren's room number four. The chamber was really a small suite, he knew, located on the northeast corner of the second floor, and, since it was at the back of the hotel rather than overlooking the main street, it was unlikely he'd be observed spying on it. He had waited for hours, it seemed, but still a light glowed within. Luke struck a match, lit a cigarette, and glanced at his watch. It was after two o'clock. Surely the new schoolteacher could not still be awake!

Earlier he had watched the shadowy figure Jenny had cast against the drawn window shade as slowly she'd undressed and prepared for bed. Despite himself, Luke had been aroused by the sight of her naked form, outlined hazily within the frame of the gingham curtains billowing inward from the cool night breeze, and he had thought again of how Jenny's body had felt pressed so close to his own in the forest. Despite her unremarkable appearance, she had stirred him in some strange fashion he could not comprehend, and she continued to do so. It did not seem to matter that she was not the kind of woman he generally found attractive; she excited him all the same.

This feeling was tempered, however, by compassion, for Luke could not rid himself of the belief that something dreadful had occurred in her past to cause her to be afraid of all men. Thus he was quite ashamed of what he intended to do to her this night. It would certainly terrify Jenny further. That it might even rip the last of her sanity to shreds was something he did not want to consider.

Her icy attitude toward him when he'd retrieved her glove had told Luke that wooing Jenny to the point of marriage would take time—if she even allowed him to court her, which, in light of her fear of men, he doubted—and somehow she must be effectively silenced. Luke knew if he had less of a conscience, he would simply dishonor her so she would be forced to wed him and he might thus ensure that she keep quiet about him. But this he could not bring himself to do. Rape was, Luke thought, what Jenny had suffered in her past—and by hands that had been less gentle than his own would have been, had he himself chosen such an option.

He had pondered as well the idea of kidnapping her—or her female servant—and holding either one hostage until Jenny agreed to marry him. But this scheme too Luke had discarded for numerous reasons. Abducting Jenny was a crime for which he would assuredly hang, if he were to be caught, and it would not endear him to the public besides. Kidnapping Delcine might be another matter here in the South, but still Luke couldn't imagine Jenny, a Southerner, sacrificing herself for a woman who was obviously a freed slave, nor could he be certain that even if she did, she would not subsequently tell all the first chance she got and seek an annulment, based on the fact that he'd coerced her to the altar.

No, simply frightening her to death was the best Luke could do. He must hope it would be enough to still the girl's tongue, though he doubted it would. He had been betrayed before by a woman, although in a different manner, and now Luke trusted no female except his mother.

Surreptitiously he glanced about the dark alley behind the hotel, but there was no one around. Satisfied that no hue and cry would be raised by his actions, Luke tossed away his cigarette, took a firm hold of the drainpipe that ran down from the roof, and started to pull himself upward to Jenny's open window. He was a strong and well-muscled man, so once he had climbed the pipe, it was easy for him to grab hold of one side of the window frame and lean over to peek inside. Despite the candle that burned on the night table, Luke saw that Jenny was alone and deep in an uneasy slumber. Locking his powerful calves in place on either side of the pipe, he reached out and grasped the sill with both hands. Once firmly anchored, he released his legs, swinging over to the right so he now dangled from the window. He paused a moment to catch his breath. Then slowly he hoisted himself up over the sill and crawled into the bedroom.

Once inside, he froze, listening intently for the sound of footsteps that would tell him someone had heard his unorthodox entrance and was scurrying to investigate it, but no one came. Jenny moved and murmured in her sleep but did not awaken. Stealthily Luke crossed the floor, drawing his Bowie knife from the sheath at his waist. He eased himself into a sitting position on the bed, then roughly clamped his hand over Jenny's mouth and pressed the sharp blade to her throat.

"Don't scream, and don't try to fight me," Luke hissed warningly as she started violently wide-awake, her eyes huge and filled with panic.

Momentarily Jenny was disoriented, for she couldn't breathe with his palm shutting off her air, and all she could think about was freeing her lips and nostrils from the grip that threatened to suffocate her. Her arms flew up wildly, and only her sudden awareness of Luke's knife jabbing into her soft skin prevented her from finishing the havoc she had wreaked earlier that afternoon on his face.

"That's better," he noted dryly as, recognizing that she was helpless against his blade, she fell back among the pillows, staring up at him with fear and loathing. "I like a woman with intelligence."

His blue eyes glittered as hard as nails in the half-light as they raked her, taking in the swell of her creamy breasts above the bodice of her negligee and the pulse jerking at the hollow of her throat; and though he made no move to hurt her, neither did he loose her.

What was he doing here? Jenny wondered. Did he mean to kill her—or worse? She longed to draw the cover up around her neck to hide her shrinking body from his eyes. Then she laughed wildly in her mind at the silly idea. As though the muslin sheet would provide any protection against him!

"Please," Jenny managed to gasp quietly, her voice muffled by his palm. "I—I can't . . . breathe."

"I'll take my hand away if you promise you won't scream," Luke told her. "Not that it would do you any good anyway. Do you promise?"

"Yes, of course."

Tentatively he released her, ready to clap his hand back over her mouth if she tried to call out for help. But though her eyes flicked to the closed door separating her from Delcine, Jenny uttered no sound, half afraid Luke would murder her before aid ever arrived, for he still held his knife to her throat.

"Now you listen to me—and listen good, Miss Jennilee Colter," he said, his voice low and purposeful, his breath warm upon her skin. "I was careless this afternoon, quite careless, and neither I nor my brothers are too happy about that. I know you got a real good look at my face during the train robbery, and I know you recognized me this evening in the dining room downstairs. You're the only person—the only *living* person, that is—who could positively put me at the scene of a crime." Luke paused, allowing this frightening piece of information to sink in. Then he continued. "I'd be most . . . displeased . . . if you ever were to mention my whereabouts today—or this friendly little visit tonight— to anyone . . . anyone at all! Do you understand me?"

"Yes, of course," Jenny repeated.

"Good," Luke breathed. "I've never killed a woman, and I'd hate to have to start now. Still, if you ever cross me, there are other means of punishment."

Casually Luke let his blade trail down Jenny's body bringing it to rest beneath the lacings of her nightgown. Deliberately with a single stroke he cut the silken ties, exposing her breasts to his suddenly hungry eyes. The twin globes were full and pale, with dark honey crests that hardened perceptibly as the cool night breeze caressed them. At the sight a powerful flame of desire flickered deep within Luke's groin and began to spread through his taut loins like wildfire.

"I assure you, Mr. Morgan, that there's no need for this," Jenny told him quietly, forcing herself to remain calm. After all, if he'd really wanted to rape her, he could have done so this afternoon. "Mrs. Zee has already explained to me the futility of reporting you to the law, and, believe me, I have no wish to be made a fool of before the whole town, especially as I must live here now and can't afford to lose my job."

Luke paid no need to her words. His eyes darkened, and without warning his mouth came down on hers hard, so there was no escaping it. His hand captured one soft breast, thumb flicking its nipple. To Jenny's shame she felt the tiny bud stiffen with mingled fear and nervous excitement, spurring him on. His lips moved on hers, slowly at first, then more demandingly as his tongue darted forth to trace hotly the outline of her mouth before compelling her lips to open. Expertly he ravaged her with his mouth and tongue, made only dimly aware by her startled response that he was the first man ever to kiss her.

Defenseless, Jenny could do nothing but submit, helplessly adrift upon the tide of emotions he was unleashing within her. To her horror she found she was shivering not just with fright, but with anticipation as well. Luke's carnal lips and plundering tongue were unlike anything she had ever tasted or felt before, wakening a thousand peculiar sensations inside of her, causing her to feel dizzy and faint, as though she were too hot and having difficulty breathing. A shower of tiny sparks radiated like an ignited pinwheel from the center of the breast his fingers taunted so intimately, sending tingles of unfamiliar, uncontrollable desire racing through her body. Her head reeled.

Whimpering over this traitorous betrayal of her flesh and the shock of the things he was doing to her, Jenny attempted blindly to push Luke away, only to feel the keen prick of his blade once more against her throat.

"Sweet, sweet," he muttered against her mouth. "I didn't know how sweet you would be."

Then, before her mind had a chance to become a black chasm, filled by the brutal memories of her past, savagely he tore himself from her, shaking with the overwhelming passion she'd inadvertently aroused in him when he'd forced his attentions on her. A kiss. One kiss. That's all Luke had taken, just a taste of this woman he knew held his life in her hands. Plain though she was, there was a world of untapped and unexpected sensuality in Jenny; Luke had felt it rising within her, trying to break through her timidity as he'd ravished her lips and fondled her breast. He had not bargained for that—or for his own reaction to it. He inhaled sharply, attempting to regain control of his wild emotions, then ran one hand raggedly through his hair.

"Don't try to leave town, Jennilee," Luke warned her softly. "I'd find you, no matter how far or how fast you ran, and I'd be angry, oh, so very angry, Jennilee. And I'm sure you remember, don't you, what I told you usually follows when a woman angers a man?"

Wide-eyed, Jenny nodded, biting her lip to keep from crying out, for his very nearness after what he'd done to her, was promising to do to her if she ever disobeyed him, filled her with anger and panic. She had longed to flee from Tumbling Creek. Now, even if she somehow made enough money to do so, she dare not leave. Luke would be watching her —and waiting—ready to vent his punishing lust upon her, and Jenny knew she could not withstand another assault upon her senses. For some inexplicable reason, despite her deep-rooted terror of men, this one seemed to know just how to break through the walls that kept her safe—and sane. His mouth crushing down on hers, the liberties he had taken with her body . . . all these things that ought to have stunned and horrified her—and had—had also once more wakened the devil of desire deep inside of her, causing her to respond to him against her will and all the teachings of her youth.

She ought to have screamed or fainted or slapped his face. Instead she had done none of these things; rather, she had lain motionless beneath him, acquiescing to his demands. Now she wanted to die of shame. What would her mother have said, if she'd known of her daughter's disgrace?

"I won't say anything about you," Jenny promised, averting her eyes from Luke's as she tried to cover herself. "Now, please, just go away, and leave me alone."

"I'll go, Jennilee," he consented, laying his hand against her throat and pressing his fingers into her cheeks, compelling her to look at him. "I'll go. But I'll be back; don't you doubt that for a minute."

Then he kissed her again, swiftly, harshly, and slipped out into the night.

Chapter Five

The sight of Jenny's new home was not cheering, and as she glimpsed it through the trees, her heart sank and all her concerns about staying in Tumbling Creek returned more vividly than ever.

She didn't really know what she'd expected, but it certainly wasn't the rough-hewn, run-down log cabin that came into view as Mr. Peabody swung the carriage onto a bumpy dirt drive, then moments later pulled to a stop before the house. Of course Jenny had known from its description in the school board's advertisement that the place would be small—and it was—but she'd never dreamed it would also be so crude and in such disrepair.

The short picket fence that surrounded the cabin was old and dilapidated. Several of the boards that composed the enclosure were split, and a few sections here and there had fallen down entirely. Weeds had taken over the lawn and were waist-high. What could be seen of the yard was littered with debris—old newspapers and bottles mostly.

Even more depressing was the house itself. Even from a distance Jenny could tell there were numerous large chinks between the logs that formed the walls. She was sure both wind and rain lashed through the cracks during a storm, and she had no doubt the roof leaked as well.

It was a most depressing greeting on top of everything else she'd suffered recently, and Jenny was hard-pressed to hold back the tears that pricked her eyes as she remembered Faxon's Folly in its heyday and Aunt Hetta's stately home on Peachtree Street in Atlanta.

Mr. Peabody cleared his throat with embarrassment.

"I had no idea," he explained awkwardly. "I haven't been out here since last May, when Miss Underwood returned to Chicago."

Privately Jenny thought it was no wonder her evidently much-refined and snobbish predecessor had gone home, but she said nothing of this.

Instead, reminding herself that she needed this job, she lifted her chin determinedly.

"There's really nothing wrong that can't be fixed, Mr. Peabody," she said, carefully assessing the work that would be required to make the cabin livable. "With the right tools Moses can repair most of the damage outside." Jenny didn't even want to think about how the inside looked. Perhaps it wasn't as bad, and, at any rate, the condition of the house gave her an ideal opportunity to ask for an advance against her salary. "If you wouldn't mind advancing me a month's wages, Mr. Peabody, Moses can ride back into town with you and buy what we need to get started."

The head of the school board was so grateful Jenny didn't intend to pack up and leave immediately at the sight of her new home that he was only too happy to give her the money.

Moses, his lower lip pushed out twice its normal size at the thought of his mistress being forced to spend even one night in such an awful place, unloaded the trunks from the buggy and carried them inside. Then, after obtaining from Jenny a long list of purchases to be made, he rejoined Mr. Peabody in the carriage and headed back to town.

Jenny waited until the vehicle was out of sight, then she and Delcine moved slowly toward the cabin, walking up onto the front porch, which had warped, uneven planks and was dangerous to tread upon. Carefully they crossed it to peer inside the house.

Moses had left the door open. It sagged pathetically on its leather hinges, one of which was almost worn clean through, and it appeared that rats had gnawed its bottom edge.

The sunlight streaming in through the open doorway revealed there was no foyer; the parlor was entered directly.

Tentatively Jenny and Delcine stepped inside, relieved to find the floor at least was real, made of puncheon rather than the hard-packed earth that served so many in the Midwest. But it was filthy all the same, coated with a thick layer of dust and dotted by the bodies of several dead flies and their excrement.

One small window was set next to the door; two others flanked either side of the fireplace on the adjacent, left-hand wall. Glass was precious in this part of the country and cost dearly, so thin sheets of cured rawhide served in place of panes. Had it been clean, the skin covering the apertures would have admitted a relatively bright, filtered light. As it was, except for the sun beaming through the entrance, the room was in shadow.

On a small table next to the door sat a kerosene lantern, along with a box of safety matches. After checking to be certain there was oil in the corroded tin base of the lamp, Jenny lit the wick and turned it up so a pleasant glow flooded the parlor. A battered old sofa and two upholstered chairs, three more occasional tables and a tea table took on recognizable shapes.

To her right another door opened into the bedroom, which contained a bed with a foul, straw-stuffed mattress; two scarred night tables, one with a broken leg; a rickety chiffonier with warped drawers; a cedar-lined armoire, one door of which had pulled away from its hinges; and a dresser with a crazed mirror.

These two rooms formed the major part of the cabin.

Attached to the back wall of the parlor was a gallery—or dogtrot, as Jenny would soon learn the Ozark natives called it. This was basically just a short, narrow hall that led to the kitchen.

Here to their delight, for they'd expected to find a primitive fireplace, the two women discovered a cast-iron stove for cooking. There was also a large tin sink with a pump, near which stood a relatively new icebox. In one corner was a table with four chairs. A small closet with shelves served as the pantry, and a trapdoor in the floor lifted to give access to stairs leading to a root cellar below.

At least, Jenny thought, the kitchen, which was obviously much newer than the rest of the house, could easily be put to rights.

Taking off her bonnet and rolling up her sleeves, she turned dejectedly to Delcine.

"Well," Jenny said with a sigh, a tiny, forlorn sound that spoke far more eloquently than words, "we've made do in the past with what we had, so I guess we'll manage somehow. Look in those cupboards, Delcine, and see if you can find some cleaning equipment. I don't think Miss Underwood would have taken anything like that with her when she left, so perhaps there'll be some old rags, a mop, and a bucket at least. That way we can get started, and we won't have to wait for Moses to get back."

An examination of the cabinets soon proved Jenny's assumption was correct, and, armed with an array of tools, the two women set to work.

The pump was rusty, but with Delcine's help Jenny was able to fill both the dented tin pail they'd found in the cupboard under the sink and the shallow basin itself. Then, wetting their rags in the sudsy water produced by a bar of strong lye soap, they started to scrub down the kitchen. Dust and cobwebs flew, coating them both with a fine layer of grime.

Delcine, who had a pretty voice and knew a number of old tunes, sang as they worked, and Jenny, her spirits lifting along with the swirling clouds of dirt, soon joined in, in her own soft tones beautifully dulcet. Delcine, who'd never heard her mistress sing, decided perhaps Moses had been right after all about the reason Kingston Colter had called his youngest daughter after the delicate brown wren that warbled so enchantingly.

They finished one melody, and without thinking Jenny began another called *"Plaisir d'Amour"*—"The Joys of Love," a traditional French ballad she'd learned as a child and hadn't thought of in years. Instead of singing it in its original language, she sang it in English.

"The joys of love are but a moment long.
The pain of love endures a whole life long.

Your eyes kissed mine. I saw the light in them shine.
You brought me heaven right then when your eyes kissed mine.

My love loves me and all the wonders I see.
A rainbow shines in my window. My love loves me.

And now he's gone, like a dream that fades with the dawn.
But the words stay locked in my heartstrings. My love loves me."

For some reason the old folk song made Jenny think suddenly of Luke Morgan and the way his gaze had held hers first on the train yesterday afternoon and then again last night, when he'd so brazenly accosted her in her hotel room. Yes, now that she thought about it, it was indeed as though his eyes had kissed her own. And had he "brought her heaven right then"? Jenny didn't know. She knew only that she'd felt something strange and frightening yet vital and exciting come to life inside of her when he'd looked at her, as though she'd been a flower lashed but not broken by a storm.

What nonsense! Furiously she gave herself a mental shake. Luke was a wanted man, perhaps even a murderer, despite the fact that Mrs. Zee had said the brothers never killed anybody. Why Jenny was daydreaming about him she couldn't imagine! Why, she could barely even bring herself to offer her hand to a man, much less let one touch her, embrace her, kiss her . . . as Luke had done so boldly last night. Why had she responded to him, in spite of her fear of intimacy with a man? Jenny didn't know. It just didn't make sense. The outlaw had broken into her room, threatened her life, and made highly improper advances to her. Yet—quite irrationally—she could not seem to stop thinking about him!

Enraged and confused, she jabbed her broom viciously at a dustball and with a vengeance swept Luke from her mind. The man was an outlaw, for heaven's sake! She would think no more about him.

Thus determined, Jenny labored strenuously alongside Delcine in close, companionable harmony for three long hours. Then shortly after noon there was a knock on the door.

"Howdy," someone called. "Howdy. Is anybody home?"

"Land's sake!" Jenny hissed.

Her hands flew to her hair; several long tendrils had come loose from the knot at the nape of her neck and now curled in tangled disarray about her face. She had no doubt the tip of her nose and her cheeks were smudged with grime, and her muslin dress was streaked with black where she had idly wiped her hands. She glanced at Delcine, who didn't look any better.

"Who on earth can that be?"

"Howdy. Is anybody home? Oh, here you are," a pleasingly plump, blond older woman observed with a smile as she stepped from the dogtrot into the kitchen. "Howdy. I'm Charlotte Morgan—but everybody calls me Lottie—and this here's my sons' wives, Kate and Winona." She indicated the two younger women who had followed her into the room, their arms laden with cloth-covered baskets. "You must be Miz Colter, the new schoolmarm."

"Why, yes," Jenny answered, slightly flustered and surprised. "And this is Delcine. But I'm—I'm afraid we weren't expecting visitors—" She broke off lamely, smoothing her gown a little, aware she appeared a mess.

"Oh, dear, I know that." Lottie laughed gaily. "So don't be flustered. We haven't come to tea, I assure you. No, indeed. In fact, we're here to help. My son Luke told me you'd arrived, and, knowing that clabber-headed Horace Peabody hadn't had sense enough to come out here and check on the place all summer, I figured you'd be having a hard time of it today. Why, I bet your mouth's so dry you could spit cotton, and no doubt you haven't had a bite to eat since breakfast. Open up those baskets, girls," Lottie instructed her daughters-in-law, "and show Miz Colter and Delcine what we've brought."

Kate and Winona set their burdens down upon the table and, after tossing aside the bright, checkered, covering cloths, began to take out platters of cold fried chicken, bowls heaped high with potato salad, hot baked beans, biscuits, a dish of apple pandowdy, and a large pitcher of cool lemonade. The women had also brought plates, cups, silverware, and napkins.

Jenny was stunned.

"I—I don't know how to thank you all—" she began, overwhelmed by their thoughtfulness and hospitality.

"Aw, shucks. It's the least we could do," Lottie declared stoutly, "seeing as how we're going to be neighbors and all. My husband's farm is just up the road a piece, and J.R.'s and Toby's land adjoins ours, just like Luke's. When my other two—Raif and Billy Clay—get hitched, we'll give them each a couple of square acres too, I reckon. Of course Luke's moved back home since his wife died. He's away so much he can't look after his two young 'uns properly, so I keep an eye on 'em mostly. But they're out to the fields today, with Jed—that's my husband —so we won't have 'em underfoot. Now, Miz Colter—"

"Please, call me Jenny."

"All right, Jenny, then. You and Delcine just sit right down here, and eat while it's hot. Me and the girls'll finish up this kitchen."

"Oh, I can't let you do that," Jenny protested.

"Of course you can," Lottie insisted firmly. "That's what neighbors are for. Besides, you look like you could use a breather. We won't have to do all that much by ourselves anyway. Luke and my other boys'll be here directly, then we'll really make hay."

Wearily Jenny sank down upon a chair, feeling somewhat dazed as at last her tired mind grasped the fact that the bright, cheerful Lottie was the mother of the notorious Morgan gang and that soon the cabin would ring with the talk and laughter of the outlaw brothers!

Jenny just couldn't believe it. Why, Lottie was as warm and friendly as a person could be. How could her sons be such infamous armed robbers? And Kate and Winona . . . they were fine, decent ladies, obviously well-bred and gently reared. So how could they have married men like J.R. and Tobias Morgan?

From beneath her lashes, as she hungrily helped herself to the wide assortment of food on the table and poured herself a glass of lemonade, Jenny studied Lottie's two daughters-in-law. Didn't the gregarious, flame-haired, emerald-eyed Kate and the reserved, black-haired, black-eyed Winona care that their husbands were criminals?

Perhaps all three of the women were unaware of their men's lawless activities. But, no. Mrs. Zee had told Jenny everyone in Tumbling Creek knew what the Morgan brothers did for a living.

The girl squeezed her eyes shut tightly as she recalled Luke's image, his golden, sun-streaked hair, his care-worn blue eyes. After what he'd done to her last night, how dare he show his face here? Worse yet, why wasn't she horrified by the prospect of his arrival?

You poor fool, Jenny admonished herself silently. Luke Morgan might be an outlaw, but he's still about the most gorgeous man you've ever laid eyes on. Why should he even look twice at an ugly duckling like you?

The bite of potato salad she'd eaten stuck in her throat at the disparaging thought, nearly choking her.

It was true. Why, Luke could probably pick and choose from among the most beautiful women in Taney County—if J.R.'s and Tobias's wives were any example of what a criminal might aspire to in Tumbling Creek.

No, even had she wanted to—which she most assuredly did not!—she didn't stand a chance at winning Luke's heart, Jenny reflected glumly. Then she chided herself sternly for even considering such a thing. Why, what would her mother say if she knew her daughter was sitting here daydreaming about a wanted man? Rachael Colter was doubtless turning over in her grave this minute at the very idea!

Flushing with guilt, Jenny wiped her mouth off with her napkin, then gathered up the utensils she'd used.

Lottie, standing on a chair so she could reach the top shelves of the cabinets, scrutinized the girl intently as she carried her plate to the sink and began to wash it.

Billy Clay was right, Lottie mused. Jenny Colter wasn't pretty, and she walked with a noticeable limp besides. She wasn't Luke's usual type at all. No, not at all. That was why Lottie was so interested in her and why last night she'd agreed to Luke's suggestion that she come over today to help the girl out.

When Raiford and Billy Clay had deftly managed to get her alone last evening after supper and had quietly told her about Luke's peculiar reaction to the new schoolteacher, Lottie had been at first incredulous and then disbelieving.

"Oh, pshaw!" she'd snorted. "You two are putting me on again, as usual. I thought you boys would have learned by now that you can't fool your old ma. No, siree. I've known you since the day you were born, and you were too big for your britches even then. Go on with you now. You two'll have to get up pretty early in the morning to make *me* the butt of one of your jokes!"

"It ain't no prank, Ma. Honest!" Billy Clay had asserted.

"He's right, Ma," Raiford had interjected. "I truly believe Luke might be serious about this girl. Why, I haven't seen him so mad since that time we cut off his horse's mane and tail to make a braid for Velvet Rose. I'm telling you this girl's really gotten to him. You should have seen him when Billy Clay said she was plainer than that speckled pup you've got. He liked to snapped our heads clean off! And she really is too—plain, I mean—or at least that's what Billy Clay says, and he's right, if what Luke told me is true and she's the girl we held up on the train this afternoon."

"You boys robbed a woman!" Lottie had burst out, indignant.

"Hell, no, Ma!" Raiford had hastened to reassure her. "I mean . . . well, I tried to steal a watch from her manservant, but they claimed it had belonged to her daddy, and Luke believed 'em, and he wouldn't let me take it."

"Well, I should think not!" Lottie had sniffed huffily.

Then she'd shooed both her sons away, still convinced they were talking nonsense. Not an hour later Luke had come out to the kitchen to help her finish up the dishes.

Casually—almost too casually, Lottie had thought—he'd mentioned the new schoolteacher and said he feared she was certainly going to have a mess on her hands, what with her house being such a shambles and all.

"It's be real neighborly of you to take a bit of dinner over and offer to help her set the place to rights, Ma," Luke had intimated. "Kate and Winona could go with you, and maybe J.R. and the rest of us boys could come over a little later and get that yard cleaned up."

"It appears like you're taking an inordinate amount of interest in the new schoolmarm, son," Lottie had replied, probing gingerly.

"I want Kipp to have an education, and if Jen . . . Miss Colter packs up and leaves like Miss Underwood did, Horace might not be able to find another teacher before the start of the fall term," Luke had explained, but he'd glanced away so his mother couldn't see his face.

How appalled and disappointed in him she would be if she ever learned how he had terrorized and taken advantage of Jenny last night. Lottie would be even more furious and upset if she ever discovered, in addition, that she was an unwitting part of Luke's plan to weave an ever-tightening web around Jenny, one from which she would not be able to escape. Luke knew his mother and his brothers' wives would welcome the girl warmly and view her as a prospective wife for him, since they were always trying to fix him up with a decent female. Luke hoped they would so overwhelm Jenny with kindness that she would feel obligated to keep quiet about him. If, after being befriended by Lottie, Kate, and Winona, Jenny betrayed him to the Pinkerton detectives, she would not only hurt him, but his family as well, and Luke was gambling on the fact that her inner nature was too sweet and caring for her to do that.

Neither Luke's slip over Jenny's name nor his turning aside to hide his true thoughts from Lottie had escaped her notice. Blissfully unaware of the real circumstances involving her son and Jenny, she'd felt a tiny flicker of hope ignite in her breast and begin to burn steadily, despite her amazement over the entire affair.

Since Maybelle's death Luke had consorted with nothing but whores, saying that that was what all women were anyway and that at least those at Miss Ruby's bordello were honest about it. He hadn't looked twice at a decent female.

Lottie, sensing the embittered change Maybelle's betrayal had wrought in him, had wrung her hands with despair, thinking he would never marry again and that Kipp and Sarah Jane would be forced to grow up motherless. Lottie knew Luke needed a woman's gentle touch to heal him, as did his children. Whether or not he would ever find it—or lay claim to it if he did—was another matter.

Now, contemplating Jenny, Lottie thought she understood why her son felt so drawn to the girl. It was evident Jenny's past was as pain-filled as Luke's own. Her grey eyes, like Luke's blue ones, were too old for her years, and her soft, vulnerable lips belied the outwardly brave and determined face she showed to the world.

But Lottie also sensed something she wasn't certain her son had realized. If Luke wanted Jenny Colter—and Lottie wasn't even sure he had admitted to himself yet that he might—he was going to have to court her very slowly and carefully, for she was as shy and skittish as a young filly.

I'll drop a hint to the boy, Lottie decided, for she'd already determined Jenny would be perfect for Luke. It would be a shame if he were to lose the girl because he set about wooing her the same way he robbed banks—too damned arrogantly and bold as brass!

"Well." Lottie sighed and stepped down from the chair, briskly rubbing her hands together. "That's that. Shall we get started on the parlor, girls?"

The women all nodded their agreement, then after sweeping out the dogtrot they headed toward the front room.

"Miss Jenny, Moses is back," Delcine announced, moving to the doorway as they heard the crunch of iron-rimmed wheels on the rock-strewn drive.

"So he is. Hey, Moses," Jenny called, running outside awkwardly but eagerly to greet him. "Did you get everything we needed? Gracious, I guess you did!" she observed as she stood on tiptoe to peek over one side of the ponderous vehicle that was nearly filled to bursting with barrels and boxes. Then she asked, "Who owns this wagon? I know twenty-five dollars wasn't enough for all you bought and that too."

"Nawum." Moses grinned. "But it belongs ter yo jes' de same, Miz Jenny. Ah knowed we wuz gwine ter be needin' some kind o' transportation, so Ah talked ter Mistah Pritchard, ober ter de lib'ry stable, an' he said yo could haf bof dis hawse and dis wagon fo' a hunnert an' fifty dollars, an' yo cain pay him on time fo' dem, ten dollahs a month."

"Why, that's wonderful, Moses!" Jenny cried, causing the big black man to beam proudly. "Well, the kitchen's all cleaned up, so you drive on around back. You can unload everything there, and Delcine will help you put it all away."

"Yassum, Miz Jenny. Giddyup der, Blossom," he clucked, slapping the reins on the big draft mare's back.

The wagon had no sooner lumbered around the side of the cabin than the Morgan gang rode into the yard. Jenny's mouth formed a small o of surprise at the sight of the brothers, for she'd hoped to have a chance to tidy herself up a little before their arrival. Now it was too late. Luke would see her looking like a ragamuffin and be even less impressed with her than he doubtless already was. Well, there was no help for it. Jenny would just have to make the best of the situation. Besides, what did she care what Luke thought? Gathering her composure, she stepped forth to greet the five men.

Because she had been working so hard her leg hurt, and her limp was even more pronounced than it usually was. Luke, at the sight of it, again felt a twinge of compassion for her and more than a stab of guilt over his behavior toward her last night. Still there was something about the set of her jaw that told him Jenny neither expected nor wanted anybody's sympathy, and so Luke offered none. He knew what it was like to be an object of pity; certainly everyone had felt sorry enough for him when Maybelle had run off. People's constant remarks, though they'd been kindly intended, had done nothing but continually remind him of his loss and the fact that he'd been made to look a fool by that slut he'd married. No, he'd heard enough well-meaning comments to last him a lifetime. No doubt the new schoolteacher felt the same.

Silently he studied her as reservedly she held out her hand, first to J.R. and then to Tobias. Her ladylike restraint was quite proper, but, thinking about what he'd guessed of her past, Luke knew there was more to it than that. Jenny's eyes were wide, and her body was hesitantly poised, as though she might take to her heels at any moment.

When it was his turn to take her hand, Luke smiled enigmatically at her.

With mingled dread and anticipation Jenny looked up at him, feeling her bones melt inside of her at his jeering grin, so that for an instant she thought she must be trickling down into a pool of quicksilver at his feet. She was slightly surprised to find herself still standing, her palm in his. His eyes gazed down into hers, seeming to peer right into her heart and soul, ferreting out her innermost secrets and unwrapping them to expose them to the light of day. Despite the hard lines that engraved his face, she sensed a curious gentleness in him, and she knew why he had not raped her last night, as he so easily might have done.

"Well, hello again, Miss Jennilee," he drawled.

"It's—it's Jenny. Just plain Jenny," she corrected him softly, wishing she'd had time to comb her hair and that her cheeks didn't go all hot and pink whenever a man addressed her—especially this one.

No doubt he was thinking she'd actually enjoyed his advances last night—and, oh, God, she had! For some awful, inexplicable reason she had! The thought was mortifying, and for an instant it was all Jenny could do to hold at bay the tears that threatened to spill from her eyes when she recalled her disgrace at this man's hands. She had never felt as helpless and mixed up as she did now, unable to cope with the tide of events that seemed to be ruthlessly sweeping her along in their wake. She ought to order Luke off her property, but then Lottie and the rest would want to know why he was unwelcome here, and Jenny could not bear to tell them, for how could she explain her shame to them without betraying her conflicting emotions about Luke as well?

Even now his very nearness was causing her heart to hammer rapidly in her breast. Nervously Jenny glanced down at her chest, half afraid the bodice of her dress revealed her agitation. To her relief it didn't, but, then, she couldn't see the tiny pulse fluttering wildly at the hollow of her throat, where she'd opened her collar earlier. But Luke could, and Jenny started to quiver all over, flustered, as she watched his eyes fasten on the exposed spot. Her face flushed even more crimson, and in her confusion she would have snatched her hand away rudely, had not Luke held it so tightly.

Her palm was damp in his own, and her fingers were trembling. For a crazy instant he longed to grab her up and hold her close, press his lips against her hair and tell her she had no need to fear, that he wouldn't let anything hurt her ever again. But of course he did nothing of the sort.

"I thought you said on the train that your name was Jennilee," he told her instead, frowning slightly with puzzlement.

"Well, it is . . . I—I mean, it's Jennifer Leigh. But everybody calls me Jenny. I guess I didn't make myself clear that day." She spoke in a rush, wondering whether or not she should even acknowledge his mention of the holdup and if she ought to thank him for letting her and Moses keep her father's pocket watch.

"Is that so? Well, I kind of like Jennilee myself. It's got a pretty ring to it, and I think it suits you."

Immediately Luke realized he'd said the wrong thing, for a queer, wounded look clouded Jenny's eyes, and coolly she withdrew her hand from his. Luke could have kicked himself in the hind end, for she wasn't pretty—and obviously she knew it. She thought he'd been making fun of her—as though what he'd done to her last night hadn't been bad enough!

Well, there was nothing he could say now that wouldn't make matters worse, so wordlessly he turned away, cursing himself for a fool.

What in the hell was the matter with him anyway? Jenny Colter wasn't even his type, yet each time he saw her he felt like a callow youth just out of short pants! Luke just couldn't understand his strange attraction to her, and, worse yet, it seemed to be growing stronger every minute.

Damn it! he swore silently, angry at himself for having unintentionally insulted the girl. *Why don't you just admit it to yourself? You don't really find the idea of marrying Jenny so bad, do you? In fact, even though you decided against it, you haven't been able to put it out of your mind—and that bothers you, doesn't it? You don't like these feelings she's arousing in you, do you? You might come to care for her— and that would mean risking being hurt again, wouldn't it? Imagine needing a woman—a woman to be there in the evenings when you come home so exhausted you can barely stagger through the door. A woman to greet you with a smile and a kiss and supper waiting hot on the stove. A woman to hold you close and caress you when the nights are so long and endless that you have to turn to the bottle just so you can get to sleep. A woman to care about* you, *not just the coins you toss on the table after slaking your lust. . . . Yes, deep down inside, you* do *need that, don't you?*

No, it's not true. I don't need anybody.

Don't you? his inner voice prodded relentlessly. *Then think of your* kids, poor little lost souls. *They* need a woman—a woman to take pride in their childish drawings and bandage up their skinned knees. A woman to bundle them up against the winter snow and pick wildflowers with them in the spring. A woman to laugh with them during the day and read stories to them at night and do a thousand other things a mother does. Yes, your kids need somebody. Lord knows, *you* haven't had much time for them since Maybelle died.

The new schoolmarm would be perfect for all that, wouldn't she? Not like Velvet Rose or any of the other whores you've been seeing. Of course Jenny appeals to you—and for the very same reasons nobody else would want her: She's plain, and she limps, and she's terrified of men. No other man would ever find her so alluring he'd risk your wrath in order to bed her, and even if one did and tried to persuade her to be unfaithful to you, she'd be so afraid of him and of you that she'd never, ever even *dream* of cheating on you like that bitch Maybelle!

Luke Morgan, you ought to be ashamed of yourself! his conscience retorted. You're an arrogant outlaw with a price on your head in at least five states, and you've got two emotionally scarred kids and nothing but a small, run-down farm to offer a woman anyhow. What makes you think a lady of Jenny Colter's class and upbringing would even look twice at you—much less be willing to wed you—especially after the way you behaved toward her last night? Why, she probably thinks you're nothing but a hardened criminal and no better than a backwoods cracker! It'll serve you right if she *does* report you to the Pinkerton Detective Agency!

As the notion occurred to him Luke's mouth tightened with rage, and he began to swing his scythe so furiously at the tall, weed-ridden grass in the overgrown yard that even J.R. stepped out of his way.

"What's eating him?" J.R. muttered to Tobias, jerking his thumb in Luke's direction.

"What do you think?" Tobias shot back, glancing back with a lifted brow at Jenny, who was outside airing some linens and smiling wistfully at Raiford and Billy Clay, whose playful antics reminded her of her own four dead brothers. Tobias continued grimly. "She saw Luke's face, and she knows we robbed the train yesterday. I don't mind admitting it's made me more than a little uneasy myself. Luke's certain she'll keep her mouth shut, but I tell you, J.R., I think he's grabbing at straws. For all we know, she's already wired the Pinkerton Detective Agency in Chicago."

"Hmmm," J.R. intoned thoughtfully. "Well, that should be easy enough to check on; I'll pay a visit to Stokes at the telegraph office this evening. As for Miss Jenny . . . well, I guess we'll just have to keep an eye on her and hope for the best, that's all. I just don't think I could stomach killing a woman, and, God knows, it would set the entire country against us for sure."

"Besides which, Ma would probably turn us into the law herself—if she didn't skin us alive beforehand!" Tobias put in.

"Yeah," J.R. agreed, "if Luke didn't get to us first. I don't know about you, Toby, but if I didn't know better, I'd say Luke was sweet on Miss Jenny. He's been acting downright peculiar ever since he met her."

"Yeah, I think so too. He sure didn't like the way Raif and Billy Clay were making fun of her last night, and imagine his insisting we come over here today to clean up this yard!"

"Hmmm," J.R. repeated. "It appears as though things are going to get mighty interesting around here shortly, Toby. Mighty interesting indeed. I don't believe the new schoolmarm, deep down inside, cottons much to men—especially outlaws—no matter how polite she's being in front of Ma and the womenfolk. I'd say Luke's got his work cut out for him if he hopes to win that little gal's hand and heart."

"She seems nice at least. Billy Clay was right though; she's not much to look at."

"Maybe not," J.R. assented, "but you know what Ma says: Pretty is as pretty does, and we all know what Maybelle was."

"Yeah," Tobias uttered scornfully. "I never did like that slut! Well, one thing's for certain: Those whores Luke has been taking up with lately have made him think he's the cat's whiskers when it comes to women. It'll serve him right to be given a smart set-down for a change, and I never did know a schoolmarm who wasn't good at that!"

Hearing the two men laughing heartily together, Luke scowled darkly. They looked so smug!

"What in the hell are you gawking at?" he questioned sharply, correctly guessing they'd been discussing him and Jenny Colter.

Damn them! His business was his own. He didn't need them sticking their oars in and muddying up the waters, though their lives hinged, like his own, on Jenny's silence. Luke wished he'd never told his brothers why he was interested in her, much less how he'd threatened her last night, warning her to keep quiet about them. But he'd been forced to make some kind of explanation to his brothers about the girl. Raiford would have recognized Jenny at once upon seeing her, and then they all would have been up in arms about her. There was no telling what they might have done; best to let them think Luke had already handled the matter.

Still his brothers' teasing galled him no end. It was obvious they thought he was taken with Jenny, and they were sure to give him no peace until they discovered whether or not they were right. Already J.R. and Tobias were sniggering and whispering about him behind his back, and Raiford and Billy Clay, whom Luke earlier had warned to be nice to Jenny or he'd wring their frigging necks, had monopolized her all day so he'd barely even had a chance to speak to her. It was enough to make a man want to commit murder!

For two cents Luke would get on his horse, start riding, and never look back! Then he glanced over at Jenny and knew he could not leave. He had been wrong to terrorize the girl last night; she hadn't deserved either that or the liberties he'd taken with her afterward. He might just as well have tormented a tiny bird, albeit one that had pecked him ferociously with its beak, Luke thought as his fingers idly traced the scratches on his face. He smiled to himself. Never before had a woman scorned him; even Maybelle had always been willing to share his bed— if nothing else. That alone ought to tell him Jenny Colter was something special, Luke reflected. Inexplicably his heart began to beat rapidly as he contemplated her.

To abandon her to the plots his four worthless brothers might devise if he left her alone to face them was suddenly quite unthinkable.

Chapter Six

Slowly Jenny tossed back the covers and eased herself off the awful old straw-stuffed mattress she needed desperately to replace on the high wooden bed. That was one of the things they hadn't managed to do today, though so much had been accomplished.

Now the house at least was clean and the yard no longer resembled a jungle. Tomorrow Moses was going to replace with iron hinges the rotten leather straps on the door. Then he would patch the roof and start filling in the chinks in the walls while Jenny and Delcine set to work on a new mattress and began sewing some curtains for the windows. Once all that was finished, Moses would fix the fence and repair the furniture. When this last was repainted Jenny, who was quite artistic, intended to stencil some bright designs on it to make it more attractive and cheerful. She'd decided to do some larger patterns on the floors as well, and Delcine had offered to braid some colorful rag rugs to match. In addition, Moses meant to build a small lean-to for himself onto the kitchen and make proper beds for both him and Delcine. Currently they were sleeping on pallets on the hard floor.

Quietly, so as not to waken the slumbering Delcine, Jenny drew on her robe and stepped into her slippers. Then she picked up the candle that burned always in her room at night. Stealthily she opened the door to the parlor. Creeping past the snoring Moses, she made her way down the dogtrot to the kitchen.

She set the candle on the table and filled one of the new tin cups Moses had bought that afternoon. The water tasted slightly rusty since the pump hadn't been used in a while, but it was cool and quenched Jenny's thirst.

Thoughtfully she gazed out the kitchen window, which was open so the night air could drift inside and dispel the hot, stuffy atmosphere of the cabin. The slender crescent moon shone down in a hazy shimmer of silver through the leafy branches of the trees. A little beyond, the fireflies flashed glowing sparks as they flitted from bush to bush in the darkness. The hushed sounds of the forest welled through the house. The monotonous droning of locusts mingled soothingly with the erratic croaking of frogs and the noises made by other stirring creatures skittering through the brush. They were quiet, peaceful sounds and brought with them a measure of contentment, for they reminded Jenny of summer nights at Faxon's Folly before the war, when she'd lain beneath the mosquito netting of her bed and listened to the world outside, knowing she was safe and snug beneath her covers.

Now, though her deep dread had lessened, she feared the darkness, for it was then that the nightmares came, gripping her with violent hands and wrenching her from her sleep so she awakened screaming and drenched with sweat, her heart pounding in her throat.

Five years had passed, and still the memories haunted her. Yet, no matter how hard she tried to reconstruct exactly what had happened, the most vital parts of the episode eluded her. Oh, if only she could remember! Perhaps then the horrible, blurred images she *did* recall would cease to taunt her. But the chasms of her mind when she thought of that day were like long black corridors, devoid of answers to her questions.

She sat down at the table and buried her head in her hands. As nothing in the past five years had done, today had brought home to her with sharp, painful intensity just how much she had lost during the war. Being with just a portion of the big, happy Morgan family had reminded her so much of her own parents and her brothers and sisters that Jenny didn't know how she'd been able to stand it. It just hadn't seemed fair that the five notorious Morgan brothers had come through the war unscathed while her own four brothers, decent, law-abiding men, had all been killed. But, then, the Colter men hadn't been as hard and determined as the Morgans, who'd grown up poor and had been forced to deal early on with the cruel blows of reality. Jenny's brothers had been well-bred and finely reared. Spared discomfort by their wealth, they had been schooled to enter a world of grace that had disintegrated before their eyes. They had not been prepared for war or its aftermath.

Yet Jenny had been drawn to the outlaws' family all the same, for they'd shown her kindness and consideration, and she was grateful now for that. But they'd also instilled in her a hungry desire to let go of the past and give herself the chance to belong and love again. It would be wonderful to be part of a big family once more.

She thought of Luke, then. She remembered how with the butt of his pistol he had savagely felled the large man on the train, then gunned down the conductor, wounding him severely. She recalled how he had threatened her life and taken base advantage of her helplessness. Still he had aroused her. Even now she was enticed by him as a gossamer-winged moth is lured to a burning flame. Was she attracted by a golden ray of light that would touch her gently, or was she dangerously playing with fire, deceiving herself about Luke because she was so lonely?

Why had he come this afternoon? Had he offered to help her to make up for the terror he'd caused her to experience during the train robbery and again last night? Or had there been more to it than that? If his attitude toward her had been the least bit menacing, Jenny would have suspected he'd meant to reinforce his dire warning to her about not reporting him and his brothers to the law. But it had not been so. Instead Luke had watched her ceaselessly, almost hungrily, a strange, unfathomable light in his eyes.

Ah, well. Jenny sighed. There was no point in wondering about the man's motives. No doubt he'd had his reasons, and they were not at all what she'd considered. In all likelihood it was just as Lottie had said: The Morgans were neighbors and had wanted to lend a friendly hand. Since most of the really backbreaking work had been completed today, Jenny probably wouldn't see all that much of Luke in the future. He was definitely too old to attend school, and he was doubtless out of town most of the time, holding up trains or committing various other assorted crimes she certainly did not want to know anything about.

It would be best if she put him out of her mind once and for all. Already her inner turmoil over him had caused her two sleepless nights, and despite her earlier fantasy of becoming a part of his family, Jenny knew that was only a dream. For it to become reality would necessitate her marrying one of the Morgan bachelors, and she couldn't wed any-one—especially a man like Luke, who would want every part of her in return for the ring he would place on her finger.

Somehow she must rid herself of this bewildering desire she felt for him. But that, Jenny reflected, as his handsome image once more crept unbidden into her mind, was going to be easier said than done.

Chapter Seven

In the two months that preceded the opening of school, Jenny saw Luke several times, for he had found to his annoyance that she haunted his thoughts, and he could not keep away from her. Besides, his brothers, with some perverse sense of merriment, had ordered him to watch her. After all, they'd said, it was his face she had seen; it was only right that he keep an eye on her.

Although the girl had said nothing about him or his brothers to anyone, Luke, remembering Maybelle's duplicity, did not trust Jenny to maintain her silence, no matter how badly he'd frightened her. He was certain the Ozark Mountain Railroad Company had telegraphed the Pinkerton Detective Agency about the train robbery and that it would be only a matter of time before one or more of the agency's detectives showed up to investigate the holdup. Jenny, Luke was sure, would crack under their grueling interrogation, and then if he were to be captured and bound over for trial, her testimony—if it did not put a noose around his neck—would at the very least cause him to be imprisoned for more years than he cared to count—to say nothing of what it might do to his brothers.

Having always prided himself on having a way with women, Luke was certain that, in spite of being scared of him, Jenny would eventually be flattered by his attentions and begin to thaw toward him, becoming at least his friend and perhaps more—if he decided he wanted to marry her after all. She *did* attract him; Luke admitted that, and the more he saw her, the more steadily he was drawn to her. It would not hurt to court her a little. In fact, it could only help his cause. If Jenny were to come to care for him, she would be that much less apt to reveal her knowledge of the train robbery.

Yes, in time her frozen attitude toward him would melt. After all,

Luke reasoned, no female really wanted to remain a spinster, no matter what dark secrets her past might harbor. All women wanted a man sooner or later—if only for the security he provided. But to his anger and dismay Luke soon discovered this was not the case with Jenny; despite his best efforts to please, he found himself thwarted by her at every turn.

If Jenny spied him in town, she would actually cross the street to avoid having to speak to him; Luke had seen her do so on at least three occasions! If he rode out to her cabin to lend a helping hand, she was cool and withdrawn, and invariably she pointed out to him that Moses was quite adept at chopping wood or cutting grass. The few Sundays Luke had attended church, hoping to see her, Jenny had deliberately refused to meet his eyes, keeping her gaze locked on the Reverend Thompkins instead. And the one time Luke had offered to drive her home she had politely thanked him, then informed him that she had a horse and wagon of her own and had no need of his assistance.

Luke was at first dumbfounded, then later enraged by Jenny's behavior. He did not realize it took every ounce of her willpower to resist him. He did not know that every time he smiled at her she wanted him to take her in his arms and kiss her passionately again.

Jenny, for her part, was so distressed by her feelings for him that she began to wonder if she were losing her mind. She recalled an incident in Atlanta in which a seemingly well-adjusted young veteran had suddenly gone berserk a few years after the war, and she was afraid that beneath her calm exterior she might be going as mad as he had. Certainly her inner struggle to reconcile her shattering memories with her growing attraction to Luke was proving a strain she didn't know if she could bear.

She did her best to ignore the outlaw, but ceaselessly he haunted her thoughts and tormented her being. She passed several more sleepless nights, tossing and turning as inwardly she fought herself for control of her emotions—but to no avail. Her mind and body appeared to have wills of their own, and Jenny could not seem to regain her mastery over them. Her mind dwelled constantly on Luke; her body was possessed by an odd, throbbing ache that would not be stilled.

Once, instinctively seeking to assuage the peculiar yearning that possessed her, Jenny ran her palms over her sweat-drenched nightgown, imagining they were Luke's hands caressing her. To her mortification something primitive and frightening leaped vividly to life within her. Like a fire bursting into flame, it spread through her veins so rapidly she believed for one awful, crazy moment that she was going to die. Her heart beat so fiercely in her breast that she couldn't catch her breath, and she sat bolt upright in bed, gasping for air.

After a while she lay back down and deliberately forced herself to count to ten slowly. Luke did not love her, and there could be no gentleness where there was no caring. Jenny had seen for herself that this was so.

She must keep out of his way. There was no telling what he might do to her. She was plain and crippled, not a combination designed to attract a man—yet Luke did not seem put off by these handicaps. That alone should be enough to warn her about his evil nature, Jenny thought. He was wicked and perverted, filled with an unnatural lust that fed off a woman's fear. But even she could not reconcile this highly distorted image of him with the man who'd had every opportunity to rape and kill her but who, after breaking into her hotel room, had done little more than kiss her.

Jenny pictured herself writhing beneath Luke, his mouth hard and brutally demanding against her own, his body piercing hers savagely, driving down into her mercilessly until she responded to him with passion, and she was eaten up by guilt and shame over her unladylike fantasies. She should be punished, she thought, and as though in answer to her wish, the portrait blurred, and Luke's handsome face took on the vile, ugly features of the man who had—who had . . . Horrified, Jenny clapped her hands to her mouth to muffle the screams that rose in her throat.

Yes, that was all Luke Morgan wanted of her—that and her silence—and it was not enough, would never be enough for her.

To Jenny's relief Luke seemed to have disappeared. At church she scanned the pews in search of him, and in town she looked down sidewalks nervously, but he was not there. Eventually she heard through the grapevine that he and his brothers had gone to Kentucky to pull a bank job. Oddly enough, instead of being glad he was no longer around to taunt her, she was torn in half by the idea, alternately wishing he would be caught and punished for his crimes, as he so assuredly deserved, then perversely hoping he would elude the law yet again to return to Tumbling Creek.

Yet whenever his devilish image danced in her mind, Jenny furiously shoved it aside, highly vexed with herself for her obsession with the outlaw. With a vengeance she threw herself into her new life. Work would drive that demon Luke Morgan from her thoughts!

After several long, hard, laborious weeks the cabin was now as snug as it could be in preparation for the coming winter. The door was fixed; the roof was patched; the chinks in the walls were filled. Moses had repaired the fence and the furniture also, and Jenny had painted the latter and the floors too with a rich, warm, dark brown stain that, once varnished and waxed, shone with a soft, burnished glow. In addition, she had painstakingly decorated most of the furniture and bordered the floors too with red hearts and yellow-centered flowers in shades of purple and lilac, dark blue and light blue, and white, all entwined with green-leafed vines. She and Delcine had reupholstered the sofa and the two chairs in the parlor as well, choosing a colonial-blue material to pick up the designs stenciled on the furniture. Plump lilac throw pillows and white antimacassars provided conplementary accent notes. In the bedroom a wedding-ring quilt that had belonged to Jenny's great-aunt, Henrietta, added a final touch to the bed's new feather mattress. White ruffled eyelet curtains and multicolored rag rugs completed the pleasant, cozy effect. Once they'd cleaned the thin hides on the windows so bright, diffused light could filter inside, the whole house gleamed with cheerful warmth.

Jenny, surveying her domain, felt quite proud of their accomplishments. Moses, having contrived an extremely clever bed for Delcine, one that folded up against a wall of the dogtrot when not in use, was now happily building a small lean-to off the kitchen for himself. In addition to serving as his quarters, it would double as a catchall area for the back entrance. There coats, hats, and scarves could be hung on pegs for easy access during the colder months.

Now that she was really settled in, Jenny intended to venture forth more often. She'd been to town a few times, and early on Mr. Peabody had of course taken her over to the one-room schoolhouse a short distance away, which also served as the church on Sundays. In warm weather she could walk easily along a narrow path that twisted through the trees from her cabin to the schoolhouse, but Mr. Peabody had suggested she might want to drive her wagon on the longer meandering country road, once the snow started in the winter.

"It'll still be quite dark in the mornings then, and you'll be safer on the main road," he'd told her. "The snow drifts awful badly in some parts of these here hills. Even though the path is shorter, it'll be more hazardous during the winter because no one uses it. At least if you flounder on the road, somebody is bound to come along sooner or later to help you out, and Miss Abigail will be able to see you in any event through her spyglass and will send for aid."

Jenny had thanked him politely for his concern, though privately she'd wondered if perhaps he weren't being overly cautious. She'd never seen snow and was therefore ignorant of how deadly cold and dangerous it could be under certain circumstances.

As for Miss Abigail Crabtree . . . well, Jenny wished the old spinster would mind her own business! Crabby Abby, as the girl had learned the town's more spiteful children called the elderly gossip, was the richest person in Tumbling Creek. Her father, who was long dead, had been a ship's captain back east who, after making a tidy fortune in the Orient, had come west to settle and enjoy to the fullest his remaining years in life. He'd brought his only daughter with him.

Miss Abigail, thoroughly devoted to her father, had never married and now lived alone in a big house on a hill overlooking Tumbling Creek. Her principal means of entertainment, Jenny had been informed, was spying on all the townspeople through a brass telescope her father had once used aboard his ship.

Jenny, who'd met Miss Abigail once briefly in church, had several times seen the flash of the spyglass's lens through the trees when the sunlight had caught it. At first she'd been puzzled by the bright reflection, but now she knew it was the spinster standing on the widow's walk of her house or peeping through one of her second-story windows to find out what her neighbors were doing. No one was safe from Miss Abigail's prying, and she did not hesitate to report to the Reverend Thompkins any scandalous behavior she observed so he might deliver the appropriate sermon from his pulpit on Sundays.

Jenny didn't like the idea of being spied on any more than anybody else in town did, but there was nothing anyone could do about it. Miss Abigail owned, among other businesses, the First National Bank of Tumbling Creek, and since she held the mortgages on most of the local property, no one dared to offend her.

Jenny sighed. There was really nothing more to be done in her cabin now that most of the needed repairs had been completed, and Moses certainly didn't require her assistance with the lean-to. Since she'd already finished her morning chores Jenny decided now was as good a time as any to walk over to the schoolhouse and thoroughly inspect it. She really ought to examine her desk and rummage through the bookshelves to see what was on hand. If anything must be ordered, she should see to it immediately. As it was, a shipment wouldn't arrive before the start of school, but Jenny could begin teaching with what she had and work other materials in later.

After untying her apron and laying it aside, she scrutinized herself in the mirror over the dresser to be sure her appearance was neat. Then, putting in a basket a few items she thought she might need, she set out down the winding path that led to the schoolhouse.

It was a glorious summer day, although a hint of fall was already in the air. A few of the leaves on the trees were starting to turn from green to gold and flame. Jenny knew that soon the last harvest of the season would be underway and the fall planting would begin. She wished she'd been able to plant a garden, but she'd arrived too late in the summer for that. Her cellar must remain virtually empty this year. But once the lean-to was done, she'd have Moses start digging a plot, laying out neat furrows to be planted next spring. Mr. Henshaw, who owned the feed store, had already promised her some seeds, and Moses was going over to Festus McNabb's place tomorrow to get the cow and chickens Jenny had purchased from him. Lottie, on one of her many visits, had told the girl the animals would be quite safe in the yard until after the harvest, when everyone would have a good, old-fashioned barn raising for her.

Jenny had at first protested, saying everybody had done so much for her already she didn't know how she'd repay them all. But Lottie, who, despite Jenny's reservations about their growing closeness, had become a dear friend, had insisted.

"Jenny," she'd said, "you're the seventh teacher Tumbling Creek has had in the past four years, and you're the *only* one who's acted like they was putting down roots and planning to stay a while." Of course Lottie knew nothing of Luke's warning to Jenny about not trying to leave Tumbling Creek. "The whole town's just plumb tickled pink about it." Lottie had beamed. "You don't drink like Mr. Farnsworthy—heaven forbid! We had to fire him after two months 'cause he kept getting his days mixed up and waking everyone up on Saturdays, ringing the school bell and swinging on the rope like he was an ape or something. You don't complain like Mrs. Davies; her constant whining purt near drove the entire school board insane. And you don't put on airs like that snobby Miss Underwood did. Lord, child! Everybody likes you. They're more 'n happy to help out."

Now as Jenny recalled the words she felt a warm glow invade her body, and her cheeks flushed with joy. She'd tried hard to be accepted by the tightly knit society of Tumbling Creek, and it appeared as though she were succeeding. Of course it would take a long time, perhaps years, for her truly to belong and for everyone to stop referring to her as "that foreigner, the new schoolmarm," but someday she would really be a part of the town.

Her step lighthearted, despite her limp, she rounded a bend in the path, and the schoolhouse at last came into view.

It was box-shaped, approximately fifty feet long and twenty-five feet wide. Set on stone pillars about three feet from the ground, in case of floods, it was built of smooth pine planks rather than rough-hewn logs, for it belonged to the town, and Mr. Kincaid, who owned the local sawmill, had donated the wood of which it was constructed. The roof was peaked, and at its front end it boasted a short, square, capped tower through whose apertures on all four sides could be seen a heavy iron bell. Jenny didn't know how the bell had survived the war, when almost anything made of metal had been commandeered by the military and melted down for arms and ammunition, but somehow it had. There was only one door, which was reached by means of five steps leading up to a small landing. Glass-paned windows that would prove a powerful distraction to her young charges, Jenny knew, lined either side of the building. Like everything else in Tumbling Creek, the schoolhouse was unpainted, blending in naturally with its surroundings.

Slowly Jenny climbed the stairs and entered. Just inside was a tiny, closetlike vestibule with a row of pegs along each wall for coats and hats. The bellrope hung down at one side of the door and was looped around a wooden cleat, out of the way when not in use. Set several feet apart on the wall opposite the door were two open entrances leading to the only room.

Within were four rows of benches and desks, the lids of which lifted to reveal a place for storing books, tablets, pencils, slates, chalk, and anything else a mischievous child might wish to conceal. Each bench would seat two youngsters, and after counting the number of desks in each of the four rows, Jenny determined the schoolhouse would accommodate forty pupils.

At the head of the room was a long recitation bench and a dais, where the pulpit, normally used only on Sundays, stood off to one side. Jenny's desk occupied the center of the platform. A large, cast-iron stove and a good supply of split logs filled the remainder of the area. In the corner behind the pulpit was a single tall stool on which miscreants were no doubt forced to sit. Beside that was a small table on which reposed a bucket and dipper. Directly in back of Jenny's desk was a short bookcase filled with books. Above this, on the wall, hung a big, black-painted board to which was attached a long shelf for holding chalk and erasers. A map of the United States and its territories, rolled up and tied securely with leather thongs when not in use, was nailed to the top of the blackboard.

Feeling a trifle giddy, Jenny walked up the center aisle to the dais and sat down at her desk. She gazed out over the room, imagined forty pairs of eyes staring back at her, and for one terrible instant felt an over-whelming sense of panic.

She would never be able to do it! she thought. Then she reminded herself that she must, despite her insecurities, for she needed this job. Should she be fired by the Tumbling Creek school board for incompetence, she would not be likely to find another position.

With renewed determination, Jenny opened the top drawer of her desk and removed a tablet and pencil. Then she swiveled around on her chair and began to sort through the worn, dog-eared books behind her.

It was some time later, after she'd closed the last of the primers, that she looked up to see a bent, leathery-faced old man standing at the back of the room. He was shabbily dressed, a battered straw hat on his head, a worn, checkered cotton shirt, its sleeves rolled up to his elbows, showing beneath his patched, bibbed overalls. His stout, laced brown shoes were scuffed, and he carried a staff in one hand, as though he were a shepherd.

Jenny was startled at first, for she'd been so absorbed in her task that she had not heard him come in. But then, as she rose and hesitantly walked toward him, her alarm faded. There was a wealth of wisdom, compassion, and understanding in his rheumy eyes. Seeing that, she knew he meant her no harm. Indeed, strangely enough, when he looked at her it was almost as though he knew her, inside and out, had known her since her birth and was privy to every single one of her hopes and fears.

"Howdy," he drawled, scratching his long, flowing white whiskers. "Lemme see. You must be Miz Jennifer Colter, the new schoolmarm. I heered you was a'comin', but I clean fergot. I thought nobody'd be here today. I come here sometimes, to think and to speak my piece to the good Lord. It comforts me, you see."

"That's quite all right." Jenny smiled. "I was just finishing up anyway. You're more than welcome to stay."

"Well, thankee, miss. That's right kind of you. I don't mind if I do sit a spell. It's a long trek down through them woods."

"You live around here, then?" Jenny inquired.

"Purt near longer 'n I kin remember. Yep. I guess I know these here hills better 'n anybody else in the county. I reckon you could say I'm sort a their caretaker—me and the good Lord, that is." He reached into his pocket, drawing forth a small music box. At Jenny's interested look, he explained. "The Good Book says, 'Make a joyful noise unto the Lord,' and so I do. I make these; it's part of my work. Each one's special, you see, like those I make 'em fer. Well, don't lemme keep you, miss. Good day to you."

Jenny nodded. Then after gathering up her belongings she made her way outside, wondering curiously who the old man was. She hadn't asked him, she realized. The sad sweet notes of the music box he'd pulled from his pocket earlier drifted to her ears from the schoolhouse, touching her heart as she imagined him sitting there, communing with God. It was a pretty melody, she thought, only gradually recognizing it as *Plaisir d'Amour*—"The Joys of Love," an odd song for someone to play in a church. Quietly as she turned toward home Jenny sang the words, accompanying the instrument until at last its plaintive lament died away in the distance.

After a time, inside the schoolhouse, the old-timer carefully closed the lid of the music box. Then he gazed up at the crucifix attached to the front of the pulpit. Solemnly he studied the Lord whose servant he was.

" 'And so abideth faith, hope, and love, these three,' " he quoted, his voice quiet but strong and devout, " 'but the greatest of these is love.' " He paused for a moment. Then softly, more gently, he said, "Have faith and hope, Miz Jenny, and love will come. Love will come, and it will be everlasting."

Then, nodding silently to himself, he tucked the music box back into his pocket, knowing now for whom he had made it.

Chapter Eight

The bell of the schoolhouse rang loudly, like a hammer hitting an anvil, as Jenny gave several long tugs on the bellrope before winding it around the wooden cleat that kept it out of the way when not in use. Then, her heart pounding nervously in her breast, she walked hurriedly up the center aisle to take her place behind her desk.

It was the first day of school, and she didn't want any of her students to notice right off that she was crippled. She was going to have a difficult enough time establishing her authority over a bunch of unruly children. Knowing she was physically lame often made people believe she was mentally deficient as well. She didn't want any of the older, more rowdy troublemakers to develop that mistaken notion this morning and to seek to put her at an immediate disadvantage in front of the rest of the class.

Of course some of the youngsters from town already knew she limped, but they had grown accustomed to the idea and did not now, Jenny hoped, give it a second thought.

From her vantage point behind her desk she surveyed her incoming pupils speculatively, trying to pinpoint the leaders of groups to ascertain the mischievous few who were bound to give her trouble. That big, strapping, freckled-faced boy teasingly yanking on a girl's braids was surely one of them, as was the devilish-eyed boy armed with a peashooter, who was using the smaller children as targets for his missiles. The two girls who were giggling and whispering behind their hands as they rolled their eyes dramatically at each other were doubtless note passers, and the dark, sullen boy deliberately slamming his books down upon his desk and staring around defiantly was definitely going to be a problem, Jenny concluded.

She waited until everyone had chosen seats. Then she rang the brass hand bell that sat on one corner of her desk. Gradually all talk and laughter died away, and a roomful of eyes looked up at her expectantly, taking her measure.

For one awful instant Jenny felt a wild, compelling urge to run down the aisle and out the door of the schoolhouse, to make good her escape while she still could. All her knowledge seemed to have deserted her, and she knew she couldn't possibly begin to answer the numerous questions that would soon be forthcoming from her charges. Learning of her ignorance, they would take no small delight in harassing and humiliating her, perhaps even reducing her to tears and making her appear like a fool before the whole town. The Tumbling Creek school board would have no choice then but to fire her, and what would become of her and Moses and Delcine?

Taking a deep breath, Jenny strove for composure, and a few minutes later her moment of self-doubt passed. She knew more than any other person here, she reassured herself sternly. That was why she was standing on the dais and everyone else was sitting out front, waiting for her to begin.

"Good morning, class," she addressed the room at last, glad to discover her voice sounded firm and strong. "My name is Miss Colter, and I am your new schoolteacher."

She turned and, picking up a piece of chalk, wrote her name neatly on the blackboard, then printed it underneath for the benefit of those who had not yet learned cursive writing.

"You talk funny," the devilish-eyed boy she'd noticed earlier with the peashooter announced, causing several youngsters to titter appreciatively. "Miss Underwood talked funny too. She was from Chicaaago"— he pronounced the city's name with the nasal twang of its native inhabitants.

A roar of laughter erupted from the class. Jenny, unable to prevent herself from doing so, smiled.

"What's your name?" she asked.

"Paul. Paul Henshaw."

Henshaw's Feed Store, Jenny placed the boy silently. No wonder he was armed with a peashooter; he had an endless supply of ammunition!

"Well, Paul," she said, "I talk differently from you because I'm from Atlanta, Georgia. Were you to visit my hometown, *you* would be the funny-sounding one."

Evidently this thought hadn't occurred to Paul, and he flushed red as the others hooted again, this time at his expense.

Quickly Jenny reached up and untied the map of the United States and its territories. After letting the thin leather scroll unroll and pressing on its corners so they would stay flat, she picked up the long, slender stick that lay on the tray attached to the blackboard. Efficiently she pointed out Atlanta.

"This is my hometown," Jenny stated, then amended her words. "Actually I was born here, in Jonesboro, a short distance away. But I spent the past several years in Atlanta. As you can see, it's several hundred miles from here. How many of you have ever visited a town other than Tumbling Creek?" she queried. A few hands were raised in answer to her question. "How many of you have ever traveled beyond the borders of the state of Missouri?" This time no one responded.

"In addition to Georgia and Missouri, I have been to Alabama, Tennessee, and Arkansas," Jenny continued. "In every part of the United States and its territories, people speak with their own regional accents, and if one has a highly developed ear for such patterns of dialect, one may determine a person's origins just by listening to the way he or she talks."

"Golly," somebody in the back said in a stage whisper.

"Before the war," Jenny elucidated, "two of my brothers went to Europe. In the majority of countries there English is not even spoken. Each country has its own particular language, and if you could not speak that language, you would not only sound funny"—she looked once more at Paul—"but no one would understand a single word you said."

Eyeing him closely, Jenny determined Paul had been put properly in his place, and she decided it was now time to let him off the hook. She smiled encouragingly at the boy.

"Thank you, Paul, for bringing this most interesting topic of conversation to our attention this morning."

The boy, who had been pouting slightly at having his antics so deftly countered, now sat up a little straighter on his bench and, beaming, threw his classmates a triumphant grin. Jenny felt certain she had won him to her side.

"Now, class," she went on, "the first thing I want to do today is to become acquainted with each and every one of you. So one by one, starting with that row there"—she indicated the far right side of the room—"I want each of you to stand up and tell me your name and the thing you like to do best for fun. Let's begin now, shall we?"

The morning passed fairly smoothly, and, as she watched her pupils close their desks at noon and race outside for dinner, Jenny felt her first day of teaching was overall a success.

There'd been one incident with the freckle-faced boy, LeRoy Pritchard, involving several spitballs that had somehow found their way up to the dais from the back of the room. But Jenny had casually mentioned that at the end of the week perhaps LeRoy would enjoy cleaning out the school's outhouse, since no doubt he often did similar work at his father's livery stable, and that had put a prompt end to the matter.

Matthew McNabb, the sullen boy, had proven more difficult to handle. He had at first refused to reveal his name to Jenny, and she had spent several uncomfortable minutes steadily staring him down while the rest of the class had watched in nervous silence to see what would happen. Finally, just when Jenny had thought she was going to have to walk down the aisle, snatch the boy from his seat, and march him up to the miscreant's chair in the corner, he'd told her his name. Then he'd slyly informed her that his favorite pastime was wringing the necks of baby chicks.

Since a live chick was much more entertaining than a dead one, Jenny had noted coolly, it was obvious he didn't have a lot of fun. It was certainly a pity his life was so devoid of amusement. Without further comment, for she'd made her point, Jenny had moved on to the next student.

Matthew McNabb, who had thought to earn the class's approval as Paul Henshaw had done earlier, had scowled ominously, feeling the scorn of his classmates as sharply as the sting of his father's belt the few times he'd been chastened in the woodshed at home. He'd scrunched down in his seat and vowed silently to get even with the new schoolmarm. Spying the look on his face, Jenny had sighed. One of these days, she was sure, she would open her desk to find a snake, lizard, or toad inside, compliments of Matthew McNabb. She had best buy a pair of leather gloves—just in case.

After spreading her blanket under a feathery pine tree, Jenny unpacked her dinner basket and began to munch contentedly on the chicken sandwich Delcine had prepared for her earlier that morning. There was a wedge of cheese, a sour dill pickle, and an apple as well. In addition, Delcine had included a jar of lemonade. After unscrewing the lid Jenny poured some into her tin cup and drank thirstily.

All around her her students were busily devouring the contents of their dinner pails. Here and there could be seen the trading of a slice of bread smeared with sweet applebutter for one laden with tart strawberry jam, or the earnest bartering of a peach for a pear.

Only one boy, Jenny saw, sat apart from the rest, with no friend to share his meal. It was Luke Morgan's son, Kipp. Jenny's heart ached as secretively she studied him, observing the lock of blond hair that fell across his forehead just as his father's did. Kipp's eyes were blue too and haunted by shadows that ought not to have darkened them, for he was only eight years old. There was too much sadness in the boy, Jenny thought, and wondered if he had ever recovered from the death of his mother.

By now Jenny had heard the story of Maybelle Boothe Morgan and had been appalled by it. How could the woman have abandoned her own flesh and blood like that? Had it just been Luke whom Maybelle had deserted, Jenny would have found the matter more comprehensible. After all, the man was a notorious outlaw and was doubtless seldom at home. But to leave behind two children born of one's own body and soul—no, Jenny couldn't understand that at all.

She knew she would never be able to bear a child of her own. Yet how she longed for children, while Maybelle, who'd had two of them, had spurned them. It just didn't seem right somehow.

Jenny's great-aunt, Henrietta, had once told her God had some special purpose in mind for her, that that was why she'd survived that day at Faxon's Folly. Speculatively she considered the notion. Perhaps He had denied her children of her own so she could embrace a world of them through her teaching. Or maybe, her thoughts drifted idly, He had intended her for two whose own mother had not wanted them. . . .

You've got to stop this! Jenny chided herself sharply, giving herself a mental shake. You've got to stop daydreaming about Luke Morgan! The man is a criminal, for heaven's sake, and you know better than most the brutal things men like that are capable of doing. You've just got to put him out of your mind!

But it was even more difficult to abide by that resolve now that Jenny had seen Kipp. What was the other child, Sarah Jane, like? she wondered. The little girl had not come to school today. Was she ill? Curious, Jenny tossed her apple core into some bushes, intending to ask Kipp about the matter.

Slowly she repacked her dinner basket. Then after folding up her blanket she strolled over to where the boy was seated upon a hollow log.

"Hey, Kipp," she greeted him friendlily. "Do you mind if I join you?"

He shook his head, and, after tossing her blanket over the fallen trunk, Jenny sat down beside him. He glanced at her expectantly, half afraid he'd done something wrong in class that morning, and she smiled to allay his fears.

"I wanted to ask you about your sister, Sarah Jane," she told him, aware he exhaled with relief before his eyes became hooded and wary. "I noticed she wasn't here today," Jenny probed hesitantly in light of the expression that had come over his face, "and I wondered if she were sick."

"Naw." Kipp studied the scuffed toes of his shoes. "Pa said there weren't no need for her to come to school. He didn't think she'd take to book learning so good since she wouldn't be able to recite or nothing, and, besides, the other kids might make fun of her, seeing as how she can't talk and all."

"You mean—you mean she's a mute?" Jenny asked, startled, for she had not heard this before.

"Yeah, I guess so. Leastways, she is now."

"She used to be able to speak, then?" Jenny prodded, puzzled.

"Yeah, a long time ago, before Ma—before Ma . . . went away."

In silence Jenny digested this piece of news. Kipp, she could tell, was still trying to cope with his mother's abandonment of him and her subsequent death. It sounded to Jenny as though Sarah Jane were suffering from some even more profound emotional shock. In the hospital where she'd spent so many long months recovering after that day at Faxon's Folly, Jenny had seen numerous soldiers who, like her, had been stricken by a severe trauma. One of the symptoms some of them had displayed was a loss of speech.

"Then there's no physical reason why your sister can no longer talk?" she inquired at last.

"Naw, I reckon not," Kipp replied. "Pa took her to some doctors, but they couldn't find nothing wrong with her—leastways, nothing that medicine could cure. One of 'em said it had something to do with—with Ma's leaving and that Sarah Jane would be all right, once she'd gotten over it, but I—I guess she never did . . . get over it, I mean."

"Well, perhaps there's still hope," Jenny offered comfortingly. "We'd better go in now. Thank you for talking with me, Kipp."

All afternoon and for several weeks afterward as she watched Kipp in school, Jenny's mind kept dwelling on him and his sister. In some way Jenny felt she and the two children were kindred spirits, all of them emotionally scarred and torn apart inside. Jenny had had her great-aunt, Henrietta, and Cade to see her through the worst of her recovery, but who could Kipp and Sarah Jane turn to? Luke? Lottie? Did either of them have the time, patience, understanding, and knowledge to deal with two hurt lost youngsters? Or had they simply accepted what they felt they could not change, as no doubt the Reverend Thompkins had advised them to do?

I could help those children, Jenny thought, growing faintly excited at the prospect. I lived through enough at Faxon's Folly, saw enough at the hospital in Atlanta to help them. Luke—Luke has his own demons, and Lottie . . . well, Lottie is kindness itself, but I think something like this is beyond her. Kipp and Sarah Jane need a special kind of understanding, the kind I have. I'll talk to Luke, Jenny decided. I'll make him see that he has to give me a chance to help those two children, for their sakes—and mine. I can do it. I know I can! I'll drive over to Lottie's this evening and see if he's back.

Chapter Nine

The sun had almost but not quite finished its slow descent in the sky when Jenny set out in the wagon toward Lottie's house. It was a pleasant Friday evening, and the horse, Blossom, ambled along slowly, pausing now and then to snatch a mouthful of grass from the side of the road, plodding forward again only when Jenny jiggled the reins to remind the mare they had a destination to reach before dark.

Beside the girl, on the seat, lay the rifle that Moses had bought from the town gunsmith, Mr. Ryland. Jenny didn't like the long-barreled weapon and hoped she never had to fire it. Still Moses had insisted she take it with her for protection since he wasn't accompanying her to Lottie's cabin.

Jenny had purposely left Moses behind in order to give Delcine a few hours alone with him. From the way she eyed him when she thought no one was looking, it was evident Delcine was sweet on the big black man. However, there was so much work to be done during the day that Moses doubtless paid scant attention to her. But tonight . . . well, perhaps he would at last notice her interest in him and start to court her. Jenny hoped so. Delcine would be good for him, and the two of them more than deserved whatever happiness they might find together.

It was funny how her life had changed, Jenny reflected as Blossom shuffled along unhurriedly. Before the war she would scarcely have given Moses and Delcine a second thought. To her they would have been little more than faceless fixtures, as taken for granted as the food she'd eaten or the air she'd breathed. Now they were her best friends, and Jenny felt ashamed that she'd ever owned a slave, that she'd actually believed people who had claimed Negroes were little better than animals, dumb and needing to be looked after by their white masters. Moses and Delcine were intelligent and quick to learn. If they'd been ignorant in the past, it was not their fault. The blame lay squarely on the shoulders of those who'd passed ridiculous laws making it a crime to teach Negroes what any white child, no matter how poor or backward, would have learned in school. Now, because she had taught them, Moses and Delcine were as adept at the basic skills as Jenny was. She could still recall the wide smile of pride and satisfaction that had split Moses's face the first time he'd ever signed his name. Education for all was one of the few good things to come from the war.

Since she'd earned her teaching certificate schooling had become very important to Jenny. That was one of the reasons she felt strongly about helping Luke's daughter, Sarah Jane. If, as Jenny suspected, the child's loss of speech was due to an emotional rather than a physical cause, her education was being wrongfully neglected. Besides, even a mute could learn to read, write, and cipher, and to communicate with others, using sign language. A hand alphabet for the deaf had been developed, Jenny knew, and was taught in special schools. It wasn't right that Luke, just because she didn't talk, should deny his daughter these means of enriching her life, and Jenny intended to tell him so, if he were home.

Her pulse leaped a little jerkily at the thought. She hadn't seen him for some time now. For all she knew, he might still be out of town.

The dusty country road twisted through the trees whose branches appeared to reach out to her eerily as the twilight shadows lengthened. A small wind began to sough, rustling the leaves, making them seem to whisper as Jenny passed by. When an owl hooted in the distance she glanced about wonderingly, slightly startled. Why, it was almost dark, and here she sat daydreaming while Blossom just moseyed along at her own sweet pace. Drawing herself up a little more straightly, Jenny took a firmer hold on the reins and clucked to the horse. Presently Blossom, realizing the hands that guided her were no longer idle, broke into a smart trot. The wagon rounded a bend in the road, and with relief Jenny saw Lottie's house come into view.

The girl turned onto the dirt drive, scattering several noisy chickens as she pulled up in the front yard.

"Shoo! Shoo!" she hissed to a particularly feisty hen as she hopped down from the wagon, set the brake, and looped the reins about the bar that kept them from becoming entangled when not in use.

She rummaged around in the wagon bed for Blossom's feed bag and placed it over the mare's nose. Then she walked up onto the porch and knocked on the door. Soon Lottie appeared, her face beaming with delight as she spied Jenny standing outside.

"Well, glory be!" Lottie cried, opening the door. "Come on in, Jenny, and sit a spell. Mercy, but it's good to see you! I was wondering when you were going to pay us a visit. Of course I knew you had to get settled in and all before school started, but, land's sake, child, I wasn't expecting you to be a stranger. Jed!" she called to her husband. "Jed, it's Jenny Colter, the schoolmarm. Come on out, and say howdy."

A tall, good-looking older man stepped from the dogtrot as Lottie ushered Jenny into the parlor and motioned for her to be seated.

Jedediah Morgan's hair was grey, and his shoulders were slightly stooped, but he had the wiry look of a man who worked the land for a living. His clear blue eyes twinkled as he caught sight of Jenny, and he stroked his grey beard thoughtfully as he considered her, a friendly smile playing about the corners of his lips.

"Well, I've heard so much about you that I feel like I already know you, Miz Jenny," he uttered warmly as he shook her hand. "Lottie here's spoken of you often, 'n' Kipp gives us a nightly report 'bout the day's doin's in school. I hear you've already got Paul Henshaw 'n' LeRoy Pritchard walkin' a fine line 'n' are workin' on Matthew Mc-Nabb. It sounds like you're doin' a mighty good job, Miz Jenny."

The girl blushed, hanging her head shyly.

"I—I try my best, Mr. Morgan," she stammered, remembering suddenly that Jed was one of the members of the school board.

"I reckon you do." He nodded. " 'N' everybody's jest as pleased as punch 'bout it too. It ain't jest anyone who could've straightened out those two troublemakers, Paul and LeRoy, 'n' Matt's got a chip on his shoulder so big it's a wonder he ain't toppled over from the size of it. He's a problem, that boy, that's fer shore. Festus jest dotes on him 'n' has spoiled him rotten, if you ask me. Our Kipp now . . . he's 'bout as good a kid as they come. Say, you ain't havin' any trouble with him, are you?" Jed's eyes suddenly narrowed intently, and Jenny saw where the Morgan brothers had gotten their grit and daring. "I'll wallop the tarnation outta that boy if he ain't doin' to suit you! He's mighty quiet around here, but you never kin tell what a young 'un will do behind your back. There wasn't nothin' my own five didn't dream up. But Kipp . . . well, he's had a hard time, 'n' he ain't as lively as he used to be. I almost wish he *was* more high-spirited." Jed's tone was wistful. "Don't seem right somehow, him turnin' into himself so much."

"I know what you mean, Mr. Morgan, and you're right," Jenny agreed. "Kipp is one of my best students, and I think the world of him, but he *is* too withdrawn. That's one of the reasons why I've come . . . that and—and Sarah Jane."

"Sary!" Lottie exclaimed, exchanging anxious glances with her husband. "Has she been up to the schoolhouse, bothering you? I know she follows Kipp sometimes in the mornings, but I had no idea—"

"Oh, no, Lottie!" Jenny hastened to reassure her. "It's not that. It's not that at all. I've come because I believe I can help her. Kipp told me about Sarah Jane being a mute, but he also said she used to be able to speak and that the doctors thought her problem was emotional rather than physical."

"Yes, that's true." Lottie sighed. "The poor mite just never got over Maybelle going off thataway. Something must have happened that night; we don't know what. But the doctors seemed to feel like Sary must have said something that made her think she was responsible for her mother's leaving, and that's why she ain't spoke a word since. Jed and me's done our best for the child, but . . . well, we're just plain folks, Jenny, and, as you know, we don't much cotton to foreigners in these here hills. We just couldn't bring ourselves to send Sary away to Saint Louis, to one of them special doctors who think us hill people are strange anyway."

"I understand," Jenny stated. "But, don't you see? If there's nothing physically wrong with the child; if her mind is bright but simply confused, her education ought not be neglected. Kipp told me Luke said there was no point in Sarah Jane coming to school, but that's not true! She can learn as well as the next person. I can teach her, and I'm willing to do it on my own time too, if that's what it takes. I—I lived through an emotional shock once as well, and it took me a long time to recover. I saw a lot when I was in the hospital, and I was just as devastated and bewildered then as Sarah Jane must be now. I just know I can help her, if you'll let me."

"Well, I dunno, Miz Jenny," Jed drawled skeptically, scratching his beard as he considered her words. "It's right kind of you, but—"

"Oh, please!" Jenny implored. "Just give me a chance to try! That's all I'm asking. It couldn't hurt, and I really believe it would help." Her eyes beseeched them both.

"I'm willing," Lottie declared, appraising Jenny intently and guessing what it had cost her to speak of her past. "But I don't think it's a decision Jed and me can make on our own. Sary is Luke's child. I reckon it's him what ought to have the final say."

"Yes," Jenny answered, feeling her heart start to thump queerly in her breast at the mention of Luke. Though she dreaded seeing him, oddly enough, some traitorous part of her being was actually eagerly looking forward to their meeting again. "Is he here?"

"No, he's over to his farm. He goes there sometimes when he—when he gets to thinking about the past," Lottie explained. "I don't know whether or not I'd bother him tonight if I was you, Jenny. I reckon he drinks a tot or two when he's out there."

"That's all right. I must see him." It didn't occur to Jenny that Luke might have imbibed more than a few shots of liquor. Since he was an outlaw she felt he must keep his wits about him. "If you'll just tell me how to get there, I won't take up any more of your time. I know it's getting late and you've got chores that need tending."

As they all walked out onto the porch, Jed gave Jenny directions to Luke's farm, Whispering Pines.

"Mercy!" Lottie wrung her hands worriedly as she looked at the night sky. "I hadn't realized how dark it was getting. Jenny, maybe you ought to go on home. You can see Luke another time."

"No." Jenny shook her head. She must visit him tonight, for in the morning, when she'd had time to consider her actions, she might find all the courage she'd summoned up to face Luke had drained away. Then she would never be able to help his daughter. "Sarah Jane's already missed quite a lot of school. She'll have to work hard to catch up, and I'd like to get started as soon as possible."

"Well, at least let me fetch a lantern for you, then," Lottie insisted, going back inside the house to get a light, then thrusting it into Jenny's hands. "Put it up there by you on the seat," she instructed as Jed assisted the girl into the wagon. "I know there's a moon, but it won't help much when you're driving through them trees. At least with the lantern you'll be able to see where you're going. Stick to the main road now; don't go wandering off it." Her tone was still anxious. "Oh, if only Raif or Billy Clay were here! Maybe you ought to go with her, Jed, just in case."

"Oh, no," Jenny protested. "I wouldn't dream of putting you out that way. I'll be all right. Really I will."

"Do you know how to use that rifle you're totin'?" Jed asked, his face filled with concern at the thought of her being out alone on the road at night.

"Yes," Jenny replied, remembering the long hours she'd spent with Cade, learning to defend herself after that day at Faxon's Folly. "I don't like the idea of firing it, but I know how to, if need be."

Jed's eyes glinted in the moonlight.

"Well, you kin take care of yourself, then, I reckon," he commented, but it was obvious he was still upset. "You're sure you don't want me to ride along with you?"

"I'm sure." Jenny spoke firmly. "I know you've got your stock to look after. Thank you, both of you. I'll bring the lantern back sometime tomorrow, Lottie."

"Don't you fret your head about it now, you hear? You just get home safe and sound."

"Yes, I will. Good-bye. Giddyup there, Blossom."

Slowly Jenny made her way down the bumpy dirt drive to the main road. She headed east, as though she were going home, but when she reached the crossroad Jed had spoken of, she swung south.

It was indeed hard to see as she wound through the trees, the moon playing hide-and-seek between the branches, and she was grateful Lottie had thought to give her the lantern. It cast a flickering glow in the darkness and helped to light her way. She was glad also that Blossom trotted along briskly; it was as though the mare too wanted to reach their destination as soon as possible.

Sometimes Jenny saw the eyes of animals gleaming from the bushes alongside the road, and once, a coyote ran across her path, causing the mare to dance skittishly. The coyote paid them no attention, however. More frightened of them than they were of it, it vanished into the brush as quickly as it had appeared.

Now and then came the hoot of an owl or the cry of some other wild creature, and Jenny glanced about nervously, half fearing she would be attacked by a lone wolf or bear.

At last, exhaling with relief, she saw the weatherbeaten sign that read: WHISPERING PINES. This was Luke Morgan's farm.

Jenny turned onto the overgrown, rock-strewn ribbon of a path that twisted through the dense woods. As she carefully maneuvered the wagon over the narrow drive, she wondered if she were out of her mind to have come here.

It was obvious the place had been abandoned for some time. The few acres that had been cleared for planting stretched like a barren desert in the moonlight, but the wilderness had already begun its gradual encroachment upon the fields, reaching out with tangled fingers to claim back what had been wrested from it by force.

The house itself was tumbling down. Both the roof and porch sagged, and there were jagged holes in the walls. The windows, surprisingly, had glass panes, several of which were broken. Still a light shone through one of them, and Jenny knew Luke was inside.

She pulled Blossom to a stop and, carrying Lottie's lantern, made her way up to the front door. She knocked several times, but there was no answer, so finally she tried the knob. The door opened on creaking hinges, and hesitantly she stepped inside.

"Luke," she called softly. Then, louder, "Luke Morgan."

She heard the sound of a chair being scraped across the floor in the kitchen, then suddenly he was standing at the edge of the dogtrot.

Jenny's first thought as she caught sight of his shadowed figure was that he was drunk, terribly drunk, and she felt a small fist of fear clutch at her heart as he staggered into the light.

His blond hair was tousled and unkempt; his shirt was unbuttoned, the ends hanging loose, exposing the whole of his matted, muscled chest to her startled gaze. In one hand he held a moonshine jug. He raised it to his lips, took a long swig, then wiped his mouth off on his sleeve.

Luke blinked his eyes a couple of times and shook his head to clear it, but when he again looked up he still saw Jenny standing there, and he knew she was no vision conjured up by the yearning recesses of his mind. She was real, and she was here.

How often Luke had thought about her during the past weeks and longed to see her. However, after her initial rejection of him he had kept away, waiting for her to get settled in, to grow accustomed to her surroundings, and to learn he was considered a desirable catch in Taney County, not only by the law, but by women as well. He hadn't wanted to press her. He hoped he'd already frightened her sufficiently as it was, and he hadn't wanted to terrify her to the point of cracking. She had talked to no one about him and his brothers, and the Morgan gang had quietly intercepted and sent packing the one Pinkerton detective who, in response to the Ozark Mountain Railroad Company's telegram to Chicago, had journeyed to Southern Missouri to investigate the train robbery.

Still Jenny's image had never been far from Luke's mind, and, because of his distrustful nature where women were concerned, he had not discarded his plan to win her over. Just because one Pinkerton agent had easily been disposed of did not mean the next would take to his heels so satisfactorily. Still Luke had recognized that he had a hard row to hoe where Jenny was concerned. He must go slowly with her, as his mother, after meeting the girl, had warned him.

All of Luke's instincts had told him Jenny was a lady, wellborn and well-bred, used to the finer things in life, despite the fact that she now made her own way in the world. She carried herself proudly, and her spine never touched the back of a chair. She held her tin cup as though it were fashioned from the most delicate bone china. Her white gloves, though worn and mended, were always spotless. Luke knew this was so, for he'd watched her slyly often enough on her shopping expeditions in town and at church on Sundays, feeling like a moonstruck fool for spying on her when she'd made it quite plain that she wasn't interested in him.

Yes, whatever else her mysterious background might harbor, Jenny was a lady. Before the war she had moved in a world very different from the one she lived in now, a world Luke had seldom glimpsed and had never known. And though she'd been left alone and penniless, she had not forsaken the teachings of her upbringing. Jenny was a victim of circumstance. She had not chosen her path, as Luke had. Secretly he feared she would continue to scorn him, and this feeling was beyond the realm of his experience.

He had always been confident in the past when courting women. His good looks, crooked smile, and charming manner had melted the hardest of hearts, opened the firmest of doors, and warmed the coldest of beds. All things in life had come easily to Luke. But Jenny . . . no, she would not come easily. She might not be won at all. The thought both angered and disturbed him. Luke was used to getting what he wanted.

"Well, well," he greeted her, slurring his words a little. "If it isn't the schoolmarm, come to catch me playing hooky."

Jenny's tongue flicked out to wet her dry lips. Then, furtively, she began to back away, edging toward the door.

"I—I think I should go." Her eyes were big and filled with apprehension. "I didn't realize. . . ." She paused and took a deep breath, then went on in a rush. "I see now that I've come at a bad time. I'm sorry."

Jenny turned to leave and without warning found Luke barring her way. How had he crossed the room so quickly? She didn't know. Her heart beat jerkily in her breast as she saw the strange glitter in his eyes in the lamplight.

"What's your hurry, Jennilee?" he inquired, his voice faintly mocking. "The night is young, and you've only just arrived. Sit down." He motioned toward one of the battered old chairs in the parlor. "Sit down!" he barked fiercely when she didn't move.

Jenny bit her lip, torn. Obviously she should go, but it was just as obvious that Luke meant her to stay, now that she was here. Had she been braver, she would have tried to push past him, but she did not. She was afraid that in his condition he might physically attempt to restrain her. She knew she dare not let him touch her, not the way he was now. There was no telling what he might do to her. They were totally alone in the cabin, and he was an outlaw—a desperate, drunken man. With a sinking heart Jenny realized she was utterly in his power. Oh, God, why had she come?

Warily she sidled over to the chair he'd indicated and sat down, placing the lantern on a small table that stood beside her. Her back was straight; her shoulders were square; her hands were folded just so in her lap. She suddenly remembered her previous suspicions that Luke was one of those men who fed on a woman's fear, and she realized she dared not let him see how scared she was. He was like an animal, and the smell of terror might arouse his baser instincts.

Luke guessed the pattern of her thoughts as surely as though Jenny had spoken them aloud, and the realization that she believed him to be that kind of a man made him furious, despite the fact that he had given her some cause to come to that conclusion. His lips curved with jeering amusement as he observed the stiffening of her spine, the other small movements she made to bolster her courage. But, in spite of himself, he felt a measure of respect and admiration for her. She was a woman alone with an inebriated criminal—but she had not run. He understood that kind of determined spirit—it was his own—and he was drawn to her like steel to a magnet.

Slowly he strode across the room and flung himself down in the chair opposite her own. He took another drink from the jug in his hand, his eyes never leaving her face. Then he lit a cigarette and dragged on it deeply.

"Why have you come, Jennilee?" he asked.

He liked the sound of the name he'd chosen for her, and he'd used it again deliberately, knowing his impudence would rattle her. Her fingers quivered, and she clasped them together more tightly to still their trembling. Once more she licked her lips, at a loss now as to how to begin. Half longingly she eyed the jug he held, reflecting that she could use a shot of the raw corn liquor herself. Then she dismissed the thought as abruptly as it had occurred. Ladies did not indulge in strong spirits. The results were not becoming, and the aftereffects were not pleasant. Luke would have a splitting headache in the morning, she had no doubt.

"It's—it's about Sarah Jane," Jenny confessed at last, wishing she could bring herself to tear her eyes away from his.

The way he sprawled in his chair, watching her like a hawk, set her nerves on edge. Taking another deep breath, she forced herself to recount calmly the things she had told Jed and Lottie. Luke listened impassively, his face giving no clue to his emotions as Jenny talked. Once or twice, in light of his lack of response, she faltered a little over her words, but still she pressed on, her determination to help Sarah Jane overcoming her doubts about Luke's willingness to let her do so. Finally she fell silent, waiting expectantly and wondering whether Luke had comprehended a single thing she'd said.

Just when she believed he wasn't going to give her a reply, he stubbed out his cigarette and leaned forward in his chair, his knees almost touching hers, his blue eyes piercing her grey ones. The air was fraught with tension, sharp and anticipatory, as though at any instant the highly charged atmosphere would erupt, loosing something bold and menacing, something brazen and exhilarating. Jenny eased away, sensing the turmoil that raged inside the man who confronted her so intently.

"What was the shock *you* suffered, Jennilee, that makes you think you can help Sarah Jane?" Luke probed mercilessly. "What happened in your past to make you so afraid of men—so afraid of me?"

"I'm—I'm not afraid of you, Luke," Jenny lied.

"Oh, yes, you are," he rejoined, his eyes traveling downward to fasten on her soft, vulnerable mouth. "I can almost hear your heart pounding," he claimed, his lean, bronzed visage now inches from her face, his breath warm upon her flushed cheeks. "I know your thoughts as well as my own. You're afraid I'll put my hands on you again, as I did that night at the hotel, that I'll make advances to you . . . perhaps even ravish you." He leered, his gaze raking her body, coming to rest on her heaving breasts. "You're listening to the stillness of the night and thinking how alone and isolated we are out here, how no one would hear you if you screamed, aren't you, Jennilee?"

"No," she whispered brokenly. "No."

But she knew it was true. With a small cry, unable to restrain herself any longer, Jenny suddenly sprang from her chair and started to run.

Luke caught her at the door, slamming it shut and flinging her up against it, his arms on either side of her to prevent her from escaping. His long lithe body, like a whipcord, pressed close to hers so she could feel the powerful, corded muscles beneath his skin, the furious hammering of his heart within his chest, and the hard tautness of his loins. Frantically Jenny struggled against him, lashing out at him with her fists, but he only laughed, a low, snarling sound, and ignored the blows. Savagely his hands gripped her hair, yanking it free of its confining pins so it tumbled down about her in dusky-brown waves that spilled over her shoulders and cascaded down her back to her slender hips.

She whimpered pitiably as his hot mouth found her throat, burning her flesh and setting her aflame.

"You can do as you please with Sarah Jane," he muttered, his voice thick and husky in her ear, sending shivers down her spine. "But my consent has a price, Jennilee. A kiss. One kiss. Are you willing to pay it?" He drew back slightly, his eyes searching her terrified face. "I've never raped a woman," he said. "I won't do so now, no matter how badly I want you. And I do want you, Jennilee. I've wanted you from the first moment I ever laid eyes on you. One kiss. That's all I ask."

Jenny could feel her heart in her throat, choking her. She stared at him, mesmerized, her mind numb with fear and fascination. She had kissed only one man, this man, and she had never had anyone say to her the exciting electric things Luke has just said. She felt scared and confused and yet wildly alive all at the same time. It was a feeling she'd never known before. A part of her was strangely thrilled and wanted desperately to give into him, to learn something of the mysteries shared between a man and a woman. Still she held back, remembering all too vividly that day at Faxon's Folly. She wanted to tell Luke about it, to explain to him her fright and bewilderment, her uncertainty. Perhaps then he would let her go, would give her time to collect herself, to decide what she must do. But she couldn't seem to find her tongue. His very nearness was proving too disturbing to her, too overpowering. Their closeness scattered her senses so she could not think, could only feel. . . .

"Luke," she breathed, her lips parting. "Luke—"

He mistook her whispered protest for assent, and his eyes darkened with passion and triumph. With an animalistic growl he crushed her to him, his mouth coming down on hers hard.

The fusion of their lips jolted Jenny as nothing in her life had ever done. A thousand shattering sensations pervaded her body, rushing through her veins like quicksilver. She couldn't seem to recover from the shock of it, to catch her breath.

Luke's mouth moved fiercely on hers, savoring the sweetness of her lips. God, how he wanted her! His tongue darted forth to trace sweepingly the outline of her mouth before insistently he forced her lips open to plunder the honey within.

Jenny's hands locked onto his arms, half pushing him away, half holding him close. Her head was swimming. Her heart raced as his tongue tasted her, exploring the warm dark chasm of her mouth, searching out her most sensitive places and taunting them expertly until at last she was kissing him back, her lips clinging feverishly to his, her body molding itself to his.

It seemed as though time had stopped and the earth had spun away, leaving nothing behind but a black void that contained only the two of them spiraling down into its pulsating darkness and heat. Tiny pricks of light, like stars, exploded in Jenny's mind, and she felt herself falling, falling . . . losing control of her very being.

Her bones seemed to be dissolving, leaving her as limp and pliable as a rag doll. Her body felt as though it had no spine as Luke bent her backward, his strong arms wrapped envelopingly around her, his mouth branding the slender column of her throat and seeking the moist hollow between her breasts. Her knees gave way, and she clutched him even more tightly, feeling dizzy and faint.

She could feel his warm breath upon her skin, smell the scents of corn liquor and tobacco that clung to his lips as they devoured her hungrily. Dimly she felt his teeth and tongue nibbling at the buttons of her bodice, deftly slipping them from their confining holes, and she thought crazily that with his tongue alone Luke could probably tie a cherry stem into a knot.

Her breasts ached in a way they never had before, and her nipples strained against the thin material of her gown, as though they were rigid with cold—but they weren't. They were hot and flushed, taut with desire.

Luke's hand slid over Jenny's buttocks, caressed her waist, pushed aside the edges of her bodice so there was nothing between him and her but her lacy chemise. His fingers yanked impatiently at the filmy fabric, tearing it, and some semblance of sanity returned to her at last.

Dear God. What madness had possessed her? She was about to give herself to Luke Morgan, willingly, like a common woman of the streets. In moments she would be flat upon the floor and he would be shoving her skirts up around her thighs. . . . Pictures from the past invaded her mind. Luke's hands became confused with those of a vile, ugly man laughing raucously and—and . . .

"No!" Jenny cried, starting to struggle furiously again in his arms. "No, don't! Don't! Oh, please, don't!"

But Luke was drunk, overcome by passion, and not thinking clearly. Jenny's pleas for release did not register as such in his dazed, drugged mind, and her writhing attempts to free herself only further inflamed him.

Ruthless now, he ripped her chemise, baring her breasts to his blue eyes, stark and naked with wanting.

"Oh, God, Luke, don't!" Jenny screamed, suddenly wrenching herself from his grasp and slapping him hard across the face.

Then, tears streaming down her cheeks, she once more snatched open the door, accidentally banging Luke in the head with its edge and knocking him to his knees. Not waiting to see if he were hurt, wildly she stumbled out into the night, her hands clawing mindlessly at the torn cloth of her chemise, her fingers fumbling with the buttons on her bodice.

She was intent on repairing the damage done to her gown that she missed her footing in the blackness and fell, twisting the ankle of her crippled leg in a wheel rut and sending shards of pain shooting through her body.

Inside, Luke staggered to his feet, Jenny's slap having caused his alcoholic haze to lift and the blow from the door having jarred him to his senses. Sweet Jesus! What had he done? *What had he done?* Had Jenny not defended herself, he would have raped her! He must be out of his mind! That was not how he had meant things to happen—not with Jenny. Never with Jenny.

His mother's admonition that he must go slowly with the girl rang in his ears like a death knell. Why hadn't he listened? Oh, God, why hadn't he listened? He himself had guessed there was something in Jenny's past that had caused her to be terrified of men—and he had taunted her with it, cruelly, wanting to unlock the secrets of her being. He had taken her in his arms brutally and laughed when she'd begged him to cease tormenting her with his rough kisses and caresses. Luke's belly lurched sickeningly. What kind of a man was he to do what he had done? He felt ill and ashamed, disgusted with himself. What he had just done had not been prompted by self-preservation, as his previous acts had been. No, tonight he had been motivated by sheer lust.

Luke thought of losing Jenny before he'd even had a chance to win her, and a sharp fist of dismay slugged him hard in the stomach. He realized suddenly that for some strange reason he needed her. He must find her, now, and somehow repair whatever damage he had done.

"Jenny!" he called, his voice rising as he raced out into the darkness after her. "Jenny!"

He tripped over her fallen form, and seconds later she felt the shock of his warm weight upon her. Shrieking and sobbing hysterically, she beat at him futilely with her fists, then tried to crawl away from him. But he grabbed her in his arms, cradling her head close against his chest.

"Shhhhh," he crooned in her ear as he rocked her soothingly. "Shh-hhh. It's all right now. Everything's going to be all right. Oh, Jenny, my brave, precious girl, I'm sorry, so very sorry. I don't know what made me behave like that." He spoke in a breathless rush. "I just wanted you so badly. Oh, Jennilee, my Jennilee, I wouldn't hurt you for the world—not for the world! Don't you know that, my darling girl?" he murmured, the endearments coming easily to his lips. "Hush now, sweetheart. Hush."

Gently he continued to stroke her hair and kiss the tears from her cheeks until finally she quieted, though she still trembled in his arms, her mind trying to understand the things he was saying to her, sweet things, things that made her long incomprehensibly to remain forever within the circle of his embrace. Somehow, no matter how violently he'd sought to claim her, she knew instinctively that he would die to protect her from anything—or anyone—else.

That knowledge was oddly comforting, and Jenny's chaotic mind latched on to it desperately as a jumble of ideas she had not previously considered began to tumble through her brain.

There was some measure of contentment after all in the fact that Luke was an outlaw. At least she knew he was man enough to defend that which he called his own. It was a peculiar, distorted way of looking at things, Jenny knew. But since the War Between the States the world itself had become a lawless place, a place of fear and uncertainty. Was not a man like Luke, one who dared to make his own rules, better to have in this new world than one who was too afraid to fight back? She thought of the men she'd seen in Atlanta, weak, broken men whose dreams had died with the Glorious Cause. Then she looked up at Luke, a rebel who even now risked his life in the face of all odds. The Stars and Bars might have surrendered—but Luke never had and never would.

He was the son of a poor farmer, and before the war Jenny wouldn't have looked twice at him. But now—now perhaps she needed someone like Luke. Her mother would have cringed with mortification, had she known, but Rachael Colter was dead, and Jenny was so alone. . . .

Had Luke really meant all those lovely things he'd told her? she wondered. Or was he even now laughing up his sleeve at her innocence and gullibility? If this last were true, Jenny didn't think she could bear it—not after the way she had responded to his kisses, his caresses. Was Luke serious about her . . . *was he?*

"Come on." He stood and held out one hand to her. "I'll take you home."

Shakily Jenny got to her feet, leaning against him for support.

"It's my ankle." She grimaced as he glanced at her questioningly, his eyes filled with solicitude. "I turned it when I fell."

Wordlessly he swept her up into his arms and carried her to her wagon.

"Wait here," he said, "while I get the lantern and my horse."

Numb, Jenny sat upon the seat, too physically exhausted and emotionally drained to make any further attempt to flee. With hands that still quivered slightly she smoothed her chemise and buttoned her bodice, then combed her fingers through her tangled hair. She wished she could put it back up, but her hairpins lay scattered on the floor of Luke's cabin, and she was too tired to retrieve them. She had no idea how she was going to explain her appearance to Moses and Delcine. Still she must think of something. If Moses ever discovered what had happened tonight, he would try to kill Luke—and the Negro wouldn't stand a chance against Luke's powerful Navy Colts. That was why, although she had debated revealing his threats to her, she'd never told either of her servants about Luke's visit to her that night at the hotel.

After what seemed an aeon Luke finally returned, carrying the lantern and leading his horse, Blaze, which he tied onto the back of the wagon. Then wordlessly he climbed up beside Jenny, gathered the reins in his hands, and clucked to the big draft mare. Blossom, realizing she was not being directed by her gentle mistress, pricked her ears forward attentively and set out at a smart pace.

Several minutes later they pulled up in front of Jenny's house, and the silence that had hung heavily between them during the drive now grew even more oppressive. Yet there was no time to speak. The door of the cabin opened, and light flooded the night as, lamps in hand, Moses and Delcine hurried out onto the porch, their dark eyes anxious and then startled and concerned as they took in Jenny's disheveled appearance.

"Oh, Lawd, Miz Jenny!" Moses exclaimed. "We wuz so worried 'bout yo. Wheah haf yo been, an' whut's hap'ned ter yo?" He pushed his lower lip out twice its normal size and glared suspiciously at Luke, bristling.

"I—I had an accident," Jenny reported untruthfully. "It was dark, and the wagon hit a bump in the road, and I . . . fell off the wagon seat. Mr.—Mr. Morgan," she stumbled over Luke's name, "chanced to be passing by, and he was kind enough to—to bring me home."

"Sho' 'nuff?" Moses questioned, relieved but still doubtful. Miss Jenny was acting mighty peculiar, but perhaps she'd hit her head when she'd fallen. "Is yo huht, Miz Jenny?"

"Just a sprained ankle, that's all."

"Here. Let me take you inside," Luke offered.

Jenny started to protest, but before she could get the words out of her mouth, he had already lifted her in his arms, swung her down from the wagon, and carried her into the house.

As he laid her on the sofa in the parlor, he glanced about with pleasure and approval, noting the many changes in the cabin since last he'd seen it. He liked the warm, simple, cheerful decor, which he guessed was Jenny's and Delcine's handiwork. It was strikingly artistic and beautiful, yet without pretention. Maybelle would have scorned the homey furniture, the rag rugs, and the ruffled curtains, Luke knew, for anything that hadn't come all the way from the East hadn't been good enough for her. But Luke felt a cozy, peaceful sense of belonging when he looked around the room. It was, he recognized suddenly, a place of happiness and love.

"Please don't hate me, Jennilee"—he bent and whispered in her ear. "I don't think I could bear it if you did."

Then he told Moses and Delcine good night, tipped his hat politely to them all, and departed.

"Where are your manners, Miss Jenny?" Delcine queried severely after Luke had gone. "You didn't even tell Mr. Morgan thank you for bringing you home."

"Why, I didn't, did I? I—I guess that . . . fall must have shaken me up more than I'd realized," Jenny uttered lamely, but she found she couldn't meet Delcine's piercing eyes.

"Well, you can send a note around tomorrow, along with a little something special to eat. A jar of that strawberry preserve we made would be nice," Delcine rambled on as she stripped off Jenny's socks and shoes. "Moses, whut is yo standin' 'round lahke a fool fo'? Fetch me dat bucket undah de sink. Fill it up wi' some water, an' po' some salt in it, den set it on de stove ter git warm. We's gwine ter hafta soak Miz Jenny's ankle. It's all swelled up lahke a hen egg."

Delcine's tone was cranky, but her eyes when she gazed at Moses were filled with love, and Moses, though he grumbled under his breath as he shuffled off to do her bidding, had a similarly smitten look upon his face. Jenny was struck by a pang of wistfulness at the sight. It appeared as though her scheme to leave the couple alone this evening had worked. Yet even as she wished them joy her heart ached with loneliness, and, unbidden, Luke's handsome face crept into her mind.

Please don't hate me, Jennilee, he'd implored. *I don't think I could bear it if you did.*

She remembered the feel of his mouth upon her own, his hands upon her breasts, and her body tingled once more with the unaccustomed and confusing desire she had felt in his arms. Hate him? No, she couldn't do that.

Despite all her wishes to the contrary, Jenny was terribly afraid she was falling in love with him instead.

Chapter Ten

The nightmares came again that night, echoes of voices and places, hushed and far away.

Once more Jenny stood at the edge of the gravel drive leading up to her father's plantation, Faxon's Folly. Through the branches of the bristly, coniferous pines, the fragrant, glossy-leafed magnolias, and the sweet, pink-blossomed mimosas, she could see the house rising up tall and proud in the distance, like a gleaming white pearl nestled in the hollow of the land that lay at the base of the rolling hills etching a gently curving line across the vast horizon.

The morning air smelled fresh and clean, rich with the scents of the forest, the earth, and the dew that lay in glistening beads upon the ground. Jenny inhaled deeply, savoring the aromas of ongoing life about her, the spring budding of the trees and flowers, renewed growth fed by the decaying leaves and twigs of autumn.

The world was a place filled with complex mysteries, yet they seemed the simplest of puzzles: birth, life, death, and rebirth, an unending circle in time, perfect and complete. God had planned it all very well, Jenny thought, knowing that for all things there must be opposites, for how could there be beauty if there were no ugliness offered up in contrast?

Reflectively she considered the profound notion, certain it held some special meaning for her, as though it were a reply to one of those questions men often asked but to which the answers were always tantalizingly just beyond reach.

She stretched out one hand to pluck a violet bloom from its stem. How delicate and fragile it was, as soft and smooth as silk, its color as vivid and yet diffused as though it had been stolen from a rainbow. Carefully she tucked the flower behind her ear, then turned to gaze again at Faxon's Folly, which shimmered like a mirage beneath the early morning sun.

Her parents sat upon the slatted swing on the front porch, surveying their domain. Her brother Niles, smoking a cigar, lounged against one of the Ionic columns that lined the veranda. His wife, Honor, perched upon the steps, was surrounded by a group of children who were listening intently to the story she was telling. Nearby, Dulcie and Fayrene swayed languidly back and forth in rocking chairs and fanned themselves listlessly in the summer heat, watching as their husbands, Jenny's brothers Rushford and Prescott, tried to tame one of the hot-blooded stallions raised on the plantation. In the gardens Jenny's sisters Evangeline and Melantha walked with their husbands, Joe Frank and Cade. On the lawn Jenny's brother Alex laughed and played croquet with her sister Bliss and their friend Lonny Ridgeway.

As one, they all looked up and saw Jenny standing there. They smiled and waved, beckoning to her, and, hitching up her skirts, she began to run down the winding road to Faxon's Folly.

When she had gotten halfway there the horror she had experienced in previous dreams erupted. With fearful expectation she cowered and tried to stop what she knew was coming—but she could not. A big black beast from hell, blood spewing from its nostrils, suddenly lunged from the cover of the trees, knocking her to her knees, then trampling her into the ground. The blossom behind her ear fell to the earth to be crushed into a million pieces; scattered petals and leaves lay upon the grass, destroyed by the sharp hooves of the unholy animal that had dared to mock God's handiwork.

For a long time Jenny peered uncomprehendingly at the violet's remains. Only moments before it had been whole and lovely. Now it was a shapeless thing, without symmetry or grace. Tears pricked her eyes for its loss, and rage at its despoiler welled up in her breast.

Slowly she managed to clear her mind of the devastating effects of the blow and to struggle to her knees. But when she could once more stand Jenny discovered she was all scratched and bruised. She could scarcely breathe for the excruciating pain crushing her ribs, and her legs were broken, their splintered bones sticking through her flesh. Blood seeped down both the limbs, redder than the rich clay of Georgia, and she slipped perilously in the warm dark liquid as she managed somehow to struggle on toward Faxon's Folly.

But the home she knew and loved so well had disappeared. In its place stood a shell-ridden ruin, acrid smoke billowing from the windows, yellow-orange flames consuming the walls and roof.

As though somehow her mangled legs were no longer a part of her body, Jenny started to run, panic clutching her in its fist as each step brought her closer and closer to the old plantation.

One by one she found the members of her family, but when she called to them they did not hear her, and when she touched them, turning them around to face her, she saw they were nothing but dust-covered skeletons.

She screamed and screamed again, but no sound issued from her open mouth. She glanced about wildly, searching for some means of escape from the unreal scene—but there was none. Ghostly forms had clawed their ways up out of the earth and were cavorting around her in a circle that kept growing smaller and tighter the harder Jenny tried to flee from its confines. Nearby, a vile, ugly man pranced about, chortling fiendishly, and the devil himself seemed to drop down out of the grey, smoke-filled sky, swinging his silver scythe at her viciously.

At one corner of the misty-edged tableau her great-aunt, Henrietta, floated like a specter, one hand stretched out accusingly, her finger pointed straight at Jenny.

"Where are your schoolbooks, Jennifer?" the elderly spinster asked, her tone reproving and severe. "You must study diligently if you're going to pass your examinations and earn your teaching certificate."

Jenny stared at her great-aunt, appalled. Couldn't she see what was happening around them? Didn't she care that all they'd ever held dear was gone, that everyone they'd ever loved was dead?

Jenny parted her lips to cry out beseechingly for help. Then she saw that Aunt Hetta too was dead. Her body lay in a plain pine coffin. Her hands were clasped upon her breast, and she had a camellia clutched between her stiffened fingers. There was no one left, Jenny realized, to save her from the devil and his gruesome apprentices.

Once more she tried to run, but she had worn her damaged legs out earlier, and now they refused to move at all. The demoniac figures closed in around her, reached out to grab her. . . .

Hysterically Jenny screamed, sitting bolt upright in bed, her heart jerking in her throat, sweat drenching her nightgown. Her candle had guttered in its socket, and she was alone in the darkness. Again she screamed and then again, her body rigid with fear, her fingers ripping frantically at the bedclothes.

In minutes Delcine was there, an oil lamp in her hands to chase away the shadows. At the doorway, his many years of training preventing him from entering a white woman's bedroom, Moses hovered, his dark eyes meeting Delcine's anxiously. She shook her head and pressed her lips together firmly, silently warning him not to speak. Then she set the lamp down upon one of the night tables and drew Jenny's shivering form into her arms.

"Hush now. Hush, Miss Jenny," she crooned. "It was just a bad dream. It was all just a bad dream," she insisted softly as she stroked the girl's hair and rocked her soothingly. "There isn't anyone here who's going to hurt you. You're safe now, Miss Jenny. You're safe. Moses and I are here, and we wouldn't let anything happen to you, I promise." Delcine glanced up at Moses. "Go out inter de kitchen an' fix dis chile some warm milk," she whispered. "Put a shot o' dat brandy in it. Dat'll quiet her down so's she cain git back ter sleep."

Moses nodded wordlessly, then scurried away to do Delcine's bidding. Presently they were able to stop Jenny's whimpers and her shaking, and, after lighting another candle to replace the one that had burned out, Delcine tucked the girl back into bed. They watched for several minutes to be certain Jenny was once more deep in slumber, then tiptoed from the room and eased the door shut.

Moses put his arm around Delcine's shoulder and hugged her close.

"Ah guess mah po' li'l lamb ain' neber gwine ter git ober dat tur'ble day," he said, his voice quavering. "Ah jes' doan know whut ter do ter hep her. But Ah sho' wish she could fo'git it, Delcine. Ah sho'ly does."

"Ah knows it, Ah knows it." Delcine sighed. "Yo's a good man, Moses, in spite o' all dem things Ah tells yo when Ah'm tryin' ter git yore 'tention. Why, jes' yo bein' heah is a comfort ter Miz Jenny—an' ter me too," she confessed shyly. "But Ah reckon aftah ternight yo already knows dat. Ah love yo, Moses, more 'n Ah cain say. Ah'm right proud ter haf yo fo' mah man."

"An' Ah'm jes' as proud ter haf yo fo' mah woman, Delcine," Moses replied. "It might o' took me some time ter figger out dat Ah loves yo, but, now dat Ah knows it, Ah ain' gwine ter eber treat yo wrong. Why, Ah want ter mah'ry yo, gal. Jes' as soon as Ah cain git a few dollahs saved up ter build us a li'l place o' our own, Ah want ter jump ober de broom wi' yo."

"Hmph!" Delcine snorted, but there was a twinkle in her eye all the same. "Yo ain' neber saved a penny in yore life! An' Ah ain' gwine ter wait 'round till doomsday ter mek yo mah own. No, wait, lemme finish." She deftly fended off Moses's protests. "Now de way Ah sees it, Mistah Luke's gots his eye on Miz Jenny—oh, yassah, Ah saw de way he wuz lookin' at her ternight. Men! Dey's sech fools; Ah jes' doan know whut dey'd do wi'out us women. Mistah Luke's jes' lahke yo wuz, Moses, purt neah stone blind when it comes ter whut he feels inside. He doan know it yet, but he's in love wi' Miz Jenny, 'n' Ah'm tellin' yo dat sooner o' later he's gwine ter mek her his woman. Den Ah 'spects he'll tek some o' dat money he's been a'stealin' an' build her a great big ole house out on his land. Den, if'n yo wuz ter ast him real nice, Moses, why, Ah reckon he might jes' let us haf his ole cabin. Ah heah it's purt nigh ruint, but wi' yo bein' right handy wi' dem tools an' all, Ah guess yo jes' might—an' Ah say *might*, Moses"—her voice was choked with laughter—"be able ter fix it up good 'nuff ter suit me. Yassah, yo jes' give thin's a li'l bit o'time, an' see if'n dey doan all wuk out jes' fine."

Moses shook his head, incredulous.

"Well," he drawled, "if'n dat doan beat all—Mistah Luke an' Miz Jenny! Why, Ah neber would o' believed it! Mah, oh, mah." Then suddenly his eyes widened with comprehension. "Why, does yo think dat wuz whut wuz gwine on ternight? Dat dey wuz a'spoonin' an' din want us ter know 'bout it? Wuz dat why Miz Jenny wuz actin' so flustahed an' her haih wuz sech a mess?"

"Ah reckon so. But doan yo say nothin' ter her 'bout it now, yo heah? Mistah Luke's gwine ter haf his hands full 'nuff, tryin' ter git Miz Jenny ober her feah o' men, wi'out yo buttin' in an' mekin' a fool out o' yoreseff, maybe eben gittin' yoreseff shot! It din huht Miz Jenny none ter be kissed, eben if'n, as Ah 'spects, Mistah Luke *did* git a might rough. He wuz sorry fo' it aftahward, believe me. Ah neber seen a man look so shamefaced as he done when dey drived up inter de yahd. 'Sides, his mama will keep him in line. She likes Miz Jenny, an' she'll mek sho' Mistah Luke's intentions are hon'rable. Now dat's 'nuff o' dis talk. It's late, an' we's gots ter git up early in de mohnin'. Get on back ter bed now, yo heah?"

The big black man hung his head and shuffled his feet sheepishly.

"Does yo want—does yo want . . . well, whut Ah mean is," Moses stumbled awkwardly over his words, "Ah'd lahke it more 'n anythin' in de world if'n yo wuz ter—wuz ter join me, Delcine . . . dat is . . . if'n yo wants ter."

"Moses," Delcine breathed, a sweet, knowing smile of love and happy expectation curving on her lips, "yo is a fool fo' sho'! Ah thought yo neber wuz gwine ter ast me!"

Quietly, their arms about each other's waists, they walked out to the small lean-to and slowly, savoring each precious, beautiful moment, began to undress. Then they slipped into the narrow bed together, their bodies pressed close in the darkness. While Moses and Delcine made love feverishly for the very first time and then did it all over again, abatedly and more gently, Jenny slept and dreamed once more.

Only this time when the nightmares came and she screamed soundlessly for help, a wild, wayward wind swirled in like a cyclone from the
west, and Luke Morgan, mounted on his huge chestnut stallion, Blaze,
galloped from the trees and swept her up into his arms, carrying her far
away from all her fears and the secrets of her past.

BOOK TWO

Wayward Wind
A'Calling

Chapter Eleven

On Sunday, Jenny, Moses, and Delcine went to church as usual. Although Jenny had been reared as an Anglican, due to her English heritage, Tumbling Creek was so small there was only one denomination of religion practiced by its residents, who were mostly Baptists. Thus each Sunday she was forced to sit through a service that was very different from her own, and in all the months she'd lived in town, Jenny had never quite managed to accustom herself to this new method of worship. The Anglican Mass was splendorous to behold, making the Baptist service seem austere in contrast.

Each time she saw the Reverend Thompkins in his plain black frock coat and stiff white round collar, Jenny thought wistfully of the brilliant, ornate robes and stoles of the priests who had conducted Mass in Atlanta. Then she had been able to tell at a glance the season of worship, for the colors of the priests' garments had been different for each. She missed the comforting familiarity of the Eucharist, in which all had participated, the words all had spoken, many from memory, in response to the priests.

Jenny longed to kneel at the altar rail to be blessed and to taste the sweet, watered wine all had drunk from a single silver chalice, to partake of the holy wafers that had melted upon her tongue. Here in Tumbling Creek a tray laden with tiny cups of grape juice and a dish of hard bread that must be chewed were simply passed from person to person.

She yearned for the pungent aroma of the incense burner and the deep tolling of the sanctum bell during the most solemn moments of prayer. It seemed odd merely to bow her head in prayer when she was used to kneeling, and her hands felt naked without her rosary. She was used to a short sermon that followed Mass; in Tumbling Creek the sermon *was* the service.

Religion was the one aspect of her new life to which Jenny was certain she would never adjust.

Inwardly she groaned as she slid onto one of the uncomfortable benches in the schoolhouse, thinking it was no wonder her young charges always squirmed in their places during lessons. Soon everyone who normally attended the service was assembled, and the Reverend Thompkins motioned for them all to stand. After the opening hymn had been sung and they'd resumed their seats, the reverend instructed the congregation to open its Bibles to the Book of Proverbs, Chapter Thirteen, Verse Twenty-four, and he proceeded to drone on for over two hours with his sermon of the day.

"He who spares the rod hates his son, but he who loves him is diligent to discipline him!" the reverend thundered from the pulpit, banging his hand down upon it for emphasis.

Jenny, as she attempted to stifle a yawn, guessed Abigail Crabtree had duly reported to him the fact that she'd spied Matthew McNabb committing some new atrocity, for which his father, Festus, again had failed to reprimand him. It was true Festus spoiled the boy, but, Jenny decided, it certainly was neither the reverend's nor Miss Abigail's place to try to correct the matter.

Jenny, on the few occasions when she'd spoken to Festus about Matthew's obnoxious behavior, had been careful to limit her comments to the boy's activities in school. She had twice found a snake in her desk. Fortunately both the reptiles had been harmless, but she feared she might not be so lucky a third time. Festus had promised to talk to Matthew, but Jenny had known it would do little good. The boy had been incorrigible since his mother's death during a wagon accident some years past.

Festus, who'd been driving the vehicle when it had overturned, killing his wife, had blamed himself for the mishap that had taken Matthew's mother from them. It was his fault, Festus felt, that the boy had no gentle hand to guide him, and consequently he'd allowed Matthew far more rein than was wise.

Everyone knew of and sympathized with the reasons behind Festus's leniency with Matthew, but they disliked the youngster all the same. Almost everyone in town had been the recipient of his malicious machinations at one time or another, and since the townsfolk knew Kipp Morgan had also lost his mother yet had not turned into a miscreant, Matthew suffered from the comparison. Still Jenny was certain the boy was not deliberately evil, that he was simply starved for attention, and she hoped Lacey Standish, the dressmaker, whom Festus had been hesitantly courting, would be able to help Matthew.

Now as Jenny studied the child, sulking in his seat, she sighed. No doubt Matthew, who was bright, had realized today's sermon was directed at him and his father. Miss Abigail and the Reverend Thompkins, Jenny mused, had best be on their guards. Then she pressed her handkerchief to her face to hide her sudden smile as several notions of how Matthew might seek his revenge occurred to her. Privately Jenny thought it would serve Miss Abigail right to be taken down a notch or two; she certainly deserved it for spying on everyone and making their lives miserable! The old bat had already informed half the town that Luke had driven Jenny home the other evening. All morning Rosanne Durrell, alias Velvet Rose, Luke's purported mistress, had shot dagger looks at Jenny from beneath her outrageously plumed bonnet.

Instead of making her ill at ease, however, the harlot's glares had, much to Jenny's consternation, secretly sent her hopes soaring. The thought of Luke wanting to court her was most flattering and caused her heart to leap with pleasure, even though her happiness was tinged with distress. Luke's interest in her must indeed be serious if Velvet Rose were mad enough to consider her a rival, for the prostitute was extremely pretty. Surreptitiously Jenny studied her, imagining her locked in Luke's powerful embrace, and to her mortification she felt a horrid stab of jealousy that made her itch to scratch the tart's eyes out. Despite the fact that she was not at all sure she wanted him for herself, Jenny didn't want Velvet Rose to have Luke either.

Casually the girl glanced about at the congregation, searching for some sign of the man who dominated her thoughts, but he was nowhere to be found. His appearances at church were desultory at best, and there had been a brawl at the Razorback Saloon last night. She ought to have guessed he would not be present. No doubt he was home, nursing a splitting headache.

Orville Ascot, however, caught her eye and nodded at her in what he perceived to be a man-about-town fashion. Jenny blushed, sternly repressed her desire to giggle, and returned her attention to the Reverend Thompkins.

Orville Ascot, of Ascot & Sons (Fine Furniture), was a gangly, red-faced man with an Adam's apple that bobbed up and down in his throat most noticeably whenever he was nervous or excited. He was a few years older than Jenny, but he seemed younger, for his father, Cormick Ascot, was highly disappointed in both his sons, whom he considered failures, and he continually derided them. Gaylord, the older of the two brothers, merely laughed at his father's rebukes and went on his merry way. Orville, however, cowered and clung to his outwardly foolish and fragile mother, Eunnonia, who, in reality, had both the mind and constitution of an ox.

The Ascots were quite well-off, for theirs was the only furniture store for miles around. Cormick was an honest, down-to-earth businessman who'd worked hard to make his way in the world. Unfortunately during his climb to the top Eunnonia had discovered she lacked sophistication and had attempted to correct the matter by acquiring those airs and mannerisms she mistakenly believed marked one as a member of the *bon ton.* All these affectations she'd drummed mercilessly into Gaylord's head until he'd become little more than a snob and a dandy; and, much to his detriment, Orville attempted to ape his brother in all things.

Clothes that appeared well tailored and stylish on Gaylord simply looked ill fitting and comical on Orville. The dainty, foppish gestures that were so elegant and graceful when employed by Gaylord took on all the qualities of vigorous wing flapping when imitated by Orville. The witty and often droll remarks Gaylord regularly directed at friends and acquaintances alike sounded silly and just plain mean-spirited when uttered by Orville, who could never understand why all his jokes fell flat. He was in every respect a well-intentioned but ridiculous copy of his brother. No respectable woman in town had ever looked twice at Orville, much to his mother's chagrin, and even after the war had produced a shortage of men, this calamity had remained unchanged.

In the past Eunnonia had wept and pleaded with Gaylord to settle down and beget heirs to carry on the Ascot dynasty—but to no avail. He'd disdainfully begged her to release the lapels of his jacket before she crushed them and then had dryly observed that her dramatic scenes bore all the aspects of a badly acted tragedy. He would marry when he was ready, he'd said, and no amount of nagging would prod him to the altar before then.

Thus had poor Orville become Eunnonia's only hope for grandchildren.

Willy-nilly, she'd thrust him at one reluctant female after another, only to see all her fine plans and expectations dashed by one of his stupid comments or his clumsy movements. What woman would be flattered to learn her eyes resembled two chunks of hard rock candy? What woman would enjoy having her new morocco slippers trod upon by two left feet? These things Orville had said and done—and worse, much to Eunnonia's despair.

But then Jenny Colter had come to Tumbling Creek, and hope again had burgeoned in Eunnonia's stout breast. The new schoolteacher came from good stock; that was obvious. But she was plain and crippled too. She would doubtless consider herself lucky to attract even Orville's attention. So Eunnonia had reasoned, and she had instructed Orville to pursue the girl.

Had she known how, like a drill sergeant, Eunnonia had issued orders to the hapless Orville about wooing her, Jenny would have been furious. But she did not know, and so whenever he accosted her she tried hard to be nice to him, despite the fact that his obtuse behavior often made this difficult.

Now once more Jenny sighed. She felt certain Orville would be waiting outside for her after the service, intent on asking her to accompany him to the church's fall social and bazaar this coming week.

It was the custom in the Ozarks each Sunday for all the bachelors, young and old, who were courting to exit from the church first and to form a single line outside the door. Then as the ladies left the building those men who were interested in an eligible female would pay their respects to her and make arrangements for an outing together later on. If a woman had a steady fellow, courtesy dictated that no other would-be beau approach her—and a man who dared to break this unwritten rule usually did so at the risk of a black eye, a split lip, or worse! But if a woman were unattached, any gentleman might offer her his arm and beg for the pleasure of her company, and she was free to accept or reject him as she wished. Widows, spinsters, and schoolgirls alike eagerly looked forward to running this gauntlet—provided of course that they knew they would not promenade past it without receiving a single compliment or an invitation.

"And now let us bow our heads in prayer," the Reverend Thompkins announced, bringing Jenny with a start back to the present. "Amen."

"Amen," all chorused.

With audible sighs of relief the congregation noisily folded up its hymnals and put them away in the desks. Then everyone began talking and laughing at once, calling greetings to friends and neighbors, reminding fellow committee members about meetings, and admonishing children to behave as all edged slowly toward the exit, pausing at the door to shake hands with the Reverend Thompkins and commend his sermon.

As she expected Jenny saw Orville Ascot in the line outside. His tie was too tight. It had pushed his Adam's apple up higher than usual and made his face even redder. He looked like a scarecrow in his suit, for both the sleeves of his jacket and the legs of his trousers were too short. A shock of lanky, mousy hair fell into his eyes, and he shoved it aside, then wiped his oily palm on his pants before taking Jenny's hand in his.

"Howdy, Miss Jenny." He positively glowed at her, for she was the only woman beside his mother who'd ever treated him kindly. "You sure look nice today. There ain't too many women who can wear that shade of brown. It kind of looks like an autumn leaf after it's curled up and died, don't it?" He paused awkwardly for a moment, then stammered in a rush, "I was—I was hoping you'd go to the church social with me this week. Otherwise Ma say's I'm gonna have to take my niece Louella. She's so durned ugly nobody else'll ask her 'cause they'd have to put a burlap bag over her head before they took her out. Will you go with me, Miss Jenny? Will you?"

The girl had half hoped, half feared that Luke would ask her to go with him, but he had not been in church, though he must have known all the men would be issuing their invitations today. Well, at least she would be safe with Orville. He didn't have gumption enough even to hold her hand more than a few seconds, much less to kiss her until she was breathless and aching with desire—as Luke had done. Besides, no one else was offering to take her.

"Of course I'll go with you, Orville," Jenny consented, trying to disguise the expression of disappointment on her face.

She needn't have bothered, for Orville didn't even notice.

"Gee, thanks, Miss Jenny," he gushed. "I'll see you Friday evening, then, around five."

He was so excited he didn't even wait for her reply but stumbled over his own feet as he hurried away to inform his mother of the outcome of his invitation.

"That will be fine, Orville," Jenny called, shaking her head ruefully at his inept attempt at courtship.

Poor Orville! She would rather remain a spinster, Jenny thought, than marry the likes of him! Still put off by his behavior, she turned and began to make her way through the crowd toward her wagon, looking around for Moses and Delcine, who'd wandered off after the service. Although she searched for several minutes, Jenny couldn't find them, and at last she decided they'd walked home.

Gathering up her skirts, she started to climb into her wagon. Halfway up she paused abruptly, seeing Luke Morgan perched upon the seat.

"Morning, Jennilee," he drawled, smiling that lazy, crooked grin of his. Then when she didn't respond he asked, "Well, are you just going to stand there giving the whole town a good look at your petticoats, or are you going to join me up here?"

Jenny flushed, mortified. Then, as she realized even her ankles must be showing, she hurriedly scrambled up to sit beside him, still trying to catch her breath. As usual whenever she found herself in Luke's presence, her heart began to thud queerly in her breast and her pulse leaped wildly at the hollow of her throat.

"You—you startled me," she explained to cover her confusion.

"Did I?" he remarked teasingly, as though he'd spied her earlier, peeping about the church to see if he were there.

Then he clucked to Blossom and slapped the reins down firmly upon her back to let the mare know who was in charge. Briskly the wagon started to move forward.

Jenny's face flamed again as everyone turned to stare at them. Luke, however, tipping his hat politely to the ladies and whistling nonchalantly to himself, didn't seem to care about the attention they were attracting as he deftly guided the horse and wagon through the congested mass of vehicles that filled the schoolyard.

Already Jenny could see the more gossipy women, their eyes gleaming with speculation, their hands cupped to hide their mouths, starting to whisper to each other about her. Eunnonia Ascot was absolutely seething with rage, her bosom swelling with indignation, and poor Orville looked as though he'd been hit in the stomach with a sledgehammer. Miss Abigail was in such a hurry to get home to her spyglass that she nearly trampled the Reverend Thompkins beneath her horse and carriage. Velvet Rose, her mouth turned down mulishly at the corners, flounced off in a huff when Luke didn't even so much as glance in her direction; and as this did not go unobserved by those present, Jenny wished she could melt into a puddle when several of the men began to chuckle with amusement and various of their ribald comments reached her ears. Luke, however, did not seem to hear them. He just went on whistling tunelessly between his teeth.

Shyly Jenny stole a peek at him from beneath her lashes, then eyed her hands clasped tightly in her lap. What was he thinking, she wondered, and why had he chosen to drive her home today? She longed to satisfy her curiosity about these things but dared not speak before they reached the main road. The crowded schoolyard was too public a place for conversation. Anyone might overhear them, especially as she was sure all ears were pointed in their direction.

The wagon wheeled past Horace Peabody, who was having difficulty maneuvering his buggy out of a deep rut on one side of the lane leading from the schoolyard to the road. As he caught sight of them his eyes widened with surprise and his mouth gaped, causing Jenny to peer back at him nervously. For the first time it occurred to her to consider her position in Tumbling Creek.

Luke was a notorious outlaw. She was a schoolteacher. The townspeople might not look kindly upon her hankering after a criminal. After all, she was supposed to set a good example for the children she taught, and hadn't the notice advertising her position requested "a young lady of unimpeachable morals?" Was it possible Luke might cause her to lose her job?

The thought was frightening, for if she were to be turned off without a reference, how would she and Moses and Delcine live?

But, then, Jenny reflected, it wasn't as though Luke were her beau or anything. Why, he'd never even asked her out. Still he'd kissed her—and she'd responded to him with a passion she hadn't known she'd possessed. Oh, if only she didn't feel so strange and bewildered whenever she thought about him! If only his very nearness didn't affect her like heady dandelion wine! After the way he'd behaved to her, first at the hotel and then again last night, she ought never to see him again—but she couldn't seem to bring herself to tell him that.

From beneath her lashes she contemplated him curiously once more, only to find he was watching her too. Wickedly he smiled, and she blushed.

"Are you mad at me about the other night, Jennilee?" he queried, his voice low.

"N-no, I guess not," she answered so softly he almost didn't hear her.

"Then will you go with me to the church social this Friday evening?"

Jenny's heart sank at the request that earlier she'd awaited almost eagerly. Now silently she cursed both Orville Ascot and Luke—Orville for asking for her first and Luke for being so dilatory with his invitation. She thought briefly of telling Orville she couldn't go with him after all, but she didn't want to hurt his feelings. Besides, she fumed indignantly, it would serve Luke right if she turned him down! Then maybe next time he wouldn't be so tardy about asking her—not that she would have gone with him anyway, Jenny assured herself stoutly! Still she felt a little shiver of fear chase up her spine at the thought of refusing Luke's invitation. He was a man used to getting his way. Maybe he would call Orville out and shoot him! Then she rebuked herself sternly for allowing her imagination to run away with her. Why, the very idea of the two men fighting over *her*—plain Jenny Wren—was ludicrous! She wasn't the type of woman men died for.

"I'm so sorry, Luke," Jenny apologized at last, hoping he wouldn't be angry with her, "but I've already promised Orville Ascot I'd go with him."

"I see," Luke replied, his voice clipped. His hands tightened on the reins, and a muscle started to work tensely in his jaw. "I didn't know you and Orville were courting," he remarked in the strained silence that had fallen.

In fact, it had never occurred to him that he might have to compete for Jenny's attention. Luke found he didn't like the idea one bit.

"We're not," Jenny corrected him quickly. "I mean . . . he's walked me home from church a couple of times, that's all."

"I see," Luke repeated dryly—and he did.

He knew Eunnonia Ascot, and he could guess the insensitive workings of her petty mind. No woman in town would have her stumblebum son. But Jenny, plain and crippled, would doubtless consider herself fortunate to attract any man, even if it were only Orville—or so Eunnonia would have reasoned.

The notion made Luke so mad he believed he could spit nails. He forgot entirely the fact that he'd once had such ideas about Jenny himself. Now whenever he thought of her it was hard to remember she really wasn't pretty. Instead he recalled the delicate planes of her heart-shaped face, the sprinkling of freckles across her upturned nose, and the way her countenance just seemed to light up when she smiled. He thought of her courage and her gallant spirit, the way she just kind of grew on a man, wrapping herself around his heart so sweetly and unobtrusively that it was hard to remember when she hadn't been a part of him. It was gut-wrenching now to think how empty his life would be without her. It was harder still to recall that she limped. Now her awkward gait was simply endearing. It made Luke want to hold her close and protect her from the cruelties of people like Eunnonia Ascot. Why, the snobby old bitch ought to be horsewhipped for even *thinking* her gawky, tongue-tied son was good enough for Jenny!

Wordlessly Luke turned the wagon onto the drive leading up to the cabin and pulled Blossom to a halt before the house. To her surprise Jenny saw that his stallion, Blaze, was tied up at her front porch. Why, Luke must have ridden over to the cabin, then walked to the schoolhouse in order to drive her home.

Wonderingly she gazed at him as he helped her down from the wagon, his hands strong and powerful around her waist.

"It was nice of you to bring me home, Luke," she thanked him, trembling a little at his touch, wishing he'd release her yet perversely hoping he'd go on holding her forever.

His blue eyes were boring into her grey ones so mesmerizingly she was having trouble breathing. There was something so unfathomable, so . . . *intense* about the way he was looking at her that she couldn't even seem to think. Would he ask her out again? He must know her barn raising was coming up soon. Would he ask permission to court her, tell her he wanted to be her beau? A million exciting prospects raced through her half-expectant mind.

However, when Luke finally addressed her, it was as though he had poured a bucket of cold water all over Jenny. Instead of the pleasant fantasies she'd dreamily imagined, he doused her with the hard reality of his demanding masculinity.

"Don't go out with Orville Ascot again," he ordered flatly, a sharp terse edge to his voice.

"W-what?" Jenny stuttered, stunned.

"You heard me. I don't want you seeing Orville Ascot anymore."

Jenny was so shocked by his words and so enraged at having deceived herself about him like a starry-eyed schoolgirl that she lost her usually even temper. Why, the man was impossible! He had no manners, no finesse, no—no anything! He drank too much. He'd kissed her savagely, attempting to take liberties with her that no decent man would have dreamed of taking. He'd shown up today and caused her to be an object of speculation among the entire town. Why, she might even lose her job because of him; Mr. Peabody had looked none too happy at seeing him in her wagon! And now, with no words of wanting, needing, or—most of all—loving, he'd presumed—and oh, how casually!—that all he had to do was issue a command and she would fall at his feet like every other besotted woman in Tumbling Creek! The very audacity of the man!

"What's it to you whom I see, Luke Morgan?" she snapped, incensed. "You don't own me! You're just mad because Orville asked me to the church social first! Well, I'm glad he did! I wouldn't have gone with you anyway! Orville is—is the nicest man I know, and you're just an—just an outlaw! I'll see Orville any time I please, and you can't stop me!"

"Can't I, Jennilee?" Luke lifted one eyebrow devilishly. Then he backed her up against the wagon, causing her heart to leap with fright and yet an odd anticipation as well. "Well, we'll just see about that," he muttered threateningly, his mouth turned down sardonically at the corners.

Jenny's pulse fluttered wildly. He was going to kiss her, she thought. He was going to kiss her! But he didn't, and to her everlasting shame she discovered she was terribly disappointed. Not only that, but she knew from a sudden flash in the trees where the lens of Miss Abigail's telescope had caught the light that the spinister was spying on them. Good Lord! What would the old bat have to report to the Reverend Thompkins this week?

"Take your hands off me, Luke!" Jenny hissed, mortified by her churning emotions and the disgraceful idea that next Sunday the reverend would be preaching a sermon directed toward her. "I don't ever want to see you again!"

Luke merely laughed.

"You don't mean that, Jennilee," he told her calmly. "You're just riled because you're not going to the church social with me. I'd be mad too if I had to go with that bumpkin Orville."

"Why, you—you— Oh, I can't even think of anything bad enough to call you!" Jenny sputtered indignantly.

"And here I was thinking you'd be ever so grateful to me for ridding you of that oaf." Luke shook his head in mock disbelief at her behavior, but when he spoke again there was a serrated edge of determination to his voice. "I will, you know. You wait and see. Friday evening you'll be eating supper with me and Orville will be nothing more than an unpleasant memory."

"Why, if I thought that were true, I'd—I'd poison your food!" Jenny declared untruthfully.

Luke threw back his head and howled with amusement.

"Jennilee," he breathed, his eyes suddenly serious, "you're a woman after my own heart. I do believe you're a bit of an outlaw yourself."

Then without warning he bent and kissed her, tenderly and all too quickly, so there was no time for her to resist.

"I suppose you think I enjoyed that." Jenny spoke tartly, once his lips had left her own and she'd managed to regain her composure.

"I do," Luke retorted smugly, "and I'll bet Crabby Abby does too."

Then he swung up into his saddle, waved irreverently at the spyglass in the distance, and set his spurs to Blaze's sides.

"Friday evening," he called back over his shoulder to Jenny. "I like fried chicken and buttermilk biscuits—the kind you make with flour, not arsenic!"

With an expression of disgust Jenny watched him go, thinking she must have been daft to have imagined herself in love with Luke Morgan. Why, the very idea! She hated the man! She was certain of it!

Well . . . almost.

Chapter Twelve

The following Monday after lessons Jenny waited expectantly at her desk while the schoolhouse emptied of her young charges. Then she smiled encouragingly to the lone child who remained.

"You may bring Sarah Jane inside now, Kipp," she said kindly.

"Yes, Miss Colter," the boy answered, then obediently stood and, fists balled up in his pockets to hide his nervousness, shuffled toward the door.

Kipp didn't know if he were happy or not about his father having given his permission for Miss Colter to teach Sary after school. Of course it would be wonderful for Sary to learn to read, write, and cipher. But she was as skittish as a butterfly, and Kipp, who loved his sister dearly, knew she'd be upset by the forthcoming attempts to pry her from her shell.

He didn't know why Sary didn't talk anymore, but he felt certain she'd suffered as deeply as he had over their mother's disappearance and death, and he didn't want her hurt further.

It was painful to know Ma hadn't wanted them, hadn't really even loved them. She'd told them often enough, when no one else had been there to hear, how they'd ruined her figure and proved such a burden to her. Little good-for-nothings, she'd called them, though they'd tried so hard to please her. They'd never amount to anything, Ma had sneered. They'd be white-trash farmers or no-good outlaws, just like their father, living in a hovel and scratching in the dirt to make ends meet, or hiding here and there, always on the run.

How Kipp and Sary had cringed when Ma had said such hateful things to them. But worse than that had been the times when she'd fought with Pa, jeering at him cruelly and laughing in his face when he'd grown angry.

"You promised me you'd amount to something, Luke Morgan!" Ma had hissed, her voice as evil and menacing as a sibilant snake's. "That you'd get your law degree and take me away from this stinking hellhole of a town! That we'd live in a fine big house in Springfield or Jefferson City or Saint Louis. That I'd have pretty clothes and a maid to wait on me hand and foot. Hmph! Some provider you've turned out to be! You —with your grandiose schemes! I should have listened to my brother, Tully, and never married you. I should have gone away with Tully like he wanted me to. Tully had friends—important friends! *They'll* all amount to something; you mark my words!"

Ma had always wanted things, expensive things. She'd never understood about the war and how it had smashed men's dreams to bits, leaving the splintered pieces lying on the ground. It was her continual berating that had driven Pa to stealing. But by then it had been too late. Ma had eventually run away, and sometime later she'd died. Pa hadn't seemed to care about anything after that. He'd grown moody and started drinking, and Kipp and Sary had gone to live with their grand-parents, Jed and Lottie.

Still, since Miss Colter had come to Tumbling Creek, Pa had paid a lot more attention to them. He'd taken an interest in Kipp's schooling, wanting to know about each day's lessons, and now he was letting Miss Colter teach Sary too. Kipp thought his father must be sweet on Miss Colter. At any rate, Pa certainly took a great deal of care with his appearance these days. Why, just this morning he'd told Grandma Lottie to brush up his courting clothes, that he was having supper with Miss Colter at the church social. Grandma Lottie had been smiling and humming to herself ever since. Kipp wondered if Pa were planning to marry Miss Colter. He kind of hoped so. It would be good to be a real family again, and Miss Colter was nice. She was sort of shy and hurting inside like Sary. Maybe she could help Sary after all.

"Come on, Sary." Kipp held out one hand to his sister. "There ain't nothing to be afeered of. You'll like Miss Colter, and she won't try to make you talk none either. She promised."

Sarah Jane gazed up at her brother solemnly, then carefully tucked her small hand securely in his. She *was* scared—just a little. She didn't get on much with strangers. They didn't understand why she couldn't speak to them. But Kipp wouldn't lie to her; he loved her. If he thought Miss Colter was all right, then she was, Sarah Jane reckoned.

Slowly the two youngsters entered the schoolhouse, and as Jenny caught sight of them she felt her heart turn over in her breast and a queer lump rose in her throat, choking her. Sudden tears stung her eyes, and with difficulty she held the shining droplets at bay. All her slowly rising hopes about Luke crumbled like ashes, leaving a bittersweet taste in her mouth, because she knew now that he couldn't possibly be interested in her. All this time he had simply been cruelly amusing himself with her so she would keep quiet about him, just as she'd feared. He had to have been. She was only plain Jenny Wren, and Luke's wife must have been breathtakingly beautiful, for Jenny needed no one to tell her the precious little girl standing before her was a tiny replica of Maybelle Boothe Morgan.

Sarah Jane's hair was as white-gold and silky as flax, falling in soft waves to her waist. Her skin was peaches and cream, unmarred by a single freckle. Beneath her gently arched flaxen brows her dark wide eyes were like two amethysts, the violet crystals fringed by feathery black lashes so heavy and thick that they seemed almost like snow-laden pine boughs. Her nose was delicate and finely chiseled. Her pink mouth was as full and sweetly curving as a rosebud. Everything about the child was so slender and graceful she appeared to be a fragile porcelain figurine.

Never had Jenny felt as ugly and clumsy as she did now. In her mind she imagined her dusky-brown hair had turned the color of mud. Her misty-grey eyes were like shards of opaque concrete. Her freckles had grown so in size that they were now huge, hideous spots. Her upturned nose belonged to a pug dog, and her generous mouth was a crimson slash in her face. Her lame leg made her move as though she was dragging a ball and chain behind her.

No, she decided, her heart sinking, there was absolutely nothing about her to attract a man like Luke, a man who had known, loved, and cherished the beauty of a woman like Maybelle.

For one awful moment Jenny wished she had never offered to teach Sarah Jane, had never wanted to help the child. Then she remembered that no matter how lovely this little girl was, she was hurting inside; she was filled with pain and sorrow. The mother she so resembled had deserted her. What a cross she must bear. Every time she looked into a mirror Sarah Jane must be reminded of Maybelle. With that thought in mind Jenny knew what she must do. She turned and removed a book from the shelves behind her desk. Then she walked from the dais to the center aisle of the schoolhouse.

"Hey, Sarah Jane," she greeted the little girl softly. "I'm Miss Colter, but I think that during our lessons you and Kipp may call me Jenny, for I hope we are going to be friends." She said nothing about Sarah Jane not speaking. "Come, and sit by me." Jenny indicated one of the hard benches as she slid onto it. "You too, Kipp. Today I want to read you both a story, and you must be able to see the words in order to learn. There are pictures too."

When the children were seated beside her Jenny opened the book she held in her hands, being careful not to break its spine, for it was new and had only recently arrived with a shipment of boxes that had been brought up the White River. Decisively she leafed through the book's pages until she found the chapter she sought.

"This story was written by a man named Hans Christian Andersen," she announced. "It's about a young boy like you, Kipp, and a little girl like you, Sarah Jane. It's called The Snow Queen."

Then with feeling, making each of the characters seem to come alive, Jenny began to read, her index finger moving beneath the printed lines, pointing to the words as she spoke them aloud.

Kipp and Sarah Jane listened intently, enthralled. No one had ever read a story to them before, especially one with pictures, though Grandpa Jed often told them tall tales in the evenings, his eyes gleaming with such merriment that they knew he was teasing them. Still they liked to hear Grandpa Jed's stories, even if they weren't really true.

There was the time he'd tangled with a wildcat.

"Why, you shoulda seen him. He had railroad spikes fer whiskers, pointed yellow fangs purt near as long as my arms, 'n' claws sharper 'n a razor. He was a'hissin' 'n' a'spittin' 'n' as mad as fire. But I grabbed that ornery ole puss up by the tail, swang him around in a circle, 'n' throwed him clean across Devil's Holler!"

And the time he'd fought a bear.

"That big, woolly critter stood twenty-five-foot tall at least. Why, he growled so loud and fierce that his breath blowed down a whole mess of mountain pine trees. He swiped at me with his paw, but I was too fast fer him. I jumped up on his back, took hold of his ears, 'n' shook his head back and forth till all his teeth plumb rattled right out onto the ground!"

And the time he'd battled a boar.

"He were a real mean fat pig, that one were. Why, he musta weighed more 'n a good-sized boulder, 'n' he had little squinty eyes and tusks like Bowie knives too. He come straight at me outta the woods, just a'snortin' 'n' a'squealin'. But I didn't flinch a muscle. No, siree. I got a right smart grip on his snout, then, quick as lightnin', I heaved him over, straddled him, 'n' hog-tied him 'er he even knowed what were happenin'."

Still, no matter how much fun Grandpa Jed's tales were, they were nothing like the story Miss Colter was reading. It was all about a snow queen who was the most beautiful lady in all the world, for everything about her was composed of dazzling white crystal snowflakes that made her glitter so brilliantly she was blinding to behold. She lived in a magnificent palace built of snow, ice, and wind. It was illuminated by a rainbow of sparkling, colored lights that shone in the northern skies. But though the snow queen's beauty was spellbinding and her riches were many, she was not content, and, instead of being warm and kind and generous, she was cold and cruel and selfish, for her heart was made of ice.

At last Jenny finished the tale and closed the book. Then she looked down at Kipp and Sarah Jane, who were staring up at her, wide-eyed with wonder, their faces sad yet thoughtful and heart-wrenchingly filled with hope.

"Even though she was the most beautiful and richest lady in the whole wide world, the snow queen was still very wicked, wasn't she?" Kipp finally asked gravely.

"Yes, Kipp, she was," Jenny returned just as seriously.

"But it wasn't—it wasn't the little boy and girl's fault at all, was it—that she was so terrible, I mean?" Kipp stammered hesitantly, his troubled eyes beseeching. "I mean . . . the snow queen was already evil even before they came into her life, wasn't she?"

"Yes, she was," Jenny repeated, holding her breath as she saw both Kipp and Sarah Jane slowly but surely beginning to understand why she had chosen to read this particular story to them.

"And it—it didn't really matter how hard the little boy and girl tried to please her, did it?" Kipp continued. "She—she never would have truly . . . cared for them anyway, would she?"

"No, Kipp, she wouldn't have. But you mustn't hate, or even blame, the snow queen for that. It was just her nature. She couldn't love anyone but herself, you see, and in the end she was all alone. We must pity people like the snow queen, for, no matter how beautiful they are or how much money they have, they are the unhappiest persons in the world."

Jenny fell silent, then, waiting for Kipp and Sarah Jane to absorb this fact. Then, longing to comfort them both, she carefully eased her arms about the youngsters' shoulders and hugged them close. They did not resist her embrace, as she'd half feared they would. Instead, with the innocent trust and faith that belongs only to children and small animals, they snuggled up beside her, responding to the love she was offering them like thirsty trees soaking up the rain. A still, peaceful sense of contentment enveloped them all, and they were breathless in its wake, filled with joy and awe at their feeling of togetherness.

From the entry of the schoolhouse Luke quietly studied their bowed heads, so near to one another. Then he tiptoed cautiously outside, not wanting to disturb them and feeling a slight twinge of guilt, as though he had intruded on something very private and special. He had arrived earlier to take Kipp and Sarah Jane home, but he'd become so engrossed in the tale of the snow queen that he'd stood in the vestibule, listening to the melodious rise and fall of Jenny's voice as she'd read aloud.

Luke too had grasped the significance of the story, and sudden tears now pricked his eyes at the delicate sensitivity Jenny had displayed in showing his children they were not to blame for Maybelle's desertion of them or for her death. With what deep perception Jenny had seen as well that Maybelle was to be pitied instead of despised, for she would never have been a happy woman. Nothing he could have done would have changed that; Luke understood that now.

How he'd hated Maybelle for her betrayal of him! Now his feeling of enmity toward her dissipated to be replaced by sorrow and shame that he'd allowed his bitterness to blind him to the needs of his children. No matter what she'd been or done, Maybelle had been Kipp and Sarah Jane's mother, and they had loved her. When she hadn't returned their affection they'd thought themselves unworthy of her. They hadn't been old enough when she'd abandoned them to realize the fault had lain with Maybelle instead of them.

Inwardly Luke cursed himself for a heartless fool for not paying more attention to his children, for being so wrapped up in himself and his own loss that he had not recognized the terrible feeling of confusion and the dreadful burden of culpability that had settled on the helpless, frightened shoulders of Kipp and Sarah Jane when Maybelle had left and later died.

But Jenny had seen—and Jenny had cared. She had cared enough to traverse the dark and dangerous wilderness of a country road so she might confront him about his children. She had cared enough to brave his drunken advances and to go on seeing him afterward, as no other woman of her gentleness and breeding would have done, so she might stretch out her firm but loving hand to Kipp and Sarah Jane.

Suddenly Luke realized how much he had come to care for Jenny Colter, had come to care for her with every fiber of his being, every ounce of his heart and soul. He liked the freckles on her nose and the smile that seemed to light up her whole face. He admired her warmth and her loyalty, her courage and her never-say-die spirit. He wanted to come home at night and see her standing there, waiting for him, soft and sweet in the lamplight. Before he had determined to woo her simply to ensure her silence about him. But now he saw that Jenny was much more to him than just a loose-tongued female he couldn't trust. She was the very air he breathed; she was life itself. In his heart Luke guessed he'd always known the truth; he just hadn't wanted to admit it to himself. Now he wanted to shout it from the rooftops.

I love you, Jenny Colter! I love you!

For the first time in his life Luke knew a fear that almost made his heart stop. He was afraid of losing Jenny, afraid she might not return his love.

Just an outlaw, she'd called him—and rightfully so. What did he, Luke Morgan, have to offer a woman like Jenny Colter? He thought of all the gold he had hoarded away and knew it was useless to him in his pursuit of her. Jenny's love would not be bought; it must be earned. It must grow from dancing eyes and muffled laughter, whispered words and warm embraces, and silent moments and shared memories. It must be strong enough to withstand the best and worst of times—as his love for Maybelle had not.

How strange it was, Luke thought, that Maybelle, whom once he'd loved, he now pitied, and Jenny, whom once he'd pitied, he now loved.

How much more difficult his courtship of her must be now that he'd realized these things. Before, he'd had nothing to lose but time—and perhaps his life if she'd revealed her knowledge about him. Now he must risk his heart and soul as well—and those were the things that really counted, the things that made a man what he was.

Well, nothing worth having ever came easily, they said. But before it was all over Luke meant to make Jenny Colter his, even if it took him a lifetime to do it!

He just had to, for he was suddenly quite certain he couldn't live without her.

Chapter Thirteen

Sarah Jane sat very still next to her father upon the wagon seat as she considered the enlightening story of the snow queen and the questions Kipp had asked afterward. She understood now that she ought to feel sorry for her mother, and she did, but that didn't lessen her fear of Maybelle or the dark, horrifying man she knew only as One-Eyed Jack.

Sarah Jane's mind drifted back to that awful day when her mother had run away. Pa had been gone for many weeks, Sarah Jane remembered, and they weren't expecting him back for several more. He was often away for long periods of time, leaving Ma to grow bored and restless.

On this particular day Ma abruptly left the farm, saying she was going into town. Kipp and Sarah Jane were all alone then. At first they were not afraid. It was still light outside, and as long as they remained close to the house, they were safe. But gradually the shadows began to lengthen and dusk settled. The children were hungry and wished Ma would return to fix supper (which would not be much anyway, for she hated to cook), but she didn't appear.

Finally Kipp looked through the cupboards in the kitchen. Finding some bread, cheese, and fruit, he set this out for their evening meal. After they ate they lit an oil lamp and huddled together in the parlor, talking and singing and playing checkers to pass the time.

It grew later and later, and at last night fell, enveloping the cabin in a shroud of darkness. Outside, wolves and coyotes started to howl, and in the distance could be heard the high-pitched scream of a wildcat. An owl hooted. Kipp and Sarah Jane stared at each other, wide-eyed with fright. They spoke in whispers, as though somehow the night creatures would hear them otherwise and know they were all alone in the house. Their imaginations started to run wild as the creaks and groans of the settling cabin filled the silence. Sarah Jane was sure there was a bear in the kitchen. Cautiously, their hearts beating fearfully, she and Kipp tiptoed down the dogtrot to peer through the kitchen doorway. The room was empty, and the children exhaled audibly with relief.

Kipp said they'd best wash up and get to bed, and this they did. But slumber eluded them both. They weren't used to sleeping with the lamp lit, but they were afraid to extinguish its flame, afraid of being plunged into inky blackness when Pa wasn't there to chase away the monsters that lurked in the shadows.

They listened intently to the sounds of the night, their ears straining to hear the crunch of wagon wheels on the drive that would tell them Ma had come home. But still she didn't arrive.

Finally they grew too tired to maintain their vigil any longer. Their eyelids drooped, and sleep overtook them.

Sometime later Sarah Jane awoke with a start. It was dark because a draft had blown out the lamp, and she could see nothing. Shivering, she slipped from her bed. The floor was chilly against her bare feet, and her teeth chattered. Quietly she drew aside the curtain that separated her bed from her brother's.

"Kipp," she whispered. "Kipp."

He didn't answer, and though she hissed urgently in his ear and shook him several times, he only mumbled irritably in his sleep and refused to get up.

Sarah Jane had heard a noise—she knew she had!—and it must have been loud in order to have wakened her. There was someone or something inside the house; she was sure of it! She didn't know what to do. She glanced about wildly, terrified, then decided she must hide. Quickly she pulled Kipp's blanket up over his head, hoping he would go unnoticed beneath the quilt. Then she scurried into her parents' adjoining room, climbed inside her mother's armoire, and eased the door shut.

She didn't know how long she crouched there, but presently she heard muffled voices, and her heart leaped to her throat. Whoever or whatever was out there would get her! Then slowly she relaxed, overwhelmed by joy. It was Ma! Carefully Sarah Jane opened the door of the armoire just a crack and peeked out slowly to make certain. The soft silver glow of moonbeams illuminated her parents' room, and she saw her mother locked in the embrace of a man. At first Sarah Jane thought it was her father, and she almost cried out with delight, making her presence known. Then the man turned. His face was cast into the half-light, and Sarah Jane spied him clearly.

Softly she gasped, for it wasn't Pa! This man had hair as black as night, a drooping mustache, and a hideous scar upon his dark visage. A black patch covered one of his eyes.

Sarah Jane's heart plunged to her toes, and her belly roiled, so she thought she was going to be sick. Why was her mother letting the strange man kiss her and so obviously enjoying it? Ma's head was flung back, exposing her creamy throat to the man's lips. Her eyes were closed, and she was laughing, the chuckle low and animalistic. The man was saying she was the queen of hearts, and she was calling him her one-eyed jack, writhing against him as his hands ripped away her bodice and chemise to cup her breasts.

Sarah Jane knew she shouldn't be watching, that what was happening was terribly wrong, but she couldn't determine any way to creep from the armoire back to her bed without Ma and the man seeing her. So she stayed where she was, her eyes squeezed tightly shut as she thought of how angry Pa was going to be when he found out what Ma was doing.

Soon the creaking of the bed and other sounds reached Sarah Jane's ears, noises such as those Ma and Pa made during those times when Kipp and Sarah Jane weren't allowed in their parents' bedroom. Sarah Jane wasn't at all sure what went on then, but she *did* know it wasn't allowed unless you were married. Once, she'd overheard some of Ma's friends talking in the parlor, and she'd learned Tammie Jo Watkins had done it and wound up in the family way (whatever that meant) and had to be sent away in disgrace because she didn't have any husband.

Wasn't Ma worried about that happening to her? Sarah Jane wondered. But, then, Ma had a husband, so perhaps it wasn't the same after all. Then Sarah Jane remembered Pa saying Mr. Peabody had disowned his wife for doing it with another man, and her apprehension returned.

After a time the strange moans and movements ceased, then Ma and the man started talking again. Sarah Jane's ears pricked up as she heard her uncle Tully's name mentioned. She didn't like Uncle Tully, who was Ma's brother. He was always telling wild stories like Grandpa Jed, except that Uncle Tully's tales were always about being rich and famous someday, because he had important friends. Pa said Uncle Tully was a pompous ass and a fool. Pa didn't like him either.

"Well, are you coming with me or not, Maybelle?" the man asked Ma, once more capturing Sarah Jane's attention.

"What would the queen of hearts be without a one-eyed jack?" Ma rejoined, laughing.

Then both she and the man rose from the bed and began to dress. To Sarah Jane's consternation she saw her mother remove a carpetbag from beneath the bed. Ma set the satchel down on a chair, then headed for the armoire. Sarah Jane's breath caught in her throat. In moments she would be discovered! She cowered behind Ma's clothes, but Ma saw her anyway and dragged her from the armoire, shaking her so violently Sarah Jane felt that any minute her head was going to topple right off.

"What're you doing in there, you stupid little brat?" Ma snapped. "How long have you been spying on me, you snot-nosed sneak?"

"I—I wasn't spying on you, Ma. Honest!" Sarah Jane protested, scared.

Ma looked wild. Sarah Jane had never seen her so mad.

"Don't you contradict me!" Ma spat, giving Sarah Jane another shake. "You're just like your pa—good for nothing! Why you ever had to be born I don't know! Jesus!" she cried, turning to the man. "Now what're we going to do? The dumb little snitch will tell Luke everything —I know she will!—and he'll come after us for sure—him and his frigging brothers!" She wheeled on Sarah Jane again. "If you know what's good for you, you won't breathe a single word about me and . . . One-Eyed Jack. Do you hear me! I'm getting out of this stinking hellhole of a town, and your pa and his kin aren't going to stop me! You tell anybody what you've seen tonight, and I'll come back here, and I'll —I'll cut your tongue clean out of your head! Do you understand me, Sary?"

"Maybe we ought to go ahead and cut it out anyway, now, just to make certain the little bitch won't talk," the man drawled, staring down wickedly at Sarah Jane, his one eye hard. "What do you think, Maybelle?" He raised one eyebrow speculatively. "I'm not afraid of Luke Morgan, but I don't fancy having him and his brothers dogging my tracks either." He drew the knife at his waist, then caught Sarah Jane's jaw in a vicious grip. "Stick out your tongue, girlie. Come on! Stick it out!" he ordered.

Quivering with terror, Sarah Jane at first refused to comply with his demand, but he pinched her cheeks so hard she finally had no choice but to give into him. He grasped her tongue between his fingers, then pressed the sharp edge of his blade down against the sensitive skin. Sarah Jane tasted blood, and tears welled up in her eyes as she gazed up pleadingly at her mother. To her horror Ma was smirking, as though taking a mean delight in Sarah Jane's plight.

"Go ahead! Cut it off!" Ma insisted. "It'll serve the sniveling slut right! How dare she spy on us like that!"

"Don't be a fool, Maybelle," the man uttered dryly. "What do you think Luke Morgan will do if he comes home and finds his kid's tongue cut out of her head—and learns you stood there watching it happen and egging me on?"

Ma shuddered, glancing about nervously, one hand at her throat.

"That's what I thought," the man said wryly. Then he glared once more at Sarah Jane. "I'm going to let you off the hook this time, girlie," he told her. "But if you ever open your mouth again; if you ever even so much as *whisper* to a single soul, I'll be back to finish what I started. Now get on back to your bed!"

It was three days before Grandpa Jed and Grandma Lottie came to the cabin to visit and found Kipp and Sarah Jane all alone in the house. By then Kipp had realized his mother was gone for good and that something was horribly wrong with Sarah Jane. She hadn't spoken a word since the night Ma had left.

Sarah Jane had never talked again. It broke her heart to remain silent when her father and everyone else she loved implored her so desperately to answer them. But she thought of One-Eyed Jack's terrifying threat to return and cut out her tongue, and she kept still.

Now, thinking about how hearing the story of the snow queen had helped her understand her mother somewhat, Sarah Jane sighed wistfully. She wondered if Miss Colter knew a tale about a one-eyed jack too. It would be ever so nice if she did. Perhaps then Sarah Jane could learn whether or not that evil man had truly meant those dreadful things he'd told her. If his gruesome warning had been intended simply to frighten her, then maybe it would be all right if she once more spoke every now and then. Until she discovered the truth of the matter, however, Sarah Jane daren't breathe a word.

It was far better to stay quiet than to lose her tongue to the sharp blade of One-Eyed Jack's knife.

Chapter Fourteen

For the fifth time in as many minutes, Jenny impatiently yanked the pins and peach-colored ribbon from her hair. She would never get it right! Oh, if only Delcine, who had spent the afternoon assisting with the preparations for the church social and bazaar, would come home! She could help Jenny put up her hair and fix the bow. Delcine's deft fingers would practically fly as she swept up Jenny's tresses, pinned them into place, and threaded the narrow length of satin through them. No matter how hard Jenny herself tried, she just couldn't seem to make anything come out right. Her curls all seemed to have gone askew, and she either wound up with too much ribbon left, making a bow so big it could have adorned the neck of a cow, or she ended up with too little, so there wasn't enough remaining for a bow at all!

Well, there was nothing else to do, she determined, but to leave her hair down, pull the top and sides up at the back of her crown, then tie the strands together to form a cascade of ringlets that would tumble down her back. She would look about seven years old, but at least she would be able to manage the simple style and the ribbon and bow.

Her fingers shaking with nervousness and wrath at her incompetence, she hurriedly ran her brush through the locks, neatly sweeping up the top and sides and wrapping a piece of thread about the whole securely. To her further chagrin Jenny saw that she had gotten the cascade too far forward; it looked as though she had a small fountain gushing up out of the middle of her head!

Frantically she tugged at the bound section of hair until it lay smooth and flat at the back portion of her crown. Then she slipped the ribbon beneath the mass, drawing it up to where the cascade began. There she tied it in a knot to hide the coarse thread, finishing it off with a bow that was finally decent. Once that was done, she picked up her small, silver-handled looking glass and turned her back to the mirror over the bureau so she could view the results.

The bulk of her unbound hair fell freely in soft waves to her hips. The part she'd secured with the ribbon formed a thick length of shorter curls down the middle. The bow's wide loops lay on either side of the top of the cascade, its trailing ends intermingling all the way down with the ringlets. With a sigh of resignation Jenny bit her lip. She looked just as she'd thought she would—like a schoolgirl! But it would have to do. It was getting late, and there wasn't time to try anything else.

Once more she faced the dresser. She set the looking glass aside, picked up her comb, and pulled a few tresses loose at her temples so wispy tendrils brushed the sides of her cheeks. Then critically she again surveyed herself in the mirror.

Her peach muslin gown was more suited to spring than to fall, but it was the prettiest dress Jenny owned, and there had been no time or money to make another. It was simply cut, with a high neck; a fitted bodice; long, narrow sleeves; a tight, gathered waist with a sash that tied in a big bow at the back; and a full skirt composed of four tiers of material, each wider than the last. Slender strips of delicate ivory lace adorned the neck of the dress and each sleeve from shoulder to wrist. The bodice had a sheer, wide, V-shaped panel composed of the finest, dainty tatting and edged with matching lace. Beneath could be seen a diffused but tantalizing glimpse of Jenny's ripe round breasts. The hollow between these was emphasized by eight tiny pearl buttons that were set down the front of the gown from neck to waist. Where the third and fourth tiers of the shirt joined was a wider band of the intricately worked lace. Beneath her skirt Jenny's two petticoats rustled provocatively. The dress was meant to be worn with hoops too, but these were now out of date and would have made her look even more old-fashioned.

A light wool shawl, peach silk stockings, matching morocco slippers and reticule, ivory gloves, and an ivory lace fan completed her ensemble.

Jenny wished she had a heavier evening wrap in case it really turned cool, but she didn't feel her one much-mended brown cloak was fancy enough to go with her gown and so decided against wearing it.

Once more she sighed. It was so evident her dress was all wrong for the season that she almost wished she'd donned one of the plain, serviceable gowns she wore to school each morning. But in her eyes none had been attractive enough for the festivities, and Jenny had especially wanted to look her best this evening. After all, even if Orville

Ascot's clothes never seemed to fit him, they were the most expensive to be found in Tumbling Creek. Only Abigail Crabtree dressed better than the Ascots.

Jenny frowned at herself crossly in the mirror.

"Admit it, Jenny Colter!" she chided herself sternly aloud. "You couldn't care less what Orville thinks. It's Luke Morgan you want to impress, and he isn't the least bit interested in you. You're a source of amusement for him, that's all, and you'd better get that through your head before you make a fool out of yourself over him and lose your heart and your job both in the process!"

She grimaced with self-disgust at the words, then childishly stuck her tongue out at the knowing, accusing reflection in the looking glass.

"Don't make faces at me," the image retorted loftily. "You know what they say here in the Ozarks: 'You better dance with the feller what brung you.' You're going to the church social with Orville, and that's that!"

Still Jenny remembered Luke's promise that she'd be eating supper with him tonight, and her heart beat erratically in her breast.

"Miss Jenny. Miss Jenny, I'm home."

Quickly the girl turned at the sound of Delcine's voice and headed toward the parlor.

"Here I am, Delcine," she said.

"My, oh, my, Miss Jenny!" Delcine beamed, a wide grin of pride and delight splitting her face. "Don't you look fine! Turn around." Jenny slowly pivoted obediently while Delcine, her hands held to her mouth, shook her head with disbelief. "I declare, Miss Jenny," she uttered approvingly, once Jenny had finished whirling about for her inspection. "I don't remember when I've ever seen you look prettier. I reckon that old Orville Ascot will just plumb burst his buttons when he sees you!"

Jenny blushed, hanging her head shyly. She wondered if Luke would do the same.

"Did you get your supper fixed?" Delcine asked.

"Yes, but, Delcine, I told you I wanted to take ham instead of chicken. Orville—Orville's right partial to pork," Jenny lied, knowing full well that the real reason she hadn't wanted to fry chicken was because that was what Luke had demanded she bring.

"Land's sake, Miss Jenny!" Delcine rolled her eyes reprovingly. "You know we don't have any pigs, and even if we did, we wouldn't have been able to butcher one today. Besides, that fat old lazy hen belonged in the frying pan. All she did was eat! Yes, ma'am. She hadn't laid any eggs for weeks now, or if she did, she hid them so well Moses and I couldn't find hide nor hair of them. Well, let's go see how everything came out." Delcine started down the dogtrot to the kitchen.

"I'm sorry I wasn't here to help you," she went on, glancing back over her shoulder at Jenny, "but the Reverend Thompkins and Miss Abigail were issuing orders like they were running an army, and I didn't dare to sneak away until the last piece of ribbon was tacked up. You're lucky you had to teach school today! But just wait until you see the booths, Miss Jenny. They look mighty fine, even if I do say so myself. The church is going to make a lot of money, what with all the stuff everybody's made to sell. The quilts alone must have taken hours and hours of work.

"Mercy, Miss Jenny! Is that your supper in this basket here?"

"Yes, why? What's wrong with it?"

"Nothing. I doubt if I could have cooked it any better myself," Delcine stated as she lifted the cloth covering the basket to peer inside and sniff at the contents of the dishes. "But, Miss Jenny, you were supposed to pack your supper in that paperboard box I left on the table."

"That old thing!" Jenny exclaimed. "I wondered what that was for. But, Delcine, it's tacky looking. The basket is so much prettier."

"Miss Jenny, I'm just a fool," Delcine confessed, her expression contrite. "I plumb forgot how you missed out on all the parties and such because of the war. If your sisters had been here, they'd have known what to do. They used to write Miss Henrietta every other week about some barbecue or fancy ball they'd attended. Don't you ever remember them going to a box supper?"

Jenny's brow knitted with concentration as she tried hard to recall. Her sisters had been older than she was. Still vaguely disjointed bits and pieces of conversation and laughter came to mind. Suddenly, dismayed, Jenny clapped her hands to her mouth.

"Oh, Delcine," she breathed, stricken. "I was supposed to decorate the box, wasn't I? So Orville would know it was mine, and he could *bid* on it at the social!"

Good Lord! No wonder Luke had been so cocksure about eating supper with her this evening! He planned to outbid Orville for her box! Jenny was certain of it.

"Oh, Delcine. Now what am I going to do?" Jenny wailed ruefully, her eyes starting to fill with tears at her stupidity. "There isn't time to fix the box properly. Orville will be here any minute!"

"Now don't you fret, Miss Jenny. We'll think of something," Delcine insisted as hastily she began transferring the contents of the basket to the box. She glanced at the bow in Jenny's hair. "Have you got any more of that peach ribbon left? And what about that old straw hat of yours, the one with the silk flowers on it?"

"Yes. Yes!" Jenny nodded, following Delcine's train of thought. "I'll fetch everything right away." Jenny scurried to her bedroom to rummage around in the trunk at the foot of her bed. Moments later she returned to the kitchen, ribbon and hat in hand. "Oh, hurry, Delcine, hurry!" she urged, wondering agitatedly what time it was.

"Cut those flowers off that hat," Delcine ordered as she closed the box and expertly positioned it upon the trailing length of ribbon.

She drew the slender strip of satin up on either side, tying it into a knot on top of the box. Then, as Jenny handed her several of the small, multicolored silk flowers, she laid them down squarely on the knot. When she had the stems all arranged to her satisfaction, she bound them together with the ribbon and finished the whole off with a large bow.

"Well." Delcine stepped back, sighing, as critically she surveyed her handiwork. "It won't be the fanciest box there, I reckon, but, then, simplicity can sometimes be prettier than a cartload of finery."

"Oh, thank you, thank you, Delcine!" Jenny hugged her friend close. "Now, hadn't you better go and get ready yourself? If I'm not mistaken, that's Moses coming up the path to the lean-to."

"Gracious!" Delcine's hands flew to her hair, then smoothed the folds of her everyday gown. "And I'm not even dressed!"

"Use my bedroom," Jenny offered. "The mirror's crazed, but you can still see yourself."

"Thanks, Miss Jenny," Delcine called over her shoulder as she raced away.

Slowly Jenny picked up the plainly decorated box that contained the supper she'd fixed. Then she walked into the parlor, gathered up the rest of her things, and sat down to wait for Orville.

Several minutes later he proudly arrived in the Ascots' carriage, his mother apparently having sided with him against his brother, Gaylord, in the inevitable dispute over who should drive the family buggy that evening. His hair was still wet from washing, or else, Jenny thought wryly, he'd used an inordinate amount of oil of Macassar to slick it back. His tie was too tight, as usual, and his bony wrists protruded prominently from beneath his cuffs as he presented Jenny with a small bouquet of late-blooming flowers.

Orville swallowed hard, and his Adam's apple bobbed up and down several times before he finally managed to speak.

"You look—you look pretty as a—as a peach, Miss Jenny," he stammered, flushing.

The compliment was an obvious one, due to the color of her gown, but still Jenny smiled, knowing it was a miracle he hadn't added, "One without the pit, I mean," as she'd fully expected.

"You're looking mighty fine yourself, Orville," she returned politely as he helped her into the carriage.

He clucked to the horses, and the showy, fine-boned greys set off at a brisk clip. Jenny knew she should feel honored to be riding in a real buggy to the church social, for the vehicles were costly and few and far between in the Ozarks. Still she would have given anything to have been sitting beside Luke in his wagon drawn by his two big draft horses who couldn't have stepped lightly if their lives had depended on it.

Idly she imagined Luke holding her and Orville up on the main country road. But instead of robbing them Luke forced Orville to relinquish his place in the carriage. Then the outlaw climbed in and drove Jenny into the woods to kiss her passionately and declare his love for her.

She frowned at the foolish notion, knowing a man of Luke's lusty appetites wouldn't stop there. Drunk, he had nearly ravished her once. She had no reason to believe he wouldn't try again, given the chance, and she simply couldn't allow that to happen. Not only would her disgrace be absolute and mortifying, since Luke wasn't her husband, but he didn't love her. To be taken under such circumstances would be a shameful experience, even if he used her gently—and Jenny, remembering that night at his cabin, was half afraid he would not. No, she did not want to share Luke's bed, no matter how empty and lonely her own might be. There was some comfort after all in the fact that she was unwed; she could hide behind the modest skirts of her spinsterhood forever, without fearing she would be forced to lift them. Even a man like Orville, should he ever by some miracle prevail upon her to marry him, would eventually lose all patience with her and demand his husbandly rights.

Jenny shivered at the thought, causing Orville to ask solicitously if she were cold. She shook her head negatively in response. Though it was autumn and the leaves had turned to red and gold, a touch of summer's warmth still lingered, and the nights, though cool, were not unpleasant. Still she drew her shawl more closely about her, as though to ward off a man's caresses.

The church social was already in progress when Jenny and Orville at last reached the outskirts of Tumbling Creek. For the first time that evening Jenny's eyes sparkled as she saw how the small town had been transformed. There wasn't a single false storefront that had been left untouched by the decorating committee. Giant paper flowers and streamers, all done in harvest colors, made the streets resemble a fall garden. Even the hitching posts had been wrapped with ribbon. Here and there on the sidewalks sat straw-stuffed scarecrows, whimsical expressions stitched upon their countenances and autumn's bounty tucked in their hands. One held a huge pumpkin in his lap. Another bore acorn squash and Indian corn. Booths were everywhere, large signboards proclaiming their wares, and already many were doing a booming business. Mr. Henshaw had opened up his roomy feed store, having cleared a space for socializing, eating, and dancing, and it was there the main body of the crowd had gathered.

Orville managed to wedge the buggy in between several other vehicles that choked the dusty main street, the livery stable already being filled to overflowing. Then he assisted Jenny from the carriage, and they started down the plank sidewalk toward the lights and the laughter.

Everywhere friends and neighbors called greetings to them, and their progress was slow as they stopped time and again to chat and to examine the contents of various booths.

Ceaselessly Jenny's eyes searched for a glimpse of Luke, but either he hadn't come, or he was holed up in the Razorback Saloon, for she didn't see him anywhere. Her heart sank at his absence, causing her to realize just how much she had looked forward to his being here. She chided herself mentally for desiring his company. It was unkind of her to be plotting to rid herself of Orville's company when he had been nice enough to bring her in the first place. To make amends for her lack of charity, Jenny tucked her arm in Orville's. He beamed down at her and walked a little taller.

At the feed store Jenny set her box supper down on the table reserved for this purpose, noting with a twinge of unhappiness that hers was the plainest box there. In fact, when she compared it to all the other elaborate creations displayed on the table, she almost wished she hadn't come to the church social at all. The silk flowers and peach bow that had looked so pretty when Delcine had arranged them earlier now paled in comparison to the boxes adorned with multitudes of bright ribbons and many-hued flowers, stuffed satin hearts and streamers of lace, tiny birds and little dolls, and other intriguing ornaments. Jenny's was the only box there that had not been painstakingly covered with gay paper, and its stark whiteness made it stand out like a sore thumb.

She sighed. Well, there was nothing to be done about it now. Already

Mayor Drucker was calling for everyone's attention, holding the first of the many boxes up high in the air so all might view it easily.

"Gentlemen. Gentlemen," he intoned. "This beautiful red, white, and blue campaign was instigated by a woman who knows more about politics than even I do." The feed store rang with laughter, for the box belonged to the mayor's wife. "Now, seeing as how I want to be reelected, and since I want to be able to go home tonight as well"—everybody present chuckled appreciatively—"I'll start the bidding off at one dollar."

"Aw, you kin do better 'n that, Mayor," someone shouted teasingly from the back, promptly raising the bid to two dollars.

Since the unwritten rules dictated that a man must at all costs buy his wife's or sweetheart's box, and since this was the only time it was considered proper—and indeed desirable—for other men to pretend to be in the running for an attached female, several of the gentlemen present continued good-naturedly to bid against Mayor Drucker. Finally to everyone's amusement he was forced to pay fifteen dollars to eat supper with his own wife. Mrs. Drucker, blushing and smiling, stepped up to claim her box, then sat down patiently to wait for her husband.

"Now this lovely affair with its dainty frills and furbelows was designed by a lady as clever with her needle as she is with a skillet." The mayor always mentioned something to give those assembled a clue to the woman's identity. "What am I offered, gentlemen, for this 'seamly' supper."

Everybody groaned at his play on words, but Lacey Standish, the local dressmaker, nevertheless glowed as Festus McNabb, who'd been tentatively courting her, bid higher and higher for her box.

At last Jenny saw with a small sense of panic that Mayor Drucker was raising her own box above his head. For one awful moment, as all studied Delcine's efforts with the simple silk flowers and peach ribbon, Jenny wanted to run and hide. But of course she did nothing of the sort. Instead she grit her teeth and stood her ground, pretending she didn't care that her box wasn't as pretty as the others.

"Now you plain-spoken fellows will be especially interested in this," the mayor began, "for I have it on good authority—from my daughter, that is—that this concise lesson in art was planned by an intelligent female who 'books' no nonsense. What do you say, gentlemen, to this 'classy' cooking?"

To the crowd's delight young Paul Henshaw stepped up manfully and yelled, "Fifty cents," causing everyone to roar with laughter and Jenny to flush crimson with embarrassment. Not to be outdone, LeRoy

Pritchard then hollered, "One dollar," shooting his classmate a smug glance. Somehow the two pranksters must have convinced Matthew McNabb to go along with the joke, for he then loftily announced that his schoolteacher was worth at least a dollar fifty. Jenny couldn't help the smile that curved upon her lips at the boys' antics, despite the fact that Orville's ears had turned beet red and across the room his mother's bosom was swelling ominously.

"Fi-fi-five dollars," Orville stuttered, glowering at the youths.

"Ten dollars," Paul instantly rejoined.

To Jenny's mortification the boys kept right on bidding, egging Orville into offering even greater amounts of money for the plain white box Mayor Drucker held above his head. Those gathered in the feed store howled with jollity at each new bid, none making any attempt to stifle the precocious youths since it was all in fun, and Orville could well afford to pay a high price to share Jenny's supper.

"Twenty-five dollars," Orville managed to get out, his voice now revealing ill-concealed anger at his being made a fool in front of the whole town.

"Thirty dollars," LeRoy Pritchard promptly shot back, smirking.

Those gathered in the feed store waited expectantly, barely suppressing their merriment at Orville's plight. Almost defiantly he declared, "Fifty dollars," glaring at his youthful competitors, as though daring them to go even higher.

Jenny glanced nervously at Orville, suddenly realizing he was not enjoying this and hoping the boys would stop tormenting him. She looked over at them beseechingly, giving a small shake of her head as she saw Matthew McNabb about to open his mouth. Already the cost of Jenny's box was more than any of the others had been. She ought to have been thrilled, and secretly she was, but her joy was mingled with pity for Orville. It really wasn't nice that he'd been made the butt of the youths' teasing. To reassure him she gave his hand a slight squeeze.

"Don't bid anymore, Orville," she whispered. "Paul and the others can't possibly pay what they've offered up to this point. If they bid again, ignore them. You'll win by default, I'm sure."

"The bid is fifty dollars . . . gentlemen." The mayor scrutinized the errant boys, his eyes twinkling as they bent their heads together conspiratorially. "Do I hear sixty?"

"One hundred dollars—in gold," a cool, mocking voice drawled lazily from the back of the room.

Jenny frowned at Matthew censuringly, then saw that he was just as surprised as she was by this new bid. A dead silence fell upon the feed store as everyone turned, craning their necks to see Luke Morgan standing in the doorway, his thumbs hooked in his belt, his hips tilted provocatively. Jenny gasped, her body starting to quiver all over as she recognized that it was he who had made that last outrageous bid. He smiled at her triumphantly, and Orville scowled. Imagine Miss Jenny being forced to eat supper with a common criminal! But there was nothing Orville could do about it. He knew there was no way he could top a hundred dollars—especially in gold.

"One hundred dollars going once," Mayor Drucker proclaimed, banging his gavel down upon the counter. "Twice." The hammer thudded again. "Sold to Luke Morgan," the mayor declared with a final whack.

Slowly, feeling as though her legs were going to give way at any moment, Jenny walked up to the small platform where Mayor Drucker stood and claimed her box. Then, avoiding all eyes as the crowd in the feed store began to buzz excitedly, she made her way toward Luke, scarcely aware of Orville at her side.

"Evening, Jenny. Ascot." Luke grinned, but his eyes were as hard as nails as he stared at Orville challengingly.

"You—you had no—no right, Morgan," Orville sputtered indignantly. "Miss Jenny came with—with me, and I'm—I'm gonna eat supper with her!"

"Face it, Ascot: You lost. Now start walking," Luke ordered tersely.

"Is—is that the way you feel about it, Miss Jenny?" Orville asked, swallowing anxiously, his eyes imploring as he looked over at her for guidance.

Jenny gazed at him quietly, torn. He seemed so much like a forlorn little puppy that she didn't want to hurt him. What would happen if she refused to share her supper with Luke? Would the church have to refuse his money? She didn't know.

"You heard what I said, Ascot," Luke uttered warningly, his hands sliding down casually to rest on his Navy Colts. "Start walking."

Jenny didn't know whether or not Luke would actually shoot Orville, but she was quite certain she didn't want to find out.

"Please, Orville." She laid her hand upon his arm. "I don't want any trouble."

To her dismay Orville shook off her gentle touch and stomped away without another word, his face bitter. Jenny was left alone with Luke.

"Let's go outside," he suggested, offering her his arm. "I think we've given this town enough to gossip about for one evening."

Dumbly Jenny allowed him to lead her away. What had she done?

What had she done? A notorious criminal had practically branded her his woman—in public—and she had let him! Oh, why hadn't she protested his bid, rejected him, done something—*anything!*—to let people know she wasn't willingly receiving his attentions. What was everybody thinking about her, *saying* about her? And, worse yet, what would Horace Peabody and the rest of the school board do in light of Luke's act?

"Why so still, Jennilee? Surely you're not miffed at having to eat supper with me rather than Orville."

"Yes. Yes, I am," she said. "What you did wasn't nice, Luke, and you know it. Besides, you're an outlaw, and I'm a schoolteacher. I have certain standards I must uphold, and you've done your best to make a mockery of them and me. Why, I won't be surprised if the school board fires me! After what you did here tonight Mr. Peabody and the others probably think I'm no better than . . . Velvet Rose."

"Bite your tongue, Jennilee," Luke commanded softly. "You're not Velvet Rose, and I've never, ever thought you were. I'm surprised you even mentioned her name, you being such a lady and all. Furthermore, nobody in this town is going to fire you for being seen with me. I happen to be considered quite a catch here in Tumbling Creek, outlaw or not. Besides, my pa is on the school board, and so is my brother J.R., and they sure as hell aren't going to go along with any plan to ride you out of town on a rail. As for me not being nice . . . why, I've never claimed I was. Now let's find a place to sit down so we can eat. I'm feeling mighty lank."

Luke glanced about but decided there really wasn't anywhere he could be private with Jenny. Finally he spread a blanket in his wagon bed, and they climbed in and sat down there. Jenny, knowing how he would grin when he saw the supper she'd prepared, reluctantly began to unpack the contents of the box that had caused such a furor.

"I don't even know why you bid on it," she remarked tartly as she contemplated the silk flowers and peach bow. "It was the plainest one there."

"Well, I'm not much for fancy wrappings," Luke commented. "I kind of figure it's what's on the inside that counts."

At his words Jenny's breath suddenly caught in her throat and her heart seemed to jerk to a halt, for without warning she could hear clearly a sweet voice from her past saying, "Now, Jenny, looks aren't everything . . . you're beautiful inside, and that's what's really counts . . . any man worth having knows beauty is just like a rose. After a time it starts to fade, and no man wants to get stuck with a thorn. You wait and see . . . one night some handsome young gentleman will take your hand in his and say, 'Jennifer Leigh Colter, I love you. . . .' "

To her horror huge tears suddenly welled up in Jenny's eyes, and, despite the fact that she tried desperately to stop the flow of crystal beads, they started to roll down her cheeks.

"What is it, Jenny?" Luke questioned sharply, appalled. "Was it something I said? Something I did? For God's sake, woman! What's wrong?"

She gave a ragged little sob that tore at his heart. Then she sniffed and fumbled in her reticule for a handkerchief.

"I'm sorry," she apologized. "I don't know what got into me. It's just that what you—what you said reminded me so much of something someone else once told me . . . in another time, another world . . . before the war ruined everything that was beautiful and beloved—" She broke off abruptly, biting her lip.

"To whom did it belong Jenny—that voice from your past?" Luke's tone was harsh, his breathing rapid, his jaw tense as he waited for her response.

Whomever she was thinking of, the man must have been one hell of a lover, Luke thought, for Jenny's memories of him to be so strong, so poignant that she was moved to tears when she recalled him. Luke was eaten up with jealousy. Jenny had never looked at him with the sad, longing expression she now had upon her face. What did he really know about her anyway? He had thought her untouched, a virgin. God! For all he knew, she might have had a dozen lovers before the war—and afterward, when the Yankees had taken whatever they'd wanted.

"Who was he, Jenny?" Luke pressed again insistently.

Gently Jenny shook her head, smiling tremulously.

"Not he, Luke. *She*. It was something my sister Bliss once said that you reminded me of."

"Oh." He was suddenly deflated, as though he were a balloon that had just been punctured. He felt stupid and ashamed. "I didn't know you had any family. I guess I . . . just always assumed you were an orphan."

"No." Jenny spoke quietly, still caught up in the past. "My father was murdered by Yankee renegades. My mother died sometime later of a fever and heartbreak."

"Any brothers?"

"Four. They were all killed during the war."

"I'm sorry, Jennilee, so very sorry." Luke's voice was softer now and filled with contrition. "I didn't know."

"No, I know you didn't. Look, Luke. Do you want to eat or not?" Jenny resolutely pushed aside her sorrow and smiled again, more bravely this time. To fend off any more of Luke's probing questions she offered him a plate piled high with buttermilk biscuits. "They had some arsenic at the apothecary, and I made these especially for you!"

Luke grinned, picked one up, and bit into it with relish. Savoringly he chewed it. Then suddenly he began to make choking sounds and clutched his throat with one hand, as though he were being strangled.

"Luke!" Jenny cried with alarm. "Luke, what is it?"

He didn't answer. Instead he dropped the half-eaten biscuit and keeled over as though he'd indeed been poisoned.

"Luke! Luke!"

Filled with panic, Jenny scrambled to her knees and bent her ear to his chest to see if he were still breathing. To her disgust she could hear the low rumbling of laughter in his breast. She jerked away as though she'd been shot, flouncing back on her haunches. Jenny hurled every epithet she could think of at him, then she dumped the whole plate of biscuits in his lap. After brushing them off, Luke propped himself up on one elbow and winked at her.

"My, my. That's some temper you have, Jennilee. And such language too," he admonished her. "You have definitely been spending too much time with those three mischievous boys who are, I hear, the terror of the schoolhouse. How much worse can one outlaw be, honey?"

Then, before she realized what he was about, he caught her in his arms.

"Stop it, Luke," Jenny hissed as he nuzzled her neck, causing her to shiver with nervous excitement in the darkness lit only by the wavering torches that lined the street. "Someone will see."

"Let them," he growled. "I want you, Jenny girl, and I want the whole damned world to know it!"

Then he kissed her passionately until the earth spun away from beneath her feet, and Jenny was falling, falling, with nothing but Luke to hold on to.

Chapter Fifteen

In the end it was not Jenny's fear of being seen that brought her to her senses; it was the horrifying pictures from the past that swirled up to engulf her, so Luke's lips and arms became mixed up with those of the men who had—who had—

"Don't Luke. Please," Jenny whispered as she wrenched herself free of him.

He sat up, regarding her thoughtfully for a time. Then finally he spoke.

"I asked you once before, Jenny." He deliberately refrained from using his pet name for her. "And now I'm asking you again: What is there in your past that makes you so afraid of men—so afraid of me?"

"Please, Luke." She turned away from his piercing blue eyes. "I—I don't want to talk about it."

He glanced down briefly at the scattered biscuits, then looked back up at her, one eyebrow raised.

"Were you raped?" he inquired bluntly.

"No. Oh, God, no!" she burst out, then flushed with mortification because he had even mentioned such a thing to her.

Her reply had been so definitive Luke knew it was the truth.

"Then I don't understand—"

"Please, Luke," Jenny begged once more, her tone almost hysterical. She bit her lip, as though to stifle her rising tide of emotions. "Just—just leave it alone. Please."

"All right. Have it your way, then. I see you fried the chicken I requested." His tone lightened to one of mock playfulness as abruptly he changed the topic of conversation. "What else have you got in that box?"

Gratefully Jenny removed the rest of the dishes from the box and set out the plates, cups, silverware, and napkins, trying hard to hide the trembling of her hands as she did so. She was sure Luke noticed, but he said nothing. Thankful, Jenny assumed he'd decided to drop the subject of her past. He chatted amiably to put her at her ease again, and eventually she responded brightly, though he saw that her body was still tense.

A million questions lay on the tip of his tongue, but resolutely Luke held them back. His mother had warned him several times that he must go slowly with Jenny. Now he saw that it was going to take more than just that. Whatever had happened in Jenny's past had scarred her deeply, perhaps irreparably, leaving her with an almost tangible horror of men. Luke would need more than just patience to win Jenny's heart. He would need kindness and understanding too—the things she had shown to Kipp and Sarah Jane. He would need to discover the reason for Jenny's fear, as she had sensed the cause of his children's pain. Only then could he help her. Only then could he demonstrate to her that the act of love, shared by two who love, was not something to fear, but something to embrace eagerly and cherish.

Everything Luke had ever wanted he had reached out for unhesitantly, knowing it was his for the taking. Now inwardly he cursed himself for rushing Jenny, for allowing his desire for her virtually to obliterate his common sense. It seemed as though every time he got close to her, he couldn't still the frantic beating of his heart, the taut racing of his loins. But he must try. He would lose her otherwise. He knew he would.

Silently Luke groaned. Jenny was going to need an inordinate amount of sweet talk, hand holding, and gentle kisses and caresses before she gave her all to a man—if she ever did—and he didn't know how he was going to be able to restrain his passion long enough to sustain this when he yearned to make her his. Well, he would just have to do his best. That was all there was to it. Luke loved Jenny and wanted very much now to wed her, but something told him she wasn't about to say yes to anyone—much less *him*—as long as she feared the marriage bed.

Speculatively he looked over at her and smiled.

"Tell the truth now," he demanded. "Did you really fix this supper all by yourself, or did Delcine cook it?"

"*I* made it, I'll have you know," Jenny informed him loftily. "Delcine was busy helping with the booths and decorations."

"I just wanted to be sure I was complimenting the right person. You did a mighty fine job, Jennilee," Luke observed, wiping his mouth off with his napkin. "I don't remember when I've eaten such a good meal—and in such pleasant company."

Inwardly Jenny glowed at his praise and his flattery, but outwardly she only made a face at him.

"I hope your mother and your sisters-in-law don't hear you say that," she teased, "since they are all excellent cooks!"

"But not nearly as pleasant company!" Luke retorted, laughing. "It's obvious *you've* never tried to eat with my parents and Kipp talking a blue streak or with J.R. glaring down the table at you every time you even look at his wife or with Toby thinking so hard about some damned new invention of his that he doesn't even know he's got guests in his house!"

Jenny laughed.

"I enjoy spending time with your kin," she stated firmly. "I'm used to a large family and children making lots of noise."

Though he cursed himself afterward, Luke couldn't seem to stop the words that tumbled from his lips.

"You ought to be married, Jennilee, with kids of your own."

Jenny's face whitened, as though he'd struck her, for, of all the things she'd considered when contemplating her strange, budding relationship with Luke, she'd never given a single thought to the fact that she was unable to bear children. Of course a man like Luke would want as many sons as possible to carry on his name—and daughters too. J.R. and Tobias already had several youngsters. Jenny took a deep breath.

"I—I can't have any children, Luke," she confessed, her voice low, her heart slowly shattering inside of her. "I had an—an accident shortly after the war ended. There was some sort of internal damage done . . . both my legs were broken too. The left one was . . . badly crushed. It never healed right."

"I'm sorry, Jennilee. Christ!" Luke swore, then shook his head wryly. "This does seem to be my night for apologies, doesn't it? How awful for you. I know you'd be a wonderful mother. Why, you've done wonders for Sary in just the few days you've been working with her. Already she can write her name." Luke's hard visage softened at the remembrance. "You should have seen her face the other evening when she showed me. God! I'd give every cent I ever stole to have been the one to put that light in her eyes!"

Jenny's heart ached with pity for Luke at this admission. Despite all his daring, his mockery, and his laughter, she knew that beneath the mask he showed the rest of the world lay wounds as bitter and deep as her own. Sometimes, when his eyes were so full of pain and looked as ageless and timeworn as they did now, she wanted to reach out to him and hold him close and speak of the love for him she felt slowly blossoming inside of her.

"Sarah Jane loves you dearly, Luke," she told him. "Why, I've seen her eyes light up that way at just the mention of your name. You mean the world to both her and Kipp."

"I reckon so. It's just that after Maybelle died I went a little crazy, I guess, and I lost touch with Kipp and Sary. It was wrong; I know that now. But I just don't seem to know how to be a father to my kids, Jenny. I know they need me. Jesus! They needed a mother too, but they never had one! You're so good with children, Jenny. I've seen how Kipp and Sary respond to you. What can I do to make it all up to them?"

"Love them. Spend time with them. Listen to them—not just to what they say, but to what they *don't* say as well. Children are people, Luke, just like everyone else, and they want the same things everybody else wants: love, understanding, sharing, a sense of belonging, a home, time to be a part of life, and time to be alone. That's all you need to know. They'll figure everything else out on their own."

Tenderly Luke took Jenny's hand in his.

"What made you so wise, Jenny Colter?" he asked. "How old are you? Nineteen? Twenty? Twenty-one? Too young, I know, for such a world of wisdom to be inside that pretty head. Yes, I said pretty, and don't you dare to contradict me!" he ordered sternly. "I've grown quite fond of heart-shaped faces and freckles recently, and I won't hear anything said against them!" He paused, then continued. "My folks are here, with my kids. What do you say, Jennilee? Shall we go and find them and show Kipp and Sary the time of their lives?"

"Yes, oh, yes, Luke!" Jenny cried. "I would enjoy that more than anything in the world, and I just know the children would love it!"

"Then that's what we'll do." Luke felt as though his chest would burst with the sudden happiness that filled him to overflowing. "Come on, Jennilee. I'll race you to the feed store!"

The townspeople thought them both mad. Jenny knew they did as she, awkwardly, and Luke, gracefully, ran down the sidewalk, breathless with laughter. But, for the first time in her life, Jenny didn't care what people thought. Let them stare. Let them talk. Nothing mattered as long as Luke was by her side.

If he had done nothing else, he had brought joy back into Jenny's life, and for that alone she would have raced him to the ends of the earth.

They found Jed and Lottie in the crowd at last, and after hearing his plan Luke's parents were glad to relinquish his children to him. Kipp and Sarah Jane were so excited they danced about impatiently, eager to be off.

"Grandma Lottie said we had to stay in the booth with her, so she could keep an eye on us, 'cause Grandpa Jed's been over there swigging corn liquor and telling tall tales to all his old cronies again. But now *we* can see the sights too, Pa, can't we?" Kipp bubbled over with enthusiasm.

At his son's words Luke felt as though someone had punched him hard in the belly. To think if it weren't for his attraction to Jenny, he'd be over at Miss Ruby's bordello, in bed with Velvet Rose and missing this precious moment in his children's lives.

"Pa"—Luke turned to Jed—"don't you think your friends are tired of hearing about that wildcat, or is it the bear story this time?" Luke forced himself to smile to hide his deep feelings of anguish and shame at being such a failure as a father.

"Now, son, I ain't any worse 'n the rest of 'em," Jed protested sheepishly. "Shoot fire! Perkin Farlow's told that damned whopper of a fish tale more times 'n I kin count—you'd think a marshal would have better sense—'n' Andrew Watkins has gone on 'n' on 'bout a rattler what was bigger 'n an alligator!"

"Hmph!" Luke snorted. "Toby and I were up at the Watkinses' place that afternoon, and that rattler wasn't anything but a little old garter snake!"

"Why, son, I'm surprised at you!" Jed chuckled. "You ain't supposed to accuse us old folks of fibbin'! Ain't that right, Miz Jenny? You two run on along now, 'fer you purt nigh ruin my standin' here 'n' I lose my turn at the moonshine jug!"

"You heard Jed. Go on, the lot of you!" Lottie put in, beaming. "Jenny, that dumb old Orville was fit to be tied after what happened over supper, and he went on home to sulk. But don't you worry none. Luke'll see you get back to the cabin safe."

Orville! Jenny's hands flew to her mouth. Why, in all the excitement she'd forgotten all about him!

"Hey," Luke whispered in her ear, as though guessing her thoughts, "I thought we weren't going to dredge up any more bad memories."

"Orville's not a bad memory; he's my escort!" Jenny wailed, distressed.

"Not anymore." Luke grinned. "Come on now. We're missing all the fun."

Against her better judgment and giddy with a strange wild delight she'd never before experienced, Jenny allowed him to sweep her away, Kipp and Sarah Jane following hard on their heels.

They visited one booth after another, *ooh*ing and *aah*ing over the fine handiwork that was on display. There were gorgeous quilts and intricately crocheted shawls, elaborate tatting and lace, and beautiful dolls.

Luke wanted to buy one of these last for Sarah Jane, whose eyes grew wide with wonder as she realized her father was waiting for her to choose whichever doll she liked best. There were several lovely porcelain ones with delicate faces and ornate gowns. But, trembling with excitement, Sarah Jane pointed to a brown-haired rag doll dressed in gingham, with a cheery smile and freckles on its cotton face. Luke didn't need anyone to tell him the doll reminded her of Jenny. Jenny must have thought so too, he guessed, for she blushed and gave Sarah Jane a hug.

At a booth manned by Mrs. Kincaid, whose husband owned the sawmill, Kipp selected a horse carved of wood.

"It looks like Blaze, Pa, don't you think?" the boy inquired hopefully.

"You're right, son," Luke answered, making a mental note that it was time Kipp and Sarah Jane both had ponies.

Christ! Luke cursed silently to himself. Maybe they already did. His father had put him on his first pony when he'd been five years old. Luke would have to talk to Jed and find out if he'd done the same for Kipp and Sarah Jane. Jesus! Luke went on swearing at himself. What a fool he'd been, throwing away the best years of his life with his children. Thank God, Jenny had opened his eyes in time!

He looked down at her and gave her hand a gentle squeeze. She smiled. Then Luke spied a booth whose shelves were filled with music boxes.

"Wait here with the kids a minute, Jennilee. I've seen something I want," he said.

Moments later he returned with one of the delicate little boxes, which he handed to Jenny.

"It's for you," he told her simply.

She started to refuse it, then closed her mouth abruptly. She didn't know what Luke felt for her, if he really cared for her, as she hoped, or if he were just amusing himself with her, as she feared. But if tonight were all she ever had of him, Jenny wanted something to remember him by.

"All right," she agreed, shyly accepting his gift. "Thank you."

She studied it silently, observing the hearts and flowers stenciled on its lid. It would go well with everything else in her house, she thought. No doubt that was why Luke had chosen it.

Carefully she tucked it into her reticule, and it was only later, long after the most wonderful evening of her life had ended and Luke had driven her home and kissed her good night, that Jenny opened the lid of his present.

And then she cried with the mingled happiness and sadness that only the deepest of emotions brings, for it was the music box she'd seen in the old-timer's hands that day at the church, the one that played the bittersweet melody of *"Plaisir d'Amour"*—"The Joys of Love."

Chapter Sixteen

"Are you ready, Sarah Jane?" Jenny asked, smiling encouragingly at the little girl.

Sarah Jane's eyes were anxious, but she nodded in reply.

"Then you may begin," Jenny said.

Slowly Sarah Jane opened her tablet. Then she sat quietly for a moment, chewing on the end of her fat, stubby pencil as thoughtfully she considered the task before her. Today she must write out the entire alphabet, and the only letters she felt truly certain of knowing were those in her name. Still for the first time in her life she was not afraid. If she failed, Jenny would only make her do it over. Jenny wouldn't frown or yell at her angrily or—worst of all—slap her and call her a stupid, worthless brat. No, Jenny would smile sweetly and say, "Well, that's *almost* right. Shall we try again, Sarah Jane?" Then she would turn to a clean sheet in the tablet.

But Sarah Jane wanted to get it all right on her very first attempt, just to please Jenny, so she worked hard at forming her letters.

Jenny watched patiently, holding her breath each time Sarah Jane hesitated, then exhaling with relief when the child managed to print the correct letter in the proper order.

At last Sarah Jane was finished and held up her tablet for inspection. Quickly Jenny's eyes scanned the alphabet: *A, B, C . . . X, Y, Z!*

"Oh, Sarah Jane, that's wonderful!" she exclaimed, hugging the little girl close. "They're all there, all twenty-six of them, and they're all in the right order!" Jenny picked up the pencil and drew a large star on Sarah Jane's paper, then added a big 100%. "You must take that home and show it to your father," she directed. "He'll be so proud of you!"

Sarah Jane laughed soundlessly, clapping her hands together with delight. Being praised for her work was a new and most satisfying

experience, and Sarah Jane treasured it, glad she had pleased Jenny.
Kipp had been right after all; Jenny was ever so nice. She was also the
first real friend, besides Kipp, that Sarah Jane had ever had. Shyly she
reached up and planted a soft kiss on Jenny's cheek and was rewarded
by another warm hug and a kiss on the top of her head. Sarah Jane's
eyes glowed in response. How she longed to tell Jenny about One-Eyed
Jack! Jenny, Sarah Jane felt sure, would know what to do about him.
But even as she considered doing so, Sarah Jane dismissed the idea. If
Jenny learned about the evil man, he might come back to Tumbling
Creek and hurt her as well! Sarah Jane wouldn't be able to bear that,
not when Jenny had been so good to her.

The child and the woman were so engrossed in each other that it was
some time before they observed the strange man standing at the back of
the room. When they finally did see him Sarah Jane shrank back into
the protective circle of Jenny's arms. The little girl wondered if One-
Eyed Jack had somehow peered into her mind, and, perceiving her
thoughts, had sent a winged henchman to remind her of his gruesome
warning.

The man was big and brawny. He wore a battered old hat pulled
down low over his piercing eyes. His face was grizzled with unshaven
whiskers, and over his suit he wore a long duster that bore the stains of
travel. It was unbuttoned, and the way it hung from his slightly stooped
shoulders made him resemble a large bird of prey.

Sarah Jane shuddered a little and hid her face, hoping the man
wouldn't notice her.

"Howdy, ma'am." He addressed Jenny, touching the brim of his hat
politely. "Are you Miss Colter?"

"I am," she replied. She too was frightened by the stranger, but,
sensing Sarah Jane's fear was greater than her own, Jenny was ready to
defend the child, if necessary.

"I kind of figured you were. A fellow in town told me I'd find you
here. I'm Gus Grissom, with the Pinkerton Detective Agency, ma'am."
The man pulled a badge of identification from his pocket and walked
toward Jenny, displaying it openly in his hand and making no protest
when she took it from him to inspect it. "I'd like to ask you a few
questions."

"What about?" she queried after she'd carefully examined his badge
and returned it to him.

"The Morgan gang, ma'am. I understand you're right friendly with
Luke Morgan."

Jenny stiffened again with apprehension, pondering her dilemma meanwhile and wondering who had told him about her relationship with Luke.

Obviously the detective hoped to elicit as much information as he could from her about the Morgans, but Jenny wasn't certain she wished to tell him anything. Luke's recent behavior toward her had led her to believe he was serious about her, that he wasn't just amusing himself with her or, worse yet, attracted to her because he was one of those men who thrived on a woman's fear. If she revealed anything she knew about him or his family to this agent, however, she would doubtless destroy any feelings Luke had for her, and in her heart Jenny knew she couldn't bear that—not now, not after he had given her the music box that held such meaning and promise. Besides, she didn't want to hurt Luke's family by turning him in to the law.

She decided to wait and see what the detective wanted of her. If his questions were innocuous, she would answer truthfully. If they were not, she would be forced to lie.

"I—I am acquainted with Mr. Morgan, yes," she agreed, once she was sure of her composure, "but not very well. I've only lived in Tumbling Creek a short while."

She pinched Sarah Jane lightly, silently warning her to keep still, for although the little girl did not speak, she might make some involuntary movement that would inadvertently reveal to the agent that Jenny was hedging on this.

"I understand that, Miss Colter, but I warn you for your own safety to tell me what you do know about the gang. Luke Morgan and his brothers are outlaws, wanted in several states and territories for armed robbery and other assorted crimes. They are dangerous men, and unfortunately they've managed to elude every single one of my predecessors. Mr. Allan Pinkerton, the founder and president of the Pinkerton Detective Agency, is none too happy about that, ma'am. He sent me down here to take care of the matter, and I aim to do just that. That means taking the Morgan gang into custody.

"Now I'm fairly certain the brothers held up the Ozark Mountain Railroad Company some months ago, stealing a shipment of gold intended for the stock exchange in Kansas City. I understand you were on that train when the theft occurred. Did you recognize any of the outlaws who robbed you, Miss Colter?"

Jenny started slightly, for she'd thought the incident long forgotten, especially since Marshal Farlow, the town lawman, hadn't even bothered to question anyone about it.

"I wasn't personally robbed, but, no, sir, I did not know any of the men who held up the train," she reported falsely, hoping the color hadn't drained from her face. "I only saw two men, and they wore bandannas over their faces. But I'm positive neither were members of the Morgan family, Mr. Grissom. These men were dark-haired and dark-skinned, and the Morgan brothers are all blonds."

The detective eyed her sharply, assessingly, and Jenny was afraid she had not fooled him with her half-lies.

"Are you aware that protecting a fugitive by withholding information from the law is a criminal offense, Miss Colter?"

"Yes, I am. My brother-in-law is one of the finest attorneys in Atlanta. I assure you I would aid you if I could, Mr. Grissom, but unfortunately I've never seen either of those two men again, and I'm certainly not hiding anyone in my cellar, though you are free to search my house if you like. Since it is Luke Morgan you are interested in, however, I would suggest you pay a visit to his farm, Whispering Pines. If you haven't already received directions to the place, I'll be happy to give them to you."

Luke, Jenny knew, would not be there. She merely wished to be rid of Gus Grissom as quickly as possible, and she hoped that by offering to help him in this manner, no matter how useless her assistance might prove to be, she would speed him on his way.

"I have been there already, Miss Colter, as well as to Mr. and Mrs. Jedediah Morgan's cabin and to those of J.R. and Tobias Morgan. I found nothing." The agent's voice was grim. "In fact, I am beginning to comprehend why my predecessors failed in their line of duty. No one in Tumbling Creek seems to know anything about the Morgan gang."

"Well, I'm sure that's understandable, sir," Jenny remarked warily. "The Morgans have a lot of kith and kin in the Ozarks. They are all noted for their hot tempers and long memories. One man who dared to speak out against them was tarred and feathered, and nobody else cares to experience the same fate, myself included. Now if you'll excuse me, I'm very busy and must get on with my work."

Nervously she shuffled her papers together. Then she opened Sarah Jane's tablet and with her pencil pretended to check the child's spelling of the alphabet, hoping the detective couldn't see the star she'd drawn and the 100% she'd written on the page earlier. The letters swam before her eyes, and Jenny swallowed hard, wishing violently that Gus Grissom would go away. Instead he gazed at her speculatively for a long time. Then he spoke once more.

"It won't do you any good, ma'am, to throw yourself away on Luke Morgan," he stated sternly. "Sooner or later he'll either be caught and hanged or be shot to death by a lawman. Pardon me for saying so, Miss Colter, but . . . where will you be then? Think, ma'am. You're a spinster and a schoolteacher. Because he's one of their own, Tumbling Creek might look the other way as far as your relationship with Luke Morgan goes. But should you ever find yourself in need of another position, I believe you'll find other folks aren't so charitable when it comes to hiring the . . . woman of a notorious criminal."

"How dare you insult me in such a fashion, sir!" Jenny jumped to her feet indignantly, her face flaming. "I am not, nor have I ever been, to Luke Morgan what I comprehend you intended to imply, and you are no gentleman to have suggested such a thing to me! I must ask you to leave these premises at once! Moses!" she shouted, agitatedly. *"Moses!"*

In moments the big black man stood in the doorway, breathless from having run as fast as his legs would carry him from the fields to the schoolhouse at Jenny's cry.

"Ya—ya—yassum, Miz Jenny!" he rasped, panting for air and eyeing her worriedly.

"Moses, make certain this . . . man is escorted to the edge of our property, and see that he leaves it and doesn't return," she instructed frostily, her voice clipped with a rage she prayed masked her fear.

"Yassum, Miz Jenny."

Gus Grissom glanced at Moses measuringly, taking in the stout shovel the Negro was holding purposefully in his hands. Then he looked back at Jenny and shook his head pityingly.

"You're making a grave mistake, Miss Colter, one I'm sure you will come to regret deeply."

"I don't think so, Mr. Grissom. It is you who have erred, sir," she informed him haughtily, her eyes shooting sparks like flint, "and you may be certain I shall report your reprehensible conduct to Mr. Pinkerton himself!"

That gave the agent pause. Allan Pinkerton had an extremely high regard for women in general and an especially soft spot for ladies of quality who'd fallen on hard times and were now forced to support themselves. Why, the Pinkerton Detective Agency had been the first in the United States to hire a female detective! No, Mr. Pinkerton would not approve of Gus's handling of Miss Colter at all!

"I . . . regret that you mistook my meaning earlier, ma'am," the detective apologized. "I'm sorry to have inconvenienced you. Good afternoon, Miss Colter."

Jenny waited until Gus Grissom had stepped outside, mounted his horse, and started off down the path leading to the main road. Then she nodded to Moses.

"Follow him," she commanded softly, inwardly trembling at her actions. "Once he's out of sight, I want you to take Blossom and the wagon and go over to Jed and Lottie's house. Find out where the Morgan brothers are, and get word to Luke. Tell him what's happened here. That man will watch us. I'm sure of it! And I don't want Luke to come here and walk into a trap. He'd think I set him up." She wrung her hands anxiously. "Don't fail me, Moses. I'm counting on you."

Though his face was troubled, Moses smiled tremulously.

"Ah ain' neber let yo down yet, Miz Jenny, an' Ah ain' 'bout ter start now. Yore man'll be safe. Ah promises yo dat."

"He's not my man, but thank you anyway, Moses. Sarah Jane"— Jenny turned to the ashen-faced child—"I don't believe we'll continue with our lesson today. You come on over to the cabin with me, and I'll fix you a warm cup of chamomile tea. Then Moses can take you home. All right? Don't forget your tablet, honey, and don't you fret now, you hear? Your father will be safe. I promise. Why, he's smarter than *ten* of those Pinkerton agents, and he'll give that one the slip too, just as he has all the others!"

But even as she spoke the words Jenny's heart filled with fear. Gus Grissom hadn't appeared to be a man who would give up easily. No, he'd reminded her all too vividly of the bloodhounds her father had once raised at Faxon's Folly, and they'd been dogs that would continue the chase until they'd dropped dead in their tracks from sheer exhaustion.

Still shaking, she took Sarah Jane's hand and began to walk toward home. A strong gale was starting to rise, rustling the branches of the trees and sending several dying leaves whirling through the air like dancing wraiths. The gusts whipped Jenny's skirts about mercilessly as she and Sarah Jane started to run down the narrow, overgrown lane. Droplets of rain began to splatter upon them, and presently they were soaked through.

To Jenny's fanciful imagination it seemed as though the wayward wind caressed her mockingly and whispered triumphantly in her ear, calling out to her to come and join it while sweeping her secure little world far beyond her grasp; and the rain was like cleansing tears, washing away her past and leaving her alone to face the future.

Suddenly the full import of what she'd done dawned on her, and with growing trepidation she realized she'd set her feet upon a path from which there could be no turning back.

It was against the law to withhold information about a crime or a fugitive. By defending Luke Morgan, Jenny had become as much of an outlaw as he!

Chapter Seventeen

It was late when the knock sounded upon the lean-to door. Jenny, Moses, and Delcine, who were huddled around the kitchen table, sharing a pot of warm tea before retiring, jumped fearfully at the noise and gazed wide-eyed at each other.

Then carefully, so he wouldn't scrape his chair across the floor, Moses got to his feet and edged his way over to one of the cabinet drawers, from which he withdrew a sharp butcher knife. With his fingers held to his lips to caution Jenny and Delcine to be silent, he tiptoed toward the lean-to.

The knocking came again, louder and more urgent this time.

"It's Luke, Jenny," a muffled voice hissed. "Let me in!"

"Oh, God," she breathed, staring at Moses accusingly as she ran to the door.

The Negro was hurt by her lack of faith in him and told her so, his dark eyes reproachful.

"Miz Jenny, Ah swear Ah done took dat message ter Mistah Luke mahseff. Ah done tole him not ter come heah, dat dat Pink'ton 'tective wuz pro'bly watchin' dis house. But dat Mistah Luke . . . why, he's jes' as muleheaded as they come. Ah knowed he wuzn't listenin' ter a blamed thing Ah done said!"

"Well, Moses, that's because you weren't saying anything I wanted to hear." Luke grinned devilishly as he slipped into the kitchen. "Trim the wick on that lamp, Delcine, and turn it down low, so we won't cast much of a shadow against the curtains. That way, if there really *are* any prying eyes out there, they won't be able to count the number of people inside this room."

He turned to Jenny, his eyes devouring her hungrily.

"Oh, Luke, you fool!" she wailed softly. "How *could* you come here tonight? I warned you to stay away! I just know that awful man is out there in the woods somewhere, watching this house!"

"Well, if he is, he's damned good at his job, because we hunted for him for well over an hour and couldn't find hide nor hair of him. But don't you worry, sugar. Raif and Billy Clay are still searching for him. If he's out there, they'll find him. He could just as easily be spying on my folks' place, or J.R.'s or Toby's cabins. Ma's still madder than a hornet about that buzzard coming around today, and so are Kate and Winona." He glanced at Moses and winked, remembering what the big black man had said about Jenny loftily ordering the agent from the schoolhouse. "I hear tell *you* sent Mr. Grissom away with a flea in his ear too!"

Jenny blushed, then snapped tartly:

"Well, I don't know why I did! I ought to have directed him straight out to those caves I've heard are on your property. I don't doubt that that's where you've been hiding all afternoon! Isn't it?"

"You bet. There's nowhere safer. My brothers and I know those caves like the backs of our hands. Even if you *had* betrayed me, I'm afraid Mr. Grissom would have gotten hopelessly lost before he ever found us. One poor sap of a detective is buried out there. He fell into a chasm and starved to death before we finally managed to locate him." Luke's voice had turned grim. "Hell of a way to go, and for what? Nothing!

"Look here, Jennilee," Luke continued. "I don't have much time. I've got to get out of town and lay low for a while. I only came to say good-bye. I couldn't leave without telling you that and letting you know I'll be back as soon as I can. So don't you go getting any ideas about that dumb Orville while I'm gone, you hear? I'll definitely horsewhip him, and I'll—I'll . . . well, I'll think of something to do to you too! Maybe I'll start coming to school and give you a harder time than Matthew McNabb does!"

Jenny's heart thrilled at Luke's words. He must care for her a little. He must! Why else would he have risked his life to tell her good-bye? If he were simply amusing himself with her, surely he wouldn't still be hanging around, chancing being captured. Surely he would have just upped and left, not giving her feelings a second thought.

"If you do, I'll smack your palms with my ruler and sit you in the corner—with a dunce cap on your head!" she shot back impudently. "Oh, Luke. You will be careful, won't you? Kipp and Sarah Jane need you so. Sarah Jane printed out the entire alphabet this afternoon, and all her letters were correctly formed and in the right order too. She was going to show you her paper this evening. She was so proud."

Luke's mouth tightened.

"That's just one more thing to chalk up to those damned Pinkerton agents!" he snarled. "God! How I hate those bastards!—pardon my language. Someday I'll even the score, and I mean it! You give Sary a kiss for me, Jennilee, and tell her I'll be home soon. Hear that owl hooting? That's Raif. I've got to go. Damn! I'm so frigging mad right now I think I'll murder that Pinkerton detective if I see him!"

Luke's eyes were suddenly dark, and his voice was husky as his eyes roamed over Jenny longingly. He was going to miss her—more than he would ever have thought possible.

"But you won't kill him, will you!" she breathed as she tilted her face up to his. "Mrs. Zee told me you never killed anybody."

"Well," Luke began, suddenly wanting Jenny to know the truth about him. She had a right to know, he thought. "Zenobia's correct about that up to a point, Jenny. We don't ever kill anybody who doesn't draw on us first and who doesn't stand a fair chance at proving himself the better shot. I *have* killed men, lots of them, though it was mostly during the war. So don't you ever think I haven't, Jenny," he uttered warningly.

"I'm an outlaw, just as you've reminded me on several occasions, and if one of these nights you decided to lure me here and turn me over to the law, you'd get a nice fat reward of a thousand dollars for your trouble.

"You think about that while I'm gone, Jenny. You could be letting yourself in for a lot more than you expect by keeping silent about me— even if I *did* insist on it! Don't worry about me; I didn't mean those hateful things I said that night at the hotel. I don't want you to be imprisoned as my accomplice, so if that agent comes back here asking questions, you tell him the truth."

Luke glanced over at Moses and Delcine, who were sitting silently at the table, taking everything in: the grim, caring expression on Luke's face and Jenny's heart in her eyes.

"You take good care of this girl for me," he told them. "Don't let her throw her life away because of me."

Then he kissed Jenny swiftly, violently, yearningly before he reluctantly tore himself away from her and slipped out into the night.

From the door of the lean-to Jenny watched him go, saw Raiford emerge from the shadows to meet him. Quickly the two men mounted up and rode off, and soon they were swallowed up by the trees and the darkness. Silently Jenny urged them on as they made their escape, and only when she heard no hue and cry raised in pursuit of them did she allow herself to breathe a sigh of relief. Gus Grissom would not catch his quarry this evening, it appeared. But he would have other chances, and perhaps the next time Luke would not be so lucky. Jenny's heart leaped to her throat at the thought of him dangling from the end of a rope or bleeding to death from the well-aimed bullet of some lawman's gun, and she did not know how Kate and Winona stood the endless, gnawing days and nights of not knowing whether their husbands were dead or alive.

Would Luke return to her, as he'd promised, or would he instead be shipped home in a pine box—as so many Jenny had loved had been? She did not know, and she did not believe she was strong enough to bear the strain of not knowing.

She went to bed, but sleep eluded her. The wind that had blown desultorily all evening suddenly increased in intensity, and the drizzle became a deluge as the sky opened up to disgorge its contents.

The old cabin shook and shuddered as the gale pounded at the doors and windows, driving the rain so savagely against the cured rawhide sheets covering the apertures that Jenny was forced to get up and close the shutters. The drops pounded upon the roof, but the violent tattoo was not soothing, for all she could think about was Luke, outside, trying to make his way through the storm and the blackness. Thunder boomed, and Jenny cringed beneath her quilt. Lightning cracked so loudly she knew it must have struck one of the tall mountain pines in the woods. Still the rain roared down, and a small fist of fear clutched her heart, for floods were not uncommon in the Ozarks. If the tempest did not abate, there was a real possibility that it would cause the rivers, creeks, and springs to rise and overflow their boundaries.

For the first time since she'd arrived in Tumbling Creek, Jenny wished her house sat upon higher ground. She thought of Luke's farm, Whispering Pines; the acreage stretched to the White River, and she wondered if morning would find the ramshackle cabin still standing. Surely Luke had built the place upon a hill. Jenny tried to recall whether or not this was the case, but she had only seen the house once, and it had been dark then. She could not remember, and she did not know why it was so important for her to do so—except that she hoped Luke's farm might someday be her home.

Her home! A thrill of wild anticipation chased up her spine at the idea. She imagined herself living at Whispering Pines, with Luke, Kipp, and Sarah Jane. The tableau was a happy one. She saw herself cooking and cleaning, reading to the children in the evenings and mending one of Luke's shirts by the lamplight. Then Kipp and Sarah Jane went to bed, and she was alone with Luke. His eyes met hers across the parlor, and Jenny shivered, unable to complete the scene. Their bedroom lay beyond, and she knew she could not bring herself to enter it, no matter how badly she wanted to. Her many recollections of love as it was meant to be were overshadowed by the single memory of that horrible day at Faxon's Folly. The deep scars that had been left upon her body and soul as a result had yet to fade.

Jenny thought of Luke's lips upon hers before he'd gone this evening, and she longed to taste them again. But she recalled too his drunken caresses and his savage kisses, his hands tearing at the bodice of her gown and her chemise that night at his cabin, and she knew there was a darker side of him that would always evoke the pictures from the past that haunted her, tormented her, and filled her with such fear.

She loved Luke, Jenny realized, but she could never give to him all that he would desire of her in the end. What she remembered of that day at the plantation was still too vivid in her mind. Time had not healed the wounds it had left. But perhaps Luke could—if only she gave him the chance to do so. Jenny didn't know. She knew only that she felt more torn and confused than she had ever felt in her life.

She listened to the wind outside, how it howled relentlessly, then dropped to a plaintive sigh, and as she had earlier that afternoon Jenny imagined it was speaking to her, whispering in her ear, mockingly, sweetly, challengingly, victoriously—like Luke, a combination of many emotions that called to her ceaselessly, demanding of her all that she was afraid to give.

Chapter Eighteen

The days passed slowly after Luke's leaving, each one seeming much like another, their sameness making Jenny realize just how much he meant to her and how he had filled her world with his presence. She missed him more than she would have thought possible, and the strange yearning she'd felt when he'd kissed her now deepened to a physical ache that would not be stilled.

She told herself it was useless, that despite her feelings for him or his for her, nothing could come of their relationship when she was unwilling to commit herself totally to him—but it didn't help. Some part of her went on hoping that somehow it would all work out.

It was quite dark now in the mornings when she rose to prepare herself for school, and cold too. Jenny shivered as she washed and dried herself hurriedly. Though Delcine had heated the water, there was no stove in Jenny's bedroom, and the warmth from the fireplace in the parlor did not extend to the farthest corners of the cabin. Quickly she slipped into her clothes, then made her way gratefully to the cozy kitchen.

Bitter black coffee was brewing on the stove, and after pouring herself a cup Jenny sipped it savoringly, wondering as usual if Luke were warm and safe. There had been no word of him or his whereabouts.

Having finished her coffee, Jenny set her empty tin cup down on the table. Then she moved to the parlor to gather up her things. There in the corner the small pine tree that Moses had felled earlier that week waited to be decorated for Christmas. Every evening she and Delcine worked on completing the ornaments they were making, tiny dolls and stuffed animals, cardboard stars and paper chains. They would have strings of cranberries and popcorn too, and gingerbread men and candy canes. Jenny was also knitting gifts for each of her students, gay little sacks she would fill with treats. After the hard rock candy had been eaten, the bags could be used to hold marbles or jacks.

Glancing at the clock on the mantel, Jenny saw that she must hurry if she didn't want to be late. Quickly she went outside to the wagon Moses was just bringing around the corner, her shoulders hunched against the blast of cold wind that assailed her as she scurried toward the vehicle

She studied the dark grey sky and the frost upon the ground curiously as she walked along, wondering if it were going to snow and what it would be like when it did. Already it was colder than it had ever been in Atlanta. Thank heavens, they had finally gotten the barn up several days ago. At least the animals need not be out in such weather, Jenny thought, shivering. She had been disappointed that Luke had missed the barn raising. She had hoped that somehow he would mange to attend the first party she'd given in her cabin, but he had not. His absence had taken some of the glow from an otherwise happy event.

Upon arriving at the schoolhouse, Jenny rang the bell several times. Then she started a fire in the cast-iron stove. Presently everyone was assembled, and class began.

Jenny listened with half an ear to her pupils' recitations, automatically correcting mistakes and rewarding sincere efforts with praise, her mind constantly on Luke. She scarcely even noticed that Matthew McNabb, sensing her distraction, had ceased to pay attention. With a sharp pocket knife the boy was carefully slicing a large square hole in the pages of the hymnal in his desk. The book was thick, so it was going to take time to achieve the desired result. But Matthew was patient; he could wait for the revenge he had planned for Crabby Abby, who had caused him and his father to bear the brunt of one of the Reverend Thompkins's fire-and-brimstone sermons. Matthew smiled devilishly to himself. Crabby Abby sat in his seat during church. Was she ever going to be in for a surprise, come spring!

Surreptitiously he glanced up at Jenny, wondering if she had yet spied his machinations. No, she was daydreaming again. She certainly had been doing a lot of that recently. She must be in love, Matthew decided, thinking about how his father had been mooning over Lacey Standish lately. Well, maybe the old man would get up enough gumption to ask the dressmaker to marry him. Matthew hoped so. He liked Lacey. The one time he'd tried to put something over on her she'd smacked him on the head with a pincushion and threatened to tie him up with her measuring tape. She was like Miss Colter; she didn't take any sass, but she was a good sport.

Matthew sneaked another look at Jenny, whom he had come to admire. He remembered how she'd looked at him that time in church when the reverend had been preaching at him and his father, and he thought she would get a real good laugh out of the revenge he was plotting against Crabby Abby. Nevertheless, he continued his cutting secretively, just in case.

It was snowing by the time school let out for the day and Moses arrived to drive Jenny home. They gazed wonderingly at the white crystal flakes, turning up their faces and stretching their hands out to touch the snow. When they finally reached the cabin Delcine was already outside, tramping about in the thick powder and giggling. Jenny and Moses climbed out of the wagon to join her, racing about and shouting and laughing, throwing snowballs at each other and letting themselves fall backward to the ground to make the snow angels Jenny had heard about from her students. The three of them built a snowman too, according to the instructions Jenny's pupils had given her. Amazed to learn she knew nothing about snow, had never even seen it, the youngsters had been delighted by this discovery. There was now something *they* could teach their teacher!

Once the snowman was finished, Jenny topped it off with an old hat and scarf that belonged to Moses, prompting Delcine to claim it looked just like him. But Jenny was in love too, and to her there was only one man the snowman resembled. She wondered where he was now and if he thought of her, as she thought of him.

Far away in the Black Hills of the Dakota Territory, the subject of Jenny's thoughts tossed the remains of his coffee into the campfire and held his hands out to the inviting heat of the blaze. He glanced about warily, for even though he and his brothers had chosen their hiding place well, he still could not bring himself to relax his vigil. The gulch that surrounded them was secure enough, and Luke was certain no Pinkerton detective had followed them to this place, but that knowledge did not lessen his worry. Rather, it increased it. The Black Hills belonged to the Sioux Indians, and they didn't take kindly to trespassers.

"What a hell of a way to spend Christmas," he remarked wryly, voicing aloud the thought shared by all five Morgan brothers.

"Yeah. Ain't it just!" Raiford put in glumly, wondering if Emmalou Ivey had found someone else to squire her to the holiday festivities that were no doubt being held in Powder Springs.

"It's a downright shame we couldn't get home," Tobias said. "I'll bet it's just about broken Ma's heart—to say nothing of how the rest of the womenfolk feel, and the kids."

The others mournfully agreed, but there was nothing any of them could do about it. Luke, standing a little way apart from the rest, crossed his arms over his chest and chafed them briskly against the dreadful cold.

Goddamn all Pinkerton agents to hell and back! This would have been his first Christmas with Jenny—and he had missed it! Luke's fingers itched to wring the neck of the detective who, like a bloodhound, had dogged the Morgans' tracks ever since they'd made good their escape from Tumbling Creek. So far the brothers had managed to find out little more about the man than his name, Gus Grissom, and the fact that he was damned good at his job, being relentless in his pursuit of them. Twice they had attempted to ambush him, but the wary agent had not fallen into the traps they'd set for him.

Luke's mouth tightened grimly at the thought. Just now, he would have given anything to be sitting at home with Jenny, his past washed clean, as though it had never been, so he needn't run and hide like an animal from men like Gus Grissom, men who hunted him ceaselessly, as others stalked game.

What was Jenny doing now? Luke wondered. Teaching school, no doubt. Damn! What a wonderful time they'd had at the church's fall social and bazaar. She had started to thaw toward him then; Luke knew she had. It made him angry to think he'd been unable to follow up on that to soften her a little more. Instead he'd been forced to flee from town. If he'd stayed, he would have been able to press his attentions on Jenny, to call on her, to court her properly, and perhaps he would have succeeded in winning her heart.

Now doubtless by the time he got back to Tumbling Creek—if he ever did—she would have hardened herself against him once more, and he would have to start all over. It was enough to make a man want to tear his hair out by the roots!

Why had he ever become an outlaw? Luke wondered. He had been reared to respect law and order, not to flout them. What had so changed him and his brothers? Luke didn't know, but they had taken to living by the gun—and perhaps would die by it.

The war had affected them all; he knew that. Certainly the horrendous raid on Lawrence had been the turning point in his life, the fork in the road where he had gone left instead of right. He thought back to that day, remembering, wondering how things might have been if he hadn't ridden out of town with Colonel Quantrill—and kept on riding long after his commanding officer had met his death in Tennessee. . . .

Chapter Nineteen

Lawrence, Kansas, 1863

Gazing at his short, slender frame, his sharp, pale grey-blue eyes that looked as though they were used to keeping a close watch on a roomful of unruly youngsters, one might easily have guessed that before the war Colonel William Clarke Quantrill had been a schoolteacher. But no one, Luke mused as he studied his commanding officer speculatively, would believe the man was now the leader of a guerrilla band of soldiers irregularly attached to the Confederate Army. No, one had to know Quantrill and his past to understand how he had come to be in charge of the four hundred and fifty men who rode behind him, their horses kicking up a cloud of dust as they galloped across Missouri toward the Kansas border.

Despite his deceptive build, Quantrill was tough and wiry and clever too. He hadn't always been a schoolteacher. At one time he'd earned his living as a professional gambler, and the expressionless face and nerves of steel that had once stood him in such good stead at the poker table now served him just as well in dealing with his men. Fond of hunting, he was a crack shot besides, and few in his rowdy bunch could touch his expertise with both a pistol and rifle.

While living in Lawrence with John Sarcoxie, the son of Chief Sarcoxie of the Delaware Indians, Quantrill had used the alias Charlie Hart, and had further honed the skills that had allowed him to gain control of those who followed him. Easily bored, he had taken to frequenting the North Ferry Landing, a gathering place for loiterers, drifters, troublemakers, and outright criminals. There he had fallen in with a gang of border ruffians who for the reward money had tracked down runaway slaves and returned them to their Missourian owners. All the while Quantrill had managed to maintain his abolitionist facade among the strongly antislavery citizens of Lawrence, who'd learned nothing of his covert escapades until he'd been arrested and indicted for them. He'd escaped before his trial, however, and, thumbing his nose at the law, had fled from town.

Luke, after considering all this, thought perhaps Quantrill's authority was not so incomprehensible after all. Unruly youngsters often grew up to be wild, dangerous men who, like children, needed a stern eye and hand to discipline them. The former schoolteacher had both, as those who'd attempted to cross him had soon learned—much to their misfortune.

Now, three years later, Quantrill was leading his loosely knit band of marauders back into Lawrence, the stronghold of the Free State of Kansas.

Fifteen days ago more than two hundred men had been killed in Missouri by Union renegades. Sometime later a group of women associated with various of Quantrill's men had been arrested by General Thomas Ewing, a Federal commander headquartered in Kansas City. Rumor claimed the women had been suspected of being Rebel spies and had been wanted for questioning. Before they could be interrogated, however, the decrepit old building on Grand Avenue that had served as their jail had collapsed during a storm, an unfortunate accident that had killed several persons. Three of the victims had been sisters of Bloody Bill Anderson, Quantrill's right-hand man.

For these two incidents, among others, the notorious Bushwhackers, as the guerrillas were known to their enemies, intended to exact the South's revenge.

Lawrence was their target because it was the primary headquarters of the Kansas Jayhawkers, those Northern sympathizers who were, in reality, little more than highly disorganized hoodlums using politics as their excuse to commit unpardonable crimes and mayhem across the Missouri border. Besides being the main mustering point for the Red Legs, as the Jayhawkers were also called, Lawrence was the place from which they disposed of the property they'd stolen. In charge of all these operations were General Jim Lane and his cohorts Jennison and Montgomery, among others.

Quantrill's Raiders, as they were later to be known, meant to kill General Lane and as many of his men as they could in the attack upon the town.

As they neared the Kansas border Luke's hands tightened upon the reins of his big chestnut stallion, Blaze. He glanced over at J.R., who was deep in conversation with Frank James and Coleman and Jim Younger.

Frank didn't look too happy, but Luke knew this had nothing to do with the forthcoming assault. Frank was mad because his hotheaded brother, fifteen-year-old Jesse, had not been allowed to come with them. Luke didn't understand why Frank was so upset. It was not as though Jesse had been singled out for insult. Quantrill had ordered all the new recruits to stay behind in Missouri. Raiford and Billy Clay were cooling their heels at home as well, and frankly Luke was glad. Raiford was as wild as Jesse James, and Billy Clay had a mouth that didn't know when to shut up. Both of them often irritated Luke.

"Hey, J.R.," he hallooed, smiling wryly as all four of the men turned in their saddles to look back at him. "How much longer before we can take a break?"

J.R. squinted his eyes against the glare of the scorching afternoon sun and the gritty dirt being stirred up by the horses.

"Another mile, maybe," he grunted, then turned to resume his conversation with Frank James and the Youngers.

Luke swore under his breath. It was hot enough to fry eggs on a rock, and his mouth was parched and tasting of sand, despite the red bandanna he had wrapped about his face. Sweat was streaming down his neck and back, and his shirt was plastered to his shoulder blades. He longed for a cool drink from his canteen and for a moment considered dropping out of the cavalcade to quench his thirst. But he didn't want to listen to J.R.'s sharp comments about his disorderly behavior if he did so, to say nothing of the public dressing-down he might receive if Quantrill spied him, which was most likely, since the colonel didn't miss a trick. So Luke clenched his teeth and pressed on. Unlike some of the others, who appeared nigh to fainting in their saddles, he could last another mile without difficulty. But that didn't mean he had to like it.

He muttered irritably to himself again, staring hard at Quantrill's back.

Tobias, who rode at his side, peered at him owlishly, his spectacles glinting in the light.

"Better not let the colonel hear you say that," he chided. "He's liable to kick your carcass into next week."

"Well, it's the truth," Luke retorted, not in the least abashed. "He acts like we're a bunch of cattle or something, for Christ's sake! I'm surprised he isn't back there flogging those stragglers into line." He jerked his thumb toward the tail end of the troop, where a few of the newer men lagged behind, unaccustomed to the smart pace Quantrill set.

"Don't worry," Tobias droned dryly. "The colonel will whip them into shape fast enough, once we reach the border. Those who don't toe the mark will get their marching papers quicker than you can blink; you wait and see. There isn't room for any slackers on this mission."

"You kin say that agin!" another man, Larkin Skaggs, asserted as he rode up to join them. "The colonel jest gave the word. 'Look lively or git! This here's a raid, not a friggin' tea party!' "

Luke snorted with disgust. He didn't like Skaggs, a brutal thief and killer who would shoot his own mother for a few pennies. Not even deigning to speak to the man, Luke set his spurs to Blaze's sides and galloped on ahead. Skaggs's eyes sparked dangerously at the insult.

"What in the hell's eatin' him?" he snarled to Tobias, his face mean and surly. "He acted like he smelt sumpin' not fit fer his purty nose."

Tobias smiled enigmatically.

"I reckon it was you, Larkin," he drawled before he too urged his horse forward through the crowd of mounted men.

Skaggs cursed them both soundly as he watched them go, but he made no move to ride after the two brothers, as he normally would have done, in order to extract forcibly an apology from them. Luke was as rapid and deadly as a rattlesnake with the Navy Colts he carried, and Tobias's talent for handling explosives was already legendary. Skaggs didn't much relish the idea of being gunned down like an animal, should he dare to challenge Luke, or of being blown to kingdom come, should Tobias happen to take offense. Besides, the Morgans hung together, and if he started a fight with one of them, he'd have all five of the brothers breathing down his neck. The oldest three might practice a little restraint under Quantrill's cold eye, but Raiford was an absolute maniac. There was no telling what he might do, and Billy Clay was just fool enough to go along with him.

Irately Skaggs spat in the dust, then cantered on down the line to pass along the colonel's orders to those who had better learn to keep up —or else!

It was midafternoon when, near Aubrey, Quantrill and his raiders crossed the border from Missouri into Kansas. By then the day was sweltering and tempers were short. The colonel, realizing his men were perilously close to fighting among themselves, shouted the command to halt.

"We're in Kansas now, men," he noted for the benefit of those who hadn't as yet made any forays into the state.

" 'Bout time, Colonel!" someone hollered from the back.

A wave of laughter and a few low cheers rippled through the ranks. Quantrill frowned.

"We'll rest here for the time being," he continued as though there hadn't been any interruption. "Then we'll press on. We ought to reach Lawrence by dawn tomorrow." He turned to one of his officers. "Lieutenant Gregg."

"Yessir?"

"Find these men for me." Quantrill handed him a list of names. "I want to see them."

"Yessir. Right away, Colonel."

While Quantrill was relaying instructions to the spies he intended to send into Lawrence ahead of the rest of the soldiers, Luke was busy drenching himself with water from his canteen.

As the liquid dripped slowly down his golden, sun-streaked hair, soaking his shirt, he sighed with relief. Then with his bandanna he wiped his face and the back of his neck. After that he took a long swig from the container, savoring the cool drink as it trickled down his throat. He yearned for another but reluctantly recapped the canteen, knowing the water would make him sick if he drank too much of it in the searing heat. He hung the container over his saddle horn, then sat down upon a nearby rock to roll himself a cigarette.

Carefully he sprinkled a bit of tobacco from his pouch onto the paper, deftly curling one edge over and licking it to seal it shut. He lit up and inhaled deeply, watching silently as Coleman Younger slowly approached him.

Luke grinned. Though Cole was fast becoming Frank James's best friend, even he must have gotten tired of listening to Frank bitch about Jesse being left in Missouri.

"Jesus, it's roasting," Cole observed unnecessarily as he sank down beside Luke. "I reckon now I know how a turkey feels on Thanksgiving."

The redheaded Cole was always "reckoning" something. Those who knew him claimed they could distinguish his voice in the dark by that one word.

"Yeah," Luke said. "There isn't anything worse than Kansas in August. Sometimes I believe it's the devil's own playground."

Cole laughed shortly.

"Those frigging Jayhawkers sure are going to think so, once we get through with them! I've never seen the colonel so riled up."

"Me neither," Luke confessed. "But, then, it isn't every day those damned Red Legs kill two hundred of our men—to say nothing of the women buried alive when that building collapsed."

"That was an accident, Luke," Cole pointed out.

"I know it was, but try telling that to the others." Luke indicated the rest of the men milling about the temporary camp. "Some of them lost their sweethearts in that cave-in. Besides, it never would have happened in the first place if the Kansas City authorities hadn't arrested the women—or at least had put them in a better jail. Someone must have known that rickety old building wasn't safe."

"Probably," Cole commented. "Well, war is hell. I'll be glad when it's all over."

"What're you going to do then?" Luke inquired curiously, for it was a question he'd often asked himself and to which he had no real answer.

Cole shrugged, then smiled ruefully.

"Keep on being a rebel, I reckon. I don't know much else."

"Neither do I, Cole," Luke remarked thoughtfully as he dragged on his cigarette. "Neither do I."

Captain J. A. Pike of the Ninth Kansas Volunteers, Company K, glanced up irritably at the sound of a commotion just outside his door. What the devil was going on? Whoever dared to interrupt his early supper had better have a damned good reason for doing so!

"Yes, Sergeant, what is it?" he barked curtly as the intruder opened the door and presented himself.

"I'm sorry to disturb you, sir, but I thought you should know a large command has been spotted about a half a mile away from the post," the anxious officer explained.

"Confederates?" Pike questioned sharply, one eyebrow raised.

"We don't know, sir. They're not in uniform."

"How many are there?"

"Four—maybe five—hundred."

Alarmed, the captain stood, tossing his napkin down upon his half-empty plate. He didn't have nearly enough soldiers to combat such a huge force, and he didn't like the odds. Still he knew the unidentified troop was not part of the regular Union Army. He would have been informed about it otherwise.

"Sound the call to arms, Sergeant," he directed at last, deciding to investigate the matter, regardless of his lack of men. "Let's go take a look."

Luke's eyes narrowed intently as he studied the blue-uniformed Federals lining up into neat columns on the prairie in the distance. His muscles tightened. His blood raced with excitement. Were they going to fight?

"Make no attack unless fired upon!" Quantrill's order was shouted back along the ranks. "Make no attack unless fired upon!"

Captain Pike was too far away to hear the words, but it was clear to him that the far-off cavalcade meant to take no hostile action against his small post. Vastly relieved, he himself made no attempt to engage arms, justifying his decision on the grounds that he was still unsure about the identity of the unfamiliar band. Dyed cloth was scarce and expensive; many soldiers were having to make do with the butternut-hued homespun in which the passing men were clothed. For all Pike knew, they were an irregular outfit attached to the Union Army, and he certainly didn't want to open fire on them, then discover he'd made a terrible mistake.

"It appears as though they're heading toward Olathe or Lawrence," he mused aloud. "Private," he called to one of his new recruits, who ran forward hastily and snappily saluted, "take a horse, and get over to the next post on the double. Alert the commander there about what we've seen. Maybe he'll know who those men are and whether or not we need have any cause for concern about them."

"Yessir, Captain."

The young private, like so many other nameless, faceless soldiers who form the rank and file of an army, was impatient for advancement and eager for recognition. He was also unused to the ungodly heat of a Kansas August, during which the more astute natives would no more have thought of galloping a horse at breakneck speed over several miles of rough, rolling terrain than they would have dreamed of fouling their only water hole. The private pushed his hard-laboring mount through the Flint Hills until it was foaming at the mouth, gasping for breath, and drenched with lather. At last, unable to go any farther, it collapsed and died.

It was over two hours before the private, on foot, managed to reach the next post, only to find it was as understaffed and uninformed as his own. Its commander sent messengers to both Fort Leavenworth and Fort Riley, but by then it was too late.

Dawn was breaking over Lawrence, and Quantrill and his guerrillas were waiting just outside of town.

Quantrill smirked cruelly to himself as he listened to the reports being delivered to him by Lieutenant William H. Gregg, who, along with five other men, had been sent ahead last night to scout out the surrounding area and to make sure the town had not been warned of their approach. It was now clear to Quantrill that the sacking of Lawrence would be as easy as shooting sheep in a pen.

The town's only defense consisted of the Fourteenth Kansas Cavalry, an ill-organized bunch of green recruits, most of whom were stationed on the other side of the Kaw River; and the Second Colored Regiment, a group of runaway slaves who could scarcely be considered soldiers. In addition to this, the mayor of Lawrence, Brigadier General George W. Collamore, had foolishly decreed that all the town's guns and ammunition be kept locked up in a central arsenal, so few of the citizens were armed.

"Gather around, men"—Quantrill motioned to his officers—"and listen up. These are your objectives," he explained as he distributed hand-drawn maps of Lawrence, which had been divided into sections with designated targets clearly marked. "I want guards posted on every road leading out of town and the ferry linking Lawrence to the military post across the Kaw cut off. No one is to escape. Kill every man you see, including the young 'uns. Remember: Today's drummer boy is tomorrow's soldier, and some troops are so desperate for recruits that they're taking them at fourteen now. Try to get the men on those lists first, however; they're the ones we really want.

"Make sure you don't harm any women; we're Southern gentlemen—not rapists. And don't murder any kids; we're not baby killers either. That's all. Now mount up and let's ride!"

It was five o'clock in the morning and the sun was just peeking over the horizon when the Bushwhackers entered Lawrence. They were a fearsome sight as quietly they penetrated the outskirts of town, coming from the south, boldly trotting up the main street, Massachusetts Avenue. Quantrill, at the head of the column, was on his favorite sorrel. Beside him were Bloody Bill Anderson, the bridle of his horse adorned by scalps he'd taken in the past, and George Todd, muttering under his breath about what he intended to do to Lawrence's "damned nigger stealers."

All was still, for most of the residents were yet asleep—unaware this day would be their last.

Luke shivered a little at the thought, for he did not enjoy killing, especially when the victims were helpless and unsuspecting. Then he reminded himself that the two hundred Missourians murdered fifteen days ago by these Union renegades had had no warning of their fates either, and his resolve hardened.

Just before Quantrill and his men reached Lawrence's business section, the colonel fired a single shot. This was the signal for a separate detachment to begin murdering several Federals who, for lack of better accommodations, were slumbering on the front porches of various houses on Berley Street.

Almost simultaneously the main body of the force reached a large clearing where numerous tents had been erected. This was the camp of the Second Colored Regiment. The Negroes who composed its ranks never had a chance. Within minutes they were all set upon by the Confederate marauders, who worked swiftly to silence any alarm that might otherwise have been raised.

Then, shrieking the wild Rebel yell for which the South was infamous, Quantrill and William Gregg charged down the street, the colonel firing left and the lieutenant firing right. The rampage had begun in earnest.

It was a morning Luke was to recall in vivid detail for the rest of his life, for never again was he to see such frenzied carnage as he saw that day.

Before the town's residents became aware of what was happening, the band spread rapidly through Lawrence, dragging its citizens from their beds and shooting many of them in cold blood.

During the first wave of the brutal onslaught, a squad of soldiers headed for the mayor's house, planning to take him prisoner. After kicking in his front door they caught his terrified wife, and, despite Quantrill's orders to the contrary, after she untruthfully informed them that her husband wasn't home, they beat her up and threatened to kill her if she didn't reveal his whereabouts to them. Brigadier General Collamore, impervious to his wife's screams of terror, climbed out a back window and, together with a neighbor, Pat Keefe, who was crouched behind some bushes in the back yard, hid in the well under the house. There the two men were overcome by poisonous gases and were asphyxiated, as was a third friend, Captain J. G. Lowe, who went down after them minutes later.

The raiders, ignorant of the mayor's fate and incensed by his escape, set fire to his house. Then, with the raucous cry of "Yip-Yip-Yaw" that was to become the trademark of Quantrill's followers, they galloped after the colonel.

By the time they were assembled in front of the Eldridge Hotel, which Quantrill initially intended to use as his headquarters, Captain A. R. Banks, the provost marshal of Kansas, was already standing on the balcony, waving a white bed sheet that served as a flag of surrender.

After robbing all the building's inhabitants Quantrill acceded to their demand that they be taken prisoner and sent them under heavy guard to the City Hotel, which was run by Nathan Stone, a man who'd often befriended the colonel when he'd lived in Lawrence. Quantrill then ordered the Eldridge Hotel to be torched and set up his headquarters at his old friend's establishment. There the colonel discovered a relative of Nathan's, Miss Lydia Stone, in tears over the loss of her diamond ring, which had been stolen from her by one of the guerrillas. Her description of the thief fit Larkin Skaggs. Since the ring had been a gift to the woman from Quantrill after she'd nursed him through a debilitating illness, he was infuriated by its theft.

"Captain Morgan," he tersely addressed Luke, who stood nearby, awaiting instructions, "find Larkin Skaggs, and escort him here personally. I want Miss Lydia's ring returned immediately."

"Yessir, Colonel."

Luke saluted smartly. Then, dodging bullets as he opened the door, he ran outside to attempt to locate Skaggs.

Last night had brought no relief from the heat, and, now that dawn had broken, the air was positively stifling. It was so hot and humid that Luke could scarcely breathe as he urged Blaze through the horrifying melee that now choked the panic-filled streets. Adding to his sense of impending suffocation was the fact that the town arsenal had fallen in the first wave of the attack, and acrid smoke from the subsequent explosions and fires hung in a black cloud over Lawrence. Luke smiled grimly to himself. Tobias was doing his job well, it seemed. His eyes watering, his lungs burning, Luke scanned the crazed throng, searching for some sign of Skaggs, but the man was not to be found.

Luke reached into his breast pocket for the map of Lawrence that Quantrill had given him earlier. Perhaps from it he would be able to determine Skaggs's whereabouts. His red-rimmed eyes still blurring from the smoke, Luke peered down at the paper. Its lines and names wavered before him, but finally he managed to make them out. Cursing, he refolded the map. Skaggs's detachment was clear on the other side of town, and even that didn't mean Skaggs was with it. The man was notorious for disobeying orders.

Luke nudged Blaze forward, reins between his teeth, pistols drawn and ready to shoot, if necessary. But, amazingly enough, he was largely ignored as he made his way through the cacophony and confusion.

It was insane, he thought. Men were being gunned down right and left, and yet no one paid any attention to him. They had all gone stark, raving mad. Luke saw one man shot at point-blank range in the doorway of his own home. His murderer, still lusting for blood, kept right on pumping bullets into the man's body. A few moments later, whooping wildly, the killer noticed the brand new boots the corpse was wearing and began to tug them from the dead man's feet.

Everywhere Luke looked the story was the same. The male citizens of Lawrence were being marched out of their homes at gunpoint and shot. Even worse was the sight of several helpless men, their hands tied behind their backs, being flung into the red-hot conflagration rapidly consuming the town. Here and there the human torches staggered from the flames, only to be shoved back in by the drunken Bushwhackers, who, having broken into the saloons, were now beyond all mercy or reason.

As though out of their minds with fever, the Rebels smashed out shop windows and kicked in front doors, looting stores and houses indiscriminately of their contents, then burning the buildings to the ground.

Women were crying and screaming hysterically as they tried to save their belongings or to reach their husbands' dead bodies, only to be forced back by Quantrill's men. Children were bawling with terror. Luke saw a murdered youth lying in the street, his corpse riddled with bullets. The boy couldn't have been more than eleven years old.

Luke's stomach roiled. This savage butchery was not revenge; it was a nightmare.

"Luke! Luke Morgan!"

As he heard his name called above the din, Luke turned in the saddle, his eyes raking the row of houses from which the shout had come. Incredibly he spied Coleman Younger trying to shove a large piano through an open doorway. Nearby, an anxious-looking woman stood, wringing her hands as she mutely regarded the licking tongues of orange engulfing her home.

"Reckon you could get down off your horse and give me a hand here?" Cole asked as Luke rode into the yard.

"Jesus!" Luke swore. "Have you gone crazy, Cole?"

"Yeah, all this killing has just about driven me insane. I've done my share of it; don't misunderstand me. But, for God's sake, Luke! Enough is enough! I ain't cut out for murdering women and kids—or for leaving them without a roof over their heads. Do you know some asshole actually made this poor lady set fire to her own house? Christ! I just can't believe it. Now are you going to help me get her piano out of here or not?"

Luke was highly gratified to find someone else who felt as he did, and, temporarily postponing the matter of Larkin Skaggs, he dismounted to assist Cole with the heavy instrument. Unfortunately even he and Cole together couldn't budge it. They did, however, manage to salvage a few other pieces of the woman's furniture, which they stacked in a vacant lot by her house. There the weeds were waist-high and made walking difficult. Luke, heading back toward the yard, tripped and fell over a rolled-up carpet concealed by the tall prairie grass. As he did so, much to his surprise, the rug gave a loud groan of pain.

"Oh, my! Are you hurt?" the woman, Mrs. Fisher, exclaimed, her voice unnaturally shrill as nervously she ran to help Luke up.

Her eyes strayed worriedly to the lump now plainly visible in the middle of the carpet, and almost pathetically she attempted to hide it with her skirts.

"No, ma'am." Luke got to his feet and brushed himself off. "But I'm afraid your rug may be. Why don't you check and see while Cole and I stand guard," he went on noncommittally. "I'm sure it's a very valuable carpet, and we don't want anything to happen to it, do we, Cole?"

"No, we don't," Cole assented, meeting Luke's gaze squarely.

Mrs. Fisher's eyes filled with tears of understanding and relief as she looked at the two men.

"What are your names?" she inquired, her voice quivering with emotion.

"Luke Morgan, ma'am."

"Coleman Younger."

"My husband—the Reverend Fisher—and I thank you for his life. We will remember your kindness and pray for you always."

"That's right nice of you, ma'am." Luke cleared his throat awkwardly, suddenly embarrassed and ashamed of himself in light of the woman's fear of him and her overwhelming gratitude now that she knew he didn't mean to murder her husband, who was concealed in the rug. "Well, I guess I'd better be on my way. Cole, you haven't seen Larkin Skaggs by any chance, have you? Quantrill wants him. He stole a ring from Miss Lydia Stone, and the colonel's madder than hell about it."

"Yeah, I saw the bastard. He was robbing a kid. A kid, goddamn it!

The boy only had a dime, and Skaggs killed him for it. Then he threw the boy's little brother into a blazing building."

Luke closed his eyes, remembering the bullet-ridden corpse of the eleven-year-old youngster he'd seen.

"Thanks, Cole," he said, his mouth tightening with anger as he swung up into his saddle. "Be seeing you."

Shortly thereafter Luke spied Skaggs and several other men racing down a side street. Setting his spurs to Blaze's sides, Luke galloped after them, reining the horse in sharply as he watched them barge into one of the houses that lined the avenue. Quickly he dismounted and went inside. There he discovered Skaggs holding his gun on three terrified females.

"Where are you hidin' him, bitch?" Skaggs demanded of one of them, his voice ugly, as Luke pushed his way through the group of men. "We know he's in here; we saw him come in. Now where is he? You'd better start talkin', you stupid slut, or I'm gonna beat it outta you."

"I don't know to whom you're referring," the woman, Mrs. Reynolds, insisted bravely, one hand at her throat, as though to ward off the wickedness that emanated from Skaggs. "My husband, Doctor Reynolds, is out of town. There's no one here but me, these other two ladies, and my husband's aunt." She indicated a fourth figure Luke had not previously noticed. "Now, please," she continued, her voice tremulous, "go away, and leave us alone. As you can see, my husband's aunt is not at all well."

The old lady under discussion was sitting in a wheelchair, her morning bonnet slightly askew, her lace shawl stretched tightly across her shoulders and flat bosom. She did indeed appear quite pale and ill. Beside her, on a table, sat a disorderly assortment of medicine bottles and spoons. Luke's glance passed over them disinterestedly before suddenly he realized all the bottles were full and the spoons were clean. He stared harder at the old lady and with difficulty suppressed the grin of admiration for the enterprising three women that started to curve on his lips as he noted the faintest shadow of a beard on the "aunt's" face. Luke would have staked his life on the fact that the old lady was, in reality, the good doctor himself or one of his friends.

"Skaggs," Luke drawled, breaking the tense atmosphere in the room, "the colonel wants to see you. Now! And you'd better pray you haven't lost Miss Lydia Stone's diamond ring in all the ruckus, because it was a personal gift to her from Quantrill himself, and he isn't too happy about you stealing it. Next time you rob somebody, you'd better make damned sure they aren't friends of the colonel's—or defenseless kids."

He rested his hands lightly, almost casually on his Navy Colts, his eyes hard.

"Shove it, Morgan! These four hussies are hidin' a man in here somewhere, and I aim to find him. You tell Quantrill I'll be along in a minute."

"Not a chance," Luke uttered softly. "The colonel ordered me personally to escort you back to the City Hotel, and that's just what I intend to do—one way or another."

Skaggs's eyes narrowed as he contemplated Luke intently. The wheels in Skaggs's brain churned furiously. Ominously he scowled. His pistol was already in his hand; Luke's guns were still in his tied-down holsters. The son of a bitch! Who in the hell did he think he was anyway? Skaggs pondered the question wrathfully. He ought to shoot the insolent bastard right now. Surely even Luke Morgan wasn't that fast.

"You want to bet your life on it?" Luke queried mockingly, his voice low.

A strange shiver of fear ran up Skaggs's spine at the words. Why, it was as though Luke had read his mind! Nervously Skaggs licked his lips, then slowly he returned his revolver to its holster.

"Let's go, boys," he growled to the rest of the men. "We kin take care of these whores later." He glared evilly at the frightened women, mentally marking their faces so he would know them again.

Then, muttering further obscenities not fit for ladies' ears, he and the others left the house. Luke, smiling, tipped his hat politely to the three females, who were slowly exhaling with visible relief.

"My compliments, ladies, and to you, sir." Luke nodded to the figure in the wheelchair.

Then without another word he too departed, his spurs jangling as he swaggered toward the door.

Back at the City Hotel, Luke found Quantrill mounted up, ready to ride, and issuing orders to his officers to round up the rest of the band as soon as possible. Those men who refused to comply with the command to cease battle were to be left behind to the mercy of the Union forces that were even now thundering at breakneck speed toward Lawrence.

Eventually the Bushwhackers assembled and began to head toward the outskirts of town.

Larkin Skaggs, enraged over having to return the ring he'd stolen, waited until Quantrill was well down the road before breaking away from the cavalcade and returning to the City Hotel. Once there, Skaggs, jeering menacingly at Miss Lydia Stone, shot and mortally wounded her relative, Nathan, before anyone could stop him. But a small boy with a rifle, the brother of the two youths Skaggs had murdered earlier for ten cents, managed to nick him with a bullet, causing him to sway perilously in his saddle. As he finally lost his balance and toppled from his horse, a Delaware Indian killed him and with a shout of glee hacked away his scalp amid the loud, unnatural cheers of the gathered townspeople who were still alive.

The marauders paused only once before leaving Lawrence. At the home of General Jim Lane, who, though the primary object of the Rebels' attack, had somehow miraculously managed to escape, the troop drew to a halt.

Quantrill's blue eyes glittered coldly as they raked Mrs. Lane, who had bravely stepped outside to greet them. Her bearing proud and triumphant, she returned the colonel's ravaging gaze unflinchingly.

"Give your husband my compliments, madam," Quantrill sneered icily, longing to wipe from her face the victorious smile that curved upon her lips, "and tell him I should be most happy to meet him."

"That I will do, sir," she returned just as coolly, then added tauntingly, "I am sorry it was not convenient for him to meet you this morning."

The colonel's mouth thinned with ire. Sharply he gave the order to ride on. The Confederates broke into a gallop, leaving the devastated town behind. They had killed one hundred and eighty-five men that day and destroyed one hundred and fifty-four of the best buildings in Lawrence at a property loss of one and a half million dollars.

It was just shortly after noon.

Striking south, the guerrillas crossed the Wakarusa River by way of Blanton's Bridge. Then after passing through Prairie City they retreated to the safety of the Sni Hills in Missouri. In the process several of Quantrill's soldiers were cut down and scalped by the Delaware Indians who hounded their heels in relentless pursuit. Others, too wounded to keep up, were callously left behind to be killed by the vengeful Federals who followed. Four raiders were captured and, near the small town of Lone Jack, hanged. A sign warning "Don't cut them down!" was tied to the corpses.

Two years later the war was over and Colonel William Clarke Quantrill was dead. But Luke and his brothers—and others like them—kept right on riding and by doing so firmly planted their feet upon the road to outlawry.

Chapter Twenty

The Black Hills, Dakota Territory, 1870

The cold sting of snow against his face returned Luke to the present. It had been summer in his mind and scorching. The snow that fell now was light, but he could tell by the darkening of the sky that the worst was yet to come. He and his brothers must find some sort of shelter—quickly.

Sharing each others' thoughts from long experience, the Morgans silently doused their campfire, gathered up their supplies, and rolled up their saddle packs. Then they mounted their horses and began to retreat even farther into the Black Hills.

It was unlikely that they would be attacked by a band of Sioux Indians in this weather, but still the brothers kept a sharp eye out. It was better to be overly cautious than less so. Besides, even though they had seen no sign of the Pinkerton detective dogging their tracks and they believed he'd given up the chase at last, there was always the chance that he was still following them. From what little they had seen and guessed of him, he appeared to be a relentless sort.

It was bitterly cold because of the wind, which whipped through the hills unmercifully, each gust seeming to jab a hundred stinging needles into the Morgans' bodies. Several times they were forced to pause, dismount, and hold their gloved hands over their horses' noses so the frozen nostrils of the animals would thaw and they could breathe freely once more.

As the brothers rode on in silence, for it was almost impossible to be heard now above the roar of the gale, Luke wondered again why he had ever ridden on with Colonel Quantrill that fateful day at Lawrence. As so many other men had done Luke could have returned home instead, could have mended the torn fabric of his life, finished his study of the law, and gone into politics as he had planned. Why had he not?

He had loved Maybelle once. Only gradually, during the war and afterward, had he come to see the selfish, grasping nature beneath her beauty. Still he had wanted her. He had not known, then, of her numerous infidelities with the enemy in his absence. No one in Tumbling Creek had dared to tell him, at first because he was a soldier fighting a bloody war and they had not wanted to add to his burdens. Later, they'd been afraid of his temper and his skill with his powerful Navy Colts. Only J.R. and Tobias had hinted of Maybelle's betrayal. But Luke had not believed them, and the three brothers had come to blows, nearly destroying their relationship before J.R. and Tobias had apologized and, shrugging, let the matter drop.

Still it had been obvious to Luke that his brothers had scorned his wife, and a seed of doubt about her had been planted in his mind to germinate and grow. He had taken to spying on Maybelle, and finally he had discovered the terrible truth about her. When he'd confronted her with her sordid behavior, she'd faced him, undaunted, smiling derisively, though a flicker of fear had lain deep in her eyes. Enraged, he'd struck her across her lovely, laughing face, but she'd only gone on mocking him, had actually dared him to beat her for her sins. Sick and disgusted, he'd turned away, his love and desire for her tasting like ashes in his mouth.

By then the war had ended and the Yankees had been everywhere, grabbing control of the South, raising property taxes to drive the Rebels from their land and putting darkies in their places. So one night when J.R., grim-faced, had slammed his fist down hard upon a table and sworn he wasn't going to take it anymore, the rest of his brothers had not hesitated to agree to his plan to rob a Northern bank. They'd managed to save their farms, but by then the excitement of outlaw life had been in their blood and they'd gone on with their private war against Yankee "law and order."

In some dim corner of his mind Luke had known nothing but a rope or a bullet lay ahead on the path he and his brothers had chosen. But, like all criminals, he'd told himself they would not be caught, and once they had enough money to set themselves up for life, they would cease their lawless activities—with none the wiser about their past.

Luke had wanted desperately to make something of himself, to prove to Maybelle that she was wrong about him being a nobody with nothing to offer her. He'd hoarded his share of stolen loot like a miser, intending to build the big house his wife wanted and then refuse to allow her to set foot in it. When she came to him on her knees, he'd planned to scorn her—as she had him.

But Maybelle had not waited for Luke's plans to come to fruition. She had abandoned him and their children instead, had run away with another man and made Luke a laughingstock. When notified of her death in a Saint Louis brothel, he'd felt cheated of his revenge, and some all-consuming desire to have the last word had caused him to bring her body home and to bury her on his small farm, which she'd so despised.

Now he bitterly regretted his past. This was no life for a man, being hunted like an animal, forced to run and hide, to live off the land, to take what could be had and move on, though he was hungry and thirsty, sweltering or freezing, and tired, oh, so tired. Luke wanted to settle down, to spend time with his children, and, most of all, to have Jenny by his side—forever. Somehow he must find a way to put his life right and make her his wife, even if it meant turning himself in and standing trial for his crimes.

Luke set his jaw in a hard, determined line. When he got home—*if* he got home—he would mend his errant ways and win Jenny's hand and heart. That was what was important now.

He willed his numb fingers to keep hold of the reins, his bone-weary body to remain in the saddle. Jenny's face loomed before him, beckoning him on, and somehow he found the strength to urge Blaze forward through the falling snow.

Chapter Twenty-one

Tumbling Creek, Missouri, 1871

The snow that had lain thick and white upon the fallow ground was melting now as with the coming of spring each day the sun shone more strongly, its glowing rays of golden warmth gradually dissipating the grey of the winter sky until a pale, pale blue stretched endlessly above the far horizon. Here and there patches of damp dark earth showed upon the surface of the land. The muddy spots squished beneath Jenny's boots as she took once more to walking the winding path that led to the schoolhouse. Presently the first green shoots of new awakening sprouted. Early flowers budded, then bloomed, daring to brave the frost that yet remained, a reminder of winter's enveloping shroud of silence.

Birds began tentatively to twitter, softly at first, as though afraid to break the stillness of the woods, then louder as the forest was filled with the sounds of groaning branches, shuddering to shake free their icy burdens. The frozen creeks and springs were thawing, ice splitting to let their long-suppressed laughter gurgle forth, and with sharp cracks icicles snapped and fell to the ground, where their pointed crystal shapes grew smaller and smaller, until all that was left were little puddles upon the earth. Water trickled in quiet rivulets down slowly unfurling leaves and evergreen boughs, at each tip forming pools whose droplets dripped with a soft, steady *plop, plop, plop* upon wet grass, spongy moss, and creeping vines below.

Animals crept from their winter hiding places, sniffing the air, their eyes taking in the wonders of spring, their tails twitching. Hesitantly paws and hooves stepped forward, sinking into the earth, leaving deep prints behind as their owners lumbered and bounded this way and that, some hungrily foraging for food, others frolicking with delight at being released from confining lairs.

With the coming of spring there was work to do. Like the beasts of the woods, Jenny took stock of her surroundings. The roof and walls of the cabin must be repaired where they had been damaged by winter storms and snow. Sections of the fence, knocked askew by strong, cruel, whipping winds and heavy drifts, must be mended. Trees must be chopped down and cut into logs to replace those used during the cold months past. The pounding thump of Moses's hammer and the rhythmic pumping of his legs turning the whetstone with a whir as he sharpened his ax filled the air, mingling with the distant noises of the forest.

Jenny caught her breath as, once, after climbing the ladder and edging his way up the wet roof, Moses slipped and nearly fell, and she called a warning for him to be careful.

She and Delcine were busy with the inside of the house, for spring cleaning took a great deal of time. There were cupboards to be emptied of their contents, scrubbed, and restocked; winter clothes and bedding to be carefully folded away, nestled with sweet-smelling sachets inside of Jenny's two cedar-lined trunks, which would keep moths at bay; spring garments and linens to be unpacked and aired; shutters to be opened and hide-covered windows to be washed and dried; furniture to be dusted; rugs to be taken outside and beaten; and floors to be thoroughly swept of mud and dead leaves tracked in during the cold months.

Once all this was accomplished, there was the garden to be hoed to even up the furrows Moses had plowed last fall, and the planting to be done.

Everything seemed so glorious and alive that Jenny and the two Negroes, who had all been born and reared in the deep South and knew little of the seasons farther north, did not recognize the small signs that told the natives of the Ozark Mountains that winter was not done with them yet.

The old-timers, emerging from their shacks in the hills, felt the crisp, chilling bite of the air. They saw the way the new leaves curled and early flowers bent, as though to protect themselves from yet another onslaught of harshness. They noted the faint blue of the sky that did not darken to a deeper azure with the passing days. They observed that the ground hogs had not yet come out of hibernation, that the buzz of insects did not fill the air; and after they had replenished the supply of logs in their wood boxes, they closed the doors of their cabins firmly and, puffing contentedly on their corncob pipes, settled back to wait a little longer before venturing outside.

The farmers began their spring planting, but when the first fruits and vegetables of their gardens took root and put forth growth, they covered the tender young shoots carefully with stout barrel halves at night to protect them from frost, and their eyes scanned the sky worriedly for telltale traces of greying. The winter wheat, emerging in waves of green in the sprawling fields might survive, especially if it were that hard-stemmed variety of Turkish origin, brought to America by Russian Mennonites and planted in the fall. But other seedlings were not so hardy. Tomatoes particularly were prone to freezing.

Jenny knew nothing of this, however, for what was grown in the milder climes of the deep South, provided it did not fall prey to bugs and disease, and the soil was good, generally flourished with abundance, come spring. There sudden cold snaps were few and far between.

So, once the work on the house was finished, she told Moses and Delcine they could hitch Blossom up to the wagon and go into town for supplies.

The morning sky was slightly overcast, but as it was early April, a month when rain was welcome and expected, Jenny and her servants thought nothing of the thick, rolling clouds gathering on the distant horizon. A spring shower was in the offing, that was all, and, though Jenny suggested Moses and Delcine might want to wait until the rain had passed before venturing forth, the two were obviously glad to escape from the confining cabin, where they'd had little privacy during the winter, and were reluctant to postpone the trip into town. Hoping they didn't get too drenched, Jenny waved until they were out of sight. Then she gathered up her satchel and old brown coat, and made her way to the schoolhouse.

She was surprised as she hurried along to notice how dark it had suddenly grown, and she wondered if perhaps she ought to have insisted Moses and Delcine remain at the house. It appeared as though a real thunderstorm were brewing. Anxiously Jenny glanced at the sky. It was a most peculiar shade of grey, she thought, and the clouds that earlier had seemed to promise rain now looked ominous and forbidding, massive and bloated as they were and streaked with sickly wisps of white.

Shivering a little, realizing the temperature had dropped several degrees in as many minutes, Jenny opened the door to the schoolhouse, laid her bag of books and papers on her desk, then set about building a fire in the cast-iron stove. Presently the tinder and kindling caught flame, and after adding a few small logs to the fire, she closed the grate, rubbing her hands briskly to warm them.

Outside, all was hushed and still, as though a thick, muffling blanket had been wrapped about the schoolhouse, enclosing it in a cocoon of silence. Jenny wondered where her students were, for, though it was yet early, usually a few children had arrived by now. But when she looked out of one of the windows that lined both sides of the building, she saw that the schoolyard was empty.

Perplexed, she walked to the vestibule at the front of the edifice, unwound the bellrope from its wooden cleat, and tugged on it several times. The clapper struck the iron bell harshly, causing it to peal forth, but still no one came, and as the last of the ringing died away, Jenny recognized that the wind had come up forcefully and it was doubtful anyone had even heard the bell.

A cold prickle of foreboding suddenly chased down her spine, and, almost running, she scurried down the aisle to the platform at the back of the schoolhouse. There, with the bucket of water that stood on a small table in one corner, she quickly doused the fire in the stove. Then she retrieved her satchel and donned her cloak.

The wind was by now so horrendous it ripped the door of the building from Jenny's hands three times before she managed to shut it firmly, and she was nearly pummeled to her knees by the gale as she descended the stairs, clutching the railing to keep from falling.

Propelled by each unrelenting gust, she raced down the path to the cabin, barely getting inside before the first of the snow flurries started, like a horde of ghosts risen up to terrorize the countryside.

Some primitive instinct warned Jenny this was no ordinary storm, and feverishly, after putting her bag of books and papers in a chair, she rushed back outside, getting as many logs from the woodpile as she could carry. Driven, she made trip after trip, not caring that her body soon grew so numb from cold and exhaustion that she did not even feel the pain when, once, she tripped and fell, scraping her hands and knees on the rough bark of the logs she dropped as she stumbled.

At last, since the snow was now falling heavily and being whipped into blinding eddies by the wind, and the woodpile was virtually depleted anyway, Jenny closed the door of the house. Then she secured the shutters on the windows and laid fires in both the parlor and the kitchen.

After that she sat down to wait, shivering, as she wondered what had become of Moses and Delcine.

* * *

Their ride into town started out pleasantly enough, for, despite the overcast sky, neither Moses nor Delcine much minded being rained on —as long as they were together. They loved Jenny dearly, but being penned up in the cabin with her all winter had not been easy for them. The brief moments of lovemaking they had snatched during the day, when she taught school, had been all too few, for they took pride in their work and had felt guilty about shirking their duties. In the evenings it had been impossible to slip away into the woods for the sweet, stolen hours they'd shared in the fall, for the winter cold and snow had not been conducive to lying on the ground, lost in embrace. Sometimes Delcine had crept into the lean-to at night, sliding into bed next to Moses and drawing warmth from the heat of his body, but this had not been often, for Jenny was a restless sleeper, given to prowling the house at odd hours when slumber eluded her.

Though Moses and Delcine were not ashamed of their relationship, neither did they wish to flaunt it before their mistress, for it would, they felt, hurt her—not because she didn't care for them and wish them every happiness, but because she was lonely, and their being a couple would make her feel even more excluded and alone. For this reason Delcine had suggested to Moses that they wait to get married. When Jenny was settled, with a husband of her own, that would be the time for them to jump over the broom.

Meanwhile they were content, and as they sat on the wagon seat together, Delcine tucked her hands into Moses's pocket and hummed gaily under her breath.

She was glad to be going into town, for though Missouri had originally been admitted as a slave state to the Union, the majority of residents of Tumbling Creek had not been slaveholders and had fought for the Glorious Cause primarily because they hadn't liked a bunch of foreigners—and Yankees at that—trying to dictate to them how to run their affairs. Moses and Delcine were always treated decently in town, even if they didn't have the words "mister" or "miss" tacked before their names.

"Ah sho' hope Mistah Henshaw remembahs dem seeds he promised Miz Jenny last yeah." Moses spoke, breaking the companionable silence between them. "An' Ah doan want ter fo'git dem flowah cuttin's Miz Standish said she'd give Miz Jenny neithah. Dat yahd ain' nothin' but grass an' trees. A few flowahs will perk it up right nice."

"Ah'll git dem," Delcine told him. "Ah's got ter stop at Miz Standish's dress shop anyways. Miz Jenny is gwine ter be needin' some new bonnets an' sech dis spring; Ah doan care if'n she do say otherwise. Dat chile's clothes is in pitiful condition! She ain' neber gwine ter ketch Mistah Luke if'n she keeps scrimpin' on her 'pearance. Ah knows he's already sweet on her, but it woan huht none ter give him a li'l nudge or two in de right direction."

"Lahke yo done gived me?" Moses glanced at her and chuckled.

Delcine grinned.

"Well, it's de truf. A man doan know his own mind, an' dat's a fact. It's up ter a woman ter mek it up fo' him."

"Yo sho' is uppity, gal," Moses teased. "Whut meks yo so sho' yo din chase me till *Ah* ketched yo?"

Delcine blushed.

"Hmph!" she snorted disbelievingly, but Moses could tell she was pleased all the same. "If'n Ah'd o' waited 'round on yo, Ah'd be a ole maid by now!"

"Is dat a fact?" Moses asked, his dark brown eyes twinkling.

"Yassah, it is. Now mek dat lazy ole hawse git a move on. Ah doan lahke de looks o' dat sky; it's a peculiar color, an' Ah doan want ter be caught in a thunderstorm."

"Dat doan look lahke no thunderclouds Ah eber seen," Moses said, eyeing the darkening firmament worriedly as Delcine shuddered, feeling suddenly how the temperature had dropped. "Giddyup der, Blossom. Giddyup!"

They were two-thirds of the way to Tumbling Creek when the snow flurries started and the savage wind began to snarl its way through the hills. Still, knowing the town was closer than the cabin, they pressed on grimly. Moses, though he didn't usually do so, used his whip on the mare, urging the animal into a gallop.

They hadn't gone far when Blossom, wild-eyed with fear, slipped on a wet patch on the ground and stumbled. Simultaneously one of the wagon wheels hit a large rock, causing one side of the vehicle to fly upward, nearly unseating them. The wagon landed with a terrible jolt in a rut, and the rear axle snapped, so the vehicle careened into the ditch that ran alongside the country road. Moses and Delcine, who had yet to regain their balance, were thrown violently from the wagon seat. Delcine rolled out onto the soft damp earth, and, except for being momentarily stunned from the blow that knocked the wind out of her, she was unharmed. Moses, however, was tossed backward into the wagon bed, where he struck his head sharply against one side of the vehicle. He lay there crumpled in a pitiful heap, blood spurting from the wound near his temple.

"Moses! Moses!" Delcine cried, scrambling to her feet and staggering toward him blindly, the gale almost sending her toppling once more.

Her cloak whipped about her wildly with each gust. She was sure Moses was dead. To her utter relief when she reached him, Delcine discovered he was still breathing. But he was unconscious all the same and could be of no help to her. She bit her lip, thinking hard.

The wagon was useless now, sitting at a crazy slant, the rear axle broken and one of the rear wheels at an odd angle, its hub dislodged. They would have to leave the vehicle. But Blossom, who'd been pulled into the ditch along with the wagon, had gotten to her feet and was now standing quietly between the shafts. Praying the mare had not been lamed when it had stumbled and fallen, then been dragged some distance afterward, Delcine quickly freed the animal, keeping a tight hold on the reins as she led it around to the back of the vehicle. She tied Blossom to the good rear wheel so the mare couldn't run off, then she removed its bulky harness, leaving only its bridle. After that she climbed into the wagon bed to search Moses's pockets for the small knife she knew he always carried.

Ignoring the growing numbness in her hands, Delcine sliced through the long leather checkreins and lines until they were short enough for her to manage from the animal's back. She knotted the four ends still attached to the bridle together, then looped them over the horse's neck. One of the trailing straps that remained bound to the wagon wheel she tied to the bridle so Blossom still could not escape.

"Oh, Lawd, gimme strength," she beseeched aloud as she positioned herself behind Moses, her arms beneath his own, her hands clasped firmly around his chest.

Groaning, Delcine slowly dragged the big black man to the far end of the wagon bed. She opened the tailgate, then rolled Moses over so he lay facedown upon it, and, tugging on the mare's bridle until the animal was pressed up next to the rear edge of the vehicle, she heaved Moses across Blossom's broad back. After that she mounted the horse and nudged it gradually away from the wagon, pulling and shifting Moses's bulk as she did so, so he lay draped in front of her, his arms and legs dangling on either side of the mare. She leaned forward and, straining to reach it, untied the useless strap from the bridle, releasing the animal from the wagon wheel. Then, digging her heels hard into Blossom's sides, Delcine headed toward town.

Afterward she never remembered the terrible, grueling ride into Tumbling Creek, how she'd stumbled up to Doc Mercer's place, screaming and pounding frantically with her half-frozen hands upon his door. She only vaguely recalled the sudden warmth of his office as the startled physician, catching her before her knees gave out, carried her inside. Obediently she drank the vast quantity of brandy he forced down her throat before darkness swirled up to engulf her and mercifully she fainted, her last thoughts of Moses, lying, injured, on the doctor's long examining table, and of Jenny, all alone in the cabin in the woods.

Chapter Twenty-two

Wichita, Kansas, 1871

"I tell you we've lost that frigging Pinkerton agent—we haven't seen hide nor hair of him in weeks—and we need the money that stagecoach is carrying," Raiford insisted, glowering at his three older brothers.

"Keep your voice down, you fool!" J.R. spat, glancing around the tavern of the Buckhorn Hotel, run by Henry Vigus and his wife. "Do you want someone to hear you?"

Raiford scowled with disgust.

"I doubt seriously if even *you* can hear me—what with that damned music box blasting away!" He jerked his thumb at the loud instrument. "Christ! A person can't even hear himself *think* in here—much less eavesdrop on our conversation!"

"He *has* got a point, J.R.," Luke observed dryly, eyeing the noisy contraption with amusement. "Why don't we go outside—where it's quieter?"

This being the general consensus, the Morgan brothers pushed their chairs back from the table and headed out the door of the long, low, single-story hotel.

It had rained earlier, and the wide streets were thick with mud, churned up and slung in every direction by passing horses and vehicles. Deep wagon ruts and chuckholes had filled up with water, making it even more difficult to traverse one's way through town—especially without being splashed.

Officially founded in 1870, Wichita was a new town, without even enough residents to qualify it as a third-class city. But progress was well underway, and the streets, despite being mired, bustled with activity.

Located at the junction of the Big and Little Arkansas Rivers, on the

Chisholm Trail, the town had once been the home of an army outpost known successively as Camp Davidson, Camp Butterfield, and Camp Beecher. But this had been abandoned in 1869. Now Wichita was a popular resting place for cattle drovers en route with their vast herds to Abilene, farther north.

Since it was still a relatively raw and uncivilized place, the majority of buildings were crude, particularly the original church, which also served as the schoolhouse. It was constructed of rough-hewn tree trunks rather than smooth planks, and, instead of being laid one on top of another, the logs stood side by side, so the walls of the edifice resembled a stockade. It had a sod roof that was so heavy it was already causing the building to buckle slightly beneath its weight, and Luke, as he studied the church in the distance, thought the two slender wooden crosses jutting up from either end of the roof and its small, high-set, glass-paned windows appeared incongruous in comparison with the rest of the schoolhouse. Jenny would have been appalled by it, he decided.

As he and his brothers trudged along the street—for there were as yet no sidewalks—his eyes swept the rest of the town speculatively. Although he was not keen on Raiford's scheme to rob one of the many stagecoaches that came through, Luke also realized the Morgans were short of funds and could not subsist much longer on the few coins they had between them.

There had been a fire recently, during which the W. P. Rouse queensware store and the John Peyton saddle and harness shop had burned, but Luke saw many other businesses, their false storefronts lining the main street of town. There were various signs: Grocery, Tin Shop, Hardware, and Liquors (Wholesale and Retail). There was a combination restaurant and cigar store and, next door, the two-story Southern Hotel that made its competitor, from whose premises the brothers had just departed, seem lacking in comparison. There was a place called City Laundry, which was run by a pretty young widow, Catherine McCarty, whose oldest son, Henry, would later change his name to William Bonney and, as Billy the Kid, become an outlaw far more infamous than any of the Morgans.

The most imposing edifice of all was the large, clapboard Empire House built by William "Dutch Bill" Greiffenstein just last year. The main portion of the hotel was three stories high, lined front and sides with numerous, evenly spaced, glass-paned windows. Several chimneys jutted up from the slant-sided, square-topped, flat roof. The rear addition was similar, though it was more modest, having only two stories. A wide plank porch ran along the entire front of the building. There stagecoaches belonging to the Cannon Bill line, operated between Wichita and Dodge City, often stopped. It was one of these vehicles Raiford proposed to hold up some distance from town.

Luke still wasn't sure whether or not this was a good plan. It was true that the Pinkerton detective, Gus Grissom, appeared to have grown weary of the chase, but nevertheless Luke remained uneasy about the agent's whereabouts. In addition, Wichita, for all its brash, upstart growth, was not a lawless place. Besides several volunteer fire-fighting crews, it had an organized police department, and a new marshal, Mike Meagher, had recently been appointed. He earned seventy-five dollars a month and was said to be good at his job. There were ordinances prohibiting drunkenness and the firing of weapons within the corporate limits of town, as well as restrictions on gambling. There was even a law against speeding, and any person riding or driving a horse, mule, or any other animal at an excessive rate was fined up to twenty-five dollars.

"Well, what do you think? Shall we rob one of the stages or not?" J.R. asked tersely, once the brothers had finished their perusal of the town.

"I don't see what else we can do," Tobias reflected glumly. "There isn't a bank, a post office, or a railroad track in sight, so all those are out —unless we want to ride up north to Newton and hold up one of the Santa Fe trains. At any rate, we've got to do something. We've barely enough left between us to settle our account at the hotel, and if we skip out without paying, Mr. Vigus will set the law on us for sure. Either way, we're going to have that damned marshal after us, and I'd just as soon have a couple of greenbacks in my pocket."

"So would I," Billy Clay chimed in.

"Luke?" J.R. turned to his brother inquiringly.

"I reckon I'll have to go along with robbing the stage." Luke spoke reluctantly. "I don't think we'll have any trouble with that. It's getting away afterward that bothers me. We'll have to come back to town and ford the river from Douglas Avenue."

"No." Raiford shook his head. "I've already checked that out. We can go on down south a ways to El Paso—it's about ten miles from here —and cross there instead."

"All right. It's agreed, then," J.R. said. "Let's head back to the hotel and make our plans. I'm getting hungry, and Mrs. Vigus is a good cook."

This was indeed the case and one of the primary reasons why, despite its appearance, the Buckhorn Hotel was a popular place. The Morgans trekked back to the tavern, heeding Mrs. Vigus's admonition that they scrape their muddy boots off outside. Then, tipping their hats politely to the proprietress, the brothers went inside and ordered supper. Their leisurely meal was only briefly interrupted, when one of the town's citizens, Jack Ledford, took exception to the noisy music box, which had annoyed Raiford earlier, silencing it with a well-aimed bullet from his revolver.

Upon hearing the loud report, the Morgans all jumped to their feet and went for their guns, then sheepishly settled back in their chairs as they realized the music box, now wheezing almost pathetically to an abrupt stop, had been the unfortunate target of Mr. Ledford's pistol.

After supper the brothers retired to their single room at the back of the hotel, where they plotted their holdup of the Cannon Ball stagecoach.

Things went awry from the beginning. The morning that had started out so beautifully, the sun shining, the sky a deep clear blue filled with puffy white clouds, gradually gave way to rain. At first it merely sprinkled as the sun's rays struggled to pierce the thick, massive, bloated clouds that intermittently obscured it. Then the drops began to fall with shattering intensity.

The vast flat prairie, stretching out endlessly in all directions, its all-encompassing sweep broken only by a few scattered cottonwood trees, was still damp from yesterday's brief shower. Now the ground turned sodden, sucking at the horses' hooves as the Morgans urged their mounts across the plains.

From afar the brothers looked like ghost riders, eerie in the dark grey light, their long pale dusters drawn closely about them so they appeared hazy and shapeless, almost translucent in the rain. The faint, irregular streaks of forked lightning cut jagged pieces from the sky, illuminating the men erratically, so they seemed to travel in slow motion over the rippling prairie grass. The powerful thuds their strong, muscular horses made as they moved over the wet earth mingled with the sounds of the thunder, and it seemed as though the animals' hooves were causing the heavens to pound and echo so violently.

No wonder, then, that the stagecoach driver and his shotgun rider, spying the Morgans in the distance, riding abreast and galloping hard toward the vehicle, believed for a moment that the brothers were specters spewed up from the bowels of hell.

Frightened, the shotgun rider fired wildly at the oncoming figures, but his aim was poor and he missed them all. His eyes rolled with fear, for to him the bullets had appeared to pass right through their targets, and his hands shook as frantically he reloaded his empty weapon. The driver, cursing, lashed the team forward unmercifully in the blinding rain, hoping to ram right through the formidable barricade of men ahead.

But the road was slick and uneven. The high, iron-rimmed wheels of the stagecoach bounced precariously over the muddy ruts and chuckholes, careening this way and that, brutally unseating the terrified passengers within. At last the vehicle could take no more. With a loud crack the shaft splintered, separating from the body of the stagecoach. The panicked team, freed of restraints, raced away haphazardly, dragging the wooden tongue with them. The helpless vehicle, left without guidance or direction, swerved sharply, swayed violently on its unbalanced wheels, then crashed over onto one side.

Both the driver and the shotgun rider were thrown clear of the wreckage. The former hit his head on a rock and was knocked unconscious; the latter lay moaning, his arm broken. Inside, the passengers, although scratched, bruised, and battered, were basically uninjured. One tried to open the door of the stagecoach but quickly desisted when he saw the shadowy forms of the Morgans approaching.

Hurriedly the brothers rummaged through the baggage, the mail sacks, and the other items that had been scattered by the accident. At last they located the metal strongbox they were seeking. It was heavy and padlocked. With a well-aimed shot Luke blew open the lid, then he and the others filled their saddlebags with the contents.

"Let's get out of here!" J.R. ordered above the roar of the storm, and as the rest concurred, not wishing to waste time robbing the passengers in the deluge, the men mounted up, then headed southeast, toward the small town of El Paso.

Unbeknown to them, hot on their heels was the Pinkerton detective, Gus Grissom, who had been tracking them determinedly for several long weeks over as many miles. They were clever, the Morgans. He had to give them that. Had he not been as astute himself, he would by now have fallen into one of the many traps they'd set to ensnare him. But Gus was neither a rash hothead nor an ambitious glory seeker. He was patient and thorough and willing to wait for the right opportunity to present itself. He had witnessed the brothers' crime, and now he would take them into custody.

Gus surmised from the direction they'd taken that the outlaws were making for El Paso, where he was certain they intended to ford the Arkansas River and head for home. Grimly he set his spurs to his

horse's sides. He would beat them to the town, and there he would be
waiting with the marshal and a posse.

Luke inhaled sharply, then gritted his teeth to keep from crying out as
yet another excruciating spasm of pain from the wound in his belly
ripped through his body.

He didn't know how long he had been riding, nearly doubled over,
barely hanging onto his saddle, weary to the bone, and hurting. It
seemed like forever. Yet he was certain no more than a few days had
passed since the disastrous confrontation in El Paso.

The Morgans had escaped, as always, but the cost had been dear. J.R.
had taken two slugs—one in the arm, the other in the leg. A bullet had
grazed Raiford's skull, and Tobias's spectacles had been dislodged and
crushed in the melee. Nearly blind without them, he had to be led on
his horse. Only Billy Clay had emerged unscathed, possibly because he
was considered the least dangerous of the five brothers.

The gang had managed to get across the river and the Missouri border, for the rain that had been a hindrance during the stagecoach
holdup had proven invaluable later on. It had washed away the Morgans' trail, making the chase more difficult. Only when the sudden
showers had ceased had they cursed the mud that had revealed their
hoofprints all too clearly. Doubling back, riding down rock-strewn
creek beds, scattering leaves and twigs across a brushed path—all these
tactics meant to outwit the enemy had taken time, time the brothers
could ill afford, especially with a posse in hot pursuit. They'd needed to
ride like the wind, to reach the Ozark Mountain caves, where they
could hide and slip through the law's fingers with ease.

This they had been unable to do, for it had soon become evident that
Luke could not keep up with the hectic pace. His wound, while not
fatal, was bad, and it had been obvious that he needed a doctor's care
and rest.

"You'll have . . . to—to leave me . . . behind," he'd gasped when
J.R. had cantered back to see how he was faring. "Go on. You know
. . . the rules."

The strictest agreement between the Morgans was that one brother
could not endanger the lives of the others. Luke's physical condition
was a handicap; the rest would travel more rapidly without him,
thereby ensuring that they eluded the lawmen following them.

J.R.'s heart had ached at the thought of leaving Luke behind to face
the posse alone, should it catch him, but he'd realized there was no

other choice. The gang must either abandon Luke or be taken prisoner along with him.

"Good luck, Luke," J.R. had said, clearing his throat gruffly, unable to say anything more.

Then he'd spurred his horse forward to join the others.

Luke's only salvation then had lain in the hope that the lawmen would not notice he'd broken away from the main body of the gang, or if they did, that they would be greedy enough to continue to hound the rest instead of settling for him alone. Now he no longer even made any attempt to cover his tracks, certain the posse was indeed after his brothers rather than him.

His eyes blurred, and with difficulty he tried to focus them. He thought he was somewhere near Tumbling Creek now, but he couldn't be sure. Inexorably, as the pale, overcast spring morning had worn on, the sky had darkened, so it seemed almost night beneath the canopy of the budding green forest. What Luke could glimpse of the firmament through the branches was now a peculiar shade of grey streaked with white, and the air was chilly, the temperature having dropped considerably within the past several minutes. The wind was starting to moan and rise, and Luke shivered.

He had been born and reared in the Ozark Mountains. He knew without a doubt that a freak blizzard was about to descend unmercifully upon him and that if he didn't find some sort of shelter—and quickly— he would freeze to death.

Incredibly he spied a light glowing in the distance, and as the snow started to flurry pitilessly about him he made his way gratefully toward the bright, steady beacon, sheer determination and willpower keeping him in the saddle.

At last he reached the cabin whence the light emanated. Luke eyed the house disbelievingly, certain he must be dreaming or delirious. Then, past caring, he slid from Blaze's back and stumbled onto the front porch, where he beat with his last ounce of strength upon the door.

"Jenny!" His voice rasped hoarsely. "Jenny! It's Luke! It's Luke! For God's sake, let me in!"

Then, like a vision, a halo cast about her soft brown hair from the glow of the oil lamp within, she was there, her grey eyes wide and startled, her loving arms outstretched to catch him as he fell.

BOOK THREE

Stories Yet Untold

Chapter Twenty-three

Tumbling Creek, Missouri, 1871

Jenny staggered under Luke's weight, for though he was lithe, he was also tall, and solid muscle besides. For a moment she was afraid she would be unable to prevent him from hitting the floor. Then she gained her balance and, half dragging him, managed to get him into the bedroom, where she heaved him halfway upon the bed.

Her initial incredulity at seeing him standing outside when she'd opened the door now gave way to shock as she rolled his body over and, lifting his feet, settled him more firmly and naturally upon the mattress.

Luke looked ghastly. His unshaven face was sickeningly drained of color, except for his nose, which was chafed red from the cold, and his lips, which were tinged with blue. His hands were nearly frozen stiff, the fingers curled up like talons, and even though he was now unconscious, they did not relax. Horrified, Jenny saw the front of his duster was crimson with blood.

Knowing that if she were to help him, she must not panic, she took several deep breaths to steady her nerves and carefully gathered her wits. Then she began to move quickly but calmly to the parlor.

There she stoked up the fire until it blazed with unbearable heat, for Luke would need to be kept warm. Then she donned her coat and, steeling herself against the blast of the wind and snow, went outside to lead Blaze into the new barn. Hurriedly she divested the horse of its bridle and saddle, rubbed it down briskly, tossed a blanket over it for warmth, and made sure there was feed in the stall. All the while Jenny's mind dwelled anxiously on Luke, knowing he needed her immediate attention but also certain he would never forgive her if she left Blaze to freeze in the blizzard.

After she had done her best for the stallion, she returned to the house, where she set a pot of water to boil on the stove. Then she rummaged through the cupboards for clean clothes and linens, a bottle of carbolic acid, and a bottle of brandy.

She observed with relief upon reentering the bedroom that although Luke lay unnaturally still, he yet breathed, albeit shallowly. Deftly she eased him from the soiled duster, then unbuttoned his shirt, unbuckled his belt, and unfastened his pants. Though she had been sure he was hurt, Jenny was unprepared for the sight of the hideous wound that met her eyes. She bit her lip, for she'd seen such injuries in the hospital in Atlanta, and she knew this one had been caused by a gunshot. Tentatively she ran her hand under Luke's lower back, but to her dismay his smooth skin was unmarred. That meant the bullet was still in his belly.

Her mouth tightened grimly. Luke needed Doc Mercer—and badly, but there was no doubt in Jenny's mind that if she dared to mount Blaze and ride for help, she would not reach town in this storm. She would have to remove the slug herself. Otherwise Luke would surely die.

The operation would take time, and in the meanwhile she must do something about his frostbitten face and hands, and probably his feet as well.

Rapidly Jenny stripped Luke naked, her deep concern for his well-being overcoming her innate sense of modesty. She had viewed many men in various stages of undress at the hospital, and now was not the time for maidenly qualms.

His feet, like his face and hands, were white, with a few greyish yellow patches here and there. Feverishly Jenny tried to think what to do. Winters in Georgia had always been mild, and she'd never known anyone who had nearly frozen to death. Still, hadn't she heard you should rub snow on extremities numbed by cold? No, that could not possibly be right, Jenny decided logically, for would that not make the skin even colder? Warmth was what Luke needed, gradual warmth, as the spring sun thawed the winter ground.

She went to the kitchen and briefly immersed several linens in the pot of water now boiling on the stove. Then she retrieved the towels and, scurrying back to the bedroom, wrapped them securely about Luke's hands and feet and lightly covered his face, making certain he was still able to breathe. After that she threw a few more logs on the fire in the parlor before searching her bureau drawers for a pair of scissors, a sturdy needle, and some strong thread.

These and the washbasin she set on the night table. The she unstoppered the bottle of carbolic acid and poured some of it into the bowl.

After sitting down on the edge of the bed, she soaked a cloth in the liquid and began to clean the wound in Luke's belly gently but thoroughly. The injury was, she saw, not as awful as it had at first seemed, for there did not appear to be any damage to his internal organs. The shot had apparently been fired from some distance away, and Luke's duster and leather belt had helped somewhat to shield him. Both bore a single hole, as did the waistband of his pants and the tail of his shirt. Nevertheless the bullet had penetrated his flesh and must come out.

Her hands starting to tremble slightly, Jenny rinsed the scissors in the carbolic acid, then gingerly probed the ugly gash.

Sweat beaded her brow and upper lip as she felt slippery flesh ooze and suck where the scissors touched, and she thanked God that Luke was unconscious and could not feel the excruciating pain she must be causing him. It was all Jenny could do to force herself to continue, to watch what she was doing. Her face knitted with concentration, she tried to remember exactly how the doctors in the hospital had done this. Once she had been able to move about, although she had not yet been well enough to be discharged, she had often assisted with operations, for there had been many patients far more in need than she. Still she had never performed any delicate surgery herself, and Jenny feared she might be doing Luke a great deal more harm than good.

There! Was that it? Hesitantly she pressed the point of the scissors down against the hard spot she'd finally located. Then she parted the instrument's blades and carefully locked them about the piece of lead.

Slowly . . . slowly, she cautioned herself, trying not to let her hand shake.

Letting out the breath she'd held, Jenny dropped the slug onto the night table, then buried her face in her hands, her body quivering violently. After a few moments she managed to regain her composure. She again cleaned the wound with the carbolic acid. Then, after drenching the needle and thread with the liquid, she sewed up the gash, her stitches small and neat. Red droplets still seeped from the injury, but this did not disturb Jenny, for she knew it was better that the blood have some means of escape from the wound.

Luke would have a scar there, she thought, studying her stitches. Then for the first time she allowed her eyes to drink their unabashed fill of his naked body. He was beautifully proportioned, lean and well muscled, his chest furred with crisp, dark blond curls that trailed down his belly to the bush between his thighs. Jenny blushed as her eyes strayed quickly over his manhood. Right now it did not appear the least bit menacing. But she remembered how its hardness had pressed against her that night when Luke had been drunk and kissed her so savagely, and she shivered a little, guessing it looked quite different when he was aroused. Here and there on his torso were several old scars, so Jenny did not think one more would matter.

She folded up one of the linen squares to make a padding for Luke's injury, then she bound the whole, drawing the bandage tight around his belly. He still had not stirred. He had lost a lot of blood, she determined, and was in shock.

Jenny removed the now-cooled towels from his face, hands, and feet. Then she searched the lean-to for some of Moses's socks and a pair of his old work gloves. She put three pairs of socks on Luke's feet and the gloves on his hands. After that she bundled him up beneath the sheets and the quilt, placing two extra blankets on top for good measure.

There was nothing more she could do now but wait. Emotionally drained and physically exhausted, Jenny poured herself a small glass of brandy and drank it. She needed it, and for once she did not consider the impropriety of her actions. Then she sat down in the rocking chair Moses had built for her during the long winter months, when there had been little else to do. Despite her worry over whether or not Luke would survive, Jenny felt a deep sense of peace and contentment she had not known in years, and after a while she fell asleep, feeling safe and warm.

Luke was here—with her. Oddly enough, somehow it seemed as though this was just as it should be.

They were alone, cut off from the rest of the world, for it snowed and snowed until there were drifts so high it was impossible to venture forth, lest one flounder in the deep white softness and die. Much to Jenny's relief, for she feared his condition might have worsened while she dozed, Luke woke on several occasions during the passing hours, feverish and disoriented but nevertheless alive. Each time, she gave him a few sips of brandy and water, then watched as he drifted back into slumber. Only once did he recognize her. Then he tried to grasp her arm, and his parched throat rasped out a cracked "Jenny" before his eyes closed and he slipped into delirium.

Jenny felt awful, like an eavesdropper, as she listened to his ravings, but she could not bring herself to leave his side. Several times he moaned and cried out, and she knew in his befuddled mind he was reliving the time he'd spent with Maybelle, and the war too. Terrible, disjointed descriptions of hateful arguments, and of battles and raids emanated hoarsely from his lips, things Jenny wished she had not heard, except for the fact that they gave her a new understanding of him.

No wonder his eyes seemed so old and timeworn! Luke's past, as she had guessed, was indeed filled with as much pain—and brutality—as her own. Like her, he had seen too much, had been appalled by it, and had survived, only to be haunted by torturous memories and nightmares. Jenny's heart ached for him, and quiet tears stung her eyes. She was not the only one the war had ravaged with such cruelty.

Now she knew why the Morgans, although outlaws, killed only when forced to do so and then only those who stood a fair chance of killing them. She discovered that Luke's strength was tempered with gentleness, as she had sensed, and she now understood why she was drawn to him. Whatever he was, despite all his failings, Luke would never have been a part of something such as what had happened that day at Faxon's Folly. Moreover, if she ever were to reveal her past to him, he would instinctively comprehend her horror that day and the overwhelming terror that had held her fast in its grip, that even now continued to clutch some part of her tightly in its fist, no matter how hard she tried to free herself of it. He would even, Jenny thought, be able to help her conquer it, as no other man would ever be capable of doing.

Luke would understand that she needed time, reassurance, a deep sense of security and belonging, and, most of all, love. He would give her that—and more, for although he would take every part of her, he would give all of himself in return. She saw that now. He had been betrayed and knew the hurt it had caused. The next woman he chose must offer him her heart and fidelity, as Luke would offer his. There would be no doubts, no lack of trust between them.

Still, Jenny reflected, downcast, she had no reason to believe that woman would be her, although she hoped with all her heart it would be. She loved him—deeply—she was certain of that now, and at last she accepted it, even reveled in it, no longer feeling the urge to fight against it. There was no need to do so; there had never been any need for her to resist her heart and emotions. If only she had recognized this sooner!

Quietly she rose and replaced the cool cloth on Luke's hot brow. Then tenderly, half shocked by her own temerity, she bent and kissed his mouth.

"Live, my love," Jenny whispered fiercely against his lips. "Live."

She clung to him fervently for a minute, as though by willpower alone she could keep him alive. Then she opened the drawer of the night table, removed her Bible, and returned to the rocking chair. Often in the past, during the long months of her recovery at the hospital in

Atlanta, Jenny had found comfort in prayer. Her fingers moved lovingly, reverently over the rough, worn leather binding, the shabby, frayed silk place marker, and dog-eared, gilt-edged pages. Slowly she opened the book, letting the thin, yellowed pages fall as they willed rather than searching out a particular passage. In this manner did she always seek solace, for then, instead of simply easing her mind with words she'd read so many times that she'd memorized them, it was as though somehow the Lord spoke to her himself—even if He did not always say what she wished to hear.

Jenny smiled to herself at the thought.

Once, when she'd been a child, she had asked her mother if God truly heard and responded to each and every single prayer directed to Him, no matter how small. Rachael Colter had told her that He certainly did, but sometimes those who were doing the praying didn't like His answers.

Now Jenny glanced down at the page to which the Bible had opened of its own accord. It was First Corinthians, Chapter Thirteen. By the light of the flickering oil lamp, she began to read:

"Love beareth all things, believeth all things, hopeth all things, endureth all things. . . . And so abideth faith, hope, and love, these three; but the greatest of these is love."

Yes, Jenny thought, it is so.

Then, startled, she closed the Bible, her ears straining intently as she listened for the sound that had caught her attention, drawing her from the book in her hands. There it was again! No. It was gone. It must only have been her imagination. Still for an instant she could have sworn that borne on the wings of the wayward wind outside had been the plaintive notes of the music box the old-timer had made, playing softly the sweet, wistful melody of "Plaisir d'Amour." But it was not possible, for the instrument sat on her night table, and its lid was closed. Mystified, Jenny shook her head to clear it, then she looked down again lovingly at the man who had given her the music box.

Chapter Twenty-four

"You saved my life," Luke said as he surveyed Jenny intently, noting how pale and drawn she looked, her eyes shadowed with mauve crescents, as though she had not slept well in several days.

"No." She shook her head, smiling wanly. "It was your strong will to survive that kept you alive, Luke. All I did was take the bullet out of you and keep the wound clean, so infection didn't set in."

"Still," he persisted, "that's more than most would have done for a man like me, an outlaw. There's a price on my head, you know, dead or alive. Most people wouldn't have passed up a chance at the reward. Why'd you do it, Jenny?"

Because I love you, she thought. I love you! But she did not speak the words aloud. Instead she forced a bright laugh from her throat.

"I just couldn't let you die, Luke," she declared. "Imagine how awkward it would have been, trying to explain to everyone how you'd come to expire in my bed!"

His eyes twinkled appreciatively at that.

"Yes, I do see the difficulty there," he admitted. "However, I daresay I'd have been the envy of every man in Taney County!" He chuckled weakly, making Jenny blush. "At any rate, it would have been a far better exit than one caused by a lead slug, you must agree."

"I'm sure I don't know what you're talking about," she insisted primly, embarrassed. "However, if you're well enough for such indecorous topics of conversation, you're quite well enough to sit up and have some of this broth and to be shaved as well. You're starting to look like the old-timer!"

"Is that so?" Luke asked, rubbing his bewhiskered face. "Well, he's a good sort, even if he is a trifle eccentric. He's been the caretaker, as he calls himself, of these hills for as long as I can remember. I wonder how old he is. He must be ancient, because he wasn't any spring chicken even when I was a boy. Yeah, he's a strange one, all right. Sometimes the way he talks you'd think he was one of God's anointed shepherds or something."

"Well, perhaps he is," Jenny remarked softly, remembering how she'd thought she'd heard the sound of the music box that night while reading her Bible. It was odd how strong and true the melody had seemed, almost as though the wind had been calling to her, had carried the notes to her ears alone. And that song . . . it was as though it held some special significance for her. "Here. Let me prop those pillows up for you. Do you think you can feed yourself?"

"God knows," Luke groaned. "I feel like a newborn foal—pretty shaky. How long have I been here, Jennilee?"

"Four days."

"Jesus! How have you managed to look after me? I mean . . . with your teaching and all it couldn't have been easy. Come to think of it . . . you've been here all morning. Why aren't you at school? What day is this?"

"Monday, but I don't think anybody's coming to school today, Luke. You haven't been outside. Don't you remember the blizzard? You should; you nearly froze to death in it. The drifts are over six feet high in places. The sun's out now, but it'll still be a few days before the snow melts and the roads are clear."

"That bad, huh? Hmmm. This soup tastes good. Did you make it?"

"Yes, believe it or not, I did."

"Why shouldn't I believe it?"

"For a sick man, you sure ask a lot of questions." Jenny gave him a mockingly reproving glance, then sniffed, haughtily putting her nose in the air. "As you may recall, you weren't so complimentary about my cooking the last time you ate it. In fact, I seem to remember you choking. . . ."

Luke grinned.

"Ah, yes. The arsenic biscuits. How could I have forgotten those? You can poison me anytime, Jennilee."

"Well, I just might—if you don't behave, that is," she warned. "Now I'm going to leave you to your broth. I've got to get a shovel and see if I can't dig my way out to the barn to check on the animals; your horse is out there, by the way. He was quite cold and worn out when you got here. But I rubbed him down hard, and the few times I checked on him before it got too bad to go out he seemed to be doing well."

"I'm glad to hear that," Luke confessed. "I don't think I'd have made it home without Blaze. But . . . where's Moses?" He lifted one eyebrow inquiringly, puzzled. "You ought not be out shoveling snow."

"Well, someone must do it, and Moses isn't here. We're from Georgia, remember? And we're not used to snow—much less blizzards—especially in the spring. We thought it was only going to rain, and Moses and Delcine went into town." Jenny frowned anxiously. "I hope they managed to get there before the storm broke."

"Do you mean we're all alone here?" Luke queried, starting to grin devilishly once more.

"Yes, of course. I thought I just said as much." Then Jenny saw the look on his face. "But you needn't get any ideas, Luke Morgan," she told him sternly, somewhat alarmed. "You're much too ill yet to be out of bed."

"But, Jennilee," he teased softly, his eyes suddenly warm and dancing with mirth, "I wasn't thinking of leaving it."

She flushed, disconcerted by his teasing. Without warning her heart began to race, and she turned away so he wouldn't see the expression on her face.

"Your soup is getting cold," Jenny admonished, "and you need to eat it to regain your strength."

"Indeed I do. It isn't often I find myself snowbound with a woman. I want to make the most of it!" Luke said.

Three days later Luke had recovered enough to be able to stand, to dress himself, and to shave, a task previously performed by Jenny, who on occasion had shaved her father and brothers when they'd been too sick to do so. Luke had been nervous about this at first, but after she'd promised not to slit his throat, he'd finally capitulated and allowed her to scrape away the beard and mustache he'd grown during his illness. To Luke's surprise Jenny hadn't nicked him even once.

She was a most capable woman, he thought, thinking about how she'd dug the bullet out of his belly and coped with his frostbite. Thanks to her, he was alive—and had the full use of his hands and feet as well. This was especially important, considering his line of work.

Luke frowned. Now, more than ever, he realized he must give up his lawless ways. He had nearly been killed in the shootout at El Paso. It was a miracle he'd made it home, and it was due only to Jenny's skillful, efficient care of him that he'd survived. The next time he might not be so lucky. Besides, Luke wanted Jenny as his wife, not as his accomplice. She had already incriminated herself by lying about him to Gus Grissom. Now she was aiding and harboring a fugitive. Lord only knew where it would all end if they continued in this manner.

Dear Jenny. How Luke loved her. More than anything, he wanted to marry her now, but still he did not ask her to be his wife. Despite their growing closeness the past few days, it was evident to him Jenny had yet to conquer her deep-rooted fear of men, and he was afraid she would refuse his proposal.

When changing the dressing on his wound she'd seemed awkward and most uncomfortable, only too relieved when the job was finished and she no longer had to touch him.

Luke did not know his very nearness had filled Jenny with such yearning that she had barely been able to restrain herself in his presence. More than once, she had been tempted to tell him of her love, and only with difficulty had she prevented herself from doing so.

He was grateful to her, she was sure, for saving his life. But he did not love her, and Jenny could not bear to destroy their friendship by asking more of him than he was prepared to give. If he did not want her, his rejection of her love would be painful for her and embarrassing for him.

Time was what she needed, Jenny thought. Time to make Luke see by her actions how much she cared for him, wanted to be his. But time was what she did not have. The sun had grown stronger and warmer with each passing day, and the snow was melting quickly. Tomorrow the roads would be traversible, Jenny knew. She had already decided she must ride Blaze into town to see what had become of Moses and Delcine.

"You will be careful, won't you?" Luke asked with concern when she informed him that she wanted to borrow his horse. "I know you're worried about your servants, but Blaze can be the devil to manage, and it will be a while yet before all those drifts melt away."

"I'll be all right," Jenny asserted, though privately she had her doubts about handling the stallion.

That day at Faxon's Folly had left her with an uneasy feeling about horses, and she had not ridden since then. It was one of the reasons, she was certain, that Moses had chosen the lazy but sweet-tempered Blossom when he had purchased the wagon from Mr. Pritchard's livery stable.

"Well, don't take any chances," Luke instructed. "If the roads are still impassable, turn around, and come home."

"Yes, I will."

Inwardly Jenny smiled. How like a domineering husband he had sounded! She would be sorry when this interlude ended. Sitting in the parlor with Luke this evening, she mending his bullet-torn shirt and he reading an old newspaper, had made her feel most wifely and content. She glanced at him lying on the sofa, wondering what he was thinking. No doubt he would be glad to escape from the cabin's confines. He had been pleasant enough to her, but still Jenny was afraid he was bored with her company.

She had been most unlike herself these past few days, chattering like a magpie, trying to be witty and gay, to amuse him with anecdotes and entertain him with games. They'd played both checkers and cards to while away the hours, for, once his fever had broken, Luke had recuperated quite swiftly, much to Jenny's amazement and relief. He had, she thought, been suffering more from shock and loss of blood than anything else when he'd collapsed in her arms. Certainly his wound seemed to be healing without difficulty. This eased her mind greatly, for she'd feared her surgery might have proven inept and that gangrene would set in.

Jenny was surprised Luke had consented to let her borrow his horse, but, then, he'd always liked Moses and Delcine, and he knew she was concerned about their welfare.

Luke, for his part, had agreed to lend her Blaze merely because he was well aware of how stubborn Jenny could be, and he'd assumed she would walk to Tumbling Creek if she had to. He wished he were well enough to go into town for her, but, even though he was up and about, he was not yet up to riding. Jenny would be safe on Blaze, even though the stallion sometimes behaved in a rambunctious manner. Even if she did fall off, the horse would not run away and leave her. The worst thing that might happen would be that she would find her pretty little posterior right smack in the middle of a snowbank. Her pride might be injured, but that was all.

Luke grinned to himself at the notion. God! He wished it had snowed and snowed and snowed—and kept on snowing! He wished he and Jenny were stuck here together forever. She had been so bright and amusing these past few days, talking and laughing. Sometimes he'd ached so badly to take her in his arms that he'd been forced to look away, to pretend she wasn't there beside him, so he wouldn't blurt out his love and desire for her.

Slyly from behind the newspaper he peeked at her.

Oh, Jenny girl, Luke thought, what's it going to take to make you mind, all mine? He sighed. Maybe someone up there would look down on him—and make it possible.

Luke had no idea that even now eyes were peering down on him—through Miss Abigail's telescope. The elderly spinster's hands swiveled the spyglass about and focused it with malicious glee on Jenny's cabin.

It was Friday afternoon when Jenny closed the door of Doc Mercer's office regretfully. She would have liked to spend more time with Moses and Delcine, but she must get home before dark. She was glad her two servants had managed to reach town and find shelter before the full force of the blizzard had hit, but she was extremely sorry Moses had been hurt in the wagon accident. He had a slight concussion and had wrenched his back as well, and it was Doc Mercer's opinion that Moses should remain in bed at least another week. Of course Jenny had agreed that Delcine must stay in Tumbling Creek with him.

"Now don't you two fret about me," Jenny had insisted firmly. "I'll be perfectly fine all by myself out at the house until Moses feels well enough to come home."

"Ah sho' is sorry, Miz Jenny, 'bout dis mess." Moses had groaned. "But Ah cain' hardly move wi' dis heah mis'ry in mah back."

"That's quite all right," Jenny had told him. "You stay here at Doc Mercer's and rest for just as long as you need. I just want to get well. Back injuries take time to heal, and if you try to get up before you're ready, you'll only make things worse. Delcine, if there's anything either one of you needs, you just get it, and tell the store to charge it to my account."

"Thank you, Miss Jenny. We appreciate that."

"Well." Jenny had smiled brightly as she'd edged toward the door, hoping to escape before Delcine thought to ask her how she'd gotten into town. "I'll see you soon, then."

Fortunately Delcine had been too wrought up over Moses's condition and the wrecking of the wagon to wonder how Jenny had managed to get into Tumbling Creek, and when it had finally dawned on Delcine that Jenny hadn't had any means of transportation, it had been too late to question her about it. She'd already gone.

Now Jenny headed over to the wheelwright's shop to find out when Mr. Fairley would be able to repair the damaged vehicle she had spied on the road on her way into town. Upon discovering it would be a few days before he could drive out to fix it, she instructed him to go ahead with the work and then asked him if he would be kind enough to bring the wagon into Tumbling Creek and leave it at Doc Mercer's for Moses and Delcine when it was finished.

"Shore thin', Miz Colter," Mr. Fairley said. He squinted at her, took a chaw of tobacco, then inquired, "Ain't that Luke Morgan's horse you's a'ridin'?"

"Yes, he learned of my difficulties and lent Blaze to me this morning," Jenny replied, hoping her cheeks hadn't flooded with betraying color.

It had suddenly occurred to her that she had spent over a week alone with a man—and an outlaw at that!—and that if anyone discovered this fact, her reputation would be irreparably damaged. It wouldn't matter that Luke had been physically incapacitated the majority of the time. It would be enough that he had been with her at all—whatever his condition. People would wonder why he hadn't gone home to Lottie's house, which was less than a mile from Jenny's cabin, and they would start to talk.

She should have thought of this, Jenny realized, before she had ridden Blaze into town, but her euphoria over Luke's recovery and her worry about Moses and Delcine had driven all other considerations from her mind. Now, not knowing who else might have spied her on Luke's stallion, she wanted nothing more than to get out of Tumbling Creek as quickly as possible.

But this was not to be the case. Jenny had no sooner headed for Luke's horse than Horace Peabody, the Reverend Thompkins, and Abigail Crabtree emerged from the Hotel Van Buren, where over a cup of tea they had been having an extremely heated discussion. Mr. Peabody had been shocked and dismayed. The Reverend Thompkins had been righteous and mortified. Miss Abigail had been gleeful and adamant. Luke Morgan, that notorious, good-for-nothing outlaw, had been staying at the schoolteacher's house since the blizzard and had yet to depart! Mr. Peabody must dismiss her at once, and the Reverend Thompkins must preach an appropriate sermon this Sunday, lest other poor spinsters fall by the wayside.

"Look! There she is now—the jinxed ship!" Miss Abigail shouted down the street as she pointed at Jenny. "Ahoy, Miss Colter! Ahoy, there. Heave to, and weigh anchor. We want to come alongside and talk to you."

Jenny's first impulse was to flee, for several of the townspeople, hearing Miss Abigail's booming voice and curious about the commotion, had stepped out of their stores to see what was the matter. They were all staring at Jenny and the three who were bearing down upon her in such an alarming and purposeful manner.

Chilled to the bone with apprehension, her nerves racing frantically, her heart pounding in her throat, Jenny determined she had no choice but to brazen out the impending confrontation.

Jinxed ship, Miss Abigail called her. Good heavens. The old bat must have been spying on her and knew she and Luke had been alone at the house for days! Jenny was ruined. Utterly *ruined!*

"I took the wind right out of your sails, didn't I?" Miss Abigail, who always spoke in the vernacular of a seaman, questioned smugly as she reached Jenny. "I thought I might. What're you doing aboard Luke Morgan's horse, young lady? Well, speak up, miss! Isn't it true he's been bunking in your cabin for over a week? What? No reply, no denial of the charges? And rightfully so, I say, for even a one-eyed parrot could see that you're guilty. I've been making detailed entries in my logbook, and I know you can't refute them." She turned to Mr. Peabody and the Reverend Thompkins, who were scrutinizing Jenny's pale face disbelievingly. "There. What did I tell you? Guilty as charged! A few more shots over her bow, and she'll be done for. Well, men, why are you just standing there? Damned fool landlubbers! You know your duty! Keelhaul her, then hang her from the nearest yardarm! We run a clean port here!"

"M—M—Miss Colter," Mr. Peabody sputtered, "is—is this true?"

"Of course it is!" Miss Abigail thundered, butting in rudely. "She's taken a pirate for her captain and has run up her true colors at last!"

Jenny was so filled with panic, so afraid of losing her job that she didn't know what to do. Miss Abigail's speech had bewildered her, but she had gotten the gist of it, and she realized she was about to be fired. She could not let that happen. Summoning up every ounce of her courage, Jenny spoke rashly to defend herself.

"You and your spyglass don't know everything, Miss Abigail," she declared, her voice cold, though it trembled slightly. "Luke Morgan"— she paused to draw a deep breath, then went on in a rush—"Luke Morgan is my husband, and I don't think he'll be too happy when he learns how you've treated me today!"

Then, before anyone had a chance to say anything else, she mounted Blaze and set her heels to the stallion's sides sharply, galloping recklessly out of town.

Her three would-be jurors gazed after her, wide-eyed and openmouthed. Mr. Peabody grimaced, distressed. Then, tapping his foot agitatedly upon the road, he turned to Miss Abigail.

"Well, Abby, you have certainly set the cat among the pigeons this time! I shall be most surprised if Jed and J.R. Morgan don't ask for my resignation from the school board. This is all your fault, you know. I should never have listened to you. You and your damned telescope! If I ever get my hands on that monstrous contraption, I'll—I'll pitch it overboard! I knew Miss Colter was a lady born and bred. I don't know why I ever listened to your tales against her, Abby. Oh, dear, what have I done? What *have* I done?"

Mr. Peabody would have been stunned to learn that at that exact moment Jenny was asking herself the very same question.

She was glad Blaze had proven to be a well trained, though mischievous mount, for if she had been forced to direct her attention to the horse, she didn't believe she could have managed. Her mind was so agitated over what had happened in town that she could scarcely even think.

What had she done? What *had* she done?

After working so hard to develop a calm and controlled personality so she might function normally in life, she had been so frightened at the prospect of losing her position and being turned off without a reference that she had reacted almost without thinking. She had not stopped to consider the repercussions of her behavior; she had simply blurted out the only defense that had come to her desperate mind at the moment. *Luke Morgan is my husband,* she had said.

Well, he wasn't—nor was he likely to be—and all Jenny had done was buy herself a tiny breathing space before inevitably she must face the consequences of the tangled web she had woven. Of course she could not continue to teach in Tumbling Creek. Once it was discovered she was not only a fallen woman, at least in the townspeople's eyes, but a liar as well, it was doubtful if anyone, even a friend like Lottie, would stand beside her. Indeed she would be quite fortunate if she were not ridden out of town on a rail!

Hot tears of defeat and anger at her own foolishness stung her eyes, and Jenny brushed them away furiously, maddened by her sudden inability to cope. Without warning her whole life seemed to have gone awry.

It would be another week at least before Moses would be up and about, and in the meanwhile she was certain Doc Mercer's bill was growing. Panic gnawed at her. How would she be able to make the payments if she had no job and therefore no income? Even if she sought another position, who would hire her under the circumstances? She had been disgraced, and no one would want the likes of her in charge of their children.

Jenny thought of her cabin in the woods, of how hard she, Moses, and Delcine had worked to make it livable. Now all their labor was for naught. The house belonged to the school board, and as soon as Jenny was given notice, her home would be taken from her.

She cursed Crabby Abby with a vengeance—and Luke too, for she had to focus her rage on someone, and it seemed that he was at the root of all her troubles. Ever since she had arrived in Tumbling Creek—even before, on the train—he had been the bane of her existence. He had mocked her, threatened her, and kissed her, arousing in her emotions and desires she had not wanted to acknowledge. He had disrupted the placid waters of her being, filling her mind with strange longings and her heart with an unbearable ache. Against her will and her better judgment too, she had fallen in love with Luke, and it was without a doubt her own wishful thinking that had prompted her to declare he was her husband.

A sick feeling formed in the pit of Jenny's stomach, a hard knot of dread that was drawn tighter and tighter as she neared the cabin. Before today Luke had at least been her friend. Now she had destroyed even that between them and made it impossible ever to win his love. He would be appalled by what she had said, for it would appear that she had made a fool of him—as well as herself. That was the one thing he would never forgive. Maybelle had made him the town laughingstock and, paradoxically, an object of pity as well. What would he think of Jenny when he discovered what *she* had done?

Jenny imagined his deep sky-blue eyes boring into her own grey ones, hard, flat, and emotionless, as once or twice she had seen them, and she wanted to weep for her loss. Once more bitter tears penciled her cheeks, and again she wiped them away irately. She would not let Luke see that she had been crying; she would have his respect at least, if nothing more.

After riding into the yard and putting Blaze away in the barn, Jenny repinned her windblown hair, dismayed to find her hands were shaking and her pulse was leaping wildly. Her skirt was wrinkled too, from being hitched up because she had ridden astride, and she smoothed its folds anxiously, wishing she did not look such a mess.

She took several deep breaths and counted to ten to steady her nerves. Then she walked slowly toward the house, enveloped by an impending sense of doom she could not dismiss, no matter how hard she tried. Her heart and soul felt as though they had been stripped bare and lay vulnerably exposed, waiting for Luke to crush the life out of them. It was all Jenny could do to force herself to enter the cabin.

To her surprise she saw that the lamps were lit, for twilight had fallen an hour ago, and in the grip of her mental turmoil she had not noticed.

Luke sat upon the sofa, cleaning his powerful Navy Colt revolvers, and Jenny shuddered slightly at the sight of them, wondering irrationally if he would shoot her for the unpardonable crime she had committed against him. Of course he would not, but some dark part of her being nevertheless hoped it would be so, for at the moment she wished she were dead.

"Thank heavens, you're back!" Luke rose and came toward her as Jenny closed the door quietly and leaned against it for support, her knees feeling suddenly weak, as though they were about to give way beneath her. "It was so late I was beginning to worry about you."

She could not speak. Her wretched tongue that earlier had proven only too obliging now failed her utterly. Jenny could do nothing but stare at Luke, wanting to throw herself into his arms and seek solace from the feel of them about her. She remembered how he had held her that night at his farm, how his voice and hands had soothed her, and she yearned for that comfort now, though she knew it would not be forthcoming.

How handsome Luke is, she thought, her earlier wrath at him draining away as though it had never been and her heart turning over in her breast as she looked at him. His golden hair gleamed in the lamplight, and even though his summer tan had faded during the winter months, his skin was still naturally darker than hers and glowed like rich warm honey. He wore the shirt Jenny had mended for him last night, and it matched the blue of his eyes, making them stand out even more startlingly in his lean face. She longed to reach out and caress his cheek and, as she had done when he'd lain ill and unconscious, to kiss his mouth just once before he turned from her in disgust, any spark of caring within him for her doused by her thoughtless behavior in town. But she did nothing of the sort.

Still she must have made some involuntary movement, allowed some small sob of despair to escape from her lips, for suddenly Luke strode toward her, his eyes filled with concern. He laid his hands upon her arms, his face searching her own.

"What is, Jennilee?" he asked. "What's wrong?"

She almost broke down then, for the thought of never again hearing him speak that impudent name for her pierced her like a sharp knife, and the pain was so terrible she cried out against it.

"Don't touch me!" Jenny wept, turning aside her face to hide her guilt and anguish. "I—I can't bear it if you do."

Luke was so stunned by the unexpected bitterness of her words, which she knew he had misinterpreted, that he dropped his hands lamely to his sides, drawing away from her a little, as though she had wounded him deeply.

"What's wrong?" he questioned again, his tone terse now, lacking the gentleness it had held earlier.

Jenny knew she must be honest with him, no matter the cost to herself, for he deserved that. So somehow she gathered up the shreds of her courage and patched them together as best she could.

"Oh, Luke," she breathed, choking down with difficulty the lump in her throat. "I've—I've done a dreadful thing, and I'm sorry, so very sorry. . . ." Her voice trailed away, for she did not think she could go on.

But as Luke was gazing at her expectantly, his brow knit with puzzlement, Jenny took a deep breath and forced herself to continue. In as few words as possible she recounted to him exactly what had occurred in Tumbling Creek, sparing herself nothing in the telling of it. What she had done was wrong, and she alone was to blame. Jenny hoped she was woman enough at least to shoulder the burden of her mistake.

At last she finished and hung her head with shame, unable to bear the look of loathing she expected to find on Luke's face. In silence she waited for his wrath and disgust to fall upon her and she was quite shocked when he simply tossed back his head and laughed. As the sounds of his mirth rose and echoed through the house, Jenny's surprise became relief and then confusion.

She did not know his whole body was tingling with exhilaration, that what Luke had most yearned for and could not for the life of him figure out how to obtain had just fallen into his lap. Jenny shivered a little, for his eyes were filled with a peculiar, triumphant light she had never seen before, and when he finally stopped laughing his odd half-smile bewildered her even more.

"How I would liked to have seen Crabby Abby's face!" Luke declared, his voice still quivering with merriment. "She must have looked like a drowning sailor going down for the last time!"

Tentatively Jenny smiled as she recalled that the old harridan had indeed appeared as though she'd swallowed a piece of unripe persimmon.

"Then you're—you're not mad?" she queried hesitantly.

"Hell, no!" Luke glanced at her sharply, wondering if she knew just how much he wanted her and how her actions in town had played right into his hands. "Don't bother taking off your coat. I'm feeling well enough to travel now, if I don't get rattled around too badly, that is. We'll ride over to my folks' farm and let them know I'm all right. My wagon's there. We'll hitch up my draft horses, then drive up to the county seat and find a justice of the peace to marry us. If we hurry, we'll be back in time for church Sunday morning."

"Wh-wh-what?" Jenny stuttered, unable to understand or accept what he'd just said.

"You heard me," Luke said softly, moving closer to her once more and placing his hands on either side of her so she could not escape. "I want you, Jennilee." His voice was husky, his breath warm upon her face. "You know that; I've told you so before. Now you're going to be mine . . . all mine."

His eyes roamed over her body possessively, savoringly, as though he could almost feel her writhing beneath him. His heart thumped with excitement; his loins throbbed with anticipation.

"But, Luke, we—we can't possibly be married," Jenny whispered, all the color draining from her face.

"Why not?" His voice was softer and lower still, his face now only inches from hers. "Are you afraid I'll rob you, Jennilee?"

Yes, she wanted to scream. You'll steal my heart and my soul and give me nothing of yourself in return. But hadn't she decided days ago, when Luke had lain ill and unconscious, that she didn't care if all she ever had of him was a few precious moments and, afterward, the memories she would treasure forever?

"No, it's just that . . . it's all so . . . sudden. Are you sure? About marrying me . . . I mean? You know I—I can't have any children, Luke," Jenny reminded him quietly.

"Well, I've already got two," he told her. "I reckon that's enough for any man. Any more objections?"

"Yes." She nodded, wanting him to know the rest of it. "I'm not just plain and crippled, Luke. I've got . . . scars, bad scars, not just emotionally, but . . . physically too."

Luke shrugged.

"Who doesn't? Enough of these protests. You wouldn't be in this mess if it weren't for me, and extricating you from it is the least I can do for your saving my life. I've already got everything all figured out. No one need know *when* our wedding took place. I'll say we've kept it a secret because I didn't want those damned Pinkerton agents bothering you. Your job will be safe, although you won't have to go on teaching if you don't want to; I've got enough money stashed away to support you and keep Moses and Delcine too. And all it'll cost you in return is yourself, Jenny." He let his fingers trail down her cheek, bringing them to rest at the hollow of her throat. "That's not such a bad price to pay now, is it, sugar?"

"I don't know." She shook her head. "I don't know."

Too much was happening too quickly. She couldn't think with him standing so near, his thighs pressed against her own, so she could feel the hard evidence of his desire for her throbbing against her womanhood. His eyes darkened with passion, and before Jenny was even aware of his intent Luke caught her jaw in his powerful grip, tilting her face up to his. His mouth swooped down on hers, imprisoning it so there was no escaping from him, even had she wished to be free. Jenny no longer did, however. She realized that for better or worse her destiny lay with this man, even though he spoke no words of love as savagely he kissed her, caressed her, his hands straying over her body as though it already belonged to him and he had the right to do with it as he willed.

His tongue compelled her trembling lips to part, and almost violently he ravaged her mouth, exploring every dark corner of it, claiming it for his own. If Jenny agreed to wed him, she would never know the feel of another man's lips, but, then, she did not want to. It was Luke she loved, and he wanted her, wanted her enough to marry her, to save her from the disgrace he had unwittingly brought on her. It was not what she had hoped for, but it was something at least.

He devoured her with his mouth, raining kisses upon every part of her face and throat until she felt dizzy, as though she might swoon, and an almost unbearable ache pulsed at the dark, secret core of her womanhood. Roughly he pushed aside the edges of her cloak and unfastened the buttons of her gown. Her chemise was a flimsy barrier, disposed of with a single tear, and then his fingers were fondling her bare breasts, his thumbs flicking her nipples, causing them to pucker and harden with excitement.

Jenny was afraid of Luke's desire, still horribly frightened of that ultimate act of surrender, but somehow she must bring herself to conquer her terror. If she wed him, he would not take no for an answer.

This thought was strengthened by the fact that suddenly he released her. Panting hard, as though having difficulty breathing and regaining control of his emotions, he spoke, his voice harsh now, a muscle working tensely in his jaw.

"That is what I will demand of you, Jenny, if you marry me," he rasped, "all that . . . and more. Be sure you are willing to give it, for if you are not, I will take it anyway—and I will go on taking it, no matter if you despise me for it. Do you understand?"

She nodded, not trusting herself to speak, for Luke had left her quite faint and breathless. She was a mass of quivering sensations, passion and fear mingling within her.

"Then let's go," he said softly.

Numbly Jenny allowed him to lead her to her fate.

Chapter Twenty-five

What a short, almost furtive ceremony it was! Nothing at all like what Jenny had imagined since she was a child, when she had dreamed of floating down the grand staircase at Faxon's Folly, clothed in her mother's ivory silk-and-lace wedding gown with its filmy veil and thousands of tiny seed pearls. Instead she wore the plain, subdued mauve dress and bonnet in which she had left Tumbling Creek, although she refused to stand up in her ragged old brown coat, which she laid on a chair in Mr. Bodkins's parlor.

Mr. Bodkins, the justice of the peace, was a gaunt, middle-aged man, who asked very few questions of the couple and yawned through the entire ritual, at which Jenny was sure he might have officiated in his sleep. Apparently he was used to being wakened at odd hours to perform marriages, and he simply wanted to get this one finished as quickly as possible so he might return to his bed. He examined only cursorily the license Luke had acquired at gunpoint from a terrified clerk who was working late at the county courthouse. Then Mr. and Mrs. Bodkins and the latter's sister, Miss Venable, the couple's only witnesses, signed the necessary papers, and Jenny was legally Luke's wife.

Still somewhat dazed by all that had occurred, she glanced down at the wedding ring on her left hand. She did not know where Luke had gotten the band, though she surmised incorrectly that it was stolen. All he had told her was that she need have no fear that it had belonged to his first wife, for it had not. Jenny did not know Luke had bought it some time ago, hoping she would someday wear it.

The ring was an antique gold circlet of flowers twining on vines, each petal and leaf delicately formed. A solitary diamond was set in the center of the largest blossom, and two diamond chips reposed on the leaves on either side. Jenny thought it was lovely, and she was glad it had not been Maybelle's.

Mr. Bodkins brought the girl out of her reverie by asking the couple if they wanted to have their photograph taken, but reluctantly Luke shook his head. Jenny was sorry not to have a small memento, other than her band, of the occasion, but she realized it would be extremely dangerous for Luke to have a picture of himself made. If the print were somehow to fall into the hands of the Pinkerton Detective Agency, it would be reproduced and published in every newspaper and on every wanted poster in the country. Luke might be recognized and identified by someone who wished him ill. The agency regularly circulated to all its detectives the photographs contained in its infamous Rogues' Gallery. Started in 1859 and the first of its kind, this was a meticulous collection of the names and pictures of the most-wanted men in the United States and its territories. No doubt Luke's name was on the list, but his photograph was not—and Jenny knew he wished to keep it that way.

It was quite late, so, after thanking Mr. and Mrs. Bodkins and Miss Venable for their time and trouble, the couple left the justice of the peace's house and made their way to the hotel, where Luke had rented a room for the night. He turned the key in the lock and opened the door, then lit a lamp and checked the chamber to be certain it had a good view of the town and was easily accessible to the back stairs in case it became necessary for him to make a quick exit. Then he left Jenny, saying he was going to take the team and the wagon to the livery stable, after which he would return.

She nodded gratefully, her throat dry with sudden nervousness, for she knew he was, in reality, being kind enough to give her both a little time and privacy in which to prepare herself for their wedding night. Jenny appreciated his thoughtfulness. Not every man would have been as generous under the circumstances, and she was struck anew by her deep feelings for Luke. No wonder she had fallen in love with him.

Slowly she took off her cloak and bonnet, laying them aside. Then she removed her dress and petticoats. These she hung carefully in the armoire so they would not be wrinkled in the morning. She had no wrapper or nightgown, for, in their haste to leave Tumbling Creek, her mind had been in such a turmoil that she had not thought to pack a carpetbag. So she left her chemise and pantalettes on, glad she was slender enough that she need not wear a corset. Jenny was not vain—her plainness did not encourage such indulgence—and she saw no point in lacing herself up so tightly she could not breathe simply to make a man admire her tiny waist.

From the pitcher on the bureau she poured some water into the washbasin and sponged herself off. Then she pulled the pins from her hair and brushed it as best she could with her fingers. She rinsed her mouth out too and drank a glass of water, wishing she had something stronger to sustain her.

As though in answer to her desire, Luke reappeared at last, carrying a bottle of brandy. His breath caught in his throat as he spied Jenny. The translucent cotton of her underclothes clung to her body, giving him only the barest, tantalizing glimpse of her flesh beneath. Her hair hung freely past her waist; Luke longed to touch the soft brown cascade, to feel its waves rippling through his fingers. Her face was so pale it made her freckles stand out all the more prominently across her nose and cheeks. Her eyes were wide and scared too, and they avoided his.

"I . . . thought we should have some sort of . . . celebration," he explained awkwardly as he set the liquor down on a table. "Is it too cold in here for you, Jenny? I could start a fire in the stove."

"That would be nice," she replied, her manner as hesitant as his own.

Indeed the spring night air was cool, and Jenny shivered slightly with nothing but her undergarments to protect her. But she knew it was not just a draught that chilled her. She was afraid of what was to come, once they went to bed, and though she had reassured herself repeatedly the past half hour that Luke was not like the marauders that day at Faxon's Folly had been, fear still rose within her. Her teeth chattered, and she clenched them tightly to avoid giving way to hysteria.

Once the fire was blazing cheerfully in the stove, Luke opened the brandy and poured two glasses of it, one of which he handed to Jenny.

"You *are* cold," he observed, noticing how still she shuddered a little. He unbuttoned his shirt, took it off, and wrapped it around her. "Sit down, and drink your brandy." He indicated the two chairs drawn up to the table. "You'll be warm in a minute."

Luke unbuckled his gunbelt and hung it over the bedpost. Then, as he did nothing more threatening than stretch out in the chair opposite Jenny and pull off his boots and socks, she began to relax somewhat. He rolled and lit a cigarette, dragging on it deeply. Silently Jenny sipped her brandy, feeling the fiery liquor burn down her throat to her belly, where it settled with mellow warmth. Luke's deliberately inconsequential chatter calmed her, for he did not appear like a man about to assault her brutally. Occasionally Jenny responded to his remarks, and gradually, between the brandy and their conversation, she started to feel at ease with him again, as she had during the time they'd spent at the cabin together.

But she knew they could not continue their light bantering forever, and presently Luke's laughter did die away. His face suddenly became intense and serious, and he leaned across the table and took her hands in his.

"Jenny." He spoke softly. "Jenny." He made her name sound like a caress, and she did not try to draw away from him, for though his touch was gentle, it was also firm. He paused, then went on. "I know there's something in your past—no, I'm not going to ask you about it." He stilled her protests quickly. "It's just that I know that for some reason you're inordinately frightened of . . . the act of intimacy that takes place between a man and a woman. I do not know what caused your fear, but I *do* know I won't allow it to come between us—not tonight or any other night. You're my wife now, and I want you.

"But I also want you to understand that I won't hurt you, Jenny, at least not deliberately. There is always some pain the first time that can't be helped, but it soon passes, and what follows can be most pleasurable if you let it. Do you understand?"

"Yes," she whispered brokenly.

The sudden terror and anguish in her eyes almost dissuaded him, but since Luke knew the only way to conquer one's demons was to confront them, he stood.

"Then come," he said, holding out his hand to her.

Swallowing hard, Jenny rose and let him lead her to the bed. There he slipped his shirt from her shoulders, tossed it aside, and turned down the quilt and sheet, waiting until she lay huddled beneath them. Then he blew out the lamp and in the firelight shrugged from his pants and slid into bed beside her, his weight making the mattress shift and creak.

Jenny was so tense she felt as rigid as a board when Luke touched her. Had she been made of glass, no doubt she would have shattered, he thought. She was holding her breath too, as though she must not make a sound, lest she draw attention to herself.

"Roll over, honey," he murmured. "I'm going to rub your back."

Hesitantly, as though fearing an attack from behind, she turned over onto her stomach, relaxing only slightly when Luke's strong hands began to knead the muscles in her back. Yet after a while, when this was all he did, the tautness of her body started to slacken and Jenny began to breathe more normally. Her eyes closed, for it was difficult to remain alert, poised for flight, with the brandy seeping so warmly through her veins and Luke massaging her so soothingly.

Encouraged, he kissed her lightly, nuzzling her hair and the nape of her neck, his lips traveling gently down her spine as he went on rubbing her back. His hands slipped down to knead her buttocks and her thighs and calves. He massaged her feet, his fingers pressing against the bottoms of her arches, his thumbs tracing tiny circles on top. He kissed her toes, sucked them, causing Jenny to moan a little down deep in her throat at the pleasurable sensations he was arousing within her. Her whole body began to feel heavy and languid, as though it had no energy; yet it tingled all over.

Slowly Luke turned Jenny over so she lay upon her back. All the while he continued to kiss and caress her, kneading her arms and hands now, rotating his thumbs on her palms, rubbing each of her fingers before running his tongue down the length of each one. He massaged the front of her legs, letting his hands close over her hips and waist before sliding them up to fasten on her breasts. His fingers trailed over the twin spheres tenderly; his palms just brushed the honeyed tips stiffening beneath her chemise.

Jenny's eyes flew open, for she was startled, but before she could protest Luke claimed her lips with his own. His hands fastened in her cloud of brown hair so she could not escape from him. He was straddling her, and now he eased his weight down upon her till he lay fully pressed against her, could feel her heart pounding in harmony with his own.

His tongue darted forth to trace the outline of her mouth, then forced her lips apart. Gently he probed the dark damp cavern, searching out its secret places, tasting of the sweetness it so reluctantly yielded up as at last Jenny started to respond to him, unable to deny her love for him. Inexorably the pressure of Luke's mouth grew harder, more demanding, as he devoured hers hungrily, his tongue plundering her until she was breathless and gasping for air. His lips finally released hers to seek her eyelids, her temples, the silky strands of her hair as he rained kisses upon her fervently, giving her no time to think. His tongue swept the contours of her ear; his teeth nibbled her lobe. He muttered into the soft small shell, words Jenny only half heard, only dimly comprehended, she was so caught up in the feelings he was wakening in her.

His breath was warm, smelling of brandy and tobacco. His hands seemed to be everywhere, touching her, fondling her, arousing her desire and causing her to strain against him, wanting him now, yet half yearning to run away from him as well before he could completely ensnare her.

His mouth found hers again; his tongue intertwined with her own until it seemed as though he meant to go on kissing her forever, as though he could banish her fear and resistance with his lips alone, leaving her like molten ore in his grasp, his to mold and shape as he willed. Jenny felt helpless against him, as though all her bones had melted inside of her and her muscles had been drained of their strength, so she was formless and weak, powerless to prevent this onslaught upon her senses. She whimpered a little, longing for mercy, for respite, but there was none.

Luke's carnal, searing mouth sought her throat, lingered there a moment before moving on to that erogenous place where her nape joined her shoulder. His teeth sank lightly into her flesh, sending sparks of electricity coursing through her body, making Jenny writhe and shiver beneath him like quicksilver. His fingers fumbled impatiently with the ribbons of her chemise, half untying, half tearing them until they were freed of their confines. Luke yanked the semi-transparent garment down, baring her breasts to his passion-darkened eyes.

Jenny felt a shudder of apprehension rip through her as he appraised her, and briefly she tried to cover herself from his raking gaze. But Luke only pushed her arms away and lowered his lips to the center of one ripe, beckoning mound. His tongue shot forth to tease the hard little peak in quick, licking and swirling motions that sent circles of rising excitement spiraling through her veins.

Her heart beat too fast in her breast; Jenny thought for an instant that it would burst from its exertions. Her pulse raced wildly, hammering in her ears and her throat, making her feel dizzy and faint, as though she were too hot and had run a great distance. She had not known it would be like this, a mad thing clawing at her mindlessly, shredding all her defenses, leaving her vulnerable and exposed—and not caring that she was so.

Somehow the earth seemed to have dropped from beneath her feet, so she was plummeting through a black void, a place where time had stopped and all emotion was primitive, feral, instinctive. Her fingers crept up to entwine themselves in Luke's golden hair, drawing him even closer as he sucked her nipple, his teeth grazing the taut button and making her feel crazy inside, as though she had been turned upside down and shaken. His mouth scorched its way across the valley of her chest, imprisoning the bud of her other breast, causing it to unfurl and blossom as readily as its mate had done. On and on he taunted it with his lips and tongue while his hands cupped the soft full globes. His thumbs glided sensuously over her areolae, mingling with the feel of his mouth as he claimed them both, then, one after the other.

Deep within the moist, hidden chasm of Jenny's womanhood, a small spark flickered into being, smoldering like an ember before suddenly it erupted into flame, threatening to consume her like a conflagration. A low cry emanated from her lips as Luke's mouth slid down her belly, his hands pulling at her chemise, tugging it down so it bunched around her waist.

"No," Jenny pleaded softly, twisting her body in his arms. "No, please, I don't want you to look at me."

"But, why?" Luke asked, puzzled, his voice thick with passion. "I want to see you, all of you."

"No, you don't." Jenny shook her head, tears starting in her eyes. "I —I told you I have scars, Luke, awful, ugly scars. . . ."

"I don't care," he reassured her, feeling her tense once more. "I don't care, Jenny darling. They can't be any worse than my own."

His fingers encircled her ribcage, finding and tracing tenderly the odd, slender, arc-shaped ridge that puckered her flesh there, as though part of a stirrup had bitten deeply into her skin. Gently Luke kissed the white mark, trailing his tongue along the length of its curve.

"It's like a crescent moon," he said, "more beautiful than any of mine. Scars are interesting, for each one has a story behind it. Someday you'll have to tell me this one's tale. Will you do that, Jenny?"

"I—I don't know. Perhaps." She spoke so quietly he almost didn't hear her.

Luke's hands moved lower still, easing her chemise and pantalettes down smoothly over her hips, his mouth kissing her all the while, his voice soothing her shaking body, her fear.

"Just relax, Jenny . . . relax. I'm not going to hurt you. Hmmm. You smell good, like honeysuckle. My brothers and I used to suck the blossoms every spring . . . sweet, sweet."

There were more scars on her belly, tiny, pale, and faint, like a scattering of stars—or the studs that could sometimes be found on hand-tooled saddles. Was that what had caused them? Luke wondered as his lips caressed each one.

He felt Jenny shudder as his hands pulled her underclothes down past her thighs, her knees, then removed them completely. Luke saw for the first time her legs, both of them scarred, the left limb savagely marred and twisted. How had it ever mended at all? he wondered, for it looked as though it had been irreparably crushed. Someone must have worked hard to save it, and Jenny had been extremely fortunate it had healed so well.

She must have spent months learning to walk again, Luke thought, his heart filled with admiration for the willpower and bravery it had taken for her to overcome this handicap.

Suddenly he realized how still Jenny was, scarcely even breathing, and it came to him that she was waiting for him to turn from her in revulsion. Instead, as he had done earlier, Luke bent his head and kissed each scar and indentation that marred her long legs. The limbs must have been beautiful once, supple and graceful, and his heart ached for her loss.

"Jenny, oh, Jenny," he breathed, "don't shrink from my touch like that. I'm not repelled by what I see. Don't you understand that these legs, whatever they've suffered, are a testament to your deep inner strength and courage? Do you know how many soldiers I saw with scars like these during the war—and worse? Do you know how many of those men simply quit trying, gave into the pain and torment that racked their bodies and minds—and died? Never be ashamed of these legs, Jenny girl. They show you're a survivor, like me."

The tears that had stung her eyes earlier now rolled slowly down Jenny's cheeks at Luke's words. It was so difficult for her to grasp the fact that this man she loved, so handsome and virile, was her husband. It was even harder still to comprehend the sweet things he was saying to her, the fact that he was not at all repulsed by her plainness, her scars.

"Oh, Luke, Luke," she whispered as softly he kissed the tears from her face.

He lay atop her now, his hands beginning to nudge her thighs apart, causing her to quiver once more with fear as inexorably the images from the past rose up to haunt her, to destroy this moment. She could feel his nakedness, his hardness pressed against her, frightening her.

"Don't, Luke. Oh, please, don't," Jenny begged as his fingers started to stroke rhythmically the length of her womanhood, tugging gently at downy brown curls, fondling the swells and folds of the dark places secreted therein.

"Why?" Luke asked quietly, gazing into her blank eyes, dimmed and shadowed with terror. "Whom do you see, Jenny? Tell me. Tell me." His voice was urgent in her ear.

"I—I can't. I don't know. They're ghosts . . . hideous ghosts."

"Don't think about them," he commanded. "Remember happy times, Jenny, happy things. Think of the church social, the arsenic biscuits. Ah, yes. That makes you laugh, doesn't it?" he teased, nuzzling her, kissing her.

Deftly, while she was slightly relaxed, he slipped his fingers inside of her, explored the warm moist chasm of her being. Jenny gasped at being touched so intimately and would have protested against his invasion of her, but Luke brought his mouth down over hers once more, shutting off her words.

"I won't hurt you," he repeated against her lips, his voice a husky murmur. "Don't be afraid."

His tongue pierced her mouth, ravaging her, swirling in and out between her lips, mimicking the movements of his fingers that readied her for him. His thumb flicked the little mound of her desire, causing it to ache and throb with wanting. Involuntarily Jenny strained and writhed against him, not knowing what she sought but instinctively sensing Luke did, that he could bring to fulfillment the pleasure and pain mingled within her. She felt wet and heated where he touched her, and she blushed at this evidence of her passion for him, the specters from her past driven from her mind.

Jenny could not think, could not remember, not now. She could only feel, engulfed by the emotions sweeping her along wildly in their wake, as though she were being buffeted by a strong, wayward wind. Her whole body felt as though it were on fire; she could feel the sparks showering within her, little embers of desire growing hotter and hotter, threatening to consume her.

She shivered and moaned and licked her lips, a mass of overwhelming sensations flooding her being. She felt as though at any moment she were going to explode from the tumultuous feelings crowding in on her, making her feel strange and dazed, as though her head were about to burst.

With some primal instinct Luke sensed her readiness to receive him. The tip of his maleness sought her, found her, entered her. Jenny had suffered internal injuries in her past, he knew. That was why she was unable to bear a child. So he did not expect to find the sheer membrane that would have marked her as a virgin, and he did not. Still her passage was tight and narrow, and he knew no man had trespassed here before him.

"A moment's pain, sweetheart," he muttered. "That's all, I promise."

Trembling with passion and the effort it had taken to control himself, Luke drove into her so deeply Jenny felt as though she were being impaled by him, split asunder by his stabbing assault. A sharp blade of agony knifed through her, and she cried out with shock and surprise at the hurt. But Luke muffled her incoherent whimpers with his mouth, restraining her body with his own as she lunged against him, unwittingly aiding his possession of her.

"Shhhhh. Shhhhh. The pain will pass," he insisted.

For a time Luke lay buried within her, unmoving, accustoming her to the feel of him inside of her. Then slowly he began to thrust in and out of her, powerfully, the muscles flexing sinuously in his back and arms as he supported himself above her so his weight would not crush her.

At first Jenny struggled against him, but presently, realizing she was helpless beneath him, she ceased to fight and began to give into the pleasurable feelings he was wakening within her. The terrible, burning ache that had devoured her earlier was gone, as though Luke had filled some void inside of her, had quenched the flames that had blazed through her body like wildfire.

Now she clung to him, her arms wrapped about his back so she could feel the rippling of his corded muscles as he spiraled down into the hidden core of her being. Instinctively she arched her hips to meet his own; his hands locked beneath her, assisting her with the motion.

Jenny felt something slowly beginning to build inside of her, growing stronger and stronger, as though she were rushing toward the edge of a cliff and was powerless to prevent herself from falling. She grew rigid at the sensation, for it made her feel as though she were losing control of herself, and after fighting it briefly at last she managed to hold it at bay. Presently it slipped away. She clutched Luke tightly, feeling the sudden stiffness of his body, the long, sighing shudder that shook the length of him as his release finally came and he spilled his seed within her, gasping with delight. A small sob of disappointment escaped from her lips as she recognized that it was over, that there would be nothing more. She felt cheated somehow, as though there were something she had missed, something she had not quite been able to grasp.

Gradually Luke withdrew, smiling down at her tenderly in the firelight, sensing she had not reached the climax he had so enjoyed.

"It will be better the next time, Jennilee," he told her, "when you are not so frightened and tense. Then you will know the full measure of your womanhood, I promise."

She did not then comprehend his meaning. Not until later, much later, after the last of the brandy was gone and the fire had died to ashes in the stove, when Luke took her yet a third time, did Jenny finally understand the joys of love.

Then she wept softly with happiness, wondering why she had ever feared the man who lay sleeping so peacefully by her side.

Chapter Twenty-six

It felt so strange to awaken and find Luke sharing her bed. Jenny was startled at first to discover herself locked in his embrace, and she gave a small cry, made a sudden sharp movement, wondering what imprisoned her so. Then she remembered, and her face flooded with color as she recalled last night in every detail. Of course. It was Luke, her husband, who lay beside her. It was delightful, Jenny thought, to wake up next to him, to feel his belly pressed against her back and his legs entangled with hers. One of his hands was wrapped in her hair; the other held her close, palm cupping her breast.

At the thought of the things those hands had done to her not so long ago, Jenny blushed even more crimson, feeling warm and tingling all over. No wonder her sisters had always looked forward so eagerly to sharing their husbands' beds! The emotions and sensations Luke had aroused in her just a few hours past had been like nothing Jenny had ever before experienced, and she felt shamelessly as though she could not wait to make love with him again, if only to be certain she had not dreamed the wondrous feelings they'd shared.

Had she really become that wanton woman who'd sprawled so nakedly, and finally so unabashedly, beneath him? Had those nails raking his back in ecstasy and that voice hoarsely urging him on toward the end really been her own? She shook her head a little with disbelief, half afraid she must have imagined the whole torrid episode during a brandy-induced stupor.

Gingerly Jenny eased herself from Luke's grasp, hoping not to disturb him, for he needed his sleep. Despite his assurances to the contrary, she knew he really hadn't been well enough to make the long drive to the county seat, and their exertions last night could not have been good for his injury. She longed to examine the wound but contented herself with a glance at his bandage, relieved to see it was not blood-soaked, as she had feared it might be. Her stitches had held, then; the gash had not broken open.

Quickly Jenny washed and dressed, marveling at herself as she did so. It did not seem possible that her body still looked the same, had not been altered in some manner. She had expected to find herself changed in some way, but she was not. Her scars were still there; Luke's kisses had not made them disappear. But somehow now the marks did not disturb Jenny as greatly as they had before. They were indeed her badges of courage, as Luke had said. She would never be ashamed of them again. Her breasts were still shaped as they had been before Luke had molded them to fit his lips and palms. And, except for a tiny twinge of pain between her thighs, a reminder of the virginity Luke had taken, her womanhood appeared untouched, as though he had never stroked its curls and secret places and buried himself within its dark moist chasm.

"You're just as beautiful in the morning light as you were in the darkness." Luke's low, throaty voice roused her from her reverie.

Jenny whirled, flushing, as hastily she slid her chemise over her head and began to pull on the rest of her garments.

"What's your hurry, sugar?" Luke asked, smiling lazily. "You're not still shy with me after last night, are you?"

"A little," Jenny confessed. "It's all so new and—and strange to me."

"But wonderful too, I hope."

"Yes, that also," she admitted bashfully. "How is your injury, Luke? I've been worried about it all morning."

"Better, I think, despite our . . . ah . . . activities last night. Are you hungry, honey? Shall we go downstairs and get some breakfast?"

Jenny nodded, swallowing hard and turning away as Luke rose to wash and dress. So he wouldn't think she was studiously ignoring him, she busied herself with tidying up the room a little and gathering up their belongings, making sure they weren't leaving anything behind. Still she could not prevent her eyes from straying once or twice to her husband's fine figure as he stood before the bureau. Once, Luke's glance caught her own in the dresser mirror, and Jenny's heart turned over in her breast at the realization that this handsome man truly belonged to her now—and she to him.

They ate in the hotel dining room, then walked down the street to the livery stable, where they retrieved the team and wagon. In no time at all, it seemed, they were on their way home to Tumbling Creek, the wedding certificate that was proof of their marriage tucked securely in Luke's pocket.

They chatted amiably during the drive, finding out as much as they could about each other, for Luke insisted it would appear strange if they didn't even know each other's favorite color and dessert. Abigail Crabtree was sure to cross-examine them to be certain they were really wed. It turned out that Luke was partial to blue, while Jenny preferred lilac. But they both liked apple pie topped with vanilla ice cream. They found they had many other things in common as well, which led them to believe their marriage would work out even better than they'd hoped.

It was already dark when they reached Tumbling Creek, so they headed straight for Jenny's cabin. After a late supper they made love long into the night and then fell asleep, smiling, not caring what tomorrow would bring.

The Reverend Thompkins was quite nervous, for, despite Abigail Crabtree's stout insistence that Jenny had lied about being married to Luke in order to save her job and reputation, the reverend was not so certain this was the case. The Morgan brothers were, he thought, extremely unpredictable in their behavior, and it was indeed just possible that Luke had wed the girl and kept the marriage a secret. If this were so, he was not going to be happy at all to hear his wife had been branded a scarlet woman, and the Reverend Thompkins had no desire to be the target of Luke's rage. Thus, just to be on the safe side, the reverend had prepared two sermons for this Sunday morning. The first, an inflammatory diatribe on the wages of sin and fornication, he would give if he discovered Miss Abigail was right about the schoolteacher and chastisement was in order. The second, revolving around the wedding in Cana, would be his speech, however, if he found Miss Abigail did not in this instance know it all—as she would like to think!

The minute the Reverend Thompkins spied Luke and Jenny driving into the churchyard, he was glad he'd had the foresight to prepare the second sermon, for it was obvious to him from the thrust of Luke's jaw that the outlaw meant to set matters straight once and for all.

His hand outstretched in greeting, the reverend hurried forward, intending to forestall any unpleasantness.

"Good morning, Luke. Miss Jenny. I was hoping to see you both here today. I—I wanted to apologize for my behavior in town the other afternoon. It seems there was some sort of misunderstanding. . . ." His sentence trailed off expectantly.

"You bet there was, Robert," Luke declared, his voice cold, indignant. "I'm certain you did not deliberately mean to insult my wife—"

"Oh, no, Luke. No siree!" the reverend insisted. "As I told you, it was all just a mistake. Why, I wouldn't offend Mrs. Morgan for the world; indeed I'm most sorry to have done so. I didn't know—"

"No, of course you didn't." Luke relented slightly, biting his tongue to keep from laughing at the stricken expression on the Reverend Thompkins's face. Then Luke thought of what Jenny would have suffered this morning if he hadn't been there to marry and protect her, and his jaw hardened once more. "We kept our marriage a secret, Robert," he explained, "because I didn't want those damned Pinkerton agents hounding Jenny the way they do Kate and Winona. However, since the cat's out of the bag now, so to speak, we'd be pleased if you'd make a general announcement this morning and give us your blessing."

"I'd be happy to do so," the reverend said, fingering his tight round collar as though it were choking him.

He was more relieved than ever that he'd written the second sermon, and he longed to throttle that busybody Miss Abigail for her prying and meddling. Well, she would get her comeuppance today!

The Reverend Thompkins didn't know how right he was. Matthew McNabb had finally finished whittling a large hollow space in the hymnal he intended to substitute for the one Miss Abigail normally used. Earlier he had crept into church, and, after glancing about slyly to be certain his actions were unobserved, he had carefully pulled from his pocket a big fat bullfrog with bulbous eyes. He had secreted the unfortunate creature in the mutilated book, then he'd closed the volume and placed it in the desk, taking away Miss Abigail's usual copy. He had then made good his escape, rejoining his father and Lacey Standish outside. Now, certain he would not be caught, Matthew's sole concern was whether or not there was enough air inside of the hymnal for the bullfrog to breathe. He frowned. No doubt he should have punched a few holes in the cover, but it was too late now. Everyone had already started toward the church.

All took their seats, quieting obediently when the Reverend Thompkins informed them he had a few announcements to make before starting the service. The most surprising of these was that Luke Morgan and Jenny Colter, who had been secretly wed, now wished to make their marriage public knowledge. Several loud gasps greeted this news, and everybody turned, craning their necks to get a glimpse of the couple. The sudden attention made Jenny blush, and Luke put his arm around her protectively.

After all the talk had died down, the reverend pronounced his blessing on the two. Then he instructed the congregation to stand and turn to page 314 in its hymnals. Miss Abigail, who was somewhat nearsighted, reached into her desk and pulled out her book, peering down at it closely as she opened its cover. The bullfrog, blinded by the sudden light that proclaimed its freedom, leaped wildly from the hymnal, smacking Miss Abigail in the face before it bounced off her bosom and rolled onto the floor, where it poised momentarily, stunned and dazed. Miss Abigail let out several loud shrill shrieks before she swayed, clutching her throat, and fainted, having the good fortune to be caught by Horace Peabody as she fell. Unaware of the commotion it had instigated, the bullfrog hopped away while Mr. Peabody, clucking with distress, laid Miss Abigail down on the bench and began lamely to wave his handkerchief in her face.

Several youngsters spied the rapidly escaping bullfrog and pointed it out to their parents, and the entire church erupted with laughter as it realized the cause of Miss Abigail's swoon. Everyone present had one reason or another for wishing to see Miss Abigail brought down a peg or two, and none could repress his delight at her ignominious descent at the hands of a bullfrog.

Luke, seeing an ideal opportunity to prevent Jenny from being mercilessly interrogated by the more curious, gossipy members of her sex following the service, grasped her hand and, amid the cacophony and confusion, led her swiftly down the aisle.

Matthew McNabb, slouching nonchalantly in his seat toward the rear of the church, positively beamed as when she passed him Jenny favored him with a long slow wink and a conspiratorial smile before leaving the church.

Chapter Twenty-seven

All summer long, with the help of his brothers and Moses, who had by this time fully recovered from his injuries, Luke worked on the big house, as they had taken to calling the home he was building for Jenny. It sat on the crest of a bald-knobbed hill on his property, so no trees obscured its view, and it was the first thing one saw in the distance after turning onto the winding drive leading up to Luke's farm, Whispering Pines.

In the eyes of the Ozark natives the place was a veritable mansion, for it was two stories high and constructed of smooth planks purchased from Mr. Kincaid's sawmill rather than rough-hewn logs. Outside, the facade was plain and unpainted, for Jenny had wanted the house to blend in with its surroundings like the other structures in Tumbling Creek, and she had overridden Luke's suggestion that they whitewash the clapboard. Both stories bore wide, welcoming verandas that circled the entire house, and shutters framed the long, narrow, glass-paned casement windows. Two sets of French doors on each floor provided access front and back. In addition, the entrances were hung with real screen doors, and there were real screens on the windows as well, so during the summer months the whole house could be opened up to catch any cooling breezes.

Inside, downstairs, were a foyer and two parlors—a formal one for company and a smaller, cozier one for family—a combination library and study for Luke, a dining room, a large kitchen with a breakfast nook and pantry, and a small washroom. Upstairs were five bedrooms and three more washrooms.

Jenny could hardly wait for the house to be finished, for Luke had given her a free hand and purse in the decorating of it. Already she had ordered draperies and carpets, fabrics and furniture, and the oil lamps that would hang in each room.

Even more excited than Jenny about the house were Kipp and Sarah Jane. They accompanied her on numerous shopping expeditions, bubbling over with enthusiasm as they selected the items to go in their bedrooms. Each having a private room was a novel experience for the two youngsters, who had always shared one in the past. Kipp wanted a bold, brown-and-blue log-cabin quilt for his new bed; Sarah Jane chose one of Dresden-plate design with a mixture of bright, cheerful colors that complemented her ever-present rag doll.

Delcine was busy as well, picking out this and that for Luke's old cabin, which he had given to her and Moses. After it was refurbished they meant to jump over the broom, and Luke and Jenny would hold a large party that would serve as a combination housewarming and wedding celebration for all of them.

Sometimes Jenny felt so happy she pinched herself to be sure it was all real. Luke now lived with her at the cabin that belonged to the school board, but Kipp and Sarah Jane were still staying with Lottie and Jed, since there wasn't room for the youngsters at Jenny's place. Soon, however, they would all be together in the new house, a real family. Jenny could scarcely believe she wouldn't wake up some morning to find she'd dreamed the whole thing.

Only one dark cloud marred her newfound happiness, and that was the thought of the Pinkerton detective, Gus Grissom. Luke had heard through the grapevine that the agent had suffered a broken leg, severe frostbite, and pneumonia during the blizzard and had gone home for a lengthy recuperation. Still Jenny fretted that the man, once he'd recovered, would return to Tumbling Creek to attempt to take her husband into custody. Luke only shrugged away her fears, saying he would handle the matter if and when it arose, but Jenny's fear that Luke might someday be arrested led her to consider all sorts of rash ideas to avoid having him taken from her.

"Toby could set off some kind of explosion or something to make it look like there'd been an accident. Then Kate, Winona, and I could claim you'd all been killed," she suggested hopefully. "We could hold a burial service for you and everything, so no one would be the wiser."

"Jenny"—Luke smiled wryly and shook his head ruefully—"don't you know how many outlaws have considered doing something like that or have actually carried such a plan out? It never works. Sooner or later word always leaks out that the 'dead' man is really still alive, and then those damned Pinkerton agents come sniffing around like always to find out the truth of the matter."

"Well," she continued, only slightly daunted, "perhaps we could bribe Mr. Grissom to go along with the scheme."

Luke laughed outright at that.

"Jennilee," he said, "I do believe you really are an outlaw at heart! It's obvious you know very little about the Pinkerton Detective Agency. Allan Pinkerton is a monomaniac. His sole aim in life is to catch criminals. Don't you think he's thought of the possibility of his men being bribed to make false reports to the home office? Believe me: Even if Mr. Grissom's integrity could be bought, it wouldn't be long before the entire plot started to unravel at its seams. When outlaws are killed representatives from the Pinkerton Detective Agency are sent out to identify positively—and to photograph as well—the dead bodies before burial. If they're already in their graves by the time word of their deaths reaches the home office, the coffins are dug up and opened so the identification process can still be carried out. Then the pictures are published in newspapers and circulated among lawmen for further verification of identity."

"Why, that's—that's absolutely gruesome," Jenny choked out, shocked.

"It may be, but it's a damned good method of preventing criminals from dreaming up plans to outwit the law, just as you're doing now," Luke stated calmly. "No, Jennilee. The only way I'm going to be able to quit my life of crime is to take my chances and stand trial for what I've done. I don't much relish the idea, but I seriously doubt the governor would even consider granting me amnesty, which is my only other alternative."

"Well, you never know until you ask," Jenny pointed out. "There's no harm in that, surely."

"No, I guess not," Luke agreed. "Still . . . I don't think too much of Governor Brown. He doesn't seem too interested in getting a whole lot accomplished. The twenty-sixth General Assembly was convened on January the fourth, but it was barely in session two and a half months before it was adjourned until December the sixth. Most of the important business was still unfinished at the time or, worse yet, hadn't even been brought up." Luke sounded disgusted. "Summer's almost over, and before you know it winter will be here—with nothing of any real value yet decided on by the state. I tell you, Jenny, sooner or later the people are going to get fed up with the government of Missouri. They're going to want to see some new blood in office."

Hearing Luke's serious and impassioned tone, Jenny laid aside her embroidery.

"Before the war you were studying law, weren't you, Luke?" she asked. "J.R. told me you were planning on going into politics."

"Yeah, I was, but it's a little late now for that."

"I don't think so. If we could get the governor to grant you amnesty or even to give you a pardon if you have to stand trial, you could still run for office. Why, you and your brothers are practically heroes in Southern Missouri. I'm sure with a little planning and campaigning you could win the popular vote with no difficulty at all."

"Do you really think so, Jenny?"

"Of course. Why, with J.R. acting as your campaign manager and Toby taking care of the funds and the rest of the details, I don't see how you could lose. Raiford's a natural salesman; he'd be great at knocking on doors and passing out leaflets. And Billy Clay . . . well, perhaps he could run errands and do other odd jobs. That's practically your whole political team right there."

"Yeah, it is, isn't it?" Luke drawled, pretending disinterest, but Jenny could tell he was excited all the same.

"I'll tell you what," she insisted, "after we have the housewarming and Moses and Delcine are settled in their new cabin, I'll take the train up to Jefferson City and plead your case with Governor Brown myself. That way, you won't have to risk your neck for nothing if the answer is no. What do you say, Luke?"

"I say you're probably wasting your time, Jenny," he replied gruffly, once more burying himself in his newspaper.

"Well"—she shrugged—"it's my time to waste after all, isn't it?"

Then, humming under her breath, she again bent her head to her embroidery, smiling happily to herself in the lamplight.

The housewarming was a huge success. Earlier that day Moses and Delcine had literally jumped over the broom together, as their ancestors had done in the past, the broom being laid flat on the ground. Then they had been duly wed by the Reverend Thompkins, who had been most anxious to make amends for his behavior on that fateful day when he'd been influenced by Abigail Crabtree.

Now the two couples stood on the front porch, greeting guests as they alighted from their wagons and buggies.

"Good evenin', sah, mizzus." Moses nodded to arriving friends. "Let me drive dat cah'ige on 'round back fo' yo. Mistah Luke an' Miz Jenny sho' will be pleased ter see yo heah."

Delcine, who was taking care of shawls and gifts, was startled and touched to discover that many of the carefully wrapped presents were for her and Moses. More than once was such a package pressed into her hands, along with words of thanks and congratulations.

"A little something for you and your new husband, dear. I certainly appreciated your taking the time to stitch that hem for me, Delcine. I doubt if even Miss Lacey could have done a better job."

Or, "Delcine, I can't thank you enough for bandaging up Johnnie's knee when he fell out of that old oak tree at school. I wanted you and Moses to have a little something from us. Best wishes on your marriage, dear."

Or, "I don't think we'd have made it through the winter, what with Emmett being laid up with his leg and all. It was right kind of Moses to cut that firewood for us. Here's a little something to show our gratitude, Delcine. We hope you two will be very happy together."

Then, talking and laughing, the ladies and gentlemen swept inside, beckoned by the welcoming lights that glowed gaily in the twilight, mingling brightly with the flashing of the fireflies that flitted in and out of the fragrant, white-blossomed honeysuckle Jenny had planted along the veranda.

The house rang with the sounds of loud, vibrant music, hands clapping, and feet stomping. The strings of the fiddles and banjos sang, blending melodiously with the plucking of mandolins, the hammering upon dulcimers, the wailing of French harps, the buzzing of Jew's harps, and the slapping of spoons upon knees. Bass harmony was added by the low notes of a catgut-strung board-and-washtub and the breathy blasts of a moonshine jug. Keeping time right along with all the rest was the scraping of thimbles across an old metal washboard.

Those who had worn their clogging shoes had formed a circle and were swinging their partners, their toes and heels beating a clattering rhythm on the wooden floor as they danced.

In the dining room the long, heavy table was laden to groaning. There were two punchbowls, one of which bore the definite taste of moonshine, and many plates of food. A large glazed ham was flanked by platters of fried chicken. There were vegetables in profusion: mashed potatoes, green beans, sweet corn, black-eyed peas, and fried okra. A gravy boat brimmed with thick white gravy, and baskets were filled to overflowing with buttermilk biscuits. Cakes and pies dotted the sideboard, along with a fluted crystal bowl of sugar-coated strawberries and a small silver pitcher of rich cream.

The doors leading from the dining room to the kitchen swung

smoothly on oiled hinges as women and young girls came and went, some carrying dishes to replace those already emptied by the hungry men, others bearing trays stacked high with dirty plates and cups.

Those gentlemen who had already helped themselves to the wide assortment of food were now gathered outside on the veranda, the air about them a thick mist as blue clouds of smoke drifted upward from their cigars, driving away ladies and mosquitoes alike. The men's jocular voices rose and fell as they exchanged the latest jokes and ribald stories that might not be told in the presence of their wives and daughters.

Inside, those women not assisting with the refreshments were sitting in one corner of the parlor, repeating gossip—old and new—while keeping a sharp eye on the children to be certain they weren't tippling on the sly from the spiked punchbowl.

It was hot and humid that late summer evening. The still air was buffeted by the constant swish of palmetto fans and scented handkerchiefs and the sound of young ladies clamoring sweetly to see the gardens (where a cool breeze was sure to be found), laying their hands beseechingly upon the arms of eligible bachelors.

After the last of their guests had been received, Luke grabbed Jenny's hand and led her toward the formal parlor, where the furniture had been pushed back against the walls to make room for the musicians and dancers. He thought she looked especially pretty tonight in a rose-colored gown of organza that Lacey Standish had made for her a few weeks earlier. Her bare shoulders gleamed above a ruffled bodice and sashed waist, and the flounced hem of her billowing skirt permitted just the scantiest glimpse of her silk stocking-covered ankles and matching morocco slippers. Her long brown hair hung freely to her waist, as Luke liked it best, and was drawn up in back with a large pink bow. The gold, heart-shaped locket, which he had given her for a wedding present, hung on a velvet ribbon around her neck.

Grinning, Luke brought out a gift from a corner where he'd hidden it earlier and handed it to Jenny. Blushing and smiling with pleasure, she opened it quickly. Inside was a pair of clogging shoes.

"Put them on," he directed, "and let's dance."

"But I—I can't," she protested, somewhat hurt that he would even suggest such a thing in light of her lameness.

"Of course you can." He overrode her complaints firmly. "If old Pop Sweeney can get out there with his wooden leg and dance, you can manage on your own two limbs."

Jenny bit back anything further she might have said, for it was true that Pop Sweeney was thumping away as loudly with his peg leg as the others were with their clogging shoes. How churlish she would appear to hold back on account of her own handicap. Jenny kicked off her slippers and stepped into the clogging shoes. Soon she was bouncing away with the rest, breathless from her exertions. To her relief no one mentioned her awkwardness; instead everyone seemed eager to help her learn the steps and delighted that she had joined in. Luke beamed with approval as he swung her around, then, winking, relinquished her to Kipp, who'd tapped on his father's waist, not yet being tall enough to reach his shoulder. Luke bowed to a thrilled Sarah Jane while Jenny curtsied to Kipp, and another dance ensued.

Finally, worn out, Jenny made her way through the crowd toward the refreshment table. Gratefully she took the glass of apple cider Delcine handed her and then sank down onto a nearby stool, fanning herself vigorously.

"Well, Miss Jenny"—Delcine eyed the crowd—"I'd say the party's a real success."

"Yes, it is, isn't it? Somehow the youngsters really add to the fun. Isn't it a lovely custom, having them attend as well as the adults? I was so surprised when Luke told me the children would be allowed to come. We never got to go to anything when I was growing up in Georgia."

"It is nice in Tumbling Creek," Delcine assented. "I'm glad we moved here and are going to stay."

"Me too," Jenny echoed, sighing. "It's good to have a family again, and it seems like this town is really home now, doesn't it? But, then, it's part of the South, and, good or bad, I guess you always cling to your roots."

At that moment the musicians struck up a rousing number, and, her feeling of pride in her homeland strong within her, Jenny joined the others in singing, swear words and all. There were several verses, but these were the two she liked best:

"Oh, I'm a good old Rebel; now that's just what I am.
For this, their land of freedom, I do not give a damn.
I'm glad I fought against it. I only wish we'd won.
And I don't want no pardon for anything I done.

Three hundred thousand Yankees lie stiff in Southern dust.
We got three hundred thousand before they conquered us.
They died of Southern fever, of Southern steel and shot,
And I wish it was three million instead of what we got."

There then followed a stirring rendition of "Dixie," which left the men clearing their throats gruffly and the women dabbing with their handkerchiefs at the corners of their eyes.

After that it seemed only natural that people should begin to gather up their belongings and head for home, calling their good-byes in soft voices that mingled sweetly with the ballad now played by the musicians and the cries of the birds, the chirruping of the locusts, and the croaking of the frogs in the distance.

After everyone had gone Luke closed the front doors firmly and, his arm about Jenny's waist, walked upstairs with her to their bedroom. In darkness they undressed and slipped into bed together, and, while they clung to each other in impassioned embrace, Luke wrapped Jenny's long brown hair around his throat and told her that he loved her.

Chapter Twenty-eight

It did not seem possible, but it was true. Luke loved her! Jenny was so happy she thought she would burst. Her husband loved her. He had said so last night, and she had whispered of her love for him in return. It had been the perfect ending to a perfect day.

"Morning, sweetheart. Are you awake?" Luke asked softly, snuggling closer to Jenny and nuzzling her neck.

"Yes, are you?" she inquired, nestling contentedly into the warm circle of his arms.

"Uh huh. But I didn't think I'd get up just yet. It's early still. What do you say, Jennilee? Are you interested in finding out what the birds and the bees and your husband know?"

"I might be." She smiled. "After all, as a teacher, it's my duty to learn new things so I can stay informed."

"Is that right?" he queried, his hands beginning to move very slowly and sensuously on her body. "Well, I've got a great deal of knowledge you might like to acquire, then. But I warn you: It will take years for you to learn it all."

"That's quite all right. I've got all the time in the world. Teach me what you know," Jenny urged, turning in his arms and tilting her face up to his invitingly.

Luke brushed her lips with his own. He touched her gently in the dawn light, tracing with wonder every plane and curve of her heart-shaped face, as though he were blind and seeing her for the first time with his hands, as though he did not know intimately each and every part of her.

"You are so beautiful," he breathed, "beautiful to me in a way that no other woman ever has been or ever will be. I love you, Jenny. I love you."

He kissed her mouth, those sweet, tender, trembling lips that parted eagerly for his tongue as it darted forth to outline the full, generous shape of her mouth before venturing inside to taste, then drink deeply of the honey within. Luke would never get his fill of her, no matter how many times he kissed her, caressed her, took her. He would always want more of her.

His lips branded her cheeks, the tip of her freckled nose, her eyelids, her temples, the silky strands of her soft brown hair. He wrapped his fingers in the long tresses and drew them across his throat. He loved the feel of them, the smell of them. Sighing with pleasure, he buried his face in the cascade billowing out like waterfall across the pillow. His tongue found Jenny's ear, and as he traced the contours of the small, curved shell, she shivered with delight. He murmured words of love and sex there, his breath warm against her skin.

His hands moved down to her breasts, fondling them with slow, featherlike strokes that made her dusky nipples spring to life at his touch. Luke enveloped the twin peaks with his mouth, lips and tongue sucking and swirling as Jenny moaned softly with pleasure, feeling tiny tingles of electricity race through her blood. His mouth swept lower still, to the small indentation in her belly, which he teased with his tongue, making her laugh and writhe beneath him. His lips trailed down along her thighs, then slid back up to the swells of her womanhood, seeking the dark, hidden chasm that lay within.

He felt that soft place quiver beneath his mouth and tongue as his fingers slipped inside of her to ease the ache for him he knew was burning there. Deftly his thumb manipulated the little round flower of her desire that blossomed at the edge of the valley he yearned to fill with his manhood, and with difficulty he controlled his passion as Jenny whimpered down low in her throat, her fingers intertwining in his hair to pull him even nearer.

"Now, my love, now," she whispered brokenly, hoarsely, unashamed of her wanting, and Luke did not wait any longer.

He rose and, poised above her, began his diving descent down into the wet, beckoning pool of her, feeling the heated waves of her being close around him, engulfing him, so it was as though he were drowning in her, being sucked down into the churning depths of her innermost self. Like breakers crashing against a beach, Jenny surged upward against him to meet his powerful thrusts, her hips arching wantonly against Luke's own.

After a time they lay still, their bodies glistening with the fine sheen of dew that gave evidence of their mating. Their hearts beat in harmony; they breathed as one. At last they slept, locked in each other's embrace.

It was late morning when they again awakened, but now they did not linger, for in the other rooms they could hear Kipp and Sarah Jane stirring, and from downstairs in the kitchen came the sound of Delcine singing as she prepared breakfast for all.

Luke and Jenny, their love for each other shining in their eyes, washed and dressed, then joined the others at the dining table. As school would not start again for several more weeks, Kipp asked permission to work with Moses in the fields, and Sarah Jane gestured with her hands to tell them that she was going to help Delcine bake cookies.

Jenny smiled, overjoyed at the children's obvious happiness with their new home and being a real family once more. Though they missed their grandparents of course, they were nevertheless pleased to be with their father again and to have Jenny as their mother now.

"Well," Luke said, "I guess Jenny and I will drive into town and get the rest of the supplies we need."

That settled and breakfast over, they all went about their projects. It was a pleasant drive into Tumbling Creek, although Jenny momentarily felt a pang of wistfulness as they passed her old cabin. Already weeds were encroaching upon the property, and the grass was waist-high. Luke, seeing the expression on her face, shook his head.

"I'll have Pa get onto Horace about it, Jenny," he told her. "Even though the place is empty now, there's no sense in letting it get all run down again. I know you and Moses and Delcine worked hard to fix it up."

"Thank you, Luke," she returned gravely, appreciative of his understanding. "It *does* hurt to see it looking so bad when it was once my home."

Tumbling Creek when they reached it was bustling with activity, for everyone was getting ready for the fall harvest and the planting season that would follow. Mr. Henshaw's feed store was quite crowded, so Jenny told Luke she would go on over to Miss Lacey's dress shop, where she wanted to pick out some material for Sarah Jane. Luke nodded, and Jenny slipped away. Once outside, she ran into Jed and Lottie, and Lottie, upon learning Jenny's destination, was glad to accompany her, leaving Jed to fend for himself.

Since Luke and Jenny's wedding, the girl had grown even closer to Lottie, who had stoutly defended their marriage, claiming she'd known about it all the while.

"Why, Abby," Lottie had firmly declared to a nosy Abigail Crabtree, "why do you think Jed and me's been so partial to Jenny all along? 'Course we knowed she was Luke's wife. You don't think my boys was over there cleaning up her yard for nothing, do you? And naturally Jed and J.R. wanted to see that she got the teaching position. After all, that's what family's for, ain't it? To lend a helping hand when it's needed? If you hadn't of opened your big mouth, nobody would ever of needed to know a blamed thing. But I guess the cat was bound to get out of the bag sooner or later. Now poor Jenny'll have them idiot Pinkerton agents hounding her the same way they do Kate and Winona!"

Now as they traipsed along the sidewalk Lottie chattered on about the housewarming last evening, saying what a good time she and Jed had had and how happy they were for Luke and Jenny, even if they did miss Kipp and Sarah Jane something fierce.

Jenny smiled.

"Lottie, you know you and Jed are welcome at Whispering Pines anytime. You don't need an invitation. Why, the children were so excited about the ponies you gave them as going-away presents that I was half afraid they weren't going to come live with us after all!"

Lottie laughed brightly.

"Well, it was the least we could do for 'em, seeing as how Luke said it was about time they were learning to ride anyway."

The two women continued to visit companionably as they entered Miss Lacey's store, where they spent nearly an hour selecting fabrics and patterns. When they left Jenny raised her hand to the brim of her bonnet to shield her eyes from the glare of the afternoon sun. To her consternation she spied Velvet Rose strolling down the street as bold as brass, arm in arm with some man Jenny had never seen before. Still there was something about his face that nagged at her, as though she ought to have recognized him.

"Lottie"—she nudged her mother-in-law in the ribs—"who's that man there, the one with Velvet Rose?"

To Jenny's surprise Lottie's eyes narrowed with intense dislike, and her lips thinned with disapproval.

"Mercy!" she snapped. "I had no idea *he* was back! That's Maybelle's brother, Tully Boothe. I sure hope Luke doesn't see him. Luke can't stand him, and, like as not, Tully'll be wanting to see his sister's young 'uns—he *is* their uncle; more's the pity—and then there'll be trouble. Come on, Jenny. Act like you don't notice them."

This was difficult, however, as it was obvious the couple had already spied the two women. Velvet Rose was whispering in Tully's ear, and he was eyeing Jenny intently, as though he couldn't believe what he was hearing about her. With quiet anger Jenny flipped open her parasol, blocking the couple's view of her. She knew Velvet Rose resented her for marrying Luke—hated her even, because from the day he'd met Jenny, Luke had not once paid another visit to Miss Ruby's bordello. There was no telling what Velvet Rose was saying about her; Jenny knew the tart would stop at nothing to even the score between them.

Well, there was little Jenny could do to defend herself from Velvet Rose's malicious tongue, and, besides, she did not care at all what Maybelle's brother thought of her. Jenny wished only that she could remember why his face appeared so familiar to her and why she felt she knew him when she was almost certain she'd never seen him before today.

The nightmares came again that night, and somehow they were even more terrifying than usual, for Jenny had not had them for some time now. She awoke screaming and ripping frantically at the bedclothes, and she did not recognize Luke when he tried to comfort her. He was horrified, not only by her violent reaction to him, but also by the fact that the candle that burned always in their room at night had guttered in its socket. He felt this was somehow the cause of Jenny's distress. Quickly he rose and lit a lamp, but its light did not help. Jenny continued to scream, staring ahead blankly, as though she did not see him at all, but viewed another scene dredged from her memories.

Kipp and Sarah Jane, wakened by the commotion, knocked timidly on the bedroom door, wanting to know what was happening, and with relief Luke instructed Kipp to run down to the little house, as they called Moses and Delcine's cabin, to fetch the pair.

"Hurry, son! *Hurry!*" Luke urged. "Sary, can you go downstairs to the kitchen and put a pot of tea on to boil for me?"

The little girl nodded, her eyes wide with fear, and scurried away to do her father's bidding, wondering what was wrong with her beloved Jenny.

At last to Luke's relief Moses and Delcine arrived. With swift efficiency born of long practice, Moses warmed some milk on the stove while Delcine talked soothingly to Jenny until gradually her shrieks and sobs ceased, and she huddled quietly on the bed, trembling.

"It's all my fault," Luke muttered. "It's all my fault. The damned candle went out—"

"Shhhhh, Mister Luke," Delcine crooned. "This isn't any of your doing, so don't be blaming yourself now, you hear? This is all on account of Miss Jenny's past, something that happened . . . oh . . . purt near seven years ago now, it's been, and you didn't have a blessed thing to do with it. Why, to tell you the truth, you've done more to help Miss Jenny than any of those doctors in Atlanta ever did."

Kipp and Sarah Jane, worried about their stepmother's welfare, crept nearer to the bed. If their father were upset, something must be terribly wrong.

"Is—is Jenny going to die?" Kipp spoke up hesitantly, his eyes big and scared.

"No, child," Delcine reassured the boy, giving him a hug. "She just had a bad dream, that's all. You and Miss Sary go on back to bed now, you hear? Moses will come tuck you in and tell you a story. In the morning everything will be just fine and Miss Jenny will be her old self again, I promise."

"All right," Kipp said, taking Sarah Jane's hand and leading her away, though she insisted on peeping back over her shoulder to be certain Jenny hadn't disappeared.

"Mister Luke, if you'll just give Miss Jenny some of this warm milk with a shot of that brandy in it, she'll be able to get back to sleep now," Delcine told him. "I'll check on the youngsters before I go. If you need anything else, just holler."

"Thank you, Delcine. I really appreciate everything you and Moses have done tonight."

"Don't you fret yourself about it. It was no trouble at all. Many's the time we've lived through Miss Jenny's bad spells, Mister Luke, and been glad to do it. I guess anybody who survived what she did is bound to have nightmares now and then."

"What was it, Delcine? What really *did* occur in her past to wound her so?" Luke desperately wanted to know the answer.

Delcine shook her head regretfully.

"Mister Luke"—she sighed—"I surely would like to tell you, but I wasn't there that day, and I reckon it's Miss Jenny's story anyhow. You'll have to ask her about it. When she's ready she'll tell you what happened all those years ago. Then maybe you'll understand why she's the way she is and you can show her how to get rid of her ghosts."

"I want to help Jenny, Delcine. You don't know how badly I want to help her. I love her."

"I know that," Delcine replied softly as she headed toward the door. "I know that. Good night, Mister Luke."

* * *

They had walked some distance from the house, and now they stood in the midst of the woods in a tiny clearing among the stand of close, gnarled trees that surrounded them. It was a solitary place, hidden from view by the feathery green boughs of pines, fringed cedars, and acorn-bearing oaks. Nearby, a clear blue spring gurgled quietly in the forest hush. Grass, moss, and creeping vines grew like a thick carpet upon the ground, and wildflowers dotted the earth in a riotous tangle of bright color. Here and there were strange rock formations with animal-like shapes.

Wordlessly Jenny sank down upon the back of what looked like a stone deer, its legs curled up beneath it, so it appeared as though it were resting. She reached out and locked her hands about its neck, inhaling deeply of the fragrantly perfumed air, for honeysuckle grew wild here. Then she turned to Luke, who was studying her silently, his hunger for her plain upon his face.

She gazed into his sky-blue eyes, knowing now why he had brought her to this place. Slowly, without speaking, for they had no need of words between them now, they began to undress until at last they were naked beneath the setting sun. Jenny held out her arms to her husband.

"Make love with me, Luke," she murmured. "Make love with me."

He needed no further invitation. Wanting her, he pressed her down upon the soft sweet grass and took her there, bathed in the pink-orange glow of the sun inexorably descending on the far horizon. But the fire of their bodies burned hotter than any celestial flame, as though the brightness of their love would never dim but would surpass the boundaries of earth and time and beyond.

Afterward they lay together quietly, whispering the words all lovers speak. Then, when he sensed she was finally ready, Luke said:

"Tell me about your ghosts, Jenny."

She stared off into the distance for a long moment, as though far away, in another time, another place. Then slowly she turned to him.

"I will tell you what I remember," she consented softly, "but it is only bits and pieces, memories only half recalled. And I can reconstruct a good part of the rest from what others concluded must have happened. But much of it is still a dark void, and out of that the nightmares come."

Then with an eerie remoteness she began the tale, speaking as though it belonged to someone else and she was but the teller of it. And as she talked Jenny wondered as always what had really happened that day at Faxon's Folly—and why?

Chapter Twenty-nine

As Jenny spoke, though he had never seen it, Luke could imagine the place of his wife's birth as it had been that day, wild and wonderful, despite all its scars, and filled with new life slowly unfurling in the aftermath of the war. And he learned too about Jenny's family, the love and security she had once known, the quiet courage they had had and she had shared, giving her the strength to go on after that day at Faxon's Folly. Luke stretched out on the grass and veiled his eyes, letting the sound of Jenny's voice wash over him unfettered, so no nuance or inflection escaped him as she told the story of her past at last. . . .

Like a blood-red sea, its motionless crests forever petrified, as though at the exact moment of their zenith they had been captured on canvas by an artist, the rich clay earth of North Georgia spilled over the rolling foothills that thrust upward from the sprawling land. Wet prisms, a legacy of the spring rain that had fallen earlier that morning, shimmered like a cascade of diamonds upon the ground, reflecting every hue of the rainbow that soared across the horizon. There a deep rose dawn was slowly unfolding, its fingers reaching out tenderly to waken the world.

The wind stirred faintly, cool and moist as it whispered to the dense, virgin forest in the distance, rustling the verdant branches of soughing pines and gnarled oaks dripping with Spanish moss. Beneath the green canopy frothy pink crabapples and fragrant white dogwoods sighed plaintively to golden raintrees and silver-barked birches. Trailing tendrils of ivy climbed and clung tenaciously to rough old trunks while, below, a multitude of ferns spread their delicate leaves wide, like feathers against the soft thick moss that carpeted the woods. At the bases of the trees a riotous profusion of wildflowers tangled like unraveled thread, their brilliant splashes of color rivaling the fading arch in the sky.

In the dark swamp beyond, thorny thickets huddled close upon the banks of the dark, muddy river that wound its way through the countryside, the gentle lapping of its waves mingling melodiously with the voice of the balmy breeze.

Here and there the vibrant calls of mockingbirds and the rhythmic chirring of locusts sounded harmoniously as they joined in the chorus that filled the forest hush.

Glimpsing the scene from afar, one would have thought the patch of tranquil terrain a paradise, newly washed and beckoning with open arms, its wild, savage beauty only hinting mysteriously at the turbulent emotions to be found beneath its peaceful facade.

It was only when one drew nearer that one saw that this Eden too was flawed.

The frozen crests of the vermilion earth had not been naturally caused by years of spring rains pouring down in welcome, cleansing release upon the land. Instead the uneven ridges had been violently gouged out of the ground by the sharp, iron-shod hooves of cavalry horses thundering forward in invasion, by booted feet marching aggressively onward, and by the churning wheels of heavily laden supply wagons and massive iron cannons.

Upon viewing the destruction that had been wrought, one could imagine the raindrops shining crimson now beneath the rising sun were beads of blood shed when the countryside had been ripped asunder by great cannonballs and rifle shot, finely tempered swords and stabbing bayonets. One could fancy the wind wept with the cries of a thousand dead and dying soldiers who had used the earth as their battleground, scarring it forever.

There were places in the forest where the trees had been blasted and burned, their black ruins standing out starkly against the green. Places where the strands of ivy had been torn from their trunks, like a woman from her lover's arms. Places where the fairylike ferns and bright blossoms had been trampled into the ground, because men engaged in the ultimate ugliness had had no eyes for beauty then.

Here and there were breaks in the thickets where their twisted branches had been bent and crushed before the onslaught of frenzied regiments fighting for their lives, and the muddy river that sang so sweetly now had once run scarlet and reverberated with infamous Rebel yells and Yankee hollers.

The mockingbirds and locusts had been quiet then, instinctively afraid of the terrible thing that had caused their serene haven to erupt in an explosion of turmoil and death.

If one moved closer yet, one could spy the winding road that meandered brokenly through the destruction, as though, confused by its devastated surroundings, it had somehow lost its way. And if one followed the path to its end, one would come at last to Faxon's Folly.

Nestled in a sweeping hollow of the land, the old antebellum plantation appeared at first untouched by the despoliation that encircled it. Like a white pearl, the house gleamed luminously in the early morning light, its four tall Ionic columns standing like sentries guarding a treasure beneath the sun turning from flame to gold.

It had been built over a century ago by Faxon Colter, in the Classical revival style that at the time had yet to gain but a small following. It had looked nothing like the rest of the plain, rambling estates that had dotted the countryside then.

How people had laughed and shaken their heads over Faxon's foolishness as they'd gazed at the proud pillars rising up from the wide front porch to meet the lofty, triangular pediment. Faxon's Folly, they'd dubbed the house and said it would crumble like the Greek temples it resembled. But Faxon, a learned and well-traveled man, steeped in the knowledge and beauty of ancient history, had ignored the skeptics and persevered. When the place was finished, as though to mock his detractors, he'd called it by the name they'd given it.

From his grave Faxon Colter now had the last laugh after all. Towering Oaks, Shadybrook, Hunter's Point, Magnolia, Piney Ridge . . . all the neighboring plantations were gone now. Only Faxon's Folly remained.

But the price of its survival had been high.

The graceful, pink-blossomed, fern-leafed mimosas that had once lined the gravel drive were only stumps now, the trees having been chopped down by Yankee soldiers for firewood. The lovely flower beds that had once so gaily welcomed weary travelers had fallen prey to Yankee horses and mules, Yankee wagons and cannons. Only a few straggling blooms now fluttered forlornly in the breeze. The house itself was streaked with soot and pitted with jagged holes from Yankee shells. The pediment sagged at one corner where a supporting column had been dislodged; the pillar itself now leaned precariously, as though it would soon be uprooted from the porch as well. The louvered shutters that had framed the windows had been ripped from the walls and sent the way of the mimosas, and many of the glass panes were broken or missing entirely.

Inside the house, in the foyer, was a gaping wound where the crystal chandelier that had been imported all the way from France had been torn from the ceiling to be carried off by Yankee looters. Here and there on the faded wallpaper were brighter places where cherished oil paintings and daguerreotypes had once hung. Most of the furniture had been burned; what was left had been deeply scarred by Yankee cigarettes and liquor. The worn carpet bore the marks of Yankee boots and spurs. For, against the Colters' most strenuous objections, Faxon's Folly had been used for a time as the headquarters of various Yankee officers and their aides during the war. That was the only reason it was still standing.

All of this was nothing, however, when compared to what lay out back a small distance from the house.

The black wrought-iron fence that had once enclosed the cemetery was gone now, but other than this, the square of land showed no signs of abuse or neglect. The granite tombstones guarded graves that were lovingly tended by Southern hands and wept over by Southern women. Their dead were all of the past they had left to them now. The damned Yankees had seen to that, and for that Southern hearts would never forgive them. Never.

Too many had died. Too few were coming home—and many of those were coming back in pine boxes to be laid to rest beside the loved ones who had gone before them. They knew nothing now of those who remained behind, those whose hearts and lives lay shattered on the ground.

Of the seven brave young men who had ridden away from Faxon's Folly that summer of 1861, looking so handsome and dashing in their new grey uniforms resplendent with brass buttons, only one was coming home now, four years later. But that was one more than many other families would have, and so the young women who walked slowly from the cemetery to the front porch of the house smiled, in spite of their tears, and looked out eagerly over the terrain.

Seen from a distance, the Colter sisters made a pretty portrait that April morning, seated together as they were now on the veranda. Like the land and the plantation, it was only when one drew nearer that one saw that something was wrong with the picture. The dark muslin mourning dresses the women wore were outmoded and much-mended, and the soles of their flat-heeled morocco slippers were reinforced with cardboard. Their skin, once so pale and creamy and zealously shielded from the elements, gave evidence of the long hours they now spent beneath the hot sun, and their hands were those of women who must struggle to survive—red and roughened by hard work, their nails broken.

Life at Faxon's Folly had not been easy for the sisters since the war had destroyed all they had ever known. Once, they had been pampered and petted and spoiled beyond measure. Their whims had been gratified and their pranks laughed at by their indulgent father. What discipline they'd known had been rarely meted out and then by their kindly mother, who could never be angry with them for long. Above all, they had been cherished and protected by their big, teasing brothers. Now, destitute and very much alone in the world, they planted vegetables, hoed weeds, and picked cotton like field hands in order to sustain their meager existence—and thought themselves fortunate!

How they'd all cheered and sung and applauded as they'd watched their four brothers and the husbands of three of the sisters ride off to battle. They'd never dreamed that day that only one would be coming back. Weren't their men the best and bravest of all? Why, they'd have those Yankee cowards licked in no time, and what a round of barbecues, parties, and balls there would be then!

But it hadn't happened like that.

Niles had been the first to fall—at Shiloh. Rushford had been struck by a Yankee sharpshooter's bullet during the siege on Vicksburg. Prescott had gone down at Lookout Mountain, just outside of Chattanooga, and Alex had been killed during an explosion at Peachtree Creek as Sherman had advanced toward Atlanta. Joe Frank had lost his life at Five Forks, where Lee's army had been badly cut to pieces, and Lonny had died of pneumonia in the Yankees' infamous Rock Island Prison.

All of them lay in the cemetery at Faxon's Folly now—all except Alex. There hadn't been enough left of him to put in a pine box.

Only Cade was coming home.

Slowly, as the morning lengthened, the earlier cool breeze dissipated. The sun rose higher in the sky, drying up the last of the raindrops and leaving the day hot and humid, the countryside streaming.

Turbulent, reckless Evangeline, who could never sit still for long, jumped to her feet and began to pace the front porch restlessly, waving her palmetto fan vigorously to stir a breath of air.

At twenty-five, she was the oldest of the four Colter sisters, and until Joe Frank Hunter had won her heart and hand, she had been the most-courted belle in all of North Georgia.

It was easy to see why. Even dressed in her old worn and faded gown, with feathery tendrils escaping as usual from her fiery copper hair swept up in a knot upon her head, she was breathtaking. Her skin, turned to gold dust by the sun, set off perfectly her golden-green eyes alive with her lust for life; and her tall, willowy figure was as graceful as an hour-glass. Bold and beautiful—that was Evangeline. Even Joe Frank had never been able to tame her passionate spirit.

When the bodies of Niles, Rushford, and Prescott had been shipped home and their parents had been too distraught to make the necessary arrangements, it had been Evangeline who'd seen that her brothers were properly buried, Evangeline who'd insisted on a headstone for Alex, though his remains lay scattered at Peachtree Creek.

After Kingston Colter had been murdered in cold blood last year by a band of Yankee marauders, it had been Evangeline who'd rushed to the concealed place in the study where they'd hidden their precious hoard of weapons and ammunition from thieving Yankees and comman-deering Rebels alike. She'd ripped open the floorboards, grabbed one of her father's rifles, loaded it, then raced back to the parlor. There she'd smashed out the jagged remnants of a broken windowpane in the front of the house and driven off the soldiers, killing three of them in the process.

After Rachael Colter had succumbed to a long illness, following her husband to the grave, and Mammy had died too, worn out from nursing her mistress, it had been Evangeline who'd taken charge of Faxon's Folly.

And after the last of the Negroes had run off, leaving the sisters alone at the plantation, it had been Evangeline who with a martial glint in her eyes had squared her shoulders, rolled up her sleeves, and turned her hands to tasks that in the past had belonged only to those who'd fetched and carried for her all her life.

The others had at first been mortified, but they'd bent like reeds before the storm of fury Evangeline had unleashed upon them; and soon, the languid days of their youth forgotten, they'd joined in the difficult chores that had come to mean the difference between life and death to them.

Even when word had come some months past that Joe Frank had been killed, Evangeline had not broken. In the privacy of her room she'd wept for her beloved husband, refusing to allow her sisters to witness her deep grief. They were not as strong as she was, she'd thought, and if she stumbled, they would all fall. So she'd laid Joe Frank to rest at Faxon's Folly and hoped he would understand and forgive her for not burying him at Hunter's Point, which had been razed to the ground by the Yankees. Then she'd clung to her children, Little Joe and Garnet, and gone on with her struggle to survive.

Only Cade was coming home.

At the thought Evangeline's mouth tightened briefly with bitterness. Why couldn't Cade have been killed instead of Joe Frank? No sooner had the notion occurred to her, however, than she was sickened by and ashamed of it. She knew what it meant to be a widow, and she wouldn't have wished that on any woman, much less her own sister. But, oh, how she envied Melantha today!

At least I have Little Joe and Garnet to comfort me, Evangeline thought, and that's more than most have.

Both Rushford's and Prescott's wives had been left childless, Dulcie's only baby having been stillborn and Fayrene being yet a bride when Prescott had been killed. After the deaths of their husbands they'd gone home to be with their own people. Only Niles's wife, Honor, having no close kin, had stayed on at Faxon's Folly. She was inside now, supervising her three children, Evangeline's two and Melantha's little girl, Zoe Beth, who were finishing up their morning chores. Alex hadn't been married. Evangeline could only count that a blessing. There was one less woman to mourn him and one less mouth to feed at Faxon's Folly.

She sighed wearily. She would be glad when Cade got here and could shoulder some of her heavy burdens. It would be good to have a man about the house again, even if he were Melantha's husband and not hers. The place had seemed so empty since the deaths of her parents and brothers. Besides, Melantha, always moody, had been too brooding of late for Evangeline's liking.

Quietly she studied her twenty-three-year-old sister, wondering what Melantha was thinking. It was hard to tell, for, though Evangeline's every wild emotion was reflected upon her face, her sister's countenance was like a mask, closed and unreadable. Yet Melantha, like a shadowed All Hallow's Eve, had a haunting beauty all her own, and before she'd married Cade Brackett she'd rivaled Evangeline for beaux.

Melantha's hair, which she usually wore down in a snood, was a dark walnut that gleamed with rich crimson streaks when caught by the light, as it was now. Somehow she had managed to preserve her complexion better than her sisters had, and it was the color of an old ivory wedding dress, contrasting sharply with her dark, fathomless wintergreen eyes. She was tall and slender, like Evangeline, but possessed an aloof elegance rather than a willowy grace.

The small, mysterious smile men had always found so enticing now lurked about the corners of her mouth as she thought of her husband, Cade. She had never once doubted he would return to her. Cade was razor-sharp, as she herself was, able to move as stealthily as a bat winging its way across a midnight sky and capable of swooping down on his prey just as cunningly. He had never been a rash hothead like Joe Frank or a gentle dreamer like Lonny. No, Cade had always been cool and clever with his plans, just as Melantha had been when she'd determined he would be hers.

And now he was coming home.

Melantha was filled with excitement at the prospect. She wouldn't mind working so hard nearly as much with Cade there beside her. Why, he'd whip Faxon's Folly into shape in no time! Then maybe she and her sisters could have some new gowns and shoes, and the children wouldn't be so hungry all the time, and everyone could get some rest, especially Bliss, who ought not be doing anything in her condition anyway, but who labored as strenuously as everybody else at the plantation.

Troubled, Melantha gazed thoughtfully at her pregnant younger sister. Bliss looked tired, wrung out. Still she smiled cheerfully when she saw Melantha eyeing her. Nothing could dampen Bliss's sunny disposition. She was as gay as a lark in springtime. No matter how depressed or weary she might be, she always managed somehow to look on the bright side of life.

When Evangeline had hounded them into their back-breaking tasks, it had been Bliss who'd made them all laugh as they'd struggled with the highly difficult and unfamiliar chores. Their inability to cope with even such simple tools as a hoe and shovel might have proven defeating, had it not been for Bliss poking good-natured fun at their awkwardness and making them giggle, despite themselves. In the process she'd assuaged some of their grief as well.

"I swan!" Her eyes had danced with mirth. "Why, if Papa could see us now, he'd sell us downriver for sure! You were too young for such escapades, Jenny, but do the rest of you all remember the time we dressed up in those outlandish costumes and sneaked downstairs to crash Mama's masquerade ball? I believe we stuffed more cotton in our basques that night than we've picked all day!"

Ruefully they'd agreed, then suddenly burst out laughing as they'd recalled how mortified Rachael Colter had been when she'd spied them and their nigh-to-overflowing bosoms. She'd hustled them upstairs and given them a scolding meant to roast their ears but that actually had had little effect upon them.

"You, Queen of the Vikings, and you—*tsk!* What a mobid child you are, Melantha, to be sure. How like you to come as Queen as the Vampires! Is that my black bombazine? Never mind. What were you girls thinking of? If it hadn't be for Bliss being so small, I might never have noticed you. Thank God, I did! What if the Hunters or the Ridgeways or someone else had recognized you?" Rachael Colter had fanned herself vigorously at the very idea, fearing she was going to have one of her fainting spells. "You and Melantha I can understand, Evangeline. But you, Bliss! Tulle—at your age!"

"But, Mama, I'm Queen of the Fairies," the then-seven-year-old Bliss had chirped brightly and flapped her wings with such enthusiasm that her cotton padding had fallen out onto the floor.

Yes, Bliss in her own way was indomitable.

Her piquant, sunburned face was surrounded by a mop of red-gold curls that, even at nineteen, made her seem like a mischievous sprite. Her pale icy-green eyes, large and wide and filled with merriment, only furthered this impression, as did her small, delicate, childlike figure, upon which advanced pregnancy was all the more obvious.

Her older sisters were very much afraid she was not going to have an easy delivery, and silently they cursed the captain who had issued Laurence Ridgeway a pass to visit his young bride.

It was just like that irresponsible Lonny to come home on furlough, impregnant his wife, then get himself captured by the Yankees and die of pneumonia—leaving Bliss to suffer the consequences. Bliss, however, was enraptured over having a part of Lonny left to her, and Evangeline and Melantha were too kind to hurt her by voicing aloud their quite accurate opinions of her dead husband.

So Bliss sat contentedly, embroidering a christening gown for her coming baby, unaware of her sisters' uncharitable thoughts about Lonny or their fears for her. She was genuinely glad Cade was coming home, and she bore Melantha no malice at all over the fact that he had survived the war and her own dear Lonny had not. She would have her husband's child to comfort her. Even now she was beginning to experience the occasional twinges of pain that told her labor was imminent. But as the spasms didn't hurt much and she had been informed that having one's first baby was often a lengthy process, Bliss saw no reason to make a fuss just yet and put a damper on Melantha's day.

Thus, of all the sisters seated on the veranda that morning, only the youngest, Jenny, was unhappy.

It was not that she begrudged Evangeline her children, or Melantha her husband and little girl, or Bliss her coming baby, for Jenny did not. It was just that life was so unfair!

Her two oldest sisters, especially, had spent their coming-of-age years in a lovely whirlwind of barbecues, balls, and beaux; and now, at sixteen, just as she was poised on the brink of womanhood, the war had ruined everything for Jenny! Her days were spent doing nothing but hard work, and she didn't even have a husband—dead or alive—to boast of or a child to comfort her, and now she probably never would. The hateful war had killed off all the young men who might have come calling at Faxon's Folly, and those who'd survived were just too tuckered out to be bothered.

Jenny had never deluded herself with the idea that she was likely to marry someone as dashing as Joe Frank or as clever as Cade or as poetic as Lonny. But, with all the men who had flocked to Faxon's Folly before the war, she'd been sure she could catch *someone*. Now the attentions of even the most undesirable of men were vied for by the most attractive of women—and what chance did Jenny have against them?

It was bad enough to be the youngest of eight. But when all your brothers were so handsome women just swooned over them, and all your sisters were so beautiful men came to blows over them, and you were as unremarkable and out of place as a speckled hen in a barnyard of prize poultry . . . well, it just wasn't fair, that's all!

Plain Jenny Wren, Papa had called her and chuckled upon first seeing her the day she'd been born—and so she had been from then on.

What made everything so much worse was the fact that it was true. The good looks with which all the Colters had been blessed and the red hair and green eyes that were a legacy from their ancestor Faxon just seemed to have been all used up when they'd gotten to Jenny.

Her hair was the soft dusky-brown color of a pecan shell, without a trace of red, and her wide, speaking eyes were a misty grey, without a hint of green. The sun had made her look like a nut-brown maid, and there was a smattering of freckles across her cheeks and upturned nose, despite the buttermilk, lemon juice, mashed cucumbers, strawberry lotion, and other less agreeable concoctions with which Mammy in the past had attempted to eradicate them. Jenny's mouth was too generous for her heart-shaped face, and, though she was taller than dainty Bliss, she had none of Evangeline's grace or Melantha's elegance. Indeed Jenny, much to her shame and embarrassment, was often quite clumsy.

Worst of all was the fact that she was painfully shy, and when any man outside of her family addressed her, she blushed and stammered.

If she had been old enough at the time to have joined in the fun when her sisters had crashed their mother's masquerade ball, Jenny was certain she would have gone as Queen of the Wallflowers.

It was most depressing, she thought, that nobody was coming home to her, never had, and doubtless never would. She sighed, feeling as though the weight of the whole world sat squarely upon her small shoulders. Then, not wanting to spoil Melantha's pleasure this day, she tried hard to banish her low spirits.

Presently a man was seen coming up the winding drive. The sisters started forward eagerly, but even as they did so their exclamations of delight died on their lips, for it wasn't Cade. It was just another stranger, one of several gaunt-faced, bone-tired Rebel soldiers who were going home and had stopped at Faxon's Folly to beg a dipper of water or a scanty meal.

With such men the sisters always shared what they had, no matter how little it was and despite the fact that it really couldn't be spared.

Much to Evangeline's relief, however, the stranger wanted only a cool drink, and after he'd slaked his thirst with the water she'd drawn from the well, he thanked her politely and trudged on.

"A gentleman born and bred," she remarked idly as they watched him go. Momentarily her eyes hardened. "Men like that ought not have been whipped like dogs by rude Yankee scum! I think that's what I hate worst of all—knowing our brave boys were beaten by filth! Why, I don't believe there's one single gentleman in the entire Northern army!"

"That Yankee officer in town yesterday certainly treated us like dirt, that's for sure," Melantha fumed, her mouth tightening at the remembrance. "Yankee trash! No Southerner would have dreamed of accosting two unprotected ladies in such a fashion. Really! The nerve of that man! Why, if Cade had been there, he'd have killed that good-for-nothing scoundrel!" Melantha declared stoutly.

Yesterday, she and Evangeline had hitched up their pitiful, bony mule to their rickety old wagon, both of which they'd found abandoned in the woods, and they'd driven into Jonesboro to try to bargain for a few supplies they'd desperately needed but couldn't raise in their vegetable garden.

Though Confederate money was virtually worthless, they'd hoped to get a small slab of bacon for it—if there were one to be had; meat was mighty scarce these days and expensive too. They'd also needed some milk for the children.

Once in Jonesboro, the sisters had been attempting to pick their way carefully through the mass of smartly blue-uniformed soldiers and tattered homespun-clad civilians, most of whom had been gathered around the marketplace, when a Yankee officer had barred their progress.

Now as Melantha recalled him she shivered, for she felt chilled, as though someone had just walked over her grave.

He'd been tall and beefy, with long jet-black hair, bushy sideburns, and a drooping mustache, all reminding her of a wild, woolly buffalo. Though they had never seen him before, both she and Evangeline had recognized at once that he was a man to be feared, one of the many infamous Yankee officers who were the terror of the South.

He'd paid scant attention to Melantha. It had been Evangeline he'd boldly appraised, a slow, jeering smile curving his thick, carnal lips as he'd stood before them, his thumbs hooked in his belt, the tilt of his hips intentionally provocative.

"Well, now"—he'd spoken with a strange drawl that had surprised them, for they'd expected his voice to be harsh and clipped like most Northerners'—"what have we here?"

"If you please, Colonel," Evangeline had stated frostily, though inwardly she'd trembled with wrath and apprehension. "You're blocking our path."

"Is that so?" he'd asked, then chortled a little, jeering at them, the two women had thought, incensed. "You ladies all alone? Yes, I can see that you are," he'd answered himself as the sisters had silently telegraphed their fright to each other.

Before the war any number of Southern gentlemen would have come to their aid, but now there was no one to defend them from this notorious man's unwelcome attentions. What should they do?

"I'd be happy to escort you ladies to your destination," the Yankee had gone on to offer with mocking courtesy. Then his gaze had raked Evangeline's figure crudely, coming to rest on her heaving breasts. "You look like you could use a man."

She had not missed the insulting double entendre intended by his words.

"Get out of my way, Colonel!" she'd snapped, her golden-green eyes shooting sparks and her cheeks flushed.

After a tense eternity the man had stepped aside to let them pass.

Melantha had breathed a small sigh of relief, for she'd seen Evangeline's temper rising with every minute of the Yankee's insolent behavior, and she'd feared the results if he'd continued to harass them. Melantha would have frozen him with an icy, scornful stare, but she'd known Evangeline was quite capable of physically striking the officer. As it was, after they'd moved on Evangeline had turned and, much to Melantha's dismay, deliberately spat on the man's boots.

His face had mottled with rage as his friends, who'd witnessed the entire episode, had hooted and howled with laughter. His steely glare had been filled with murderous intent. His hands had clenched into tight fists at his sides, and for a moment Melantha had been afraid he would actually hit her sister. Hurriedly she'd dragged Evangeline away, forcing her into the milling mass that had crowded about the marketplace.

"I don't care if we starve! I won't go back to town again, Evangie," Melantha now asserted, "and neither will you—not as long as those Yankees are there, especially that colonel. Oh, I do wish you hadn't antagonized him, Evangie. I've heard some of the things they're saying about him, and after seeing him in town yesterday there's not a doubt in my mind that all those evil stories about him are the gospel truth! He gave me the shivers. Why, I believe that man would kill his own mother if he thought it were necessary! He's just downright wicked! When Cade gets home he can go into Jonesboro for us. Until then we'll make do with what we have."

"Well, I certainly hope Cade gets here soon, then." Evangeline sighed, feeling somewhat nervous about the Yankee officer herself and resigned to the fact that Melantha was right; they could make no more trips to town. "The children need milk. Oh, if only we had a cow! And a bit of fatback with the vegetables would help. Oh, damn the Yankees! Damn them to hell and back!"

"Evangie!" Bliss chastened, shocked. "You know Mama wouldn't approve of such language, and if Mammy were here, she'd wash your mouth out with soap! At least we're eating, no matter how poorly, and that's more than some people can say."

Briefly Evangeline longed to shake her sister silly. She loved Bliss, but sometimes her eternally optimistic behavior irritated Evangeline no end. Why, when Lonny had died Bliss had quietly folded up the letter informing her of her husband's death and actually said at least he'd passed away peacefully and among friends—as though Rock Island Prison had been a luxurious resort!

Oh, well. There was no point in starting a fight and ruining Melantha's day, Evangeline thought. Besides, Bliss would only look hurt and say she didn't know what good it did to dwell on all their troubles at Faxon's Folly when it didn't make things one whit better and so many other people were so much worse off anyway. And that, Evangeline mused with another sigh, was the truth. Grief didn't hoe weeds, and depression didn't pick cotton.

"Evangie"—Jenny looked up—"I do wish you'd stop that endless pacing and lend us a hand. Mellie and I could use some help picking the embroidery out of these pillowcases. Bliss is almost out of thread, and with just a little more she can finish the outfit for the baby."

"Oh, all right," Evangeline consented grudgingly. "But I still think it's terrible, undoing all of Mama's fine handiwork that way." She stared with a frown at the pillowcases, at the intricate designs Melantha and Jenny were slowly unraveling.

"Don't be cross, Evangie," Jenny coaxed. "You know as well as I do that if Mama were alive, she'd have suggested it herself. What a shame the christening gown Little Joe and Garnet wore was destroyed during the shelling at Hunter's Point. It was such a beautiful dress."

"Yes, it was, wasn't it?" Evangeline agreed. Then she ordered with determination, "Here, Mellie. Give me one of those pillowcases. Those da—darned Yankees aren't going to rob Bliss's baby too!"

The tense moment when Evangeline might have quarreled with Bliss passed, and soon the sisters were chatting companionably as they worked.

The day dragged on lazily, the morning turning gradually to afternoon, the warmth of the spring sun beating down on the women soothingly and making them sleepy. But none thought of retiring upstairs to join the children, now taking their naps. The sisters all wanted to be on the front porch, waiting, when Cade came home.

Once more Melantha smiled to herself.

"I declare," she exclaimed. "I'm so excited I feel like a giddy young girl sitting here waiting for my first beau to call and half afraid he isn't going to show up."

"Well, he will, and you know it. How lucky you are, Mellie! You and Evangie and Bliss! I wish *I* had a beau," Jenny uttered wistfully. Then her face blanched, stricken with remorse. "Oh, Evangie, Bliss, I'm so sorry. What cruel, thoughtless remarks—" She broke off abruptly, biting her lip.

"That's all right, Jenny," Bliss said kindly in the awkward silence that had fallen. "We all know what you meant. Joe Frank and Lonny might be dead, but at least Evangie and I were courted and wed. We have our memories to sustain us. Poor Jenny. You don't have anybody, do you? Not even a medal, a lock of hair, and a few letters bound up in faded ribbon to keep you company when the nights are so long and lonely you just wish you could die—"

Tears stung Bliss's eyes, and as though ashamed she bent her head over her sewing so the others would not see.

Evangeline's heart twisted with pain over her earlier annoyance with her sister. Why, Bliss's bright outlook on life was just a facade, her own way of coping with the depredating effects of the horrible war. Her sorrow over Lonny's death ran as deeply as Evangeline's own grief over her loss of Joe Frank. Strangely enough, the sight of Bliss weeping did not in the least gratify Evangeline, but hurt her worse than she would have believed possible. Trying to smile through her own tears, she put her arm comfortingly around her younger sister.

"Where's that happy face we all know and love so well?" she queried, giving Bliss a hug. "Jenny's situation isn't as desperate as all that, is it?" Evangeline deliberately misinterpreted the reason for Bliss's tears. "I know she lacks the red hair and green eyes for which the Colters are famous, but surely there's some man out there who wouldn't mind tweaking brown curls and gazing into grey eyes."

"That's right." Melantha joined in Evangeline's attempt to cheer Bliss. "Why, I remember one time Bubba Henry told me he thought brunettes were just downright enchanting."

Even as she voiced this lie Melantha was torn between her sisters' sadness and her own happiness. She was sorry Joe Frank and Lonny hadn't made it, but she wouldn't have traded Cade for one of them either. Was that selfish of her? Was she wicked to be glad Cade wasn't lying next to her sisters' husbands in the cemetery? Oh, God, why couldn't they all be coming home? Not just Cade, but Joe Frank and Lonny and Niles and Rushford and Prescott and Alex too? Why couldn't Papa, Mama, and Mammy still be alive and things be the way they were before the war? Now Bliss was crying and Jenny, poor Jenny . . . well, Bliss was right. Jenny didn't have anybody, not even a memory. Her girlhood had been finished before it had even begun.

"Brunettes enchanting? Oh, Mellie, you're making that up," Jenny put in, doing her best to dispel the unhappy atmosphere she'd unwittingly created. "Maybe girls like Randa Kay Wilding are—but not freckle-faced ones like me." She grimaced. "Who wants to look at a plain old speckled hen over breakfast every morning?"

"Now, Jenny, looks aren't everything," Bliss insisted, starting to smile again, much to her sisters' relief. "Even if you aren't the prettiest girl in North Georgia, you're beautiful inside, and that's what really counts. Why, you take Letty Hamilton, for example. Outside of Evangie, Letty's about the most gorgeous belle in the county—and who'd have her? She's got a tongue more poisonous than a water moccasin's, and she's meaner than an alligator to boot! She drove Grant Beauregard to drink, and Skeeter Ingram shot himself to death two months after he married her!"

Bliss's red-gold curls shook as she tossed her head with indignation at the thought. She had at one time worshiped Skeeter, though he'd never been one of her beaux, and she'd never forgiven Letty Hamilton for nagging him into an early and self-dug grave.

"It's the truth, Jenny," Bliss went on, once more her brave, pertinacious self. "Any man worth having knows beauty is just like a rose. After a time it starts to fade, and no man wants to get stuck with a thorn.

"You wait and see. The Yankees can't keep us down forever. After all of this is over the South will rise like a phoenix from the ashes, and there'll be barbecues and parties and balls once more, and the beaux will come calling at Faxon's Folly again. And one night some handsome young gentleman will take your hand in his and say, 'Jennifer Leigh Colter, I love you. Will you marry me?' And life will be gay and grand and glorious once more, just as it was before the war."

But it wasn't so—and they all knew it. Nothing would ever again be as it had been.

Only Cade was coming home.

Chapter Thirty

Was it true? Jenny wondered as thoughtfully she considered Bliss's words. Was it true that somewhere there was a man who wouldn't care that outwardly she was just plain Jenny Wren? Who would love her for herself and cherish her as she so longed to be cherished?

She sighed. It just didn't seem possible. Beauty might be only skin-deep, but it had a way of attracting a man—and keeping him around. No. Bliss was wrong. If such a man existed, Jenny would never find him, not now, not after the war had killed most all of the South's young men.

"Listen! Someone's coming!" Melantha cried joyfully, rising to her feet and interrupting Jenny's reverie.

For a moment, lost in her poignant thoughts, the younger girl could not understand her sister's excitement. Then, as Jenny watched Melantha lift her skirts and start to run forward expectantly, she remembered. Of course. Cade was coming home. Jenny stood then too, laying aside her handiwork as she moved toward the edge of the porch, her face a mixture of gladness for Melantha and sadness for herself. Dreamily she leaned against one of the pillars and wistfully imagined it was a beau of her own riding up the drive to Faxon's Folly. Her dream ended abruptly when Evangeline, her eyes suddenly dark with premonition, began to call desperately to Melantha.

"No!" Evangeline yelled. "No, Mellie, it's not him! Come back! Come back!"

Then the older woman raced after her sister, leaving Jenny to stare after them both in bewilderment, wondering what was wrong.

"Oh, God," Bliss murmured, her face suddenly ashen, her voice rising. "It's Yankees. It's Yankees! Where would Cade get a horse?"

Instantly Jenny perceived the wisdom of this. The Rebel soldiers who were coming home were on foot. The ones who were lucky had boots, but none boasted a horse. The same thought occurred to Melantha even as Evangeline reached her and a band of the hated, blue-uniformed soldiers galloped from the trees lining the road, then turned onto the winding gravel drive leading to Faxon's Folly. Alarmed, the two women studied the oncoming men speculatively for a minute, pondering what it was that they wanted. The war was over, but still the sight of a Yankee soldier struck fear into every Southern female's heart. Without warning Melantha's mouth went dry; her body and mind felt paralyzed.

"Dear God," she breathed. "It's that colonel, Evangie—the one from town!"

The sisters gazed at each other, horrified. They remembered the appalling stories they'd heard about the man. They recalled his cruel, sneering face, his dark, menacing presence in frightening detail. He was no gentleman but a blackguard of the lowest sort. Instinctively they knew he meant them harm.

"Hurry!" Evangeline ordered, despite the fact that both of them were now running as hard as they could toward the house. "We've got to get Papa's guns. Bliss! Jenny!" She motioned frantically to them. "Go upstairs, and get the children. Take them into the woods, and hide. Hide! Hurry! *Hurry!*"

The two younger girls rushed inside, not understanding what was happening but grasping their sisters' terror all the same. There had been Yankees at the plantation before, but somehow this time was different. Otherwise Evangeline would not have demanded that they hide. Evil was coming to Faxon's Folly. Jenny could feel it. Her skin crawled; her nape tingled. Even the afternoon air seemed suddenly to stifle her, suffocating her with dread.

Once inside the house, the sisters saw that their dead brother Niles's wife, Honor, who'd heard the commotion and been frightened by it, had already wakened her oldest boy, ten-year-old Niles Colter III. Trey, as they affectionately called him, was getting the rest of the sleepy-eyed, confused children up and herding them downstairs. Honor herself was yanking Kingston Colter's hoard of weapons and ammunition from beneath the concealing floorboards of the study.

Evangeline slammed the front doors shut and bolted them. Then, along with Melantha and Honor, she started loading the guns. Bliss and Jenny went out the back door, urgently propelling the youngsters to the woods.

Directed by Trey, the children rushed on ahead. Jenny came next, half afraid her father's heavy revolver, which Evangeline had hastily thrust into her hands, would go off. As she ran she scooped up little Zoe Beth, Melantha's girl, who was having trouble keeping up with the rest. Carrying both the child and the gun was difficult, but somehow Jenny managed. Bliss, made awkward by her pregnancy, lumbered along as best she could, bringing up the rear. She was breathing heavily from her unaccustomed exertions, and already it felt as though she had a stitch in her side. Searing pain shot through her body. Then suddenly her face contorted, draining of all color beneath her sunburn, and she stumbled, doubling over in agony. She screamed, a high thin shriek that cut through the now emotionally charged afternoon air like a knife.

"Jenny," she gasped. "Jenny!"

Jenny turned in time to see her sister stagger, then crumple to the ground.

"Trey," Jenny hollered. "Trey! Take Zoe Beth, and get the others to the woods. Find a hiding place, and stay there until we come for you. Hurry!"

"But, Aunt Jenny, what about you and Aunt Bliss?" the boy asked, his face sharp and pinched with anxiety.

"We'll catch up. Go on now. Hurry!" Jenny implored again, then raced back to Bliss's fallen form. "Bliss, what is it? What's wrong?"

"It's . . . the baby," Bliss managed to reply as she grit her teeth against yet another onslaught of pain. "The baby's . . . coming."

"Oh, God," Jenny muttered, her voice rising. "Oh, God, Bliss. Not now. Not now!"

"I know. I'm sorry, but I—I can't help it."

"You've got to get up." Jenny spoke more firmly, trying to retain control of her tumultuous emotions. "Do you hear me, Bliss? You've got to get up. We can't stay here."

"I know. Help me," Bliss moaned, holding out one hand.

Quickly Jenny pulled Bliss to her feet, supporting her as best she could as they lurched on toward the protective cover of the trees. Bliss bit her lip so hard she drew blood in a determined effort to keep from crying out again as excruciating spasms continued to rip through her body with each step. Her face was so pale Jenny feared that any instant Bliss would faint. At the forest's edge her water broke, and with a low wail of anguish she sank to her knees, unable to go on.

Jenny was appalled. She had never seen Bliss in such a state, and she knew very little about childbearing besides. Adding to her trepidation was her remembrance of Evangeline and Melantha's worry that Bliss was not going to have an easy delivery. Never in her life had Jenny felt so helpless. She glanced about wildly, as though expecting aid somehow miraculously to appear, but there was no one to assist her. The nearest doctor was in Jonesboro, and Mammy, who would have known what to do, was dead.

"I've got to go back to the house and get help," Jenny said, her heart-shaped face blanching at the realization, for evil was at the dwelling, waiting to crush her in its grip.

But beneath her shy exterior Jenny had a wealth of quiet courage, like a candle in the wind, flickering but alight all the same. Squaring her small shoulders bravely, she started toward the house.

"No! No! Don't leave me!" Bliss cried, clutching raggedly at her sister's hand. "I—I don't think I can bear it if you leave me!"

"But—but, Bliss," Jenny stammered, "I don't know what to do."

"You won't have to do . . . anything," Bliss rasped. "Evangie said . . . it would take a long time. By then the . . . Yankees will be gone and Evangie will be here to help me."

At last Jenny reluctantly gave way to Bliss's pleas and set about making her as comfortable as was possible under the circumstances. Then there was nothing to do but wait—and to try to hold at bay the gnawing fear that threatened to devour them both.

It did not seem possible that the lazy afternoon, filled earlier with such happiness and expectation, was now a terror-ridden nightmare. But it was. The villainous colonel had seen to that. Dark and hulking, he was the devil personified as he goaded his men on toward the plantation.

In front of the house he dismounted, tossed away his cigar, and ground it out deliberately beneath his boot. Then he swaggered up the front steps and beat resoundingly upon the doors.

"Mrs. Hunter!" he shouted. "Mrs. Hunter, you and your sisters come out with your hands up. You're all under arrest."

"On what charge?" Evangeline inquired icily from one of the parlor windows, though inwardly she was shaking.

The colonel didn't even blink as he turned to see a long black rifle barrel aimed straight at his heart through a broken pane.

"The murder of a Yankee officer and two soldiers. Is that the same gun you used to kill my brother, you bitch?" he queried softly.

Evangeline's face flamed at the insulting word even while her mind whirred with questions. *A Yankee officer and two soldiers.* She thought back to the day when the band of marauding Yankees had gunned her father down in cold blood. She had killed three of them in retaliation. Had this man's brother been one of them? Perhaps. But that was what war was all about, wasn't it?

"This rifle's dealt with a lot of Yankee scum, Colonel," she replied, "and I imagine it's going to deal with some more if you don't get off my land. Now," she commanded, cocking the hammer, thinking that perhaps if she were bold enough in her defiance, he and his men would go away and leave her and her sisters alone.

"Why, Mrs. Hunter, I do believe you're resisting arrest," he drawled.

"Unless you've got a warrant, Colonel, which I doubt, I'm not resisting anything. I'm defending my home from a pack of rascals. So don't think you can fool me with that trumped-up charge of murder. You and your men have no legitimate business here. The war's over, and this is private property. You're trespassing, Colonel, and I'm not asking you to leave; I'm telling you."

"I don't need a warrant to arrest you, Mrs. Hunter," he rejoined, his carnal mouth curling into a cruel grin. "The South is under martial law. Now you and your sisters get out here, or I'm afraid I'm going to have come in and get you."

"Do as he says, Evangie," Honor whispered, a sob in her voice, her face white with apprehension. "We don't want any trouble. Think of the children! I'll stay here, and when Cade arrives I'll tell him what's happened. He's a lawyer. He'll know what to do. Why, he'll have you out of jail in no time."

"Don't be a goose, Honor!" Melantha chided impatiently, her tone cold. "You don't really suppose that man is just going to cart us off to jail, do you? No. It's—it's just a ruse to get us out of the house so he and the others can—can—"

"Oh, Mellie!" Honor inhaled raggedly, whimpering. "You don't think—"

"Yes, I do," Melantha retorted. Then she reasoned, "Evangie never killed anybody except those soldiers who murdered Papa, and if the Yankees were going to arrest us for that, they would have done so a long time ago. I tell you that man out there doesn't want anything but revenge for his brother's death! We've all heard the stories. We all know what he is!"

"Yes, we do," Evangeline confessed reluctantly, her heart turning over in her breast. "Oh, God, I wish Cade were here!"

"Aw, come on, Colonel!" one of the soldiers bawled, obviously the worse for liquor. "We're wastin' time. Let's set the house afire. That'll git them whores out fast enough, shore as shootin'!"

"Yeah!" the others clamored eagerly, already lusting for blood—and more.

"No!" the colonel snapped, his steely gaze spitting sparks as he wheeled on the men. "Do you want someone to see the smoke, you idiots, and sound an alarm? Everything in its own time, boys. Everything in its own sweet time." He turned back to Evangeline, still standing at the window. "I don't have all day, Mrs. Hunter. Are you coming out, or aren't you?" he asked, slurring his words a little.

If Evangeline had had any lingering doubts about his intentions toward them, she did no longer. He was drunk, as drunk as the rest of his mean-looking mob, and fueled by his desire for vengeance. In that moment she knew he meant to kill them all. Melantha was right. The tales about him were enough to curdle the blood.

In answer to his question Evangeline pulled her rifle's trigger. He was prepared for that, though, and slammed himself up against the front doors so her shot merely splintered away part of the doorjamb. Then, dodging the barrage of bullets that followed, he rolled across the porch and ran for his horse. With a loud whoop he and his men opened fire on the three women.

In the beginning the soldiers galloped wildly around the house, the hooves of their well-trained cavalry mounts thundering against the earth, mingling with their bloodcurdling shouts and laughter, the loud shots that echoed from their guns. The old house shuddered as the shells thudded against its walls, and for a time the three women were afraid it might actually collapse upon them. Silently they prayed it would stand as they decided to split up, for there were numerous doors and windows to guard.

Then frantically they began to discharge Kingston Colter's weapons one after another, hastily loading and reloading, each staring with dismay at the growing pile of empty ammunition boxes that littered the rooms.

Finally, after the women had managed to kill four of the Yankees, the men withdrew to instigate a new line of offense.

On foot now they crept up on the house, using the trees and bushes as cover. This time the soldiers were quiet, eerily silent, as though well aware their earlier, jarring attack coupled with this new, stealthy onslaught would stretch female nerves, unaccustomed to the cold, calculating tactics of battle, until they were raw and screaming.

Where, before, the women inside had defended themselves desperately, now they stood frozen with fear, holding their breath as they listened intently for each little sound. Was that a door, creaking on its hinges, or was it a window sash, easing up its rungs? Were those boots in the upstairs hall or spurs jingling across the kitchen floor? Every familiar groan of settling made by the aged dwelling startled them, set their hearts leaping. The house, once so dearly beloved, now seemed as much an enemy as the men outside.

Evangeline, crouched in the parlor, felt an insane desire to giggle, to break the nerve-racking stillness, and with difficulty she fought down the hysterical laughter that threatened to bubble from her throat.

Tense and wary, she skittered like a crab across the carpet, peeked out the doorway, and motioned to Melantha, who was creeping down the stairs to the foyer.

"Get Honor," Evangeline directed quietly. "Let's barricade ourselves in Mama's dressing room. That way, we'll have only one entrance to watch."

"No," Melantha dissented, shaking her head. "You heard those men earlier. If that colonel can't control them, they're liable to set the house afire, and we'd burn to death for sure. I'd rather take my chances down here. At least from here there might be some means of escaping."

"Do you really believe that, Mellie?"

"No, but we have to try."

"Oh, Mellie! Mellie! You should have gone to the woods with the others!" Evangeline sobbed. "I should have made you go! For your sake —and Cade's."

"Hush, Evangie, hush! I wouldn't have gone, no matter what you'd said. I'd never been able to face Cade afterward. He hates cowards."

Both women realized they were speaking as though they were already dead, but neither one wanted to acknowledge that fact. They would not let go of life so easily, not just yet. But they would say good-bye to each other now—just in case.

"I love you, Mellie," Evangeline whispered, her voice choked with feeling.

"I love you too, Evangie." Melantha gave her sister's hand a gentle squeeze. "I'm glad we were sisters."

A sudden crash came from the kitchen. The two women jumped and clutched their pistols in readiness. They had long since abandoned their father's rifles, since no ammunition was left for those weapons. Soon the sisters heard an exchange of shots, then, horribly, the sound of slaps, clothes tearing, and worst of all, Honor's pitiable pleas for help. Evangeline started forward, but Melantha held her back.

"There's nothing we can do for her," the younger woman intoned dully, her face blank, as though she were in shock. "Unlock the front doors, Evangie. Maybe we can get away while they're—while they're—"

"No," Evangeline responded, her heart sinking as she turned away from one of the long windows on either side of the front doors. "They've left some men out front—"

Honor's screams ceased. The sudden silence was deafening, fraught with ill omen. Evangeline's mouth tightened.

"This is it, Mellie," she hissed, pulling Melantha into the parlor. "Get down behind the sofa."

Their mouths dry, their hearts pounding, the sisters huddled behind the flimsy barricade, waiting, waiting. . . . An eternity passed, it seemed, as they listened to the terrifying sound of boots moving through the house. Then without warning the soldiers burst into the room. From behind the cover of the battered old sofa, the women fired again and again. Two men went down, but still the others kept on coming, yelling in triumph now, certain victory was theirs.

At last the dull click of the pistol's hammer informed Evangeline that her gun was empty. Cursing, she reached for the last of the ammunition boxes, only to find it too held nothing more. The ominous quiet of Melantha's revolver told the same story.

There was nothing, then, but fear and despair.

"Yaaahooo!" one of the men howled, then chortled jeeringly. "The bitches are outta shells! The bitches are outta shells! Let's git 'em, boys!"

For a timeless moment the two women gazed at each other. Then they stood, tall and proud, as the mob closed in around them.

The soldiers were awful, reeking of sweat and gunpowder and alcohol, handpicked by the colonel from the lowest of life's dregs. The thought of their hands pawing her, their lips ravaging her own, their bodies violating hers was more than Melantha could bear. They would not have her. They would not! She had saved one bullet.

"Cade. Oh, Cade." She enunciated each word clearly, then coolly put her gun to her head and pulled the trigger.

"Jesus! Jesus!" somebody swore as they all watched, stunned, as one side of Melantha's beautiful face distorted into a pulpy mass of brains and blood, spewing out in all directions like a watermelon hit by a sledgehammer.

Her body jerked spasmodically as it fell, then lay still. Momentarily paralyzed, everyone stared at her crumpled figure. Then slowly all eyes turned to Evangeline.

"Goddamn you!" she spat, her voice rising. *"Goddamn you!"*

Then she raked her nails down one side of the colonel's grinning face as savagely he yanked her to him.

* * *

Jenny had to have help; she knew she did. Bliss's labor had progressed much more rapidly than either of them had expected, and now something awful was wrong. The baby wasn't turned right; Jenny could see a tiny foot where the head ought to be, and Bliss was in agony, shrieking and crying so loudly Jenny was certain her sister could be heard for miles. There was nothing else to be done. Despite the hateful words, the barrage of shots, the bone-piercing screams, and finally the dreadful, foreboding silence that now emanated from the house, Jenny must force herself to go back. Perhaps the Yankees were gone now. She prayed it was so.

Slowly, feeling chilled, despite the warmth of the sun, she left the protection of the woods, forcing herself to put one foot in front of the other as she made her way back to Faxon's Folly.

The first thing she saw was Evangeline. But, no—Jenny stopped dead in her tracks, stricken—that pitiful creature couldn't be her bold, beautiful sister. Evangeline was young and wild and glorious in her lust for life. This poor woman was a thousand years old, bent and broken beyond repair, and the stark blankness of her eyes was the glazed stare of the dead. Dull and lifeless, her hair straggled down about her in tangled disarray, as though she were mad; and her gown, torn and soiled and bloodied, looked as though it had been worn through hell and back. Her face was a mass of cuts and bruises, swollen, misshapen; and her legs, showing nakedly where her dress, petticoats, and pantalettes had been ripped away, seemed too weak to hold her up as she staggered dazedly across the yard, the sharp prick of a bayonet driving her on. She tripped and fell, sprawling facedown in the grass, her hands clawing at the ground—and then at the filthy, vile, ugly soldier who rolled her over and, laughing raucously, forced her thighs apart.

"Oh, God." Jenny's lips moved mechanically. "Oh, God."

Then she doubled over and vomited.

She scarcely heard the shouts as someone spied her, and it was only through a strange, dizzy haze that she saw a huge black stallion spin away from the men gathered on the lawn and come galloping toward her, appearing to move in slow motion, the devil himself upon its back. His silver saber gleamed where the sunlight struck it, following the blade's cutting arc as it swept toward her.

Unaware of her own instinctive, defensive action, Jenny lifted her father's heavy revolver and fired.

A shrill, inhuman shriek of torment split the air. The horse lunged, then reared, falling back heavily upon its haunches. Blood spewed from its chest and then its nostrils, spraying wet and sticky upon Jenny's face and hands. Another high scream shattered the afternoon, mingling sickeningly with the cries of the animal. Dimly Jenny recognized that the terrible noise was coming from her own throat.

Foam started to bubble from the stallion's mouth as, white-eyed and snorting, incredibly it lurched to its feet and leaped forward. Two steps. Three. Its knees buckled, and at last it pitched over.

Petrified, Jenny watched it topple, its massive hulk thrashing wildly as it rolled, crushing her helpless body, blotting out the sun.

"Lawd a'mighty! Are you all right, Colonel?" one of the men queried anxiously as he ran to assist his commanding officer to his feet. "That shore was some tumble, sir. Yore lucky you wasn't kilt. If you hadn't of jumped clear, that horse mighta smashed you flatter 'n a hoecake!"

"Yeah," the colonel said as he glanced at the dead animal.

He felt a twinge of regret for the stallion. It had been a good mount and had served him well. It would take him a long time to find and train another like it.

"Here's yore hat, Colonel. I brushed it off fer you," the man, Williams, noted, his eyes a little nervous, for his commanding officer was quick to punish any signs of disrespect.

"Thanks. Is that slut dead?" the colonel motioned toward the small, broken figure half concealed by the horse.

"Yessir. Leastways, I cain't feel no pulse." Williams shrugged as he raised up from his quick, haphazard examination of Jenny's pathetic form.

"Too bad. Moffatt's got a pecker that won't quit," the colonel observed dryly. "It's a wonder it hasn't fallen off. He'll be sorry he missed getting a piece of this one.

"Go round up the men, Williams. Inform Boothe that he's to bring half of them—and the woman, if Moffatt hasn't fucked her to death by now—and come on. I reckon the rest of her kin are hiding in those woods. Tell Deacon and the others to form a work detail, and get this place cleaned up. Be certain they find everything belonging to us. I don't want so much as a brass button left behind! Make sure everyone understands that, Williams, because I personally aim to shoot any man who disregards that order. Do I make myself clear?"

"Yessir."

"Good. Strap our dead soldiers on their horses so we can take them with us and bury them someplace where there won't be any questions asked. Once that's finished, you can strip the house—if there's anything of value left—then set it on fire."

"Yessir."

"Oh, and, Williams, take my bridle off Satan, and cut my saddle loose. Then round up Purdy's gelding for me. He won't be needing it. You can put his corpse on that old mule Jake found tied up out back."

"Jesus, Colonel! Purdy'd be madder 'n hell if he knew that!"

"Well, he's dead, so he won't know, now, will he? Now get a move on, Lieutenant!"

Chapter Thirty-one

The war was over, and Cade Brackett was going home. No, not home, for Towering Oaks had been home, and it was no more. A charred black ruin was all that remained of its once beautiful and comforting existence. But he was going back to North Georgia, to Melantha and their daughter, Zoe Beth, and that was enough for any man who had lived through the horrors Cade had survived, things that had made him old before his time.

It would be good to be young again, if only for a little while, to lay his head, like a child, upon his wife's breast so she could soothe away the pain and the terrible nightmares that haunted him. Maybe then Cade could weep, could shed the bitter tears pooled deep in his heart and soul, could cry, as he had not yet been able to do, for all he had loved—and lost: his boyhood friends, one after another, until none had remained; his family home, burned to the ground by the Yankees; his folks, dead of a raging fever that had swept the devastated countryside.

These wounds pierced Cade to the very core of his being and went on hurting. It seemed sometimes as though they would never heal, and even if they did, he would still have the scars—and the memories. These last were the worst of all, for he could close his eyes and his ears to shut out the world. But the memories . . . no, they were not so easily escaped from.

The train taking him south to Atlanta rumbled on, its wheels clattering rhythmically over the tracks.

Too many dead. Too many dead, it chanted ceaselessly in Cade's mind.

He rubbed his temples tiredly, trying to block out the gruesome refrain.

Sometimes he felt so torn asunder that it was hard to remember he was still alive, and at such moments he wondered dully why he was. Why hadn't he died like so many others? It was not enough anymore to tell himself he was clever and cool-headed. He had known other soldiers with those attributes, good men, brave men, men who had eaten with him, slept by him, and fought at his side. All dead now. Did he have some vital element they had lacked, or had it all been part of some master plan devised by a being greater than himself? Cade didn't know. For the first time in his life he was at a loss to understand the mysterious ways of the world.

War did that to a man, filled him with self-doubt and questions, where none had been before.

He had never been particularly religious, but now he thought there must indeed be a god who determined men's fates, and for Cade that god was the god who had gambled with the devil for Job's soul. What kind of a god was that? he asked himself. What had poor Job ever done to merit such torment? What had any of them ever done, the Johnny Rebs and the Billy Yanks?

The Negro sitting beside him studied him silently, wondering what he was thinking. Mistah Cade had always been a strange one, silent and brooding, Moses thought. But Miz Mellie loved him, and for that reason alone the big black man would have laid down his life for his companion.

Moses belonged body and soul to the Colter sisters. He had been given to them one year for Christmas as their stable boy and eventually had advanced to the position of groom. He had saddled their horses for them, ridden with them, and protected them for as long as he could remember. In later years, as they'd grown up, he'd driven their buggy to barbecues, parties, and balls; listened with one cocked ear to their giggling, whispered secrets; and watched them fall in love. When the war had come he had defended them against the undesirable attentions of the Yankee officers stationed at Faxon's Folly, and when the blue-uniformed soldiers had thrust a rifle into his hands and dragged him off to fight, telling him he was free, he had run away and tried to make his way back home. It had been difficult to get through the battle lines, however, and at last Moses had been satisfied to locate Cade somehow in all the upheaval and to offer to serve Melantha's husband.

Mistah Cade would look after him; Moses had been certain of that. The Bracketts had always been good to their slaves. Mistah Cade wouldn't let him starve, as so many of the free-issue Negroes were starving, unaccustomed, as they were, to taking care of themselves.

"Mistah Cade. Mistah Cade." Moses nudged his companion gently, prodding him from his reverie. "We's heah, sah."

Slowly Cade stood, brushing from the seat of his pants the straw with which the floor of the boxcar was littered. The train was easing to a grinding halt, whistle singing, steam hissing, and brakes squealing as the wheels grated on the tracks. With a lurching shudder that caused Cade to sway unsteadily on his feet, it came to a stop.

There wasn't any platform, for the Atlanta depot, a victim of Sherman's bloody march to the sea, had yet to be rebuilt, so Cade jumped down onto the ground amid the sooty remains of what had once been the train station.

He breathed in deeply and knew this was no dream, that he was indeed really here, for nowhere was the morning air as sweet as it was in North Georgia, damp with dew and filled with the scent of pine trees and wildflowers and rich red clay.

His grey eyes searched eagerly the crowd that milled about the starkly exposed rectangular foundations that were all that was left of the numerous warehouses that had once lined the railroad tracks. But there was no sign of Melantha.

"She woan be heah, Mistah Cade," Moses, who had joined him, pointed out logically. "Dey ain' gots de Jonesborah spur runnin' agin yet, an' eben if'n dey did, it's a long ways ter walk ter de Jonesborah depot from Faxon's Folly. Ah doan 'spects Miz Mellie gots no hawse, sah; pro'bly ain' eben an orn'ry ole mule lef' on de place. 'Sides, eben if'n der was, Ah knows she ain' gots no cah'ige. De Yankees done buhnt mos' eberthin' lahke dat fo' fahrewood."

"Yes, you're right of course, Moses," Cade answered, shaking his head as though to clear it. "I don't know what I was thinking of."

"Bettah times, Mistah Cade. Bettah times, sah."

"Yes, that was it, I suppose. Well, let's get a move on. I want to get home before dark."

Home? Yes, anywhere Melantha was waiting for him was home.

His heart swelling suddenly with joy, Cade shifted the small bundle on his shoulder and set off almost jauntily down the dusty road leading to Jonesboro and Faxon's Folly.

Nothing, not even the horrors he had seen during the war, could have prepared Cade for what he and Moses found at the old plantation.

They saw the smoke first, curling up into the sky in billowing wisps of grey, and because smoke to a soldier meant cannons and gunpowder, fire and death, the two men broke into a run, heedless of their tired feet.

It was the absolute silence that struck them first about the plantation when they reached it, for, other than the roar of the flames licking their way up the sides of the house to the roof, the place was deathly still. The happy sound of women's voices calling out to them in greeting, the shouts and laughter of children at play were nowhere to be heard.

Their eyes suddenly wide with alarm, Cade and Moses rushed up the steps and through the open front doors of the old house.

Inside, the heat blasting down the hallway to the foyer was so intense it nearly drove them back out again, but they persevered. The smoke too was so thick they could scarcely see. Hastily they ripped their bandannas from their throats, wrapping the handkerchiefs about their faces to prevent the acrid, choking fumes from asphyxiating them.

Surely the women had gotten the children safely out. Surely they had! But then why weren't they outside on the front lawn?

"You search upstairs," Cade instructed Moses. "I'll look down here." Then he began to shout "Mellie! Mellie!" at the top of his lungs.

He found her in the parlor, but she was not the Melantha he had known and loved so well. Indeed he recognized her only by the thick strands of her crimson hair that tangled around what remained of her face. For a long time Cade could do nothing but kneel woodenly beside her body, sick and stunned, unable to believe she was truly dead.

At last he wept, but Melantha was not there to soothe away his pain, would never be there again. His shoulders shook with each racking sob. He did not even care that the fire was spreading, beginning to consume the room about him. He started to cough as the smoke penetrated his bandanna, filtering up into his nostrils. He gasped for breath. His lungs burned. But still he couldn't seem to stir.

His wife was dead, had killed herself for some reason unknown to him. She still had the pistol clutched between her stiffened fingers.

"Oh, Mellie, why? Why?" Cade groaned brokenly—but there was no reply.

Entering the parlor, Moses was brought up short by the sight that met his eyes. Then, big tears starting to roll down his cheeks, the Negro moved blindly to kneel beside Cade.

"Deah Lawd," Moses mumbled, feeling as though he were going to be ill. He pressed his handkerchief more tightly to his face. "Deah Lawd. Mah lamb. Mah po' li'l lamb. Oh, Lawdy, Mistah Cade, whut's done hap'ned heah? Der weren't nobody upstaihs, so's Ah—Ah comes back down heah ter hep yo look fo' de res'. Ah found Miz Honah in de kitchen." He broke off, coughing, then went on raspingly. "She wuz— she wuz . . . well, Ah wouldn't eben haf knowed her, Mistah Cade, 'ceptin fo' her haih. It wuz so purty an' blond, lahke cornsilk. Ah—Ah tried ter git her out, but de fahre was so hot. . . . Ah couldn't save her. It din mek no dif'rence anyhows. She wuz daid too. Oh, Lawdy, Mistah Cade, whut's done hap'ned heah?''

"I don't know, Moses. I don't know," Cade repeated numbly.

"Mistah Cade, we's gots ter git out o' heah," the Negro insisted, his eyes watering and hurting from the smoke, his lungs feeling as though they were going to burst. "Ah almos' din mek it back downstaihs 'fo' dem steps done gived way. Ah 'spects de roof is gwine ter cabe in mos' anytime now. Mistah Cade, yo heah me?" Moses asked, his voice rising anxiously.

Already the open portieres hanging across the parlor doorway were ablaze, as were the drapes at the windows. If the two men waited much longer to make their escape, they would be trapped in the fiery inferno now engulfing the room.

Cade shook his head as though to clear it, then glanced around, suddenly becoming aware of his surroundings. Moses was right. They had to get out of the house immediately. Hurriedly Cade gathered Melantha in his arms and stumbled toward the foyer.

Once outside, he laid his wife's body tenderly upon the grass, noticing for the first time the freshly made prints the iron-shod hooves of horses had cut deeply into the yard. He turned to Moses.

"If the others weren't in the house, they've got to be somewhere else. See those tracks." He pointed to the marks in the rain-softened earth. "It looks as though a band of marauders has been here." Cade shuddered at the thought. With the number of deserters both the Confederate and Union Armies had suffered, there were numerous outlaws roaming the countryside, as well as desperate, dangerous free-issue Negroes the Yankees had liberated from the bonds of slavery. "Maybe the others hid in the woods," Cade suggested, though his voice revealed that he had little hope the rest had survived. His heart lurched sickeningly as he thought of his young daughter, Zoe Beth. Had she had time to get away—as Melantha had not? "We'll have to search the grounds, Moses."

"Oh, Lawd, Mistah Cade, Ah—Ah doan think Ah cain, sah. Der ain' no tellin' whut we might find. Seein' Miz Honah an'—an' Miz Mellie was bad 'nuff. But, lawdy, if'n anythin's hap'ned ter de res' o' mah lambs an' dem li'l chilluns . . . well, Mistah Cade, mah haht's already done been broke dis day. It jes' cain' tek no more."

Cade put one hand on the sobbing Negro's shoulder.

"I know how you feel, Moses. Believe me, I know how you feel. But as long as—as there's a chance the others—the others are still alive, we've got to look for them. You understand that, don't you?"

"Yassah, Mistah Cade." The big black man nodded, wiping his eyes and sniffling a little. "Doan pay no 'tention ter me. Ah's jes' plain ole plumb skeert, dat's whut. Ah din—Ah din tell yo 'fo', 'cause yo wuz so griebed 'bout Miz Mellie, but Miz Honah—Miz Honah . . . well, she wuz . . . all beat up, sah, an'—an' whoeber done it . . . well, dey—dey raped her too, Mistah Cade."

"Oh, God," Cade cursed softly. "Oh, God. No wonder Mellie killed herself! She'd rather have died than let— Oh, my brave heart." He glanced lovingly, pityingly at his wife's body. "My dear brave heart. I'm glad you were spared that at least."

Then, filled with dread, he and Moses set off to look for the others.

They found Evangeline first, on one of the side lawns. Cade didn't need to see Moses's suddenly ashen face to know she had suffered an even worse fate, if that were possible, than Honor. The Negro sank down upon the grass, retching, and Cade himself was forced to lean against a tree trunk to steady himself as he fought down the bitter gorge that rose in his throat.

Who in God's name could have been capable of such brutality? he asked himself. And why? What had any of them ever done to have deserved this? They were good, decent people, weren't they? Then why had God allowed them to suffer so?

"What kind of a god are you?" Cade roared angrily, shaking his fist at the sky. "What kind of a god are you?"

Then he buried his face in his hands, trying to get hold of himself.

After a while he pressed on grimly. He passed the dead black stallion, but it held little interest for him, for he was too distraught to notice Jenny's partially concealed form beneath the horse. He walked on, discovering Bliss, who lay at the edge of the woods, her belly ripped open, her unborn son stabbed by a bayonet.

By now Cade was beyond shock, beyond comprehension. He knew only that he couldn't move another step, could not bear to go on. But he had to. He had to know. . . .

Dear God, the children! *The children!*

He vomited until there was nothing left to come up. Then dazedly he staggered from the trees, wanting only to find a quiet refuge where he could lie down and gather together the ragged edges of his sanity before he lost his mind completely.

"Mistah Cade!" Moses's voice suddenly split the air like a shaft of shining light piercing an utter darkness. "Mistah Cade! Come hep me. Come hep me move dis heah hawse. Miz Jenny's undahneath it, and, Lawd haf mercy, sah, she's still alive! She's still alive!"

BOOK FOUR

The Outlaw Hearts

Chapter Thirty-two

Tumbling Creek, Missouri, 1871

At last, her story ended, Jenny fell silent, wondering again why she alone had been spared and thinking it was a miracle she'd survived at all. When the colonel's big black stallion had fallen on her, Jenny had suffered extensively from the impact, though fortunately she had not borne the entire weight of the huge, heavy animal. Had that happened, she would surely have been killed. Still she had not escaped unscathed.

A concussion and numerous fractured ribs had resulted from the force with which she'd hit the ground, and the weight of the horse had caused severe internal injuries in her pelvic area and crushed both of her legs. A great deal of scar tissue had formed due to the damage done to her female organs, and old Doc Whitting at the hospital in Atlanta had told her that, because of this, it was highly unlikely she would ever bear a child. Her right leg had snapped with a sharp clean break, so, after being set, it had healed without complications. But her left limb had been badly mangled, and the bones in it hadn't knit properly. It was permanently twisted. Jenny had been extremely lucky gangrene hadn't set in, for then the leg would have had to be amputated.

She closed her eyes, recalling again the terrible things she had seen, the pictures indelibly branded into her mind when Cade had lifted her in his arms and carried her from Faxon's Folly.

Had that pitiful, sprawled, and gaping body at the edge of the woods really once belonged to sunny Bliss? And that shapeless mass of cuts and bruises . . . had that bloody, crumpled heap once been fiery Evangeline? And what of those dark crimson strands that had tangled about what not long before had been someone's face—Melantha's face.

"Don't think about it anymore, Jenny," Luke ordered quietly, taking her hands in his. "Those weren't men; they were animals, savage animals! My God!" He tried hard not to think of Quantrill's raid on Lawrence. "You must try to remember your sisters as they were before that day, Jenny. They wouldn't want you to do otherwise, nor would they want you to make yourself ill with grief over them."

"I know," Jenny murmured. "I know. But it's—it's so hard to forget, Luke. There hasn't been a day in my life since then when I haven't been haunted by memories, when I haven't tried to reconstruct exactly what occurred, who attacked Faxon's Folly—and why. If I knew that; if ever I could remember, I think the nightmares would stop, Luke. It's not knowing that hurts, as though somehow I've failed Evangie and Mellie and Bliss . . . and—and the children."

"Nevertheless, Jenny, you can't keep dwelling on it," Luke insisted. "Whatever happened will only continue to elude you if you persist in attempting to remember it. Try to forget the whole episode, to put it from your mind. Then someday when you least expect it something will trigger your memory and you'll recall everything that occurred, down to the last detail."

"Do you really think so, Luke?"

"I know so. I've seen it happen during the war. That day at Faxon's Folly was so horrible your mind has blocked it out. When you're ready to confront it you'll know, and your brain will throw the right switches. Until then, Jenny, try not to think about it, for me. I love you, you know, and I hate to see you hurting inside like this. I wish I'd never asked you to tell me about it."

"No, you did the right thing," Jenny declared firmly. "Why, I feel better already, just talking about it. It's like a sickening wound that's been festering inside of me. You've helped me to open it up and rid myself of some of the infection. Thank you, Luke.

"Now, hadn't we better be getting back to the house?" Jenny changed the subject abruptly. "It's getting late, and I've got to hurry if I'm going to get my bags packed and make it to the depot in time to catch the train to Jefferson City. Come on. I'll race you down the hill!"

Governor Benjamin Gratz Brown, called Gratz by all his friends and relatives, was sixty-five years old. Married to the former Mary Ginn and the father of two sons and five daughters, he had been active in Missouri politics for a number of years, having been one of the founders and the chief editor of the *Missouri Democrat,* a well-known Free Soil paper in 1854. Few had escaped his diatribes against slavery, and he had lobbied hard to prevent the secession of Missouri before the outbreak of the War Between the States. During the war he had served as a colonel in the Missouri Volunteers, Fourth Regiment, in the Union Army and had assisted in the organization of the state's pro-Federal militia. Like Jenny, he walked with a permanent limp, having been shot near the knee in a duel with Thomas C. Reynolds in 1856.

Jenny, as she considered all of this while waiting nervously to discover whether or not the governor would see her, thought it was most unlikely that he would offer to grant Luke amnesty or even a pardon if her husband were to give himself up and stand trial for his crimes. In his valedictory message Governor Brown had proposed, among other things, the abolition of grand juries and suggested that criminals instead be charged in formal accusations made by prosecuting officers. This would eliminate the need for indictments, thus reducing the cost of criminal suits and simplifying the judicial system as a whole.

Jenny thought Governor Brown would view Luke not only as a Rebel and a Southerner, but as an expense to the state—and one that needed to be curtailed. Adding to her trepidation was the fact that she herself was from Georgia and her family had been slaveholders before the war.

"Mrs. Morgan, the governor will see you now," an aide said, bringing the girl out of her reverie. "If you will step this way, please."

As she had feared, Jenny found Governor Brown unsympathetic to her cause, and to her chagrin she was forced to return home and report to Luke that he had been right and she'd wasted her time in Jefferson City.

"However, you mustn't despair, my love," she told him. "While I was there I heard rumors that Governor Brown is going to campaign as a nominee for the vice presidency next year, so whether he wins or loses he won't be in office in Missouri much longer. I'll try again after the new governor is elected."

Luke only smiled wryly and said she must do as she pleased.

The year of 1872 passed rather quietly, for the Morgan gang, persuaded by Luke's persistent arguments, had voted to cease its lawless activities and to try to become respectable citizens again. J.R. and Tobias had been worried for some time now about what would happen to their families in the event that the brothers were captured. But they had not wanted to voice their objections to continuing their criminal existence to the others and were relieved that Luke had chosen to do so. Raiford claimed he could either take the outlaw life or leave it but that Emmalou would be happier if he left it. So the only one actually upset by the decision not to commit any further crimes was Billy Clay, who grumbled that he had no intention of settling down to become a dull farmer like the rest.

That year a number of railroad companies, several of whose bonds had been fraudulently issued and guaranteed by the state, failed. These bankruptcies caused a loss to Missouri of approximately twenty-five million dollars, the burden of which had to be borne by the taxpayers.

The matter would have been of little interest to Jenny, except for the fact that it brought Tully Boothe, Maybelle's brother, back to Tumbling Creek. She had not seen him since that day when she'd spied him in town with Velvet Rose. He had come out later that afternoon to Whispering Pines to visit the children, but Jenny had not been home, and Luke had sent Tully packing before she'd arrived. So she was startled when she opened the front door in response to a sharp knock and saw Maybelle's brother standing on the porch.

"Well, hello there," he drawled, not bothering to remove his hat, his eyes raking Jenny disrespectfully, his mouth curved into a sneering smile. "I don't believe we've met. I'm Tully Boothe, Luke's brother-in-law."

"*Ex*-brother-in-law, you mean, don't you?" Jenny asked coolly, returning his gaze.

Since marrying Luke she had acquired a great deal more self-confidence and her deep-rooted, overwhelming fear of men had lessened to simple nervousness around those she did not know. But this man was not a stranger. Now that she had gotten a good look at him up close, Jenny felt more strongly than ever that she should recognize him.

"Yeah, I guess that's right," he responded to her question. Then he grinned, spat a stream of tobacco off to one side, and wiped his mouth off on his sleeve. "Well, aren't you going to ask me in? I *am* still Kipp and Sary's uncle, you know."

"Yes, I know," Jenny said.

Reluctantly, for she was certain Luke did not want Maybelle's brother in the house, she stepped aside so he might enter. Luke was working out in the fields with Moses, but Jenny expected both men back for dinner at any minute. There was no sense in trying to deal with Tully herself when Luke could handle the matter.

"Won't you have a seat?" Jenny motioned him to a chair in the formal parlor. "Kipp and Sarah Jane are out riding their ponies. But if you'd care to wait, I'm sure they'll be home directly. Ah, Delcine"—she glanced up as the mulatto made a noiseless entrance—"this is Tully Boothe, Maybelle's brother. Would you mind bringing us some refreshments, please?"

"Whiskey, if you've got it," Tully put in rudely.

"Very well, Miss Jenny." Delcine frowned her disapproval.

Tully just grinned again.

"I don't believe that high-yellow wench thinks too much of me," he observed after Delcine had left the room.

I don't think too much of you either, Jenny wanted to reply, but out of politeness she held her tongue.

"Well, Mr. Boothe, what brings you to Tumbling Creek?" she queried instead.

"The name's Tully—and I'll call you Jenny. After all, we're practically related." This familiarity didn't sit well with Jenny at all, but she made no protest, deciding it wasn't worth arguing over; the man would be gone soon enough. "I'm just passing through," he went on, "just passing through. I missed you the last time I was here, so I was determined to stop and pay my respects. I wanted to see the woman Luke Morgan found to take my sister's place."

"I've hardly done that, Mr. Boothe," Jenny insisted, her tone frosty, "since it is my understanding that before she died Maybelle voluntarily relinquished all claims to my husband."

Tully's pale, colorless eyes glinted at that.

"You've got a sharp tongue, Jenny," he noted. "I'll say that for you. But, then, I never did know a schoolmarm who didn't. Whereabouts are you from? I don't recall there being any Colters in these here hills, and that *is* your maiden name, isn't it?"

"Yes. I was born and reared on a plantation just outside of Atlanta, Georgia. Faxon's Folly it was called."

Jenny didn't know why she'd mentioned the name, except that Luke had said she must learn to speak naturally of her past if she ever wanted its deep wounds to lessen. To her surprise Tully started slightly in his chair, and his eyes narrowed intently for a moment before smoothly he regained the insolent expression he'd worn previously. The fleeting instant of recognition passed so quickly Jenny could almost believe she'd imagined it, but she was sure she had not. For some reason Tully was familiar with Faxon's Folly. But . . . why? It was not a place about which he was likely to have heard. Now, more than ever, Jenny felt she ought to know this man.

"Have you ever been to Georgia, Mr. Boothe?" she inquired, her heart starting to beat peculiarly in her breast, fluttering with a mixture of anxiety and anticipation.

"Tully," he reminded her, "and the answer is yes. I served in the Union Army, under General Sherman. As you might imagine, that doesn't make me too popular in these here hills. I made several forays into the area, delivering messages and running various other . . . ah . . . errands for my commanding officers," he explained, and Jenny realized he'd acted as a spy. "I was part of a detachment garrisoned in Atlanta after the city fell as well."

Jenny's hopes were dashed by the obviously quite truthful reply. It was entirely possible she had seen this man on Atlanta's streets during the Reconstruction. That would account for her thinking she knew him. It might even be that he had visited Faxon's Folly during the war, when it had been used as a headquarters for various Yankee officers and their aides. Numerous soldiers had come and gone then, and Jenny had paid scant attention to any of them. There was no reason at all to believe there was anything more to the matter than that. Still something about Tully nagged at her, and she could not seem to put her finger on what it was.

Was he one of them? she wondered. Was he one of the men at Faxon's Folly that day? Jenny tried hard to remember, but as always her mind was a blank, and after a time she decided she was grasping at straws. She did not like Tully, but she thought perhaps that was simply because he was Maybelle's brother and Luke did not care for him either. She must not allow her imagination to run away with her, nor could she permit her personal prejudices against the man to cast suspicion on and condemn him without just cause.

"Tully. What're you doing here?" Luke drew up short upon entering the house and seeing his ex-brother-in-law sitting in the formal parlor. "I thought I made it clear to you during your last visit that you're not welcome here."

"Well, now, you really didn't expect me to believe that, did you, Luke?" Tully's eyes were flat and hard. "After all, seeing as how Maybelle's not here now to look after her interests, I figure it's up to me to do so."

"Really?" Luke raised one eyebrow skeptically. "I would have thought your *own* interests would be of paramount importance, Tully. But you always were one to think of every angle. A bachelor uncle looking out for your deceased sister's two kids—especially when their father is a notorious criminal—that would look real good on your record, wouldn't it, Tully? And you want to get ahead in the political world, don't you?"

"Now, Luke, you got it all wrong," Tully protested with mock hurt.

"Do I? Really? Well, then, do forgive me, Tully; I must have been misinformed. Do you mean you *aren't* state Senator Taggart's right-hand man? That you weren't, along with your war-hero boss"—Luke's voice dripped with sarcasm—"involved in the illegal issue of numerous fraudulent railroad bonds, although you both managed to cover yourselves brilliantly and to escape paying for your crimes? And you didn't subsequently—to protect your ass with the people of course—have anything to do with the instigation of the massacre at Gunn City last Wednesday afternoon?"

"I don't know what you're talking about," Tully insisted coldly. "Now, if you'll excuse me, it's obvious that I have outstayed my welcome. I came by merely to pay my respects to Mrs. Morgan and to see Kipp and Sary. I didn't come here to listen to your accusations, Luke. You've always been ready to accuse me of something, a case of the pot calling the kettle black, isn't it?" He turned to Jenny. "Good afternoon, Mrs. Morgan. It has been a pleasure. I'll see you again another time in more civilized company."

Then he departed, not in the least unnerved by the scorn and dislike that iced over Luke's eyes or the quick, involuntary movement he made toward his pistols before managing to regain control of his emotions.

Though courtesy dictated otherwise, Jenny, aware of her husband's anger, made no attempt to show Maybelle's brother to the door. She reasoned that since he had practically invited himself in, he could just as easily find his own way out. She had been taken aback by Luke's accusations, and silently she wondered if they were true.

A few days ago, on April the twenty-fourth, there had been a terrible uprising and slaughter at Gunn City, a small town on the Missouri, Kansas & Texas Railroad Company line. An eastbound train, running from Harrisonville to Holden, had pulled into the station, carrying approximately thirty passengers, among whom had been General Joe Shelby, Judge J. C. Stephenson, County Attorney James C. Cline, and his bondsman, Mr. Thomas E. Detro.

Stephenson and Cline, both implicated in the railroad bond swindle, had been indicted and were soon to stand trial. But they were not to have their day in court after all. Several unknown agitators, in the hope of further stirring up the taxpayers (who were already incensed at being forced to bear the brunt of the monies lost in the scandal), had journeyed to Gunn City to incite a riot.

These men had piled on the railroad tracks a barricade composed of rails, logs, and rocks. The train was forced to stop, and before the engineer could reverse the locomotive, the cab had been riddled with a barrage of bullets. No one had been injured in the initial assault, but the vehicle had been compelled to halt, and it had then been attacked by seventy to eighty armed ruffians, all wearing masks.

Several of the vigilantes had invaded the cab and at gunpoint had taken the engineer and the fireman prisoner. Others had surrounded the train and continued to shell it. Cursing and shouting threats and warnings, the mob had demanded that County Attorney Cline step forth. Bravely but foolishly Cline had emerged from the baggage car to appear on the platform outside, only to be gunned down in cold blood on the spot.

The crowd of men had then rushed the vehicle, breaking down its doors and smashing out its windows while claiming they intended to set it on fire. The defenseless passengers had been terrified.

"Where are the bond robbers?" one of the gang had demanded. "Turn out the bond thieves!"

Someone had spied Judge Stephenson in one of the cars and had shot him and dragged him outside. Others, bursting into the mail coach, had located Mr. Detro. Badly wounded during the fracas, he had been thrown out onto the side of the tracks and allowed to bleed to death.

Only General Joe Shelby had escaped. Hearing the agitators screaming for his blood, he had calmly called out, "Here I am. If you want me, come and get me," refusing to budge from his seat. After a great deal of argument the men had finally decided to let him go.

Learning of the incident, Governor Brown had dispatched Captain Phelan's company from Kansas City to Cass County to investigate and had, in addition, sent Adjutant-General Albert Sigel to the town to accumulate facts. The governor had also authorized the formation of a commission under the leadership of Colonel John F. Philips, of Sedalia, and Colonel F. M. Cockrell, of Warrensburg, to help quell the public disturbance.

So far the identities of the ringleaders had yet to be discovered, and as the men had been masked it was unlikely that they would now be caught and punished.

Jenny wondered what had led Luke to accuse Tully of instigating the massacre. She glanced at her husband curiously.

"Luke, do you really believe Tully was one of the mob at Gunn City?"

"Yes, I do," he replied. "The whole incident just smacks of his handiwork, and he always did run for home like a rabbit after stirring up trouble." Luke's lip curled derisively. "Even when we were kids he used to play some rotten prank on all of us, then hightail it back to his folks' house before any of us could catch him. There he'd be—hiding behind

his mother's skirts like a sissy, sniggering at us because there was nothing we could do to him with his mother looking on. The old lady's dead
now, but Tully doesn't need her anymore anyway. He's got 'important
friends' now, or so he says." Luke snorted with contempt. "I guess
Senator Taggart's important enough, but I sure wouldn't want him for
my friend—the damned Yankee bastard! The South didn't call him the
Butcher Colonel for nothing!"

Jenny's head snapped up sharply at that.

"Wh-what did you say?" she asked.

"I said the South didn't call Sly Taggart the Butcher Colonel for
nothing. Why?"

"Why, I—I don't know," Jenny said, puzzled. "It—it just seemed to
ring some sort of a bell, that's all."

"I'll bet," Luke intoned. "There isn't a Rebel alive who doesn't know
that name. Come on, sweetheart. I'm starved, and it smells like
Delcine's got dinner on the table. Hmmm. Fried chicken. My favorite.
Did you make some biscuits to go with it?"

"No," Jenny responded tartly, though her lips curved upward. "The
apothecary was closed!"

"Most inconvenient," Luke drawled, putting his arm about her waist
and nuzzling her ear. "We could have fed some arsenic to Tully and
been rid of him once and for all."

"Luke!" Jenny chided sternly.

"You're right," he rejoined, laughing, not in the least abashed. "Poison's too good for the likes of him! Ah, Delcine. That glass on your tray
is filled with whiskey for Mr. Boothe, I take it. Smart woman—taking
your time about serving it. No sense in wasting good liquor on the likes
of him!"

"No, sir, Mister Luke," Delcine grinned. "I figured you'd be home
sooner or later to put a burr under his saddle. This here's from your
own private stock, Mister Luke. I thought you'd like to have it to wash
the smell of that vermin off you."

"Delcine, remind me to give you a raise," Luke commented, an appreciative gleam in his eye.

"Yes, sir, I will," she stated firmly. "Miss Lacey's got a new dress in
her shop window, and it's just my size!"

Chapter Thirty-three

They did not see Tully after that, although a detachment from Captain Phelan's company later appeared in Tumbling Creek, asking questions that led Jenny to believe Luke had been right about Tully's involvement in the Gunn City Massacre, as people had taken to calling the incident. But popular feeling against the murdered men was so high no one was willing to assist the government, even though sizable rewards were offered for information leading to the arrest of the ringleaders of the mob, and so the instigators were never apprehended.

Governor Brown was, as Jenny had suspected, nominated by the liberal Republican party for the vice president's slot on the campaign ticket, but his ballot lost, and he retired to Saint Louis to resume his law practice. In 1873, a new governor, Silas Woodson, took up the reins of Missouri. He was the first Democrat elected to the office since the war.

Jenny had little hope that he would look any more favorably on granting Luke amnesty than Governor Brown had, and she was filled with despair that she and Luke might not ever be able to lead normal lives. Although the Morgan gang had ceased its criminal activities, the public had not stopped accusing the brothers of various offenses. If a crime were not credited to the James-Younger gang, it was invariably pronounced the work of the Morgans, no matter if a holdup the previous day on the other side of the country had made a second such event by the same outlaws somewhere else an impossibility.

Twice, Luke and his brothers were forced to take to their heels and go into hiding when lawmen arrived in Tumbling Creek, seeking to root out the notorious Morgans. The brothers escaped as usual. They knew the hills and caves of the Ozark region better than the outsiders did, but Jenny was never able to rest easy as long as her husband was being hunted like an animal.

Again she made the long trip to Jefferson City, and again she returned home to report to Luke that she had wasted her time. Governor Woodson had, if anything, been firmer than Governor Brown in his refusal even to consider her proposal. It seemed the only option Luke had was to stand trial and take his chances with a judge and jury.

Jenny bit her lip apprehensively at the thought, for even reaching the courtroom alive would be an accomplishment when the state was teeming with hotheaded youths and glory-seeking lawmen who would love nothing more than to claim they had shot Luke Morgan. And after the trial, if Luke were not acquitted, there would be little opportunity to engineer his escape. If the Morgans failed in their attempt to free him, he would most assuredly hang.

For this reason it was determined that only Luke would give himself up at this time. That would leave his brothers free to try to rescue him if anything went wrong. If Luke's trial went well, the others could always turn themselves in later.

"I think we ought to contact Gus Grissom," Luke stated as they went over the details of their plan once more. "He was damned good at his job and seemed an honest sort too. I don't think he's the type to shoot me in the back or let anyone else do it either."

"Well, Luke," J.R. grunted, "it's your neck, so we'll do whatever you want us to do. If you want Gus Grissom to take you in, then we'll get him."

"I could wire him, in care of the Pinkerton Detective Agency in Chicago," Jenny offered. "That way, maybe we can keep things a secret a little while longer. People are bound to suspect something's up if one of you goes in to send a telegram to the agency."

"She's right, you know," Tobias agreed. "The quieter we keep this matter, the better Luke's chances are going to be for staying alive to stand trial."

"All right, Jenny; you wire Gus Grissom, then," Luke consented. "You're the schoolmarm, so we'll leave the wording of the telegram to you." He smiled at her encouragingly, noting how pale and drawn she looked. "Don't worry, sweetheart," he murmured. "Everything will work out fine, you'll see."

But Jenny wasn't so sure, and, as she lay next to Luke in bed that evening, she voiced her fears aloud to him.

"Oh, Luke," she breathed, holding him close. "I love you so much. I don't know what I'd do if anything ever happened to you."

"Shhhhh," he whispered. "There's nothing to be afraid of, Jennilee.

Nothing's going to happen to me, I promise. If I can just get them to hold the trial in Taney County, or even Springfield, I'll be all right. I know I will!"

"And . . . if you can't?"

"Then I'll just have to think of something else. Either way, I'm done with running."

"Oh, Luke!" Jenny wailed softly. "Maybe we should just forget this whole mad plan. We can take Kipp and Sarah Jane and go away somewhere together . . . to Mexico or South America—"

"No, Jenny." Luke shook his head. "Missouri is my home. I was born and reared here. Everything I love is here. I won't be driven away as though I were no better than a weasel trying to break into a chicken coop! I'm a Morgan, not a coward, damn it! And that means something to me." He looked down at her upturned face and went on more quietly. "I love you, Jenny. I want you to be proud of me and what I am—not ashamed."

"I *am* proud of you, Luke! You know that!" she cried. "I know you're not a coward, and I've never thought you were."

"No, I know. But, well . . . you're a lady, born and bred, sugar," Luke insisted, "and I *am* just an outlaw, as you've told me so often in the past. And there comes a time in every man's life when he gets to thinking about things and wishing they were different. He looks back at the mistakes he's made, and he wants the future to be better, especially for his wife and kids. I've reached that point now, Jenny. I've either got to take a stand and clear the slate or keep on running, and you know what I've decided to do."

"Yes, and I'll support you in any way I can," Jenny declared firmly. "But I won't stand by and watch you die, Luke! You can't ask that of me! If it comes down to that or escaping to Mexico, you've got to promise me we'll start a new life someplace else. I don't care how we live or where we go—as long as we're together. That's all that matters."

"I know, Jenny." Luke pulled her into the circle of his arms and kissed her gently. "I know. All right, my outlaw heart. If it comes down to that, we'll do it your way. But don't ask me to throw in my hand as long as I still have a chance at winning."

"No, I won't."

"Come. Make love with me," he urged, abruptly changing the subject, and, stilling her fears for the moment, Jenny gave herself up to his all-consuming embrace.

* * *

Slowly Jenny reread the telegram she'd drafted to send to Gus Grissom in care of the Pinkerton Detective Agency in Chicago. It seemed clear enough, but still she wasn't sure the detective would comprehend her meaning, even though she'd signed her maiden name as a precaution so he would be sure to recognize her and so the name Morgan wouldn't go out over the wire.

JUNE 14, 1873
TO: MR. GUS GRISSOM
C/O THE PINKERTON DETECTIVE AGENCY
CHICAGO, ILLINOIS

HAVE NEWS CONCERNING MUTUAL FRIEND STOP WOULD LIKE TO DISCUSS SAME WITH YOU STOP IS THERE SOMEPLACE WE CAN MEET ALONE STOP ANXIOUSLY AWAITING YOUR REPLY STOP

JENNY COLTER

"Are you ready, Jenny?" Luke asked from inside the telegraph cage. "Stokes will be back from dinner anytime now, so we have to hurry."

"Yes, all right. Here it is." She shoved the piece of paper across the counter through the window to her husband. "Are you sure you know how to operate that contraption properly?" she questioned skeptically, gazing at the telegraph key. "What if you make a mistake? Won't it garble the entire message?"

"No. Don't worry. I've done this several times before," Luke reassured her. "It's all a matter of knowing the Morse code. Just trust me. All right. Here we go now."

Carefully he began to tap out a series of clicks and clacks while Jenny looked on nervously, afraid Luke would mix up the message, despite his insistence to the contrary, or that Mr. Stokes would return to the office before they had finished. Fortunately neither of these calamities occurred, and soon she and Luke stepped out onto the sidewalk, closing the door of the office behind them.

"Afternoon, Stokes." Luke nodded nonchalantly to the telegraph man as he hurried down the street toward them, pulling his key chain from his pocket and then scratching his head in confusion as he realized the door was already unlocked.

"I must be gittin' senile in my ole age," Mr. Stokes commented to Luke and Jenny. "I coulda sworn I locked that 'fer I went to dinner.

Oh, well." The telegraph man shrugged. "Ain't nothin' inside worth stealin' anyhows." He eyed Luke sharply, frowning.

"No, I don't reckon there is," Luke returned, his eyes glinting with amusement as he and Jenny continued on down the street, trying to keep straight faces.

"Oh, Luke!" Jenny burst out, once they had rounded the corner. "I declare. I had to bite my tongue to keep from laughing when I saw the look on poor old Mr. Stokes's face! Do you think he knows you picked the lock?"

"Probably. No doubt he'll spend the whole afternoon trying to figure out what we stole! Just wait until the reply from Gus Grissom comes for you. Then Stokes'll know we sent a telegram we didn't want him to read, and he'll really be mad! He hates missing out on any of the town's doings almost as much as Crabby Abby does!"

"Well." Jenny sighed, her giggles subsiding. "I still don't know but what we ought to have trusted him to relay the message. Lord only knows whether or not *you* got it right!"

"Of course I did." Luke grinned, knowing she was teasing him. "You wait and see. If the Pinkerton Detective Agency can locate him, Gus Grissom will answer all right. No doubt he still hasn't forgiven my brothers and me for eluding him during that blizzard. He'll figure we owe him one."

This was exactly what the detective thought upon receipt of Jenny's message. Gus Grissom stared hard at the wire he held in his hand, puffing on his fat cigar thoughtfully as he pondered the words on the paper. Was it possible Miss Colter had changed her mind and was ready to testify against the Morgan gang after all? No. The agent shook his head. Somehow he didn't believe that was it. He'd heard rumors claiming that Luke Morgan had married the Tumbling Creek schoolmarm. If Miss Colter *were* Luke's wife, she wouldn't be attempting to hand him over to the law. No. The telegram had to mean something else, but for the life of him Gus couldn't figure out what it was. Although Miss Colter wanted to meet alone, he just didn't think she'd be a party to an ambush.

Carefully he folded up the piece of paper and stuck it in his pocket. Then he sat down with a tablet and pencil to try to compose a response. Finally, after several attempts resulting in a wastebasketful of crumpled wads, he was satisfied with what he'd written. Chewing the tip of his pencil, he reread his reply.

JUNE 17, 1873
TO: MISS JENNIFER COLTER
TUMBLING CREEK, MISSOURI

CAN MEET AT SCHOOLHOUSE JUNE 24TH AT 3:00
STOP WILL COME ALONE STOP

GUS GRISSOM

After considering the message for several more minutes, Gus finally crossed out both *ats,* feeling as though they were not needed and that there was no reason for him to spend the extra money to include them. Then he patted his pockets to be sure he had his wallet and started downstairs to the lobby of the hotel in which he was staying in Saint Louis. He left his room key at the desk, then went outside to locate the telegraph office.

After sending his wire to Tumbling Creek he had supper at a restaurant, then returned to his room, where he settled in for the night. He wondered again what Miss Colter wanted of him. It would be nice to take the Morgan gang into custody, Gus thought. During the blizzard when the brothers had managed to elude him and the posse he and the marshal had formed, Gus had lost his way and nearly frozen to death in the Ozark wilderness. Three of his toes and two fingers had had to be amputated as a result of frostbite. Thank heavens, he still had the use of his gun hand! Yes, the way he figured it the Morgans owed him one. He would be more than happy to collect the debt. Gus had been sent to Saint Louis to investigate the James-Younger gang, but he didn't think his boss, Allan Pinkerton, would be too upset if he brought in the Morgan brothers instead.

The schoolhouse was empty because the spring term had ended. But when she was here Jenny always felt a sense of love and belonging, as though this were her special place. She knew why the old-timer spent so many hours here alone, communing with God. The quiet solitude and the half-light of the afternoon sun streaming in through the glass-paned windows, illuminating every mote of dust swirling up from the plank floor, produced a sense of peace and contentment. In the distance the breeze rustled the branches of the trees; insects buzzed, and birds chirped; and the noises combined with the warmth of the schoolhouse made her feel lazy and drowsy. Jenny almost fell asleep, but she prodded herself to wakefulness, remembering she needed to remain awake and alert.

It was three o'clock. Gus Grissom would be here any minute, and she must persuade him to allow Luke to surrender himself. Just the thought of doing this made Jenny's breath catch in her throat, for if Luke had miscalculated and the detective were the sort to shoot him in the back, he might not stay alive long enough to stand trial.

"Miss Colter."

Jenny turned. Gus Grissom walked so softly she had not heard him approach, but she ought to have heard the crunch of his horse's hooves upon the road. She glanced out the window and realized he had tethered the animal some yards away and, fearing to be ambushed, had crept up on the schoolhouse. She smiled.

"It's Mrs. Morgan now," she explained.

Gus nodded.

"I'd heard that, but I wasn't sure it was true."

"Well . . . won't you sit down." Jenny cleared her throat awkwardly and indicated one of the many benches. "We have a great deal to discuss, Mr. Grissom, so we may as well get started."

Then, taking a deep breath, she began to confide to the agent her reasons for asking him to come to Tumbling Creek.

They went to their special place in the hills, the place where Jenny had told Luke the story of her past, the place where they had laughed and whispered secrets and made love, the place they had come to think of as theirs alone.

There was no need of words between them, for they had come to know each other with a closeness that at times made their hearts and thoughts as one, and now was such a moment in their lives. Both of them knew this might be the last time they ever made love together.

So they had come here, had sought the shelter of the pines and cedars and oaks that surrounded them, tall, ancient, and majestic, standing like ever-watchful sentries to be certain they were not disturbed. Luke pushed aside the heavy green boughs to make a little path for Jenny, who preceded him into their bower. Then he let the branches drop back into place, shutting out the rest of the world.

Eagerly they began to undress each other, their fingers trembling as they fumbled with buttons and ties, then cast away their garments to stand naked beneath the setting sun.

Their bed was the sweet, soft, spongy grass and moss, the creeping vines and wildflowers that gave way beneath them, green blades bending to conform to the contours of their bodies, petals showering and scattering upon the ground to release their fragrant perfume. Tenderly

Luke pressed Jenny down upon the earth, his eyes caressing the pale honey of her flesh, every line, every curve of her that he had ever known and loved and called his. Here and there the white scars of her past stood out prominently against her skin, marring her. But to Luke she was the most beautiful woman he had ever known. Deep within her there burned such warmth and caring that she seemed to glow, and when she smiled it lit up her whole face, as the sun rising on the horizon brings light to the world. Her eyes were the color of morning dew beneath her half-closed lids, and they shone like prisms before they darkened with passion and her lashes swept down to veil them in expectation of his kiss.

He covered her mouth with his own, tasting her, his tongue parting her lips to seek the sweetness that waited therein. His hands touched her everywhere, knowing now exactly how to arouse her and what pleased her best, for these were things he had taken the time and patience to learn—as another man might not have done. This Jenny sensed instinctively, and it made her love him all the more.

She burned and shook with the onslaught of sensations that assaulted her, as though she were feverish and chilled, her body turning to fire and ice everywhere that Luke's hands stroked her. His palms glided like sensuous feathers over the dark crests of her breasts, and they stiffened with desire. His fingers drifted down her belly and slipped between her inner thighs, probing the soft, downy curls that gave way beneath his touch.

As though she could not get enough of him, Jenny explored him in return, her palms lingering on the silky mat of blond hair that covered his chest, tapering into a furry line that trailed down his belly to thicken and flourish once more between his flanks in a rough, triangular pelt. Here his shaft grew beneath the firm caress of her fingers, and she shivered a little with anticipation and excitement at the thought of the power she wielded over him at this moment.

Then she was opening her legs to him, wanting him. Strongly he thrust into her, feeling her velvet sheath envelop him like a pool of fiery quicksilver, searing him, inflaming him. He moaned and muttered against her lips and hair, age-old sounds and words that heightened Jenny's passion.

Her soft cries mingled with Luke's own, filling the forest hush with a melody known to all its creatures. A warm, tingling feeling began at the very core of Jenny's being, building until it felt as though she were about to explode from the force of it, and then she did, reveling in the waves of heat that shuddered through her body, only gradually subsiding. Almost simultaneously Luke's own release came, and he stiffened against her, lost in the blinding sensations of his own climax.

After that they were still, clinging tightly to each other, only slowly relaxing, Jenny's head cradled against Luke's chest as they fell asleep in each other's arms.

Chapter Thirty-four

Before long word got out that Luke Morgan had been taken prisoner, and as they journeyed by train from Tumbling Creek to Springfield, where Luke was to be incarcerated and the trial was to take place, Jenny was touched to see how all along the line people came to stand beside the tracks and pay their respects to her husband. She saw old men, bent and stooped, with their hats held reverently over their hearts as the train on which she and Luke were riding clattered by; women, their faces mournful, held up babies so later in life the youngsters could claim they had watched Luke Morgan on his way to jail; and children waved, their hands upraised, their eyes round with wonder and excitement at seeing a living legend.

Tears pricked Jenny's eyes at the sight of them, these poor, plain, ordinary folk, dirt farmers mostly, to whom Luke had become something of a hero and through whom they had lived vicariously, applauding his daring and cheering his victories over the powerful and the rich. His capture represented to them the end of an era, a special way of life that would never come again, and cheeks other than Jenny's own were moist with tears at the thought. Still there was hope upon their faces too. Their champion might be taken, but he was not defeated. He would never be defeated, for even death would not break his brave wild spirit, would not tame the rebel streak that had brought him to this pass.

Folk singers composed ballads about Luke's exploits and sang them as the train rolled by, and they shouted words of encouragement to let him know they were with him every step of the way.

Luke too was moved by the outpouring of affection for him. He stood for hours outside on the small platform of the private car in which they were traveling so people might not be disappointed, but would be able to glimpse him without hindrance. He smiled and waved until Jenny knew his face must be frozen from the effort and his arm aching, and she could not help but think he would make a brilliant politician.

She knew he would laugh at the idea, but his eyes would hold too that hungry gleam of yearning and anticipation that always filled them when something captured his fancy.

The sun beamed down upon him, making him look like a golden god as he stood there upon the platform. His hair glistened, shining like spun gold intertwined with silver where a few of the flaxen strands had turned to grey at his temples. Jenny noticed the deep lines engraved at the corners of his eyes seemed more pronounced than they had in the past too.

It came to her then just how far they had come in the last few years together. Yet it seemed almost yesterday when, seated upon her hard bench in the public coach of the train that had been carrying her to Tumbling Creek, she had raised her eyes to meet Luke's own, had felt her breath catch in her throat at the sight of him, and had felt desire for him leap within her, so she had never been the same afterward.

As Jenny had done so many times in the past, she stretched out one hand to touch him, to reassure herself that he was real, that he was here, a part of her, as she was a part of him, now and forever. Luke turned and smiled at her, that slow, warm, crooked grin she had come to know and love so well, and she knew then that, no matter what lay ahead for them, nothing could ever take away or diminish the love they had shared, so sweet and everlasting it would bind them together for all eternity.

When his hand closed over hers firmly yet tenderly, she could feel the strength and the gentleness mingled within him, and she knew this was the true measure of the man, the reason why all those people lined the tracks. They needed a hero like Luke, just as Jenny did, someone who embodied all their glorious dreams and their harshest realities. In Luke's eyes were both of these things, the farseeing stare of the youthful visionary, the timeworn gaze of the aged sage.

"I love you," Jenny whispered, filled with awe and happiness that this man belonged to her alone.

"I love you too," Luke breathed, longing to draw her near, to kiss her mouth, to make love with her.

Gus Grissom, standing just behind them, cleared his throat awkwardly and looked away, as though he had intruded upon something very private and special.

* * *

It was a trial that would be talked about for years to come, a trial parents would describe to their children and that children would later relate to their own offspring.

Newspapermen came from as far away as New York, hoping to get an interview with Luke or Jenny or Gus Grissom, who had achieved fame overnight as the man who'd brought Luke Morgan in.

The courthouse was packed to the rafters with spectators, all of whom had been thoroughly searched before being admitted, for no lawman wanted Luke to escape or to cheat the hangman by being assassinated by an overly zealous, law-abiding citizen. Jenny was grateful for the precautions taken, for they helped to lessen some of her fears.

It took nearly a week to select a jury, but in the end Luke's lawyer, Buzz Sawyer, was satisfied that several men sympathetic to the outlaw's cause had been chosen as jurors, much to the disgust of the state of Missouri's prosecuting attorney and the counsel for the Ozark Mountain Railroad Company.

The trial itself lasted three weeks, but by the time it was over there was not a doubt in anyone's mind as to the outcome. There simply was no real evidence presented by the prosecutors. The state was unable to produce a single witness who could positively identify Luke as one of the train robbers, and Jenny, the only person who could provide information absolutely damning to Luke's case, refused to testify. The jury debated for less than an hour and then returned a verdict of not guilty on all counts. Those in the courthouse cheered.

By late August Luke was a free man.

It did not take the rest of the Morgans long to turn themselves in and stand trial. They too were found not guilty.

By Christmas the entire Morgan family was able to sit down to dinner without fear that the holiday would be rudely interrupted by the arrival of lawmen or Pinkerton detectives. Lottie was so happy she shed tears of joy and hugged Jenny several times to display her gratitude, for she felt it was Jenny who had inspired Luke to regain his respectability, paving the way for the rest of his brothers to become law-abiding citizens again as well.

Kipp and Sarah Jane beamed at learning their father would not be going away on any more jobs, and Jed was tickled pink to discover his middle son intended to resume his study of the law and run for political office.

"I'm thinking of going after a seat in the state senate," Luke announced. "If I win, I hope I can get the legislature to pass some sort of an amnesty bill for outlaws. I believe that, more than anything, would help to cut down on crime in Missouri. I'm sure the Jameses and the Youngers would give themselves up if they thought they wouldn't have to spend the rest of their lives in prison or, worse yet, be hanged for their offenses. I know they haven't committed half the crimes of which they've been accused, and those damned dime novels don't help matters any, fabricating stories about outlaws and making the public think the tales are the gospel."

"Ain't that the truth!" Billy Clay declared glumly. "I wish I *had* robbed as many banks as those stories claim. I'd be a rich man today instead of a reformed criminal about to become a dull old dirt farmer."

The others all laughed.

"Billy Clay," Luke began, "how'd you like to do something more exciting than that? If Pa can see his way clear to sparing me a little of your time, I'm going to make you part of my campaign team."

"Really, Luke? Do you mean it?"

"Of course I do. What do you think, Pa? Can you do without him and Raif for a while?"

Jed tugged on his beard, considering, his face grave—but his eyes were twinkling all the same.

"Well, I dunno, Luke," he drawled. "I was kind of countin' on them boys as replacements for Frank and Fred, who're getting on in years now."

"Aw, Pa." Billy Clay grinned. Frank and Fred were his father's two mules. "You're joshin' us again! You know Luke's gonna have to have a campaign team if he wants to win the election, and you know he's gonna need all the help he can get."

"I know, son," Jed agreed. "I was just funnin' you a little. Shoot fire! We'll *all* pitch in to get Luke elected. Hell! Even the young 'uns kin pass out leaflets."

"Oh, can we, Pa? Can we?" Kipp pleaded.

"Sure, son," Luke consented. "Well, since it looks as though I've got my whole campaign team right here, what do you say we make a few plans and then go open some presents!"

"Yeah! Yeah!" all the children hollered enthusiastically, racing toward the parlor and the Christmas tree, the rest of the family smiling and following hard on their heels.

Had Jenny given any thought to how Luke's new career would thrust her into the public limelight, she would not have so eagerly encouraged him to go into politics. But there was little she could do about it now. She was swept away by a whirlwind of activity that left her breathless and longing for respite and quiet—but there was none to be found.

After she finished teaching school each day, she hurried home to help Luke and the others with his campaign. There were handbills and speeches to write, accounts to be tallied and checked, and a seemingly neverending parade of numerous other details to be taken care of. Jenny did not mind doing any of these things. It was her other duties she wished she could forego.

These included dinners and afternoon teas, many of which she must attend alone as Luke's representative, hoping the ladies with whom she spoke would have some influence over their husbands' votes. There were parties and balls too, more than enough to make up for all those she had missed in her youth, Jenny thought.

Lacey Standish and Delcine were kept busy sewing and embroidering, for Luke declared stoutly that it would not do for Jenny to be seen in the same dress twice. Jenny said it was nonsense, but when at an elaborate social affair she overheard two gossipy females discussing a third's gown, remarking that it was the same one the woman had worn to the opera just a few weeks ago, she was glad Luke had insisted on her having so many clothes.

With so much happening it was a wonder Jenny could even think. Still she tried hard to remember the names of the rich, powerful men who were important to Luke's campaign and their wives as well, many of whom watched her with eagle eyes to see how she was measuring up. Many a wife had ruined her husband's political career—or so Jenny was informed on more than one occasion.

Luke's opponent, the incumbent Senator Sly Taggart, was unmarried, but the few times Jenny saw him at various functions he always had on his arm one of any number of lovely, eligible young ladies with political connections, each of whom made Jenny feel like a wren being compared to a peacock. Luke said it was all in her mind, that she grew more beautiful with each passing day, but still she could not help but feel plain and bookish and more than just a little ignorant for not knowing who was who on the social register, although she applied herself to learning as quickly as possible. Senator Taggart's companions, on the other hand, appeared to be old friends with everyone and to be up on all of the latest news too, no matter how recent, secret, or scandalous.

Luke told Jenny to relax and stop worrying, that everybody who'd met her liked her and she was a tremendous asset to his career, but still she was beset by niggling doubts, and she strove even harder on his behalf. Luke was much smarter and better looking than Senator Taggart, she thought, for in assessing Sly's character she had come to the conclusion that he was much more shrewd and cunning than he was intelligent, and she found his appearance strangely disturbing. The black patch over his left eye and the jagged scar marring his cheek made him look sinister, Jenny thought. She couldn't imagine anyone finding him attractive, although apparently there were a number of females who did, for there was always quite a flock of ladies gathered around both him and his aide, Tully Boothe.

It delighted Luke to be running for office against his ex-brother-in-law's employer, but Jenny could not share her husband's enthusiasm about this. The more she saw Tully, the less she liked him, and she could not help but think that anyone capable of inciting a riot was not likely to balk at performing various other assorted, sordid deeds. She did not care for the cold, appraising manner in which both Sly and Tully eyed her and Luke the few times they chanced to cross each other's paths, and she was afraid they were hatching some evil plot against her husband. She mentioned her fears to Luke, but he only grinned sardonically.

"Tully Boothe'll have to get up pretty early in the morning to put one over on me, Jenny," he stated coolly. "I'll match my wits against his any day of the week! And as for Senator Taggart . . . well, I doubt that his slate's any cleaner than mine. If he wants to throw a little mud, I won't be the only one who gets dirty."

Jenny would have been even more alarmed if she'd realized the two men were more interested in her than Luke, but as she was not aware of this, she decided her husband was astute enough to have the matter in hand and that perhaps it was only her imagination running away with her again.

Still she shivered a little as she turned away, and once more she wondered what it was about Tully Boothe that nagged at her.

Chapter Thirty-five

"I'm shore sorry, Luke, but I doubt if any of the rest of them gentlemens yore waitin' fer is gonna be able to make it now. The news just come in over the wire: Ain't no more trains runnin' today, less'n they's already on the move, 'n' if that's the case, there won't be no stoppin' 'em. The whole state's bein' attacked by a horde of grasshoppers, 'n' the railroad tracks is so slick now with the crushed bodies, trains are jest slidin' right on by depots."

"Now, Zachary," Luke began, "I've heard some tall tales in my time, but that just about takes the cake."

"Tall tale! That ain't no whopper, Luke, I swear! It's the gospel truth!" the ticket agent insisted. "If you don't believe me, go ask Stokes over to the telegraph office. He'll tell you!"

"Jesus, Zachary! You mean you really aren't putting me on? For Christ's sake! I've got a houseful of people at home. We're having a barbecue for some of my campaign backers and their wives. Do you mean to tell me a plague of locusts is coming—that everything we own is about to be wiped out by insects?"

"Well . . . I don't know about that, Luke," the ticket agent drawled, scratching his head. "I reckon them stories might be a bit exaggerated after all. But why don't you go ask Stokes to show you the wire anyways, jest to be certain."

"No, I'll take your word for it. I'd better light a shuck on out of here." Luke climbed into the new buggy he'd purchased and gathered up the reins of the fine-blooded chestnut team he'd bought as well. "If by any chance the rest of my party *does* show up, I'd be right grateful, Zachary, if you'd have Pritchard set them up with a team and carriage and directions to my farm. Tell him I'll settle my account when I return his vehicle and horses."

"Shore thin', Luke."

The barbecue was in full swing when Luke arrived home. Beneath the towering pines and oaks a large white canopy shielded the spreading lawn from the sweltering summer sun; a cool breeze rippled through the branches of the trees, causing the awning's lacy material to flutter gently and sending its trailing white satin ribbons streaming gaily.

On one side of the yard a short, wide wooden platform had been erected. Here musicians sat upon tiered benches, playing a lively reel on their instruments. Several of the younger couples present were dancing, their shoes clomping loudly on the dais, their shouts and laughter ringing out through the afternoon.

Long tables set end to end and covered with white tablecloths draped with intertwining streamers of red, white, and blue adorned the opposite side of the lawn. Platters and bowls piled high with a wide variety of foods burdened the trestles, so their wooden legs seemed to be groaning under the weight. There was apple cider and lemonade as well as a punchbowl filled with sparkling, spiked fruit juice.

Everyone appeared to be having such a good time that Luke hated to interrupt the festivities, but he felt it was his duty to inform the others about the grasshoppers. He stepped up on the wooden platform, signaled the musicians to cease playing, and called for quiet. He smiled down at Jenny, who had appeared unobtrusively at his side. Then he explained what he had learned in town. Once he had finished, there was some discussion, with all agreeing that no doubt the reports of the insects had been greatly exaggerated and, though Luke felt a twinge of apprehension about the conclusion reached, it was voted that the party should continue. He nodded to the musicians, and they struck up another song. Jenny's brow knit a trifle anxiously.

"Luke," she said, "I think I'll have some of the women cover the dishes just in case. It really would be awful if all the food were to be ruined. If there truly is a horde of grasshoppers coming, we can just move everything inside."

"That sounds like an excellent idea, honey," he replied. "I'll get Moses and some of the other men to help me move the furniture back in the parlor."

None of them, in their ignorance, had any concept of what was about to descend on them until the locusts actually arrived. They heard the buzzing first, a low, ominous sound that presently grew louder and louder, drowning out the music, and then they saw the grasshoppers—millions and millions of them, like nothing anyone had ever imagined. The insects blanketed the sky, their bodies pressed so close together that they formed a single pale greyish green cloud that seemed almost white, for the rays of the sun glinted off the locusts' translucent wings, so the mass appeared almost like a hazy mist slowly settling over the land.

Then one by one the grasshoppers began to drop out of the firmament like heavy, giant drops of pelting rain. They alighted on every tree, every bush, every flower, and every blade of grass until they virtually covered the area, a moving carpet four inches deep and voraciously devouring anything green in sight.

Women and children screamed and ran toward the house, trying to escape from the barrage of insects. Jenny saw one lady in a white dress sprigged with green flowers trip and fall in her haste. Instantly a group of locusts settled upon her, eating every scrap of green material from her gown, leaving it full of holes. A bunch of boys, Kipp among them, noticed and pointed at the woman, laughing. Jenny would have reprimanded Kipp sternly, but as it was the first time she'd ever seen him acting just as other mischievous youths did, she was loath to repress his glee. Instead she ordered him to help the woman to the house and find her something else to wear.

Then Jenny raced on, gathering up platters and bowls and herding everyone inside. The hum of the locusts roared in her ears, but the sound they made when hitting the ground was even more unnerving, for it was as though they were battering the earth to pieces. En masse the grasshoppers were so heavy that branches snapped and broke under their weight. Wheat and corn fields were flattened and reduced to stubble in hours; vegetable gardens were mashed and stripped bare in minutes.

No one had ever seen anything like it. They were fortunate in many respects in being at Whispering Pines when the calamity struck, for Jenny and Luke had screens on their doors and windows, and this was invaluable in helping to keep the insects out of the house. Other people were not so lucky.

Once the locusts had eaten everything green in sight, they started on other types of food, and wood, leather, and cloth. They attacked the rough siding on cabins and barns; they ate the handles off tools. They devoured saddles and harnesses. They munched through quilts, blankets, sheets, coats—every covering people had used to shield their crops. At night the grasshoppers worked on burrowing their way into homes, eating the contents of pantries and cabinets, destroying furniture, and shredding curtains.

It was days before the insects moved on, and by then Jenny was at her wit's end, for she had been caring for a houseful of unexpected guests. At that moment she heartily wished the locusts had done away with Luke's political career as well, but instead the incident seemed only to have strengthened the support of his campaign backers, who had seen him as a man who could be counted on to keep a cool head in a crisis. Jenny had no doubt that if these men had their way, her husband would win the upcoming election.

Luke lost. It did not seem possible after all their hard work, but it was so. J.R., upon learning the news, was so disgusted he accidentally put his cigar out in his half-full coffee cup instead of his ashtray. Tobias shook his head disbelievingly, insisting that Luke demand a recount of the votes. Raiford gnashed his teeth and cursed a blue streak, accusing Senator Taggart of somehow stuffing the ballot box. Billy Clay just sat on an empty crate in the campaign headquarters, looking morose and glumly agreeing with anything anybody else said. Jenny was busy putting away the horns that had not been blown and the confetti that had not been thrown after all. Only Luke was not discouraged or downcast.

"For God's sake!" he swore impatiently. "You're all acting as though I'd died or something! It doesn't matter that I lost. This was the first time any of us ever attempted to conduct a campaign. We made some mistakes, sure, but that's all right. Next time we'll have some experience under our belts and we'll have a better idea of what to do and what not to do. We know now, for example, that we need to broaden our spectrum, do more extensive traveling, get our own private railway car, and work out a schedule with the railroad companies so we can visit every little station around. What we need to do now is forget this election, regroup, and get started on our next campaign. Having more time to plan things and get ideas into action will help too."

"I think Luke's right." Jed nodded gravely. "You've gotta git yore feet wet 'fer you kin learn to swim, 'n' that's a fact. That Senator Taggart, no matter what any of us may think of him personally, had some right good notions, 'n' there ain't nothin' that says we can't make use of his ideas. I think we should all sit down right now, while everythin's still fresh in our minds, 'n' jot down some plans. Jenny gal, you pull up a chair, 'n' find you a piece of paper 'n' a pencil. You kin organize what we're sayin' into some kind of legible notes so's we'll all know what we're doin'."

"All right, Papa Jed," she consented, her eyes sparkling as he winked at her, for he liked her pet name for him. "I'll do that. Now . . . let's see. Luke, I thought the baking contest Senator Taggart's committee sponsored was a good idea. It got a lot of the women involved, and the sales of the cakes and pies afterward brought in a great deal of money. Lottie, Kate, Winona, and I could put together something like that."

"That's true," he agreed. "Write that down, darling."

And so it went. Pretty soon, their doldrums forgotten, the entire family was busy drawing up the outlines of Luke's 1876 campaign.

Some miles to the north of Tumbling Creek, in Jefferson City, the triumphant incumbent, Senator Sly Taggart, who ought to have been celebrating his victory, was instead sitting in his office, his mouth tightened into a hard thin line of anger.

"Goddamn it, Tully!" he cursed. "I haven't worked my butt off for years, kowtowing to fat, pompous old asses and their silly, scatterbrained wives, just to be done out of my seat by your frigging ex-brother-in-law! If Moffatt hadn't been sharp enough to get those ballot boxes stuffed when he did, this wouldn't be my office any longer, and I don't mind telling you, Tully, that I'm none too happy about that."

"No, Sly, I don't reckon you are," Tully said somewhat nervously.

"Luke Morgan is trouble," Sly continued coldly, "and his wife is an even worse menace. We've got to get rid of her. Somehow we've just got to get rid of her. Otherwise sooner or later she'll be the end of my political career—and yours too, Tully! Damned whore! I owe her one, that's for sure! Moffatt, go round up the others so we can make plans. I want Mrs. Morgan taken care of as soon as possible."

Chapter Thirty-six

Just outside of Tumbling Creek there was a huge bare hill that was known to most everyone in the region as Big Bald. It stood out starkly among the forested knolls and ridges that surrounded it, for its smooth broad top was devoid of even a single tree or shrub. Only grass and rocks covered its surface.

It was an ideal meeting place—or so thought the thirteen men who were gathered there this late winter evening of January, 1875, for, beneath the hazy light cast by the silvery full moon, the knob's very nakedness allowed them to see for miles in every direction and spot any interloper who might attempt to approach and spy on them. This was especially important, for the men did not want to be overheard.

They were a conscienceless group, the last, die-hard remnants of the men Senator Sly Taggart had commanded during the war. They had come here this night at the instigation of their leader to do evil under the guise of good. Most men would have been appalled by this twisting of morals. But these were not ordinary men, and they had long been accustomed to dealing unscrupulously. Now they waited silently for Sly to speak.

He stared at them, thinking about how far he had come—and they with him. It was hard to believe, he thought, that he had started life in an old, run-down, two-room shack just outside of Powder Springs, Missouri, the son of a poor, white-trash dirt farmer and his tired, defeated, slatternly wife. To think if he had not taken steps to change his fate, he would even now be following in his father's footsteps, trying to wrest a living from worn-out soil unable to yield anything worthwhile any longer. How clever he had been to turn the war to his advantage, working his way up through the ranks of the Union Army. Afterward, after his honorable discharge, he had returned home to run for office and had succeeded in winning a seat in the state senate. Soon he meant to campaign for the governorship of Missouri, and then when his term was up Sly intended to win his party's nomination for the presidency of the United States! Oh, yes, he had big plans, and no two-bit outlaw and his stupid slut of a wife were going to prevent him from eventually bringing his schemes to fruition!

"All right, men." Sly faced the crowd gathered around him. "You all know why we're here. As decent, law-abiding citizens, we are fed up with the lack of law and order in Missouri, with ineffectual marshals and sheriffs who're scared of their own shadows . . . outlaws like the James-Younger gang who terrorize the countryside . . . and known criminals like Luke Morgan running for public office. Tonight we're going to do something about it by forming the Law and Order League. You men will be the group's founding members, and it will be your duty to seek out additional recruits. We will be a secret organization, working anonymously to rid ourselves of the vermin that plague us. We will have rules and regulations, passwords, grips, and the like, all which shall help to bind and identify us to each other and to those who join us in the future. We will each of us be sworn in, and once we become members of the League, we shall remain so until our deaths.

"Now"—Sly unrolled an elaborate scroll tied with red ribbon—"I want you all to join hands and repeat this oath after me:

"I, in the presence of God and these witnesses, solemnly swear that I will never reveal any of the secrets of this order nor communicate any part of it to any person or persons in the known world unless I am satisfied by a strict test or in some legal way that they are lawfully entitled to receive them, that I will conform and abide by the rules and regulations of this order and obey all orders of my superior officers or any brother officer under whose jurisdiction I may be at the time attached; nor will I propose for membership or sanction the admission of anyone whom I have reason to believe is not worthy of being a member, nor will I oppose the admission of anyone solely on a personal matter.

"I shall report all theft that is made known to me and not leave any unreported on account of his being a blood relation of mine, nor will I willfully report anyone through personal enmity.

"I shall recognize and answer all signs made by lawful brothers and render them such assistance as they may be in need of, so far as I am able or the interest of my family will permit; nor will I willfully wrong or defraud a brother or permit it if is in my power to prevent it.

"Should I willfully and knowingly violate this oath in any way, I subject myself to the jurisdiction of twelve members of this order, even if their decision should be to hang me by the neck until I am dead, dead, dead. So help me God."

Sly paused for a moment, waiting for these words to sink in. Then he went on.

"We will hold our first raid this coming Saturday night. Our target will be the home of Elijah P. Mulvaney, one of the backers of Luke Morgan's campaign. That is all."

It seemed that no one was safe anywhere these days. Sly's infamous group of night riders, who had come to be known to one and all as the Baldknobbers after word of the secret organization and its meeting place had leaked out, had thrown the citizens of Taney County into turmoil and confusion. None knew who the masked men were, but all agreed they did not want to be dragged from their beds by the vigilantes, who had burned property, beaten several of their victims, and hanged one man who had attempted to escape from their wrath and punishment.

The masks worn by the group were hideous. They were fashioned of black, brown, or grey cambric and covered the face completely, the ends being tucked inside the wearer's collar. Circular holes were cut out of the material for the eyes, nose, and mouth, then these were outlined with bright red thread, stitched buttonhole-fashion. On the top of the mask were two six-inch-long horns made of cambric and stuffed with wood or cork to make them stiff. At the tip of each horn was a scarlet tassel. Those men wishing to appear even more gruesome had added circles and streaks of white paint to their masks and horns, so they looked like the devil's apprentices. They wore their coats turned inside out as well, to help conceal further their identities, and they carried carbines and revolvers and switches.

Few were those citizens who confronted the night riders without fear, although the vigilantes had little effect upon outlaws, their primary targets—or so they claimed. Indeed public opinion was currently quite favorable toward the James-Younger gang especially. Last year Pinkerton detectives had shot and killed one of the Younger brothers, John, who'd ridden with the gang on less than half a dozen occasions, and in January overly aggressive Pinkerton agents, railroad detectives, and Clay County lawmen had surrounded the home of Frank and Jesse James's mother, Zerelda Samuel, and had lobbed a thirty-three-pound bomb through one of her windows. Afterward the men had claimed the device was meant only to smoke so the inhabitants would be forced out of the house. But instead the bomb had exploded, killing nine-year-old

Archie Peyton Samuel, Frank and Jesse's half brother, and blowing away their mother's right arm.

Luke had insisted that out of respect he and Jenny journey to Clay County to attend the boy's funeral. Although she was very much against this, since the James-Younger gang actually killed people, in the end Jenny acquiesced to her husband's desires and so got her first glimpse of Frank and Dingus James, as all of Jesse's relatives and friends called him.

It was on the way home, when the train was pulling out of the Springfield depot, one of its many stops, that Jenny saw the man, the vile, ugly man who had haunted her dreams for so many endless nights during the past several years. At first she shook her head to clear it, not believing her eyes, for the man was laughing, as he had been that day at Faxon's Folly, and she thought she must be seeing things. Then slowly she became aware of the fact that he was actually real and truly standing alongside the station, and her face drained of color. She clutched Luke's arm tightly, fearing she was going to be ill.

"Jenny! What is it, sweetheart?" he asked with concern at the sight of her ashen cheeks, her huge hurt eyes. "What is it?"

"Luke," she breathed, "it—it—it's him! The man . . . that day . . . Evangie . . ."

"Where?" he questioned sharply, to her relief understanding at once the meaning of her disjointed words.

"There." She pointed accusingly.

"Go on home, Jenny," Luke ordered, his voice stern, his lips thinning into a grim line. "I'll join you when I can."

"No, Luke! Wait!" she called.

But it was too late. He was already halfway down the aisle of the public coach, his footing steady and sure even though the train was already in motion, picking up speed as it pulled out of the depot. Her heart in her throat, Jenny watched him go, helpless to stop him. She gasped as she saw him step onto the small platform outside the car and jump from the vehicle, rolling over and over again on the ground as he landed. Then he sprinted toward the depot. She could see nothing more, for the train had passed the city limits and the wood-covered hills were beginning to obscure her view. Jenny bit her lip anxiously. There was nothing she could do now but go on to Tumbling Creek and wait and wonder, sick with worry about Luke, half hoping, half afraid of what he would uncover about her past.

* * *

It was three days before Luke returned home to Tumbling Creek. By then Jenny, although outwardly composed, was a mass of churning emotions. She longed to know what her husband had found out, yet perversely she was terrified of learning, lest the black void be ripped from her mind, forcing her to face that which she most feared.

"Well?" she asked at last.

Luke shook his head.

"His name was Harmon Moffatt, and he admitted he was there at Faxon's Folly that day, but more than that he wouldn't say. I tried to get it out of him, but he turned quite vicious and suddenly went berserk and attempted to kill me. I'm sorry, but I . . . I had to take my knife to him, Jenny. He's dead."

She shivered a little and turned away, not wanting to know any more, for she had heard tales in the past of Luke's murderous ability with a knife. He was more feared for that than his skill with his Navy Colts, and even though he had acted in self-defense, she had difficulty accepting what he had done.

Since she was not looking at him, Jenny missed the hooded expression that came down over Luke's face, concealing his thoughts from her. Had she seen, she would have known he had lied to her about discovering little, had lied because he had wanted to spare her. After all, what he had learned might mean nothing. On the other hand, it might mean a great deal.

Harmon Moffatt had had a train ticket to Jefferson City inside his duster, and there'd been a room key in his pocket too, as well as an old flier promoting Senator Taggart's campaign. Luke intended to check all these things out. After mulling over his impressions it had come to him that Moffatt had worked for Sly Taggart; Luke remembered seeing the ugly man on several occasions. He was not the type to have dealt with the public, as Tully did, but the sort of man who would have handled private business—especially the kind conducted in back rooms and dark alleys.

Luke wanted some answers, not just for Jenny, but for himself too. He didn't know why, but he had a bad feeling in his gut about all of this. The story of Jenny's past followed a familiar pattern; he'd heard other tales like it during the war, rumors of atrocities committed by irregular outfits attached to the Union Army, outfits like that commanded by Sly Taggart, the man the South had called the Butcher Colonel. Was there some connection between this and the fact that Moffatt had worked for the senator? Luke didn't know. He knew only that he must find out. If by some chance it *had* been Sly Taggart's band of marauders who had destroyed Jenny's family and the senator happened to remember and recognize her, he would have to kill her, lest she denounce him and expose his unsavory past, ruining his entire career. Sly had seen Jenny several times during the campaign. Perhaps even now he was plotting her death. The thought made Luke's blood run cold.

"Jenny, I've got to go up to Jefferson City tomorrow," he told her. "I'll try not to be gone too long. In the meantime why don't you take Kipp and Sary and go over and visit my folks for a while. You know they love to see you."

"Well, all right. I suppose I can, although I don't know why you have to keep traveling up to Jefferson City all the time, Luke. The campaign plans are coming along nicely, and you don't even have to run for office until next year." Then, seeing that he wasn't even listening to her, Jenny's mouth turned down wryly at the corners. "Luke Morgan, you aren't paying one bit of attention to me!" she accused, then burst into laughter at the startled, sheepish expression on his face. "Oh, forget it! I'll go upstairs now and tell the children to get a few things packed."

"Yes, you do that," Luke insisted. "You do that."

After she'd left the room he breathed a sigh of relief. At least at his folks' house Jenny would be safe. His heart turned over in his breast at the thought of her being otherwise. If anything ever happened to her, he didn't think he could bear it!

Chapter Thirty-seven

In his anxiety over Jenny's welfare Luke had forgotten one very important fact: This was the week his folks had planned on driving over to Stone County to visit Jed's cousin Gilbert. So, instead of being safe at Jed and Lottie's cabin, Jenny was very much alone in the big house Luke had built for her, with only Kipp and Sarah Jane for company, once Moses and Delcine had gone home for the evening. Had Luke known this, he would have been frantic with worry, but as he continued his investigation in Jefferson City, he felt secure in the thought that Jenny was being well looked after by his family.

Thus he knew nothing of the night the Baldknobbers came to Whispering Pines, their faces hidden beneath their gruesome masks, their coats turned inside out to obscure further their identities.

When they came Jenny was in the small parlor, reading, trying hard to distract herself so she would not miss Luke so badly. The children were upstairs, asleep. The house was very still and seemed bigger and emptier than it did during the day, as though with the coming of darkness it had taken on a new and almost frightening personality. It creaked and groaned, each little noise sounding like the footsteps of someone walking across the floor above her or creeping stealthily down the stairs. Had Luke been there, Jenny would never even have noticed the settling of the house, but because she was alone and it was night, her imagination played havoc with her thoughts.

Her nerves were already on edge when the masked men came, turning her fears to stark and real terror. She knew the Baldknobbers had attacked the homes of several of the men who had funded Luke's foray into the political world, for there were many who still condemned him as an outlaw, even though he had stood trial for his crimes. But Jenny had not thought the night riders would go so far as to assault Luke and his family personally. Although tamer than they had been in the past, the Morgan brothers were still feared, for the natives of the Ozarks had long memories and did not soon forget, and she had mistakenly believed this offered her and the children some protection. Now she knew it was not so.

Hearing the sound of hooves upon the gravel drive, Jenny thought at first that Luke had for some unknown reason returned home sooner than she had expected. Eagerly she rose and, laying aside her book, started down the hall to the foyer, her heart filled with joy. She had almost reached the front doors when the first of the rocks smashed through the windowpanes of the formal parlor and the dining room. She cringed and pressed herself against one wall as shards of glass flew in all directions. Then the shouting began, loud rude demands that she come out to the front porch and show herself.

Jenny's heart raced, and for a moment she knew what her sister Evangeline must have felt that day so long ago at Faxon's Folly. Hesitantly Jenny tiptoed to a window and peeked out, her worst fears confirmed when she saw the band of masked men on horseback ranged in a semicircle out front, waiting for her. Had she not been so frightened, she would have realized how strange it was that they did not call out for Luke, almost as though they knew he was not home. But Jenny was too scared to grasp this fact. She knew only that she was alone, with two small children to look after, and the notorious Baldknobbers were outside, howling for her to come out.

Shaking, she made her way to Luke's study, where with trembling hands she unlocked his gun cabinet and carefully removed and loaded one of his rifles. Then, taking a deep breath, she prepared herself to face the night riders.

There were thirteen of them, an ill omen! But Jenny did not recognize any of them in the flickering light of the torches they carried. Nothing about them gave even a clue as to their identities. Even their voices were muffled and indistinct beneath their masks, and she soon gave up all hope of finding a sympathetic friend among them.

"What do you want?" she asked, trying to quell the slight quaver in her voice and leveling her weapon at the man she had decided was their leader.

"You, Mrs. Morgan," he returned mockingly.

There was something about his voice that gave Jenny the shivers, as though she had heard it before, sounding just as it did now, and once more, eerily, she thought of Evangeline and was afraid.

Then she tried to reassure herself. The war was over, and these men were not Yankee marauders, but ordinary citizens carried away by their zeal for law and order. Surely they would not harm her. Surely they would not!

"You have no legitimate business here, gentlemen," she stated more calmly, gaining a firmer grip on her emotions, "and you are trespassing besides. I must ask you to leave these premises at once, lest I be forced to send someone for Marshal Farlow."

The Baldknobbers merely sniggered, as the men long ago had laughed at Evangeline. Jenny could feel fear rising again within her, for it was as though she were reliving the nightmare of her past, and with difficulty she once more fought down the panic that threatened to engulf her.

She stiffened her spine slightly as the leader of the gang, his saddle creaking, dismounted and began to saunter toward her, menace seeming to ooze from his every pore.

"Don't. Please, don't," Jenny begged, sensing the violence he held in check, as though he were a cat playing with a mouse before pouncing upon it viciously and putting an end to the game.

Despite Jenny's pleas, the man only continued to swagger toward her purposefully, and suddenly she knew that, despite all her hopes to the contrary, he meant to hurt her as surely as those men at Faxon's Folly had been bent upon pillage and murder. Evil was in the air now, as it had been then. Jenny could smell it, feel it.

Terrified, she pulled the rifle's trigger, staggering backward from the powerful recoil of the weapon as it discharged. The bullet slammed into the ground, kicking up a spray of dust. The leader paused, but the wide mouth-hole in his mask betrayed the fact that he was grinning jeeringly, as though Jenny's warning shot had not bothered him at all. It was obvious he did not believe she would actually fire at him, though she threatened to do just that.

"Don't come any closer," she warned. "I don't want to have to shoot you. But I will!"

The man only laughed, a low, mean chuckle that sent chills down Jenny's spine. Her flesh crawled, as though a snake had slithered over her, and for one awful moment she was afraid she was going to be sick. Then she gathered her nerve and once more steadied and aimed the rifle. She was Luke Morgan's wife; she would give her husband no cause to be ashamed of her.

The leader shifted his stance slightly, made wary now by the sudden martial glint in Jenny's eye. Perhaps she really would shoot him after all, he thought, remembering another woman, long ago, who had tried to kill him and had mortally wounded several of his men before he had captured and brutally subdued her. Some of his confidence ebbed away, and more cautiously now he moved toward Jenny, like a hunter stalking its prey.

She was so intent on watching him so he wouldn't catch her off guard that she was only dimly aware of the fact that, wakened earlier by the sounds of the breaking glass and the yelling, Kipp and Sarah Jane had crept from their beds to join her on the front porch. Now protectively they edged closer to her. Their hands gripped her skirt tightly as they peeked from behind her at the man who loomed over them like some malevolent monster. Though they were afraid, a good deal of their concern was for Jenny. The man's attention was focused on her, and each of the children, who had come to love her dearly, was wondering how best to help her. Suddenly, with a wild "Yip-Yip-Yaw" Kipp darted past her, ramming his head into the leader's stomach.

The man, unprepared for such an attack, grunted, doubled over, and stumbled backward, nearly falling before he managed to regain his balance. Then, reacting swiftly, his fist shot out savagely, cuffing Kipp on the side of his head and sending the boy sprawling.

"Kipp!" Jenny screamed. "Kipp!"

To her relief he scrambled quickly to his feet, apparently only momentarily stunned. But then to her horror, his arms flailing wildly, he assaulted the leader again.

"You leave my stepmother alone!" Kipp hollered, beating ineffectually at the man, who appeared almost amused by the boy's blows. "You leave my stepmother alone, or I'll kill you!"

At last the leader grew annoyed by this display, and with another casual swing of his fist, he punched Kipp in the jaw. The boy flew backward, then rolled head over heels once more. This time he stood up more slowly, shaking his head and reeling a little as though badly dazed, and Jenny feared a third blow might prove too much for him.

"Run, Kipp! Run!" she ordered. "Run for help!"

The boy realized this was the best thing to do, for it was obvious he was not going to be able to overcome the night riders all by himself, and, stumbling slightly in his haste, he began to race toward the edge of the woods, praying the trees and the darkness would swallow him up.

"Don't let him get away!" the leader growled to his men. "Don't let him get away!"

Then, cursing their slowness to react, he drew his pistol and fired at Kipp's small, zigzagging form. The first shot missed, and before the man could get off another, Jenny, horrified, instinctively pulled the trigger on her rifle, feeling the butt of the weapon slam into her shoulder, bruising it, as the bullet spiraled from the long barrel aimed straight at the leader. But it had been a long time since her lessons in marksmanship from Cade, and Jenny was rusty from lack of practice. Her hands wavered, and instead of hitting the man in the chest, as she had intended, she struck him in the thigh. He exhaled sharply at the impact of the slug, one hand clutching his leg as blood spewed from the wound, spraying warm and wet and sticky upon Jenny's face.

She scarcely even felt the red liquid upon her skin; her concentration was now riveted on another member of the gang, who, mounted upon a powerful gelding, was intent on riding Kipp down. Once more she raised her rifle and fired. This time her aim was true, and the night rider toppled from his saddle, allowing Kipp to make good his escape before the leader wrenched the weapon from Jenny's grasp and smacked her with it, knocking her to her knees.

She didn't mind the punishment inflicted upon her. It had bought Kipp's safety and perhaps help too. That was enough. Jenny only hoped she and Sarah Jane would still be alive when aid arrived.

"You goddamned bitch!" the man snarled, then hit her again. "I ought to kill you!"

The second blow was so savage it smashed the rifle's stock, and with a grunt of disgust the leader hurtled the broken pieces to the ground, then yanked Jenny up and shook her furiously before pushing her roughly toward his horse. She tripped and fell, and when Sarah Jane, who had been cowering off to one side, courageously ran forward to assist Jenny up, the man struck the little girl, splitting open her lip and sending her reeling.

"Stop it!" Jenny cried. "Stop it! She can't do you any harm. She's a mute! Do you hear me? She's a mute! She hasn't been able to speak since she lost her mother years ago."

To Jenny's shock the leader started to laugh raucously at what she'd told him. Then, still grinning, he bent wickedly toward Sarah Jane and whispered in her ear.

"You'd better keep quiet, you sniveling slut," he hissed. "I haven't forgotten you, you know, and if you don't do just as I've told you, I'll be back, just as I promised, and I'll cut out your tongue for sure!"

Sarah Jane froze upon hearing the evil voice that had haunted her for so many years. It was him! One-Eyed Jack! Yes, she could see now that one of the eye-holes in his mask had a black patch beneath it. White-faced with fear, she began to tremble and slid to the ground in a dead faint.

"Sary!" Jenny shrieked. "Sary! Oh, what did you do to her, you bastard?"

She started to run toward Sarah Jane's crumpled form, but the man caught her arm in a cruel grip and snatched her back.

"There's nothing wrong with her," he said. "She's just blacked out, that's all. Now get mounted up, bitch, that is . . . unless you want me to kill the kid after all."

He cocked his gun and pointed it at Sarah Jane.

"N-no," Jenny stammered, gasping. "It's—it's just that I—I don't understand. What have we done to deserve this? Where are you taking me? What do you want with me?"

"All in good time, Mrs. Morgan. All in good time."

Then the leader tossed her up into his horse's saddle, mounted behind her, and brought his skittishly prancing stallion under control, the fingers of one hard, muscular hand digging into Jenny's soft flesh where he gripped her tightly, his thumb just brushing her breast.

Jenny sat frozen as the man behind her began to shout commands to his men, ordering them to hurry, that no doubt Kipp had by this time summoned help, which would soon be forthcoming. Hastily the men retrieved the body of their fellow night rider whom Jenny had killed, and, after catching his horse, they hung him over his saddle, tying his wrists and ankles together tightly to prevent him from falling off. Then they carefully eliminated all remaining traces of their presence, picking up one or two burned-out torches that had been thrown to the ground and removing a piece of material caught on a thorny tree, which had snagged someone's coat. After that they cantered all over the yard, the hooves of their mounts cutting up the lawn and making if difficult, if not impossible, to tell one print from another. Jenny knew it would be hard to track them now, and she whimpered a little down deep in her throat, sure no one would ever find her again.

An eerie sense of déjà vu again crept over her as she watched the Baldknobbers, and she thought this was what it must have been like that day at Faxon's Folly, when there had been nothing left behind to tell Cade and Moses who had destroyed her family and why. Those men too had erased all signs of their violent intrusion upon the plantation. Jenny shivered at the idea, now more terrified than ever.

The night did not seem real. This could not be happening to her—not again!

She wondered who this man was who held her prisoner, but there was nothing about him that appeared familiar or gave her a clue to his identity. Jenny shuddered in his arms. Somehow it was even worse to think she was being kidnapped by someone she did not even know. What would he do to her? she wondered, then swiftly banished the thought, preferring not to dwell on it, not wanting to remember Evangeline and what she had suffered before she'd died.

Oh, God, Jenny prayed, if he's going to kill me, please let him do it quickly. Don't let him torment me. . . .

She bit her lip to keep from crying out and grasped the pommel tightly as the leader dug his spurs into his horse's sides, urging the stallion forward into the night, splitting away from the rest of the Baldknobbers, who were dispersing silently in groups of twos and threes.

Alone. I'm to be alone with him, Jenny realized, growing even more painfully conscious of the way the man's hand gripped her, how his thumb just rested upon the crest of her nipple.

Oh, Luke. Luke!

But there was no answer to the soundless cry of her mind. There were only the woods and the darkness swallowing them up as they left Whispering Pines far behind.

Chapter Thirty-eight

The ride was a nightmare in the darkness, but as the sky began to lighten Jenny grew even more terrified when she recognized that they were headed toward the high bluffs that marked the Arkansas border, steep, jagged promontories known as Murder Rocks.

During the War Between the States the towering bluffs had served as the headquarters for a gang of Bushwhackers headed by Alf Bolin. From their vantage point atop the cliffs the marauders had swooped down and hideously murdered numerous Federal soldiers passing by on the winding wagon road leading from Little Rock to Springfield. It was said that if a Rebel could cross the White River into Arkansas there, he would be safe, and much to the chagrin of the Union Army, this had more often than not proven to be the case. Frustrated by the gruesome success of Alf Bolin's raids, the North had finally offered a sizable reward for his head and eventually had attained that grizzly evidence of his death at the hands of a Yankee soldier.

But even now the terror of Murder Rocks lived on in the hushed tales of the Ozark natives, and because she was distraught Jenny half expected to see blood dripping from the bluffs that loomed ahead in the distance.

The man behind her had been frighteningly silent during the night, refusing to answer any of her questions, not even deigning to speak further to her, even to give a command. He had simply stared at her through the dark slits of his mask, so black that it appeared as though he had no eyes at all but was a specter from the grave. The white rings bordering the eye-holes only served to accentuate the effect.

Now slowly he drew the stallion to a halt and, pulling his pistol, motioned for Jenny to dismount, making it clear that he would shoot her if she attempted to escape.

Stiffly she slid from the horse's back, every bone in her body feeling as though it had been jolted out of position, every muscle aching, and her backside bruised and sore. She doubted she could have run away if her life had depended on it. She only hoped it did not.

She sank to the ground, watching with trepidation as the man removed his duster and turned it right side out, then tugged the hood from his face.

"Senator Taggart!" Jenny exclaimed, recognizing him at once.

"That's right." He smiled at her grimly.

"What is the meaning of this?" Jenny demanded, now more outraged than afraid.

The senator shook his head disbelievingly, short, ironic laughter bursting from his lips.

"You don't even know me, do you?" he asked. "I've risked my career and my neck for nothing. *Nothing!*" he reiterated bitterly. "You bitch! Why couldn't you have died along with all the others—like you were supposed to do?"

"What do you mean I don't know you? I—I should have died? What are you talking about? Why? Others? What others? I—I don't understand," Jenny stammered, confused.

"No you don't—unfortunately for you," Sly said, his mouth twisting sardonically. "If I'd known you hadn't recognized me, I wouldn't have made such elaborate plans to kill you. I kept wondering, you know—during the campaign—why you didn't denounce me, expose me. I didn't realize I'd changed so much. Or perhaps I haven't changed at all," he mused. "It is possible Tully was right after all. Is it possible you don't remember?"

"Remember? Remember what?" Jenny queried.

"That day at Faxon's Folly." Sly spoke coolly as he sat down beside her.

Jenny gasped, horrified, at the unexpected, shocking reply. She recalled suddenly how she'd felt as though she knew Tully Boothe. She'd been right! He *had* been there that day! And Sly Taggart . . . But there was nothing the least familiar about the swarthy, devilish-looking senator. Surely she would have recognized him if there had been. Jenny closed her eyes, trying to remember, and all of a sudden it was just as Luke had once told her. The past came rushing back in a flood of memories, swirling up to engulf her, so it seemed as though she were there once more that day at the plantation.

She saw a dark, hazy demon on horseback, riding toward her, swinging his silver saber at her. She saw herself raise her father's heavy revolver and fire. She saw blood gush from the wound in the black stallion's chest. She saw the animal stumble and fall, blotting out the sun, crushing her. . . .

"It was *you!*" Jenny cried. "It was *you* on the horse! But . . . why?"

Why? Sly thought. Why. Because of Orin. Everything I ever did was for Orin. Orin. Cold in his grave these many years past.

How had it all ever started? Sly wondered, thinking back . . . back to the beginning. What had led him to this pass?

Then he began to speak, all his pent-up anger and hatred spewing forth at Jenny, the target of his thirst for vengeance.

"It's a long story," he began, "but you're not going anywhere. . . ."

He was born Silas Taggart, he explained, but all his friends—and his enemies—called him Sly, an apt moniker, for he was indeed as clever as the proverbial fox. He had to be, being the son of a perpetually tired mother and a big, brutal father who beat him regularly until, at the age of twelve, he ran away from his home in Powder Springs, Missouri, regretting nothing but the fact that he must leave behind his younger brother, eight-year-old Orin, who had the measles and was too ill to go with him.

He would never, not as long as he lived, forget the hurt, scared look on his brother's pinched face when the boy learned Sly was going away.

"Don't leave me, Sly," Orin pleaded, clutching pitifully at his brother's arm. "Pa'll wallop me twice as hard if you're not here to stand up to him. I know he will, and I—I won't be able to bear it, Sly. God knows, it's hard enough to take as it is. But I won't have the courage to run away, like you. I—I couldn't bring myself to leave Ma all alone with the brute."

Orin had always been something of a mama's boy, though what he saw in that poor old worn-out bag of bones Sly couldn't imagine. After all, it wasn't as though she ever tried to defend them during their father's outbursts of rage. No, she just cringed in a corner and cried until Zeb Taggart smacked her a couple of times too, then dragged her into their bedroom and slammed the door. After that would be heard through the thin walls the violent creaking of the Taggarts' old straw-stuffed mattress and, sometime later, Zeb's drunken snoring.

Sly grimaced.

"Listen, Orin," he said, "I can't stay here. If I do, Pa and me'll wind up killing each other. You know that. I'm almost as big as he is now, and sometimes my fingers itch so bad to strangle the bastard that I can't hardly control them. But I'll make it up to you some way—I swear I will—and someday we'll be together again, just like we are now. Here. I want you to have my pocket knife. Take good care of it, and remember me whenever you use it."

"Gee, thanks, Sly." Orin's tear-stained face brightened a little. "I'll treat it like gold, I promise."

"You do that. Write to me now, you hear? And never forget I'll be waiting for you to join me when you can."

Despite all of Sly's hopes, life did not get any easier for him after leaving his family's shack. Work was scarce in the South, where unlimited, free labor was to be had after a man bought a slave, and, though Sly would have performed the meanest of tasks for a few pennies, no one had any use for him. A strapping, growing boy, his hunger soon became such that he was reduced to stealing, for he refused to beg, the thought of doing so a bitter reminder of his father's whining to his betters when times were hard and they couldn't pay the rent.

At first Sly's thievery was petty—a few ears of corn gleaned from the edge of a field, a chicken taken from a poorly guarded coop, a pie filched from a back porch, where it had been set upon the rail to cool. But, as he managed this ravaging without being caught, he grew bolder and progressed to more daring deeds.

By the time he was fifteen, Sly had killed his first man, a grocer who, wakened by the sound of breaking glass in his general store, grabbed his shotgun loaded with buckshot, confronted Sly, and threatened to call the marshal to him. During the ensuing struggle Sly bashed the grocer's head in with an empty pickle barrel, then relieved the cash box of its contents, stole some food, and raced out into the night.

Some months later he raped his first woman, a fourteen-year-old girl on an isolated farm. At his appearance, wary and instinctively distrusting him, she ran into her family's house and bolted the door, refusing to let him inside. She wouldn't even give him a meal, for that would mean opening the door or a window, and she was all alone at the farm; her folks were away, and her brothers were working in distant fields. Hungry and infuriated, Sly waited around until she was certain he'd gone and she came outside to finish hanging up her laundry to dry. Then he dragged her into the barn, beat her, and raped her twice. Afterward he slit her throat, fearing she would never forget his face and would give an accurate description of him to the law, whom Sly had realized, after the incident with the grocer, he must now forever evade. Though afraid that any moment the girl's family would return, he pillaged the farmhouse until he found a precious hoard of hard-earned cash beneath some loose floorboards, then he rolled some victuals and clean clothes into a bundle and moved on.

Sly always searched for money, no matter how hard-pressed he was for time, for that was his contribution to his beloved brother, Orin, whom he'd never forgotten and with whom he corresponded whenever he could. If the ill-gained funds eased Orin's lot, they were worth the risk to Sly. He was always very careful to hide the loot in some trivial and utterly useless gift so his father would not learn of it. Sly had no doubt that if he knew about Orin's secret income, Zeb Taggart would confiscate it and waste it on liquor. Once, Sly hollowed out a wooden statue of an Indian and filled it with coins. Another time he stuffed a raccoon tail with greenbacks. In his letters to his brother he told Orin where to find the caches. It was safe to do that, for neither Zeb nor his wife, Maudie, could read. But Sly and Orin could, having learned well enough the few times they'd been permitted to attend the one-room schoolhouse several miles away.

So Sly lived until the outbreak of the War Between the States—a loner, a gambler, and a criminal, constantly on the prowl and never doing more than what he had to in order to get by. That this had on several occasions included rape, burglary, armed robbery, and murder had long since ceased to bother Sly. Life had kicked him in the teeth, or so he thought, and, as he saw it, he had done nothing but kick back as hard as he could.

When finally the war split a yawning chasm down the Mason-Dixon Line, Sly, always ambitious, perceived that long-awaited opportunity was knocking on his door. Here was his chance to rise above his penny-ante dealings, profit considerably, and make something out of himself in the process. If all went as he dreamed, he could bury his unsavory past and become so rich and powerful that even if the deeds ever were discovered, the law would still be unable to touch him. Never being one to hesitate, he grasped his fate with both hands.

The South would never win the war; of that Sly was convinced. She was a languorous, decadent courtesan, was King Cotton's mistress, coddled by her black mammies and grown fat and lazy on the blood, sweat, and tears of her Negro slaves. She might have more intelligent, more highly educated officers—Virginian visionaries and South Carolinian scholars. But it was the scrappy, cold-blooded cunning learned in Northern slums, on Eastern waterfronts, and on Midwestern prairies that would prevail in the end, and Sly was a bonafide graduate of the school of hard knocks.

It was a rally in Chicago where he first spied the way to wedge himself an opening in a better world. He stared at the fresh-faced youths around him, all of them shouting and cheering and singing

"We'll rally 'round the flag, boys, we'll rally once again/Shouting the Battle Cry of Freedom," and he smiled to himself wolfishly.

God and country be damned! There was money to be made in war—and power and glory for men who knew how to win battles. His father might be a poor, white-trash farmer, kissing arse and scratching in the dirt for a living, but he, Sly, would not settle for that. Fame and fortune were out there waiting for him, and he meant to have them! After all, war was nothing but brutality, and he knew brutality inside and out.

His face hard and set with determination, he joined the long line to sign up in the Union Army.

His rise in its ranks was nothing short of meteoric. He was as competent as Sheridan, as merciless as Sherman, and he could drink Grant under the table. Moreover, he had something the three generals lacked: Sly was by now totally without morals or scruples. If winning battles meant shooting senile old men as well as young soldiers, raping terrified women, and bayoneting innocent children, then he would do it. His ambition was all-consuming, and his first taste of command vanquished the last vestiges of any gentility he might have had.

By the time he'd been promoted to the rank of colonel, Sly had been awarded enough medals to have decorated ten uniforms; he had banked a fortune in gold made on the black-market, and he had gathered under his authority a group of hard-core men as unconscionable as he was.

Tales of their infamous exploits were whispered about far and wide and in the South had earned Sly the dubious distinction of being known as the Butcher Colonel. Rebel soldiers spat upon the ground when they heard his name; women cringed at the sound of it, thinking fearfully of the dreadful, unmentionable shame that might be suffered at his hands; and small children shivered under their covers at night, certain Sly was the most gruesome bogeyman of all.

At thirty-seven, he was at the peak of his military career, and there was no stopping his quest for supremacy.

The decision makers in Washington might frown and mutter among themselves at the abominable rumors that reached their ears of Sly's vicious campaigns and other assorted and sordid related activities, but as nothing concrete could be proved against him, they were forced to keep their opinions to themselves. Colonel Sly Taggart won battles. How he did it was as unimportant as it was indeterminate. He was a hero of the Union Army, as were the men who followed him, and they, basking in his reflected glory, were as closemouthed as Sly was about how he achieved his victories and what he did afterward to his victims. At best it was unpleasant. The worst didn't bear thinking of.

But Sly *was* thinking of it, just as he had thought of it so many years ago when, his one good eye glinting, he'd listened to the report one of his men had delivered to him.

"We was out feragin' fer supplies, Colonel, jest like you ordered, 'n' we come upon a plantation—Faxon's Folly, the folks hereabouts call it. It looked deserted, 'n' there were a vegetable patch out back—we seen the corn from the road—so we moseyed on in. Well, hell. We'd no sooner got up to the front of the house than this ole silver-haired coot come a'roarin' outside, a'wavin' his hands 'n' a'hollerin' at us to git offa his land. He said the Yankees had already come 'n' gone 'n' cleaned him out in the process, 'n' he weren't given' 'em nothin' else. Well, sir, we didn't see no reason to pay no mind to the bastard—he weren't armed or nothin'—so we started 'round back. But the silver-haired geezer . . . he didn't take kindly to us ignorin' him, 'n' he run up 'n' tried to yank Orin offa his hoss. Then there were a whole lotta yellin'; Orin's hoss started a'rearin' like a wildcat; 'n', the next thing I knowed, Orin's done pulled his pistol 'n' shot that ole fool right between the eyes—kilt him deader 'n a doornail, Colonel.

"Well, sir, that oughta of been the end of it, but the son of a bitch's women was watchin' from the winders—musta been his daughters, 'cause they was all young 'n' looked kinda alike. Anyways, one of 'em ran to git her daddy's rifle, 'n' 'fer anybody knowed what were happenin' that red-haired she-devil smashed out one of the winderpanes 'n' opened fire. I tell you, Colonel, she were sumpin' else, that damned hellion. Looked like an avengin' angel with that red hair a'tumblin' down about her like it were on fire. She blowed a hole clean through Orin's chest, sir, then shot Linus in the head, pore boy. I don't think he ever knowed what hit him. Then she got Randolph in the stomach.

"Me 'n' Jake here squeezed off some rounds, but it didn't do no good. The witch put a bullet in Jake's arm 'n' one in my leg, so we figgered we'd best hightail it on outta there 'n' report back to you, Colonel."

"Thank you, Deacon. That will be all," Sly had stated coldly to mask his churning emotions.

Orin dead? No. It just wasn't possible. After all their long years apart they had barely been reunited. It just wasn't possible Orin was dead.

How glad Sly had been when he'd learned from a letter that his brother had joined the Union Army. How many strings he had pulled in order to get Orin transferred to his command. His brother was the only person Sly had ever loved, and now Orin was dead.

That red-haired she-devil. That red-haired she-devil.

The words had rung over and over again in Sly's mind, and he'd known, then, what he must do.

After diligent investigation he'd found out that all the Colter sisters except the youngest had red hair. But there was only one whose tresses looked as though they were on fire. Evangeline. Evangeline Colter Hunter had murdered his brother.

She—and those *she* loved—must pay for that.

Unfortunately for Sly's plans the war was over. Thus the fact that what he intended to do would ruin his entire career if he were caught had given him a brief moment's pause. He hadn't slipped in rivers of blood, sweltered in muddy, mosquito-ridden ditches, eaten moldy old hardtack washed down with brackish water, suffered from dysentery, lost his left eye, and had his face hideously scarred for nothing.

Still . . . Orin was dead, and the person responsible for his murder must pay.

Sly had plotted his course carefully every step of the way, taking his time and covering his tracks deep. He could afford to wait for his revenge—it would be all the sweeter for that—and precaution was necessary if he were not to be discovered and exposed.

His first move had been to request that General Sherman leave him behind in Atlanta to garrison the city after they'd taken it. Sly would oversee the Union troops there, as well as those in the surrounding areas—Fayetteville, Jonesboro, Decatur, and so forth. Once in charge, Sly had set about making himself familiar with the countryside, especially the vicinity around Jonesboro, in particular the plantation known as Faxon's Folly. He'd learned all he could about the Colters, every last detail down to the sort of material from which the unmentionables of the four sisters were made.

Before the war it had been silk; afterward it had been plain old cotton. A pity, Sly had thought. Fiery Evangeline Colter Hunter had belonged in silk, and he would have enjoyed the feel of the raw fabric as he'd ripped it from her flesh—though he hadn't minded tearing away her cotton chemise after all. For Sly had raped the woman who'd dared to reject him and spit on his boots, publicly humiliating him, and then he had killed her, because she had taken her father's rifle and ended Orin's life.

"She had to pay, you see," he told Jenny tonelessly now as she shrank away from him in horror. "All of you did. Orin was all I had, all I'd ever had. It wasn't right that he was dead and she was alive, that murdering whore!"

"But he—he gunned our father down in cold blood," Jenny whispered, stricken.

"What was one old man compared to Orin?" Sly retorted so indignantly that for a moment Jenny feared he would strike her again. Then he settled back against the rock supporting him and shrugged. "Well, it's all so much water under the bridge now, I suppose—except for you." He stared at Jenny, his good eye hard, merciless. "Why couldn't you have died that day like all the rest? It would have saved me a lot of trouble. But, no, you had to live, and now I've got to kill you too before you ruin everything."

Jenny's heart leaped to her throat. In seconds she would be dead; Sly would aim his revolver at her head and pull the trigger. But to her relief he made no threatening moves toward her.

The entire time he had been talking he had been tearing away the bloody, makeshift bandage he had wrapped about his injured leg earlier. Now, grimacing, he probed the wound gingerly. Jenny, still stunned and horrified by his revelations, watched, torn, as with his fingernails he scraped away some of the dried blood. She was sure the bullet from her rifle was still in Sly's leg. The slug ought to be removed, she knew, but why should she help this man who had so brutally murdered her family and left her crippled? Besides, if he were hurt so badly he couldn't walk, there was a chance she could escape from him. Fighting her terror and exhaustion, she attempted to gather her courage and wits. Then surreptitiously she began to examine her surroundings, wondering if she would be able to steal—and ride—the big black stallion that had brought them here.

"Don't even think about it, bitch," Sly uttered warningly, guessing her thoughts. "I might be wounded, but that won't stop me from putting a bullet in your back if you try to run. Now hand me that canteen and that bottle of whiskey in my saddlebag."

Slowly Jenny rose to do as she was bid. Apparently Sly didn't mean to murder her immediately, or he could already have done that, back at the house, anytime during the night, or just minutes past. The thought gave her a slight measure of hope that she might yet manage to get away from him. But Jenny was puzzled too. He had made it plain that he *did* mean to kill her, so what was he waiting for? She shuddered as again she remembered Evangeline and what had been done to her before she'd died. Silently Jenny vowed she would take her own life, as Melantha had done, before allowing this savage butcher to lay a single finger on her.

Squaring her shoulders determinedly, she walked over to where Sly was seated on the ground and wordlessly handed him the items he'd requested. She inhaled sharply as she caught sight of the gaping hole in his leg. It was encrusted with blood and already showed signs of developing angry red streaks. It needed to be cleaned immediately before further infection set in, and, though it went against all her principles to assist him, Jenny found she was unable to turn away, as she would have liked to do.

"The bullet ought to be removed," she observed, her voice crisp and even, her tone as professional as it had been when she'd nursed the Rebel soldiers at the hospital in Atlanta, though she longed to scratch Sly's remaining eye out. "I can perform the necessary operation, if you wish."

Sly's good eye crinkled against the rays of the rising sun as he looked up at her. With his teeth he yanked the cork from the whiskey bottle, then spat it out onto the ground.

"What do you take me for? A fool?" he growled. "I lived through the war, bitch. Remember? I know what it's like to have a slug taken out of my body. If the pain alone didn't cause me to pass out, the alcohol to lessen it would, and I don't doubt but what you'd stab me to death then without a second thought. No thanks. I'll just make do as I am. It'll take more than a little piece of lead to put *me* out of commission."

Then Sly proceeded to pour a portion of the whiskey over his injury before downing a goodly amount of the fiery liquid, something Jenny believed would no doubt bring on a raging fever. Still she bit her tongue and turned away. She had offered to help and had been rejected. Her conscience was clear now, which was more than this cruel, ruthless man could say. In fact, considering all the things he'd done, she did not know how he could sleep at night, and she was quite certain she did not want to find out.

She was startled when Sly tossed her the canteen, ordering her to drink. But then Jenny recalled that for some unknown reason he did not want her dead just yet, and her surprise lessened. Gratefully, for she was thirsty, she unstoppered the container and took a few long slow sips, careful not to guzzle the water, knowing it would make her sick, hitting her empty belly after the strenuous ride. Then she chewed slowly a piece of beef jerky Sly took from his pocket and handed to her.

"It's time to move out," Sly said, standing, wincing at the pain in his leg. Already he was beginning to feel hot all over, as though he had a fever coming on, and, despite the cool, early morning breeze, sweat beaded his brow and upper lip. He must find a means of securing the girl, should he fall into a delirium. "Get mounted up."

Once more he aimed his gun at Jenny, motioning for her to get in the saddle. Briefly she considered trying to make her escape then, but Sly must have suspected her intention, for he grabbed the horse's reins in one hand, holding them tight, so Jenny had no means of controlling the animal. Sighing, she put one foot in the stirrup and pulled herself upward. Sly shoved his pistol into his holster, then mounted behind her, his arm about her waist. Soon they were picking their way along a mountain trail, Sly apparently having some specific destination in mind.

By midafternoon Jenny discovered his objective was a blacksmith's shop in a small Arkansas town. Again her hopes rose, only to be dashed upon learning the proprietor of the forge was an unscrupulous man who had ridden with Sly during the war until the loss of a leg had disabled him. Rube Ballard not only would not help her, but he eyed her lasciviously and suggested that instead of payment for services rendered, he be allowed to take Jenny into his back room for an hour.

"She ain't much to look at, Sly, 'n' that's a fact," Rube declared as he scratched his posterior crudely, "but it's been a while since I had me one as young as her. This peg leg of mine don't sit too well with the ladies."

Jenny scarcely even minded the slur upon her looks; in fact, for the first time in her life she wished she were even plainer. Perhaps then the blacksmith would not be interested in her. She cringed at the idea of this fat, unshaven slob making use of her body and glanced anxiously at Sly, wondering if he would acquiesce to the man's unsavory request.

"I'd like to oblige you, Rube," Sly replied, "but I'm in a hurry. I'll tell you what, though: I'll pay you double your usual fee. How's that? That ought to be enough to persuade some pretty young thing to overlook your missing limb. Besides"—he eyed Jenny lewdly, sending shivers through her—"I've got plans of my own for this one. Now get on with the job, Rube; I don't have all day."

When the blacksmith was finished at his forge, he handed Sly a heavy iron chain perhaps fifteen feet in length, with a shackle at either end, both of which could be opened only with a key. Despite her protests that such measures were unnecessary, Sly fastened one of the locking rings about Jenny's left ankle, then attached the other to his left wrist and clamped the circle shut. Jenny's heart sank as she studied the bond that now stretched between them. Without the key she would now have no means whatsoever of escaping from him, and Sly had hung the device on a leather thong around his neck and tucked it under his shirt. There was no way of removing it without his knowing, for even if he were asleep, he would surely awaken if Jenny attempted to take it from his neck.

Her fear and despair at the thought was all-consuming. For the first time she was forced to face the fact that this man might well succeed in viciously ravishing and murdering her.

Trembling, she again forced her weary bones into the saddle, feeling the weight of the chain drag upon her like an unbearable burden before Sly swung up behind her and looped the iron bond about the pommel.

Chapter Thirty-nine

Sarah Jane watched her father anxiously, torn by her fear and conflicting emotions. Pa looked so tired and drawn; it was obvious he had not slept since receiving the wire Moses had sent to him in Jefferson City last night, waking up old Mr. Stokes to relay the urgent message. Pa had taken the first train home. Now he sat, slumped dejectedly, in a chair in the formal parlor, running one hand raggedly through his hair while his four brothers eyed one another worriedly and fidgeted uncomfortably.

"Kipp, tell me again exactly what happened," Luke said. "Are you sure the men were Baldknobbers?"

The boy nodded, then repeated his story for the umpteenth time, trying to remember if he had left out any detail—no matter how small—that might be of help to his father. But Kipp could think of nothing more. He had not recognized any of the men who had kidnapped his stepmother, nor did he know why they had taken her.

Luke listened wearily, his eyes closed, trying to make sense of what Kipp was saying. The night riders had terrorized several of his campaign backers recently, but it had not occurred to him that they might actually attack his own family. And what possible reason could they have had to abduct Jenny? It just didn't add up. There was something wrong somewhere, but for the life of him Luke could not figure out what it was. If only he'd had more time in Jefferson City! If only he'd been able to locate Tully. But Tully had not been home; his housekeeper had said he'd been called away on business for Senator Taggart, and she had not known when he would return.

"Why would they have taken her?" Luke asked aloud, bewildered and distraught. "Do you suppose they mean to hold her for ransom?"

"I don't know, Luke," J.R. replied, "but we must consider every possible motive. If ransom *is* the reason, no doubt we'll be receiving a note soon enough. I suggest we let Pa and Ma wait here while the rest of us see if we can't make sense of some of those tracks in the yard. The folks can send word if anything turns up here."

"All right," Luke agreed, then sighed. "Christ!" he burst out suddenly. "If only we knew who took Jenny! And why!"

Sarah Jane quivered with anguish at the words. *She* knew who had taken her stepmother away. It had been One-Eyed Jack, the same man her mother had run off with so many years ago. But Ma had wanted to go with the awful man. She had been laughing and clinging to his arm and kissing him. Jenny had done none of those things. Jenny had screamed and fired a rifle at him, and her face had been as white as death when One-Eyed Jack had struck her. No, she had not wanted to go with him; she was not like Ma had been. Ma had gone with One-Eyed Jack and had never returned. Sarah Jane's heart lurched in her breast at the thought. Perhaps Jenny would never come back either. Perhaps that terrible man would kill her! Big tears welled up in Sarah Jane's eyes. If Jenny died, it would be all Sarah Jane's fault for not telling what she knew. What a coward she was and how Pa would scorn her, once he found out she had been too afraid of having her tongue cut out to speak up when Jenny's life was in mortal danger. Jenny, who loved her and had always been so kind.

Suddenly Sarah Jane brightened, struck by an idea. She could write everything down in her tablet! That way she wouldn't have to talk, and she could still help save Jenny. Quickly Sarah Jane ran to get her tablet and a pencil, but once she returned to the parlor, Pa was already leaving, his face grim with distress. She tugged on the sleeve of his shirt, but he paid her no heed, and Grandma Lottie, who'd come over early that morning and had been crying all day, gently pulled her back, telling her not to bother her father right now, that he had a lot on his mind.

Sarah Jane's face crumpled. There would be no time now to write in her tablet. Tears streaked her cheeks as, swallowing hard, she determinedly summoned up every ounce of her courage. It was better to lose her tongue than Jenny.

P-P-Pa. Sara Jane was mortified to discover that although she'd formed the word, no sound had come out of her mouth. Inhaling sharply, she tried again.

"P-P-Pa." Her voice was just a cracked whisper at first; it had been so long since she had used her vocal cords. But still Sarah Jane persisted. "P-P-Pa. Pa. *Pa!*"

They heard her at last, all of them, and one by one they fell silent, turning to stare at her, their faces filled with disbelief and joy.

"Sary!" Luke cried, dropping to his knees before her and pulling her into his arms. "Sary!"

"Pa," she said. "Pa. I know who took Jenny. I know who took Jenny!" Her words came flooding out in a rush, as though a dam had burst within her. "It was him, One-Eyed Jack, the man Ma ran away with. But she wanted to go with him, Pa, and Jenny didn't. Jenny was so scared, Pa. I—I couldn't tell you before, because I was afraid. One-Eyed Jack said if I ever told anyone about him; if I ever even so much as whispered to a single soul again, he'd come back to Tumbling Creek and cut out my tongue."

"Oh, dear Lord," Lottie gasped, horrified, as she grasped this last. "You poor child. You poor, poor child."

"Oh, Sary. Sary, Sary," Luke repeated, tears in his eyes as he hugged his daughter close. "Don't you know I'd never let anybody hurt you like that! To think you kept silent all these years out of fear—By God! When I get my hands on the bastard who threatened you like that—One-Eyed Jack, Sary . . . was that what you called him? What does he look like? Can you tell me? Is he tall, dark, what?"

Sarah Jane nodded.

"Both, Pa. He kind of reminded me of a buffalo, a real mean one. He's got a bad scar down one side of his face, and he's—he's only got one eye, Pa. He wears a black patch over the other one. That's how I knew it was him; I could see the patch through the eye-hole in his mask."

"My God," Luke breathed, stricken, looking up at his folks and his brothers. "It's Taggart. It's Sly Taggart, and if I'm right about why he's taken Jenny, he means to kill her!" He turned back to Sarah Jane and kissed her gently, then pulled Kipp into the circle of his embrace as well. "Sary, you and Kipp may just have saved Jenny's life by your brave actions last night and today. I'm proud of you, both of you. I couldn't have asked for any better kids than you two." Then he stood and nodded to his brothers. "Let's go," he said. "This is one campaign Sly Taggart *isn't* going to win!"

The Ozark natives called it Devil's Den—and with good reason, though at first glance it appeared innocuous enough. It was just a hole in the ground, perhaps three feet in diameter or slightly larger, its edges rimmed with overgrown grass and weeds and a few straggling wildflowers. But, despite its innocent exterior, it was deadly all the same.

Some claimed the chasm was well over a hundred feet deep; others swore it was bottomless. Still others believed it was an opening to a vast, dark underground cave filled with numerous winding caverns and cold, subterranean pools. No one had ever ventured down the hole to discover the truth of the matter—or if they had, they had not lived to report their findings, and this only added to the wild tales told of the place. Many a man had lost his life here, flung down into the chasm's depths by outlaws or Rebel soldiers, and it was said that on a wintery eve one could hear the eerie groans of the dead whistling up from the hole like a moaning wind.

It was to this place of death that Sly at last brought Jenny to wait, he said, for Luke, who would surely follow them.

"And then I'll kill you both," Sly told the girl, smiling wolfishly, his face shining with sweat, despite the cool shade of the forest, and his good eye unnaturally bright. "He's been a thorn in my side for as long as I can remember. I always wanted Maybelle, you know, from the time we were just kids. But after I ran away from home I didn't get back as often as I should have, and she got tired of waiting. I guess that's why she turned to Morgan instead. But I fixed her for it. Yeah, I sure did. She was sorry in the end for what she'd done, especially when Morgan never amounted to anything. It was easy, then, to persuade her to run away with me, and once I'd had my fill of her, I sold her to some old madam of a whorehouse in Saint Louis. Maybelle wasn't so high and mighty then. No, she wasn't." Sly shook his head, remembering, then went on.

"I'd let Moffatt and some of the others have her beforehand, and it'd taken some of the starch out of her. I reckon that old bitch of a madam beat the rest out of her. But . . . what the hell! Maybelle was a whore long before then anyway. Shit! Even Tully'd had her; he'd always secretly lusted after her, the incestuous bastard. He was kind of upset about it afterward, but I told him it didn't make any difference, him being her brother and all. Christ! She'd spread her legs for half the state of Missouri. Why not Tully too?

"He's dead, you know. You killed him with Morgan's rifle," Sly informed Jenny bitterly, startling her. "It was him chasing after Morgan's little bastard the night I kidnapped you. Poor Tully. He probably never even knew what hit him. The boys said you blew the back of his head clean off. You'll pay for that, bitch. Next to Orin, Tully was the best friend I ever had," Sly declared, then took another long draught from his whiskey bottle, which he'd been nursing all day.

Numbly Jenny listened to his words, appalled by the things he was saying to her. Still she prayed he would go on talking drunkenly, fever-ishly, anything to prevent him from taking any real notice of her and deciding to use her as brutally as he had used Evangeline. Previously he had been concerned only with reaching their destination and their sur-vival along the way. But now that they were actually at Devil's Den, which spot apparently suited Sly's wicked fancy, there was nothing for him to do but drink, and she was afraid he would soon lose all sense of reason and begin to view her in a different light.

He wasn't well, Jenny thought. His leg had started to swell, and pus oozed from the red-streaked wound, attracting a horde of flies that Sly now only occasionally bothered to wave away. Jenny was certain she could smell the sickly sweet odor of gangrene too. They had traveled much more slowly these past few days, slowly enough to give her hope that Luke was indeed hard on their heels and would catch up with them at any moment. If only she could keep Sly at bay until then. But pres-ently he turned to her, his good eye glinting evilly, his lips slack with lust, and Jenny knew her time of waiting had come to an end.

She tried hard not to think of Evangeline, or Honor and Bliss, and how this man and his cohorts had savagely raped them before they'd died. But still the memories crowded in upon her, so she did not even realize it was her own screams echoing through the woods as Sly's mouth pressed against her lips and throat, and his hands tore roughly at the bodice of her gown.

Blindly Jenny struggled against him, her fingers groping for the knife he carried at his waist. There! Swiftly she pulled the blade from its sheath and stabbed downward with the weapon, hitting Sly in the back, just above the hip. She was unprepared for the shock of the knife driv-ing into his flesh, glancing off a bone, and quickly she yanked the blade free. With a snarled curse Sly arched upward in pain, so Jenny was able to inch her way partially from beneath him before his body fell back down upon her with a thud, and he tried to force the weapon from her grasp by slamming her wrist down hard upon the ground. Jenny let go of the knife, but as she did so she managed to bring her knee up, jamming it into Sly's groin. With another grunt of pain he rolled off her, and while he was trying to recover Jenny snatched the key from around his neck, breaking the leather thong that held it fast.

Hurriedly she bent to unlock the shackle about her leg, but before she could get the iron ring open, Sly scrambled over and ripped the key from her fingers, throwing it into Devil's Den in his fury.

"You bitch!" he spat. "Did you really believe you could escape from me so easily?"

Then once more he fell upon her, crushing his mouth down hard upon hers, making her long to gag and retch as he forced his tongue between her lips and with his hands finished tearing away her bodice to expose her breasts, which he squeezed cruelly. When his mouth moved to her nipples Jenny screamed again and again, wanting to die.

Then suddenly she was free, and Luke was there, his face filled with murderous rage as he began to thrash Sly with his bare hands, pummeling him unmercifully.

The two men tumbled over and over, dragging Jenny helplessly along in their wake, until she thought surely her shackled leg would be wrenched from her body from the force of the chain pulling upon it. To her utter horror she saw that her husband and his opponent were now fighting perilously close to the opening of Devil's Den, and, feeling sick, Jenny realized each man was trying to push the other in. Her heart hammered painfully in her breast, her concern all for Luke. Such was her love for him and her fear for his safety that her brain scarcely even registered what would become of her if Sly were to be the one propelled into the hole. It was not until she found herself sliding toward Devil's Den that she understood her danger.

Her hands clawed frantically at the ground, but there was nothing for her to hold on to as the grass and weeds she grasped in a desperate effort to stop her descent were simply yanked from the earth by their roots.

"Luke!" she screamed. "Luke!"

Then Sly disappeared into the chasm, and Jenny was falling, falling. . . .

She felt as though her arms had been dislocated from their sockets as, panting for breath, Luke caught hold of her wrists at the last moment, preventing her from dropping into the yawning darkness that waited below. Still the strain of Sly's weight hauling on her shackled, crippled leg was almost more than Jenny could bear, and tears stung her eyes as she gazed up into her husband's loving, fear-filled face.

"Hold on, Jenny girl." He spoke grimly. "We'll have you out of there in a minute. J.R. Toby," he shouted. "Get a rope, and give me a hand here."

"You—you don't understand, Luke," Jenny gasped, knowing he thought she had somehow been accidentally knocked into the hole during the struggle. "Senator—Senator Taggart's got my leg chained to his wrist."

"That's right, Morgan!" Sly called drunkenly from where he dangled below. "If I go, I'm taking your wife with me. If you want to save her, you'll have to pull me up too."

"Jesus," Luke breathed. "Oh, Jesus." He paused, then raised his voice. "All right, Taggart. Just keep still. We're going to bring Jenny up first." He looked into her frightened eyes and smiled encouragingly. "Are you ready, sweetheart? J.R.'s going to tie the rope around your waist, then he and Toby and I are going to haul you up. We'll take it easy so just stay calm, and everything will be okay. Here we go now. All right?"

"All right," Jenny murmured.

Slowly the three men began to pull her upward, the muscles in their arms rippling and bulging at the effort. At last they managed to haul Jenny over the edge of Devil's Den, where she lay still for a moment, sobbing with relief in Luke's warm embrace as he caressed and kissed her over and over, as though to reassure himself that she was truly safe.

"What's the stall, Morgan?" Sly hollered. "Get me out of here! I threw away the key to these shackles, so don't think you can go off and leave me here now that you've gotten your wife out."

"Okay, okay," Luke growled. "Raif, you and Billy Clay come over here, and hold on to Jenny while the rest of us pull that bastard up."

Once the two younger brothers had a firm grip on Jenny to prevent her from sliding back in Devil's Den, Luke and the others started yanking on the chain, trying to haul Sly out of the chasm—but without result. Apparently the heavy iron bond linking him to Jenny was snagged on an outcropping rock and would not be budged.

"Christ!" Luke swore furiously. "Now what are we going to do?" He bit his lip, thinking hard, then ordered, "Billy Clay, get an ax."

For several long minutes the men hacked at the chain, but it would not be broken, and finally, their brows beaded with sweat, they gave up. Luke stared at Jenny searchingly, noticing the fine lines of strain, fear, and exhaustion that etched her face, and he wondered how much more she could take.

"Toby"—he turned to his brother—"do you think you can blast that chain in half without killing Jenny?"

Slowly after considering the matter Tobias nodded.

"Yes, I think so," he asserted, "but I'm afraid the explosion will blow Senator Taggart to kingdom come."

"Do it," Luke said, his voice hard.

"Oh, Luke, no. No," Jenny protested softly. "Surely there must be some other way. He—he murdered my family, you know. But I—I don't want to be responsible for his death. . . ."

"I know," Luke told her quietly. "It took me some time, but I finally managed to put together all the pieces of that day at Faxon's Folly. I don't want Taggart to die any more than you do, Jenny. I want him to live to stand trial and be hanged for his crimes. But I don't see any other way to free you, darling, and I won't lose you. You're my love and my life." He glanced once more at his brother. "Do it, Toby," he demanded, then covered Jenny's body with his own.

For the first time in his life Tobias's hands trembled as he reached into his saddlebag for the dynamite he carried always. Carefully he removed one stick, then broke it open at the top to pour out some of the powder so the charge wouldn't be as powerful as normal. Then he replaced the fuse, and with J.R. hanging onto his legs, he leaned over the rim of Devil's Den and pushed the stick securely through one link of the iron chain.

"What're you doing, you bastard? Morgan, what're you sons of bitches doing?" Sly shrieked.

"Say your prayers, Taggart," Luke shouted back grimly. "This is the end of the line for you."

Then Tobias lit the fuse, and the four brothers backed away to take cover, leaving Luke and Jenny huddled upon the ground, waiting for the explosion.

"I love you, Jennilee," Luke whispered, holding her tightly and smiling down tenderly into her eyes.

"I love you too, Luke."

There was no time to say more. The earth erupted beneath them, slinging dirt in every direction and sending Jenny and Luke tumbling across the soft sweet grass.

After a time all was still. Then with the infamous, wild cry of "Yip-Yip-Yaw!" Luke swung Jenny up into his arms and kissed her passionately until she was laughing and crying all at the same time, knowing that at last the past had been washed clean and from now on all her memories would begin with this moment.

"Jennilee, my outlaw heart," Luke breathed into her ear, "let's go home."

BOOK FIVE

And Seek Enchantment There

Chapter Forty

The Ozark Mountains, date unknown

The old-timer falls silent, his tale ended at last, and, though he has been a long while in the telling of it, still it seems too quickly finished. The magic of the story has been so spellbinding one has not even noticed the lateness of the evening, so swiftly have the hours passed. How high the moon has climbed in the night sky, and how bright the stars sparkle against the black velvet firmament.

The hills in the distance cut a jagged line across the sky—magnificent, awesome, compelling. It is not hard to believe these are the same hills that once echoed with Rebel yells and Yankee hollers, the wild cry of "Yip-Yip-Yaw!" made infamous by Quantrill's Raiders. It is even less difficult to imagine they are the same hills where the Morgan gang once rode hell-bent for leather and where Luke and Jenny once walked the wooded paths, hand in hand, their love for each other shining in their eyes.

There is an agelessness about the hills, an undaunted spirit, a dark, ethereal quality, as though they belong to a fairy tale or a fable. But they are quite real. It is simply that they are yet a wilderness, unspoiled by man, closely guarded by those who want no foreigners to alter the unchanging and unbroken circle that is life in the Ozark Mountains.

Here the old ways are not forgotten but revered. Here the inhabitants know those things really worth having cannot be bought, but are given freely, cannot be touched, but only felt with the heart. Their lives may be simple and old-fashioned—but they are good lives, uncluttered with material possessions, far from the city's hustle and bustle. For there is peace to be found in the hills, a serenity so gentle, so sweet, a feeling of release, of contentment.

One longs to return to the special place in the hills that belongs even now to Luke and Jenny, to feel the richness of the grass and earth underfoot, to smell the fragrant scents of the vines and wildflowers, damp with the evening dew, to walk where the lovers lie beneath the soft, spongy moss, sleeping, only sleeping, awakening with the sunset. There is enchantment there.

One turns to ask the old-timer if he might lead a stranger to that magical dell, but he has risen and gone inside his cabin, and only the faint aroma of his corncob pipe lingers behind to say he was there at all. His empty rocker moves ever so slightly in the cool night breeze, the hushed creaking of its wood mingling with the rustling of the leaves, the groaning of the branches, and the murmur of distant mountain streams. A soft light glows from his window.

Feeling like an intruder now, one stands silently and, deep in thought, moves from the porch to the narrow, rock-strewn path that meanders down through the hills to the valley below. How did the old-timer learn of the tale he has told? How did he come to know it so intimately, in such detail? Clearly this must remain a mystery, for the old-timer has said all he is going to say.

Halfway down the path, one pauses, listening intently to the sound borne on the wind. It is as though somewhere—perhaps in the old-timer's cabin—a music box has been wound and its lid opened so the sweet, plaintive notes of its song echo through the hills, like a woman whispering to her man, like the ghosts of Luke and Jenny laughing softly, their voices low and filled with passion, soughing on the wings of the night.

And the melody the music box plays? It is an old French ballad called *"Plaisir d'Amour"*—"The Joys of Love."

Author's Note

There are many people the author must acknowledge and thank for their invaluable assistance with research and other contributions to this novel. They are as follows: one of the author's favorite wholesalers, Ken Richman, of Ozark Magazine Distributors, Inc. of Springfield, Missouri, for suggesting a book dealing with the Baldknobbers in the first place and for his extensive help in locating sources about the Baldknobbers, who are as notorious in the Ozarks as the Ku Klux Klan is in the rest of the South; the author's sister, Lisa Beth Freeman, for additional research on the Baldknobbers as well as for information about various regions of Missouri, Kansas, and Arkansas; the author's grandfather, William H. Stamps, who worked for a railroad company all his life and who, instead of being furious at being wakened at one o'clock in the morning, took the time to explain all about old-fashioned locomotives and railroad cars; the author's dear friend Mary Railey, a graduate of the School of the Ozarks, and her mother, Lillie Railey, for sharing so generously from their own personal libraries so many hard-to-find books about Missouri and Kansas; and, last but not least, the author's husband, Gary D. Brock, for innumerable trips to the library for information on everything from the Ozark wilderness to Quantrill's Raiders to the Pinkerton Detective Agency, for several telephone calls and hours on the computer to obtain additional materials, for pitching in above and beyond the call of duty with all the housework and the cooking, and for his unfailing patience, support, and love always.

The Baldknobbers actually existed, and stories of their famous and infamous exploits may be heard in the Ozarks today. For the purposes of this novel, however, the author has altered some of the true facts about the organization, and she hopes the natives of the Ozarks will forgive these few liberties, taken to enhance the plot of the book. The Baldknobbers were, in reality, founded by Captain N. N. Kinney, of Taney County, and twelve other law-abiding men in January, 1885, in response to the reign of terror sweeping the countryside. By this time lawlessness had become so prevalent in Missouri and law officials and the courts had proven so ineffectual in combating crime that citizens feared for their lives and property. The night meeting of the proposed vigilante committee actually did take place on Big Bald (which was bald at the time but is now covered with scrub cedar), not far from the Oak Grove (rather than Tumbling Creek) schoolhouse, and the oath sworn was actually that given in the novel, taken from the Springfield *Daily Republican,* Springfield, Missouri; Vol. IV, No. 155, December 29, 1888, in a reprint credited to the New York *Sun,* December 23, 1888. The oath was, in reality, however, drawn up by Mr. J. J. Brown, Esq., a Taney County lawyer at the time.

Originally the organization, which also had a constitution and bylaws, existed to perform good deeds. Its members, who were armed but did not wear masks, rode abroad quite openly, holding their meetings in the daylight hours, as they were proud of their participation in the order and meant only to see that justice was done. Once lawless activities around the countryside appeared to have abated, the organization was disbanded. It was later revived by a group of unscrupulous men, who, calling themselves Baldknobbers, twisted the original intent of the order and used the organization as a means to terrify actual law-abiding citizens, rousing them from their beds at night and threatening them with carbines, revolvers, and switches. These men, who carried out their activities primarily in Christian, Stone, and Taney Counties, were the ones who wore the hideous masks described in the book, and it is this particular sect of the Baldknobbers upon which the author has modeled her own. The Baldknobbers were disbanded for the last time in 1889, when several members of this by-now-notorious order were hanged.

In its heyday the James-Younger gang was both worshiped and reviled, depending upon whether or not one subscribed to the largely false and glorified stories appearing about the gang in various dime novels, which, for the most part, portrayed the Jameses and the Youngers as heroic, latter-day Robin Hoods. This was a grossly distorted image of the gang, who never gave to the poor—unless they were relatives. In reality, the Jameses and the Youngers were dangerous men who were feared by the sensible and knowledgeable, yet they continued to be regarded as heroes. Coleman Younger was truly liked and remembered because he really did attempt to help people during Quantrill's raid on Lawrence, and Frank James was so well thought of, despite his infamous crimes, that he was tried and acquitted twice by juries. Certainly the gang did not commit a good many of the holdups of which it was accused, but during those jobs the Jameses and Youngers did pull, several people were murdered, and it was only because the gang really did not shoot well that more people were not killed. The author has of course in part modeled her own Morgan gang after the James-Younger gang as well as a later group of outlaws, Butch Cassidy and the Hole-in-the-Wall gang.

Although Tumbling Creek and Tumbling Creek Cave both exist, the town of Tumbling Creek is fictional, as is Devil's Holler. What was once called Devil's Den has been opened up and excavated and may be visited by the public; we now know it as Marvel Cave. The towering, rocky bluffs along the Missouri-Arkansas border may still be seen and are still known today as Murder Rocks.

A favorite story in the Ozarks is that of the Shepherd of the Hills, and today there are numerous places in the region that have the words *Shepherd of the Hills* in their names. The author would like to think that at one of them there is an old-timer who knows the tale of The Outlaw Hearts.

Rebecca Brandewyne